Clan of Heroes

Rise of the Giants Series: Book 2

Theo Mann

The Invisible Publishing Company

Rise of the Giants Series

Contents

Chapter 1

H angman flattened his back against a tree, ducked out to peek in front of him, and pulled back before anyone could see him. He rested his head against the trunk for a minute, shut his eyes, and listened.

He didn't hear anything at first—nothing but the endless throb of thousands of insects and other creatures moving in the jungle around him.

Then he heard it. He barely heard anything at all, but it was definitely there. He heard breathing off to his left.

He peeked out a second time and made eye contact with his cousin Viking looking back at him from behind another nearby tree. Hangman pointed in the direction of the breathing and Viking nodded.

Hangman judged the distance, darted to Viking's tree, and the two men crept across another open place to a different tree to join up with Hangman's younger brother Cross and their other cousin Alien.

The four men advanced extra slowly so they wouldn't make any noise. Hangman pricked up his ears when he heard Crushers and Gorlocks rumbling in the distance, but the creatures didn't come this way.

The cousins drew their weapons as they headed deeper into the jungle. A dense patch of undergrowth covered a rise up ahead. The breathing sounds came from there.

Hangman judged the positions of the other men in the Godless scouting party. His father Shadow and his cousins Banjo, and Feather closed from farther south to surround the same mound.

The party also brought Alien's nephews, Devil, Bantam, Breaker, and Grizzly. They were the sons of Midnight's daughter Neia and her husband Cosmos.

The Godless got more than they bargained for when they discovered another group of warriors from the Renegade Clan invading the Godless' territory from the west.

Now the Godless had to attack and destroy these invaders before the Renegades made it any closer to the long camp where all the Godless women and children lived.

Hangman tightened his grip on his kukris. His brother and his cousins raised their weapons to strike as soon as they drove the Renegades out of the bushes.

Shadow and the others advanced from their side. They must have heard the breathing, too. It sounded so loud from this close up. Did one of the Renegades get injured and crawl into those bushes to hide?

Hangman didn't hold out any hope for that. The Godless had found too many signs and tracks recently. The Renegades didn't send scouting parties into Godless territory. They sent whole war parties with a couple dozen warriors each.

The Godless had their work cut out for them hitting these war parties again and again, driving them back, whittling down their numbers, and holding them at a safe distance from the long camp.

The Renegades made the problem so much worse by sending multiple war parties from multiple directions. The Godless had to go from war party to war party attacking, killing, driving the survivors to retreat, and moving on to the next attack.

Alien raised his own giant kukris, opened his mouth, and inhaled a deep breath to bellow out his war cry, but at that moment when another ten Renegades burst out of the surrounding undergrowth.

The Renegades wore some kind of matted grass coverings over their mouths to stop the Godless from hearing the Renegades breathing. The Renegades also wore leaves, branches, and other vegetation attached to their clothes to camouflage themselves.

Four Renegades pounced on top of Alien and struck him to the ground. The others attacked Hangman, Cross, and Viking.

Another twenty rushed out of nowhere and laid into Shadow's group the same way. Hangman saw it all in a heartbeat. Whoever lay hiding in those bushes breathing so loudly—he must be a decoy. The Renegades laid a trap to ambush the Godless.

Two Renegades tackled Hangman and tried to take him down, too. The first one landed on his back and made him stagger. Hangman's stumble made the second man miss his aim.

Hangman deflected the second man and pivoted sideways just enough to slam his enemy's back against a nearby tree. The guy grunted in pain, but his grip didn't loosen.

Hangman floundered out of his confusion, stabbed one of his kukris under his own arm, and impaled his enemy through the ribs.

The guy grimaced, groaned, and would have fallen off. Hangman spotted the second Renegade rushing him. The attacker raised one of the Renegade's metal weapons high to strike Hangman down.

Hangman started to throw the injured man to the ground, but Hangman changed his mind, held onto his stricken enemy, and turned his injured enemy's back to the attacker.

The attacker brought the weapon down hard and Hangman steered the injured man's head into the strike. The weapon stuck in the guy's skull and gave Hangman just enough time to drive his kukri into the attacker's eye socket.

Hangman barely had a chance to pull the weapon free before another Renegade charged him from out of the confusion. Hangman's relatives fought tooth and nail all over the area. Hangman couldn't even see what his cousins and brother were doing in the mayhem.

He looked up just in time to see his new attacker slash another metal blade at him. Hangman reacted in a split second and pulled his injured opponent's body around, but not fast enough.

The weapon came down to cleave Hangman's skull in half. He ducked and the weapon embedded in his shoulder where it met his neck. The tree saved his life. The trunk blocked the blade from sinking more than an inch into his shoulder. The blade couldn't go any deeper.

He roared in fury, shoved his injured opponent at the attacker, and the man's weight made the attacking Renegade stumble back.

Hangman followed up his advantage by tackling both of them flat on the ground. The attacker fell onto his back with his injured comrade pinning him down. The injured man stopped the attacker from getting up.

Hangman pounced on top of the injured man's body to hold them both down under his weight, scrambled to straddle the injured man across his back, and stabbed that attacker in the head, too.

Hangman looked up half-crazed on bloodlust and battle fury. His dazed brain hardly registered what his cousins were doing.

He happened to notice one Renegade standing twenty feet away from him. The man didn't engage in the battle.

He aimed some kind of small object at Hangman. Hangman didn't recognize the thing. It looked like a piece of junk he might have found in one of the ancient cities.

The thing exploded in the man's hand and something struck Hangman in the shoulder from that distance.

He felt the unmistakable sensation of something small, round, and blistering hot tear through his shoulder and burst out the other side. It ripped a perfectly round hole straight through him.

The impact jolted him back and almost knocked him over. He wavered for a second before he caught his balance.

He stared up at the guy in disbelief. Hangman's brain didn't want to accept that this Renegade actually injured him from a distance without touching him.

Hangman would have ascribed that to witchcraft, but it must have come from that object. The object, the explosion, and the injury all happened one after the other. They had to be connected.

Hangman stared at the man trying in every possible way to understand. Hangman had never seen or even heard of a weapon like this.

His first instinct told him to ask Mora about it and find out if she or the Followers knew anything about it or if they had seen anything like this in the cities. The Followers knew more about the ancients than anyone.

Hangman was still sitting there feeling that hole through his shoulder when the object exploded a second time.

The second shot tore across the side of his face, cut into his temple, razed through his hair, and kept going.

That shot whipped his head sideways, and when he looked up a second time, the Renegade strode up to him and planted the object right against Hangman's forehead.

Hangman couldn't think clearly enough even to fight back. How could he fight back against a weapon like this? It made no sense. It didn't seem to belong to this world—and yet it must because it was already here.

The man tightened his fingers around the weapon to use it again. Pain and loss of blood dulled Hangman's mind. He couldn't even raise his kukris to defend himself.

At that moment, a deep thump shook the ground underfoot. The noise of battle stopped Hangman from hearing the Crushers coming closer until they actually stomped into the area. The commotion must have attracted them.

Three of the huge creatures stomped through the trees, snapped branches, and stepped on fallen combatants lying on the ground.

The Renegades whipped around to stare as the first Crusher snatched one of the biggest Renegades off the ground, tossed the body into the air, caught the guy in its mouth, and swallowed him. The other Crushers eyed the combatants to pick out their next prey.

Everyone stared up at the Crushers in shock for a second. No one attacked them. That would be irretrievably stupid.

Right then, Alien stormed up behind Hangman, cleaved the Renegade through the skull with one of his massive kukris, snatched Hangman by the arm, and yanked him backward.

Hangman's legs failed to keep up with his much bigger cousin. Hangman stumbled—and in that moment, more of the same explosions went off behind them.

Alien jerked right and left, bellowed in agony a few times, and then bolted into the undergrowth running through the jungle.

Chapter 2

A lien let go of Hangman's arm and Hangman collapsed against another tree. Everything hurt.

He still bled from a blade cut deep in his neck. That hole tore through his other shoulder. His head pounded and blood ran in his eyes.

Alien buckled onto the ground next to him and fell on his back bleeding from multiple wounds in his sides, chest, and legs.

Alien lay there gasping, whimpering, and searching the sky overhead. Hangman couldn't sit here watching.

He blundered over to his cousin and raised his hand to touch the perfectly round wounds, but Hangman hesitated to actually touch them.

One of them sliced across Alien's ribs under his arm. Another tore through the flesh on his other side and one penetrated through his thigh.

The worst one hit him square in the middle of the chest, but it didn't penetrate.

Hangman moved his face a little closer and saw a shiny round ball of metal lodged in the bone of Alien's sternum. Blood welled all around it, but at least it didn't go any deeper.

"What is it?!" Alien husked. "What is it?!"

Hangman snapped back to his senses. "I don't know, brother. It's some new weapon they have."

"Am I going to die?" Alien choked.

"No, brother. You won't die. I promise. I'll save you."

Hangman started to straighten up. He really wished someone else would come along to treat his injuries, but Alien needed his help too much right now. Hangman was that person.

He sat back on his heels and summoned the resolve to stand up when he heard running footsteps coming closer.

He shot to his feet and pulled his kukris. His arms hurt to move, but he planted himself there to defend Alien.

Hangman slumped against a tree when Cross ran through the undergrowth. He slowed and then stopped when he saw Hangman and Alien both injured.

"Is he....is he dying?" Cross quavered.

"He isn't dying—not yet." Hangman made a quick assessment of Cross's injuries. He got hit by that mysterious weapon, but he had a slash across his abdomen and a penetrating stab wound through one of his legs.

"Help me gather leaves for the paste," Hangman told his brother. "We need to treat these injuries as soon as possible."

"Father....and the others....." Cross gulped. "They're still back there. I'm the only one who made it out....I mean the three of us."

Hangman gritted his teeth. "All the more reason we need to treat these injuries and go back for the others." He opened one of his bags and pulled out a wooden bowl with some leaf paste already in it. It wasn't enough.

He handed the bowl to his brother. "Treat Alien and yourself, Cross, but don't remove that ball from Alien's chest. Then go around, gather as many leaves as you can, and start making some more paste."

"Hey! Where are you going?!" Cross exclaimed. "You can't go back there! The Renegades still have that weapon!"

"I know they have the weapon and I also know they have our people. If Shadow and the others are already dead, then I'm Kral and we have to withdraw as soon as possible. We won't stay here to put our lives in danger for people who are already dead. Now do as I say, Cross. If you can get Alien into the trees, so much the better. The blood will attract the creatures in no time. We have to hurry."

Hangman took off running the way he came—back toward the battle Alien took so much trouble to get Hangman away from.

Hangman was the only man still walking around free with no injuries to his legs. He could move just fine below the waist. He had to go back and see what was happening with Shadow and the others.

Hangman experienced a pang on his way back there. Now he understood why Shadow never challenged Butcher for the position of Kral.

Hangman really hoped Shadow was still alive. Hangman didn't want the responsibility of his whole band's lives resting on his shoulders. Hangman didn't want to be Kral. He just wanted to be a normal man and live a normal life.

Bellows, yells, and even screams drew him to the Renegades' location long before he got to the battleground. He had to divert to a different place. The combatants must have retreated here to get away from the Crushers, but at least he didn't hear any more of those explosions.

He crept into the bushes and snuck forward to see what was happening. The Crushers weren't here anymore, but he heard them not far away.

Shadow, Bantam, and all of Hangman's cousins sat tied up on the ground. Fifteen Renegades stood over them, strode from man to man, and delivered kicks, blows, and even lashes of switches cut from the jungle.

Hangman couldn't see from here how the Renegades or the Godless got away from the Crushers.

"Tell us where your comrades are hiding!" one of the Renegades bellowed. "Tell us where they are!"

"We don't know!!" Shadow roared. "How should we know? We were fighting against you when they ran away!"

"Follow the blood trail if you're so smart," Viking snarled over his shoulder and one of the Renegades punched him across the jaw.

"Tell us where they are or we'll stake you out and feed you to the ants!" the same man snapped. "Do you think we give a damn what happens to Godless scum like you?"

"We'll never tell you where they are!" Bantam fired back. "I don't care what you do."

A different Renegade kicked him. Then the first guy withdrew and gave orders to his men to search the area—presumably to find Hangman and the others.

He withdrew and took off running back to the others. Alien must have been alert enough to hear what Hangman said about getting into the trees. Cross and Alien sat perched between two thick limbs high in the canopy.

Cross was busy smearing the paste onto his own wounds. He'd already treated Alien—all except the wound in Alien's chest.

Alien lay slumped in the crook of the two branches so he didn't have to hold himself up. His head lolled over to one side. His mouth hung partially open and he didn't open his eyes when Hangman returned.

Cross handed Hangman the bowl. "There isn't much left. We should put it on your neck first."

Hangman winced and tried not to pay attention when Cross dabbed the rest of the paste to the deep blade cut between Hangman's neck and his shoulder.

"You'll need some Gooji juice tonight," Cross remarked.

"Won't we all?" Hangman muttered.

Cross looked up and made eye contact with Hangman. "At least that cut on your face won't make you any uglier."

Hangman snorted. He didn't feel like laughing, not even at that most over-used joke.

Cross finished the paste left in the bowl and picked up a fresh handful of leaves to start grinding them into more paste. "What do you think that weapon was?"

"Something the Renegades found in the cities, most likely," Hangman replied. "We haven't seen it before, but the ancients must have had it. The Renegades couldn't come up with something like that."

"Is it witchcraft?"

"No, it can't be. Look." Hangman inched forward on the branch, took hold of the metal ball embedded in Alien's sternum, and tried to pull it out.

Alien burst to life, roared, and struggled to slap Hangman's hands away.

"Easy, brother," Hangman murmured. "We're trying to treat your injuries. You're hurt. Rest easy."

Alien crumpled back against the truck with a pathetic moan. He didn't fight back when Hangman took hold of the ball with his right hand, planted his left hand on Alien's chest, and twisted the ball extra hard. It still wouldn't move.

Alien bellowed in pain and rage again. "Be quiet!" Cross hissed. "You'll attract the creatures."

Alien paid no attention and he didn't quiet down. "Help me hold him down!" Hangman yelled to Cross. "We have to get this out."

Cross and Hangman both grabbed Alien. His position on the tree branches wouldn't let the men lie him flat. This would just have to do.

Hangman bent over, clamped his molars around the ball, and ripped his head sideways with every ounce of his strength. Alien gave one last blood-curdling roar as the ball came away. Then he really did collapse.

Hangman took the bowl and smeared paste on the wound, but Hangman already saw that it wasn't as deep or as dangerous as the others.

He was still examining Alien's injuries when Cross took the bowl back and started applying the paste to the rest of Hangman's injuries.

The pain drew Hangman's attention back to the problem in front of him. "We have to go back and help Shadow and the others. The Renegades will feed our men to the ants pretty soon. We have to stop them and rescue our men."

"How?" Cross asked. "There are so many more Renegades than just the three of us."

"I don't know how, but we have to go back. We can't leave our own relatives to die. I only saw fifteen Renegades there just now. If we free Shadow and the others, we can level the field at least partially."

"They have that weapon," Cross pointed out. "We can never level the playing field against that."

"We can't leave," Hangman repeated. "That's all there is to it. We can't just run off and save ourselves while our relatives are in danger. We'll go back and try it. If it doesn't work....."

Alien growled from his place in the branches. "If it doesn't work, the Renegade Clan will capture us and feed us to the ants. Then what will happen to the long camp?"

"The Renegades will go to the long camp either way unless we stop them here. Now come on. Finish putting the paste on yourself, Cross, and let's go. We don't have much time."

Hangman dropped down to the ground. He focused on his captured father and cousins to block the pain out of his mind. It didn't work completely, but he knew what he had to do. Retreat wasn't an option, not even with three injured men.

Alien climbed down next. He climbed much faster than Hangman expected him to. Alien closed up his features in a mask of murderous fury. He must be in a lot of pain.

He would channel that pain and fury toward the enemy The cousins just had to find the bastards.

Cross stayed in the trees while he finished treating his own injuries. He finally joined Hangman and Alien and the three cousins set off heading back the way they came.

Alien and Cross limped on the way. Hangman's head pounded and his vision kept slipping out of focus. That weapon must have injured his head much worse than he realized.

He pushed forward until he heard more yelling in the distance. He adjusted his course and slowed down so he would be ready to meet the Renegades. His brother and cousin stayed with him and followed his lead.

It wasn't the first time ever. He usually wound up being the leader if they went out alone together away from Shadow, Fang, and Butcher.

Hangman sensed his own words starting to have an effect on him. He would become Kral if Shadow died. Then everyone really would follow Hangman's lead.

He put that thought out of his mind, and a second later, the crash of breaking branches startled him to high alert.

The heads of Crushers stuck up over the canopy. The same Crushers came back to attack the cousins. The Crushers must have smelled the blood or followed the trail to track down the injured men.

No one could fight Crushers—not like this—not when the four men were injured.

Cross and Alien dove out of the way and scattered. Neither of them could run fast enough to keep out of the Crushers' reach. Hangman made a split-second decision, hesitated a fraction of an instant to make certain the Crushers saw him, and took off running.

His trick worked. All three Crushers charged him to run him down. Only his own speed saved him.

He forgot for a second why he was here and where he was supposed to be going. He didn't think of anything other than keeping far enough in front of the Crushers' enormous teeth.

Seeing something small and helpless running away from them sent the Crushers into a frenzy. They ran their fastest to track him down. The Crusher in front kept snapping its teeth at him, but he always stayed just a few steps ahead.

He blundered through the jungle not thinking about anything else until he just randomly happened to pass close enough to the clearing where the Renegades had already staked out the prisoners to the ground.

Two Renegades walked backward through the jungle a dozen yards away. They scattered pollen on the ground to lead a trail of ants to the prisoners.

Shadow and the others thrashed, protested, and cursed the Renegades. The Renegades all gathered to one side well out of the ants' path. No Renegades surrounded the prisoners at all anymore.

The ants entered the clearing. The two men scattered pollen over and around the prisoners and retreated to join their comrades to watch.

Hangman made another snap decision, veered left, and barreled straight into the clearing. He didn't even try to avoid the ants.

He hurdled over them and led the Crushers into the ants' path. The ants attacked, grabbed onto the Crushers' legs, and then the Crushers stumbled into the Renegades' group.

Hangman sprinted straight past the startled Renegades just as the Crushers came within range to snap up as many Renegades as they wanted. The ants diverted to follow the Crushers, went after them, and the Crushers trampled Renegades instead.

Hangman swerved hard, darted from one prisoner to another, cut their ropes, and moved on.

Shadow, Bantam, and the others leapt up and took off running into the jungle.

Chapter 3

The Godless didn't stop running for miles before Shadow told them to stop. Everyone slumped under the trees to rest and catch their breath.

Cross took the paste from Hangman's bag and went from man to man treating their injuries. "We should find one of those weapons and see what it is," Viking suggested. "Maybe we can figure out how to use them against the Renegades."

Shadow nodded. "I know where we can get one. We'll go back for it."

"Where is it?" Hangman asked.

"It's back at the battle site. Some of the Renegades tried to use their weapons against the Crushers. The Renegades stayed behind too long, got trampled or eaten by the creatures, and dropped the weapons there. We'll go as soon as Cross finishes."

"What will examining the weapons do for us?" Bantam asked. "We won't be able to figure out how to use them. We don't know anything about them."

"We might learn," Alien interjected. "Maybe Mora can tell us what they are and how they work."

Hangman didn't respond. At least someone else made that suggestion so he didn't have to.

"We won't know anything until we see one," Shadow went on. "We won't be able to understand them without looking at them. Are you finished, Cross?"

"Yes, Father."

Cross handed the bowl back to Hangman and the group limped and hobbled all the way back to the battle site. Hangman and his cousins never stopped searching everywhere for any sign of their enemies coming back.

Hangman heard distant screams coming from the place where he and his party left the Renegades to the ants. The screams died out after a while, but he couldn't be sure if any of the Renegades survived.

Anyone who spent any amount of time in the jungle would know what to do to avoid and escape getting eaten by the ants. Any of those Renegades could have jumped up into the trees, climbed into the canopy, and survived to fight another day.

The men spread out to search the battle site. Shadow knew exactly what he was looking for, walked straight over to one of the fallen weapons, and picked it up.

A curved wooden handle fit into the palm of his hand. A tube of metal stuck out of some kind of chamber embedded in the metal.

Hangman pointed at it. "They put their finger through there. That must be how you work it."

"What do you think *that* is?" Shadow pointed to a wheel in the chamber section.

Hangman turned the weapon over and showed his father five identical cylindrical holes. "Do you see those? Now take a look at this." Hangman took out the ball he removed from Alien's chest.

"This ball came out of the Renegade's weapon and hit Alien. This must be the thing these weapons throw at us to injure us. These tubes have three objects in them. The other three tubes are empty. This ball must come out of the weapon when it explodes. That's how it works."

"So this thing has three balls left?" Shadow's cheeks drained of all color.

"Just keep your finger off that piece right there. Don't put your finger inside that loop."

Shadow nodded, but Hangman still saw his father swallowing. Shadow told them where to collect the two other weapons. Shadow put one in his bag, gave the other two to Viking and Hangman to carry, and ordered everyone to retreat.

The men traveled for another five hours before Shadow told them to make camp. He assigned Hangman to gather Gooji sap. Shadow divided the other chores among all the other men depending on how injured they were.

Hangman came back and squatted by the fire while the stones heated to boil the water. Bantam brought a basin of water from the nearby creek and Hangman brushed his sap into it.

No one mentioned hunting. Everyone ate dried meat out of their bags.

"Do you want to go looking for more Renegade parties?" Viking asked after a while.

"We should retreat to the long camp," Shadow decided. "I want to prepare everyone to evacuate, now that the Renegades have these weapons. We might not be able to hold them off."

"You mean we *won't* be able to hold them off," Alien growled. "All our future battles will go the way today's battle went."

"All the more reason to get our women and children out of the long camp," Shadow replied. "The Renegades have been advancing steadily toward the long camp. It's obvious that's their objective. We were already losing ground long before Butcher became Kral. Now the

Renegades bring out this new weapon against us. We have to be ready to evacuate. The odds are stacked too heavily against us."

"What about using Hangman's trick of leading the creatures into them?" Devil asked.

"We don't have time for that," Hangman told him. "It would take time to find the Renegades. Then it would take time to find the right creatures. Then it would take time to lead the creatures back to the Renegades. One party of Renegades could attack the long camp while we were busy fiddling around with another party of Renegades."

"You're right, my son," Shadow replied. "We have to warn the long camp. If we have time after that, we can worry about slowing the Renegades down."

"We won't even be able to slow them down if they can kill us from a distance like this," Cross pointed out. "They don't even have to engage with us."

"We already know what we have to do," Shadow countered. "The stones are hot enough. Make the juice so it's cool enough for us to drink and go to sleep."

Viking used two sticks tied together to lift the heated stones out of the coals and lower them into the water. It sizzled and boiled for a minute until it cooled down.

Hangman didn't stay awake long enough to listen to his relatives' conversation. He went to sleep and crashed hard until Viking shook him awake in the middle of the night.

Viking poured Gooji juice down Hangman's throat and left him alone. Hangman sank into a deep, black slumber.

He didn't wake up until morning. The rest of the men woke up stiff, sore, and grouchy. No one talked while they ate and then they moved out silently.

The party headed straight east without diverting right or left. Hangman checked for signs of Renegades, but after a while, his head started to hurt so much that he didn't even do that.

He stumbled and his vision blurred. It didn't come back into focus. He lost track of where he was until Viking laid a hand on Hangman's shoulder and steered him where to go.

Hangman surrendered to his cousin's protection. Hangman couldn't even think right now. He wanted to die, but he wouldn't. If he fell and couldn't go on, Viking or Alien would carry him back to the long camp. That would be humiliating.

He lost track of everything until a Gorlock roar snapped him back to his senses. His vision cleared instantly and his head shot up. The Gorlock sounded too close.

Another roar split the jungle. Actually it was more than one roar coming from more than one Gorlock. Their heads stuck up over the canopy and they came straight toward the party.

Hangman didn't see how these Gorlocks got so close to the party without Shadow taking evasive action, but that hardly mattered now.

"Use the weapons!" Shadow hissed and clawed at his bag trying to get the weapon out. "See if you can use the weapons against the creatures!"

Hangman and Viking attacked their bags. Their cousins moved behind those three for protection.

Hangman had to think hard to figure out what to do with his weapon. His looked different from his father's.

This one had a different, squarish kind of grip. Even the long tube looked more like a square. Only the channel running down it from the end had a cylindrical shape like everything else.

This weapon didn't have a wheel. He couldn't see how many balls this weapon might be carrying. It might be carrying none at all.

Four Gorlocks spotted the party. The Gorlocks acted like they already understood that everyone in the Godless party was injured and couldn't fight back.

Hangman put his finger into the loop, raised the weapon, and pointed it at the advancing Gorlocks. He wished now that he had his kukris in his hands instead. He knew what to do with them.

Shadow's hands shook when he aimed his weapon at the Gorlocks. The Gorlocks cocked their heads, fixed their beady eyes on their targets, and shrieked.

Viking had one of the weapons with the wheel. Hangman didn't know how many balls Viking had, either. This was no good at all.

The Gorlocks broke through the undergrowth. The others crowded against Hangman's back way too close. He would have liked to shrug them off, but he didn't dare to take his eyes off the Gorlocks.

They spread out in a line abreast of each other. The three weapons couldn't kill all four of the creatures at the same time. One of the men would have to shoot at least twice and none of the men knew how to aim these things.

Shadow's weapon exploded in Hangman's ear. The deafening noise startled him out of his skin and he squeezed his weapon without thinking.

It exploded in his hand. The Gorlock in front of him screeched, reared onto its hind legs, and lunged for him, but he didn't see that the weapon damaged the creature at all.

He squeezed the weapon again. Shadow and Alien fired again and again, but nothing happened. The Gorlocks rushed the three men and the Godless party scattered before them.

All the men took off into the jungle heading in different directions. The Godless' sudden departure confused the Gorlocks into hesitating so the men could get away to safety.

Hangman met up with Shadow, Viking, and Alien under the trees. "They didn't work," Shadow panted. "The weapons didn't work."

"At least we know how to shoot them now," Viking pointed out. "The Gorlocks' skin must be too tough for these things to penetrate."

"It's true," Hangman replied. "One of the balls couldn't penetrate the bone of Alien's chest. These weapons might not be as strong as they appear unless they hit regular flesh. Some solid substance will stop them."

Shadow frowned, but right then, the men heard yells and the clash of weapons nearby.

Hangman and the others charged back to the spot. The weapons must have drawn out any Renegades in the area. Now Hangman's brother and cousins locked in a hopeless battle of eight Godless against twenty Renegades.

Hangman raised his weapon and he, Shadow, Alien, and Viking charged into the assault. Hangman sprang into line with his cousins, aimed his weapon at the Renegades right in front of him, and squeezed.

Nothing happened. The weapon clicked. It didn't explode.

He almost forgot what he was doing and looked down at the thing trying to figure it out. He squeezed again and then turned the weapon around to look down the barrel to find out what was wrong with it.

He couldn't figure it out. None of this made sense when he just used it against the Gorlocks.......unless.....

What if the Renegades developed a weapon they could use against anyone but that no one could use against them? Was that even possible?

The idea horrified him so much that he dropped the weapon right there on the ground, pulled his kukris, and plunged into the fight the old-fashioned way.

His kukris definitely worked, but only until the Renegades in front of him pulled out more weapons. He knew enough to know he couldn't fight them. He barely survived the last time.

"Fall back!" Shadow yelled. "Break away and retreat!"

Everyone obeyed his order, but some of the Godless men had to evade the weapons before they fully got away.

Hangman leapt into the branches. Shots from the weapons pinged and whistled all around him as he took off springing from branch to branch to put the battle behind him.

Chapter 4

Hangman dropped to the ground in front of his father. Shadow and the others continued to travel east. No one looked back.

Hangman didn't see what Shadow and Viking did with their weapons. Hangman didn't regret dropping his. What use was it if he couldn't harm any Renegades with it?

His father halted when he saw Hangman. "Are you all right, my son?" Shadow asked. "Are you hurt?"

"No more than I was before." Hangman cast a glance at the others. "Did you all make it out?"

Shadow nodded and made a face. "Those weapons were useless against the Renegades. Both Viking and I discarded them."

"I did the same thing." Hangman turned away. "We should go."

Shadow grabbed him. "I want you to get up into the trees and make sure the Renegades aren't following us."

"And if they are?" Hangman asked.

"Then do what you think is best." Shadow stepped around Hangman and led the others onward down the path. They left Hangman standing three with those words ringing in his head—his aching, pounding, swimming head.

He really would much have preferred to climb into the branches, curl up in some protected place, and go to sleep for a week. He really needed it, but he wouldn't likely get it anytime soon.

He took his time climbing into the canopy. Moving his arms hurt enough to keep him conscious and alert, but not as alert as he might have been otherwise.

He perched on a branch for a while and rested while he listened to the sounds around him. A herd of Stalkions didn't make it easy. They kept bellowing, pawing the earth, smashing their skulls against tree trunks, and charging each other in tests of strength.

The only good thing about their noise was that it didn't go anywhere. They stayed in one place and occupied each other. They didn't bother anyone else.

He finally got tired of waiting. He might as well go to sleep if he was only going to sit around doing nothing.

He couldn't do that, so he started traveling back westward toward the spot where the Renegades ambushed the Godless this last time.

He found the Renegades long before he got to the spot. The twenty-odd warriors who attacked Shadow's party stood around talking about how to track the Godless scouting party.

Hangman listened for a while. The Renegades didn't talk about the long camp, but that didn't mean anything.

He agreed with Shadow. The Renegades had been working their way closer and closer to the long camp for years. They wouldn't give up until they got there and attacked it.

The Renegades set off walking through the jungle heading north, met back up with another two different war parties, and turned east to track down the Godless.

Hangman tailed them in the branches for a while. Shadow told him to do what he thought was best. That left the field wide open for Hangman to use his own personal brand of creativity.

He couldn't attack the Renegades outright. That would be reckless and probably wouldn't get the job done anyway.

He tried to listen for any indication of where Shadow's scouting party might be right now. The Stalkions' roaring blocked Hangman from hearing anything.

Their noise annoyed him for a minute—until he realized. His race against the Crushers and leading them to the Renegades gave him the perfect idea.

He took off running through the branches. He had to inflict blinding pain on himself every time he grabbed a branch, but he had nothing to lose at this point.

The Renegade party grew to more than thirty men. They would run right over Shadow and the others. Then nothing would stop the Renegades from taking the long camp completely unawares.

Hangman ran all the way to the Stalkion herd. Their noise led him straight to them.

He dropped out of the branches at a distance from them, cut himself a long, straight pole, and hacked the end off to make a sharp-pointed spear. He didn't have time to do it neatly or even to do it right. He just had to go with it.

He climbed back into the branches, tiptoed along the high branches above the herd, and jumped down right in the middle of them.

This particular herd consisted of twenty huge bulls all fighting for dominance in their power hierarchy. They all rounded on Hangman in a rage exactly the way he knew they would.

One big beast charged him, gouged its horns at him, and he sprang out of the way. He stabbed his spear into the creature's hide as it passed him.

The creature roared in fury, but it couldn't get back to him before another bull rushed him. The creature lowered its head to butt him.

He sidestepped, and this time, he stabbed it hard in the neck where the soft flesh met behind the creature's ear.

The bull bellowed to shake the earth and four more Stalkions attacked Hangman. He stabbed each of them in a different place to infuriate them and started to back his way out of the clearing.

The Stalkions roared deep in their chests and the whole herd came after him. They started by stomping their heavy, powerful legs on the ground to track him down. He retreated and they picked up speed.

He eventually had to run just to keep ahead of them. He leapt over fallen trunks, smashed through undergrowth, and prayed to High Heaven he was leading the herd back to where he would find the Renegades.

He looked everywhere for any landmarks and spotted some. He was too far north. He veered westward and led the herd right into the track leading to the Renegades.

The Stalkions' thunderous footsteps vibrated the earth beneath Hangman's feet. He couldn't hear anything else to tell if the Renegades were still in front of him. They better be or he would be in trouble.

The Stalkions kept up with him much better than he expected. His pain and fatigue got the better of him and they gained on him.

A huge bull came up right behind him and tried to swipe its tusks at him. He barely dodged in time to save his life—and then he spotted the Renegades ahead.

Their eyes popped when they saw him coming straight for them at high speed. None of them reacted in time before he blew past them and the Stalkions ran right into them.

Screams, roars, and a few explosions of weapons fire echoed through the jungle. Hangman ran for another half a mile before he stopped.

He would have buckled on the ground and passed out right there. He stayed conscious just long enough to climb into the canopy before he found a quiet nook between the branches and shut his eyes in an exhausted sleep.

He woke up at dusk. He had no idea how long he might have been asleep. He could have been asleep for three days for all he knew.

He stayed where he was for a long time—long enough for night to settle over the jungle. He didn't feel like rushing to move anywhere.

He took the last dried meat out of his bag and ate it. He would have to hunt—or he might just decide to go hungry for another three days until he started to feel stronger. It wouldn't be the first time.

He rested as much as possible. He would catch up with Shadow and the others later. Shadow sent him out here knowing the danger. Shadow wouldn't expect Hangman to come back anytime soon.

He spent the time listening to the jungle noises. He heard a lot of things, but he didn't hear any Renegades.

That didn't mean they weren't here. They would always send more war parties after the Godless. Their recent success would make them bolder than ever.

He must have dozed off again because he woke up in the morning and decided to leave. His head and body still hurt, but he felt strong enough to travel.

He decided to travel through the branches, though. He would still encounter dangerous creatures up here, but at least he would be able to see and hear them coming.

He would be safe from ants and Abnormits if he passed out up here.

Chapter 5

Hangman set off, but after an hour of steady travel, he passed a river winding through the jungle. His thirst drove him insane, so he descended to the ground to drink some water.

He squatted on the bank and used one of his bowls to scoop the water into his mouth. It felt mind-blowingly good going down his throat.

He scooped some of it over his head, washed his face, and then poured more water over his body and especially his wounds.

He washed all the dirt and dried blood off himself, cleaned his wounds much better than before, and reapplied leaf paste to all of them.

He felt better after that. He actually found himself feeling almost normal while he put his bowls and the remaining paste back in his bag.

He started to stand up when a rush of moving air distracted him from behind. He barely glanced over his shoulder in time to see a massive Ridgebeak pelting out of the clear blue sky.

It collided with him full force, pinned him to the ground, and landed on top of him. He barely managed to turn around in time so he fell on his back.

He tried to grab his kukris to fight the thing, but the creature's talons held his arms and legs down. He couldn't move.

He struck out, punched at the creature's legs and feet, and even tried grabbing its feathers. The bird held him no matter what he tried.

The bird flexed its wings to lift off with him. He couldn't stand that. He couldn't let the creature take him back to its nest. It probably wanted to feed him to its chicks.

He needed some kind of weapon, so he squirmed his hand behind him trying to grab the hunting knife he carried in the back of his waistband.

The Ridgebeak didn't like him moving around. It clubbed him with its wing, dazed him for a minute, and lifted off.

It closed its talons around him to tighten its grip on him, but at least he could get his knife like this. The Ridgebeak no longer held him down on the ground.

He pulled the weapon forward, stabbed it into the creature's foot, and the Ridgebeak clenched its talons nearly tight enough to crush his ribs.

He yelled out in pain, flailed sideways, and his antics finally annoyed the bird enough that it stalled in midair, arched back, and struck him four more times with its wing.

He wilted and his head swam. He lost his grip on his knife and it fell down, down, down into the jungle far below.

He looked around trying to find it, but it was long gone. He couldn't do anything but lie here.

He still had his kukris. He could fight the Ridgebeak once he got into the nest—or he hoped he could. He might not be able to in this weakened condition.

He would have to. Staying in a Ridgebeak's nest without fighting back wasn't an option.

He decided to give it up and rest on the way there. Why waste his strength? He would plummet to his death if the bird dropped him from this height.

He definitely couldn't afford to lose his kukris at this point. He decided not to even try to draw them until he got into the nest.

He dreaded meeting the chicks while their mother stood by to make sure he didn't hurt them.

He might have dozed off again or even passed out completely. He woke up when the bird screeched and dropped into the nest high in the canopy somewhere.

He didn't even know what part of the country he was in. The Ridgebeak might have taken him hundreds of miles from his Clan's territory. That would be a nightmare.

He dragged his blurry eyes open and gulped when he came face to face with the Ridgebeak's seven chicks. They weren't chicks. They were fledglings bigger than he was.

They were almost half their mother's size, fully feathered, and they understood exactly what they were looking at when they narrowed their eyes at him.

His hands flew to his kukris, but the mother knocked him down with another swipe of her wing. She hopped around the edge of the nest to get closer to him while not interfering with her chicks' access to him.

He glared up at the chicks. He had to be careful here or risk these birds tearing him apart.

The chicks moved in. One of them pecked at his injured shoulder—the one with the hole in it. The chicks must have smelled the blood. Another eyed the gash in his forehead.

A different chick pecked him in the thigh. He kicked it in the head to knock it away and earned himself a vicious headbutt from the mother bird. What was he supposed to do—sit here and let them devour him? Not likely.

They all moved in and surrounded him. He pushed them off when they pecked him too hard, but he didn't dare to draw his kukris—not yet.

The chicks mostly just experimented pecking at him. They couldn't figure out how to actually eat something that was still alive and intact.

The mother bird screeched at them and lowered her head. Hangman couldn't let her start showing them how.

He drew his kukris in a heartbeat, slashed her across the face, launched himself to his feet, and dove for the edge of the nest. His one thought was to get out of it and hide underneath it. None of the Ridgebeaks would be able to get to him there.

He barely stood up and turned around before the mother bird pounced on him. She squashed him under her talons, but he kept his hands free.

He twisted around in her grip just as her head dove down to gouge at him. He stabbed her in the side of the head again and made her rear away from him. She shrieked in fury, lifted up on her feet, and flexed her wings to give him the pounding of a lifetime.

He took advantage of that moment, hurled himself into a sitting position, and stabbed one of his kukris into the muscle where her leg connected to her body.

She screamed even louder, but he didn't stick around long enough for her or the chicks to attack him. He dove under her body and flattened some of the chicks in the process, but everything depended on getting out of the nest.

He barely stashed his kukris back in his waistband before he threw himself over the side, grabbed the tangled mass of sticks, and flung his legs all the way over. He dangled by his arms as splitting pain tore him apart, but he just had to keep on holding on.

The Ridgebeak screeched in fury and launched out of the nest. He had to work fast and that meant pushing through the pain. He climbed hand over hand down the side of the nest and underneath it to the branches on which it perched.

He cast a desperate glance over his shoulder and confirmed his worst fears. The mother Ridgebeak launched into the sky and came swooping back around to try to recapture him. She definitely wouldn't keep him alive this time.

He scrambled onto the branch, crawled all the way up it, and tucked himself between the branch and the nest. She couldn't get to him here.

The twigs and limbs that made up the nest stabbed him in the body, but he forced himself to lie still and relax. He would probably have to stay here for a long time and that was just fine with him.

He felt no temptation whatsoever to kill these creatures for food. He could get food anywhere. His life was more important.

The mother Ridgebeak kept soaring back and forth. She tried again and again to get underneath the nest and hover there so she could grab him, but she couldn't get to him. The branches and the nest blocked her.

She finally stopped trying, but she didn't stop flying around and around the nest screeching in fury and frustration. She kept up a constant guard in case he came out.

He shut his eyes and forced himself to concentrate on calming down. The Ridgebeaks wouldn't stand guard all the time. They would eventually go to sleep.

Then he could climb down and go about his business. He wouldn't go down to the ground again. He didn't want to risk that.

Just when he started to relax, something moved above him inside the nest. He couldn't tell what it was until he felt it again—and again.

The mother Ridgebeak kept revolving around the nest in predatory circles. She never took her eyes off him. She knew exactly where he was and she wouldn't let him get away a second time.

That jostling sensation came again. He tried to look up, but he couldn't see anything except the underside of the nest.

The sensation got stronger. The nest jounced on the branch and then something sharp scratched through the limbs above him.

He looked in horror and saw the young Ridgebeak chicks clawing their way through the nest straight for him. Their talons already broke through. They would expose him in seconds.

He thought fast. Going out onto the branches would leave him vulnerable to the mother bird. He had to get away from her at all costs.

He looked around in wild panic—and realized. The only way to escape was deeper into the canopy.

He didn't give himself a chance to hesitate. He swung out onto the branch, took hold of it, and dropped to the next branch. It was a thick tree limb directly below him.

He should have been able to land on it easily, but his injuries got the better of him. He landed on the branch just fine, but his foggy brain didn't balance him in time.

He toppled, and before he could even fall, the mother Ridgebeak zoomed out of nowhere and smashed into him with bone-breaking force.

She might have been trying to grab him, but she missed and sent him careening off into open space.

He plummeted into branches, bounced off, crashed through leaves, broke off twigs, and slammed into the ground.

He barely stayed conscious enough to feel himself tumbling over and over on his side down a steep ravine, through more undergrowth, bumping over rocks and fallen trunks, and hitting different unseen objects.

He eventually fell off another steep cliff and landed hard enough to knock himself out completely this time.

Chapter 6

Hangman tried to open his eyes, but something stopped him. His eyelids stuck together. He tried to move any part of his body, but that proved too much to ask, too.

It took him a few minutes of panic before he realized why. He was lying on his stomach with his face plastered into the dirt. He only realized that because of the smell in his nostrils. He couldn't see, hear, or tell anything else about his surroundings.

He felt the pain in his body and immediately gave up on moving anything. Cuts, bruises, and gashes covered him all over the place now, not just on his face and shoulders. That fall did more damage than he realized, but at least the Ridgebeak wasn't here anymore.

That meant nothing. Lying on the ground injured and helpless was the absolute worst possible place to be. Any creature might come along and take another shot at him. Something was bound to come along sooner or later—probably sooner.

He just couldn't summon the willpower or the energy to move. Maybe all the dirt, leaves, and debris covering him would mask his scent enough to protect him.

He had no choice but to lie still and rest. He didn't even know how long he might have already been lying here. He might as well stay where he was.

He shut his eyes—or at least he stopped trying to open them. He let his whole body relax and he fell asleep again.

He woke up calmer but more uncomfortable. He didn't want to face the pain of moving his body, but he had to. He had to do something even if it turned out to be something not very useful or got him killed in the end.

He summoned an almighty effort to pry his head out of the dirt. That was the first step. Then he heaved himself onto his hands and knees.

He wavered there breathing heavily and trying to muster the resolve to wipe the dirt out of his eyes, open them, and look around. He almost lost heart when he thought about what he might see.

He flopped over onto his seat and finally used both hands to brush the dirt off his face. Dried blood stuck most of the dirt to his skin, but at least the view didn't present too much of a nightmare landscape.

He sat under a rocky overhang ten feet away from a stream. The dirt ended in a gravel beach going down to the water's edge. He couldn't see the top of the ravine. He couldn't see anything but the stream and the beach.

He heaved a deep sigh. He was alive and he could move all his limbs even if he did get re-injured. He could live with that.

He just sat in silence for a while, looked all around him, and breathed. He didn't need to do anything just yet. He would have to do something soon enough. He didn't need to hurry up to do it, though.

He eventually hobbled down to the beach, squatted by the water's edge, drank some, and used the rest to clean himself off again.

He felt better afterward and started to relax, but as soon as he did, he started to get hungry. Hunting was going to be a challenge when he couldn't move around very fast.

He would have to decide which creature to kill and how to kill it. He didn't need much when he only had to feed himself.

He turned around to survey the surroundings. He would have to scout the area to find out what creatures lived here.

He would tackle the smallest possible creature he could get away with. He didn't need any kind of physical challenge. Just staying alive would take enough of that.

He crossed the stream and headed for the trees on the other side, but he stopped in his tracks when he heard a Krakelow moving through the branches in front of him.

He didn't see it right away. He didn't have to see it. It was coming toward him.

He pulled his kukris and backstepped back toward the river. He only made it ten feet before an enormous Dushag reared out of the water behind him.

Normal-sized Dushags lunged out of the water onto riverbanks to grab people who came too close. This one must have been five times the size of every other Dushag he'd ever seen before.

It didn't lunge onto the bank. It broke the surface from right there in the middle of the stream, arched fifteen feet straight up into the air, curved its neck, and dove at him.

He stared at it in blank disbelief. He just couldn't bring himself to accept that this thing was real. It didn't look like a Dushag at all. It looked like something completely unknown.

The creature coiled its long body to aim straight for him. It would fall across the stream, across the bank, and its mouth full of teeth would fall with him right inside its mouth.

He couldn't even bring himself to raise his kukris to defend himself. If he used his usual strategy of stabbing the Dushag in the back of the throat to puncture its skull, he would already be inside the creature's mouth. The dead Dushag would slide back into the river taking him with it.

The Dushag dropped closer and closer. He could not for the life of him think of even one sensible thing to do to fight a creature this big.

His only thought was that absolutely no one in his Clan would believe him if he somehow survived long enough to make it back to their camp and tell them about this.

At that moment, right before the Dushag's mouth enveloped him, the Krakelow uncoiled from the nearby tree branches, looped through the air, and hit the Dushag right in the head.

Hangman staggered back to get out of the way, but the two creatures didn't even notice him.

The Krakelow whipped its long body around and around the Dushag's head, neck, and body. They fell across the bank and thrashed, cartwheeled, and slashed each other in brutal combat.

Hangman's back collided against one of the jungle trees. He considered running for it, but at that moment, the exact same mother Ridgebeak dropped out of the sky and landed on the bank right in front of him.

She landed facing him, pumped her wings, and eyed him with deadly accuracy.

He tightened his grip on his kukris to make his last stand, but in that instant, the Krakelow disconnected part of its length from the rest of it, whipped into the air, and coiled around the Ridgebeak instead.

The Krakelow lashed its coils around the bird's neck and body. The Krakelow wrenched its weight over to one side trying to take the bird to the ground.

The Ridgebeak screeched in fury and tried to flex her wings to fight the creature, but the Krakelow enveloped her wings with coils, too. She couldn't take off.

They crashed down sideways on the ground. The Ridgebeak turned on the monster to cut it to ribbon with her talons.

Hangman didn't wait a second longer. He spun away and took off running through the jungle. He didn't stop until the sun went down and he collapsed in exhaustion in the crook of another tree.

He woke up in darkness and listened. The jungle sounded as peaceful as it could possibly sound in the middle of the night.

A full moon shone down through the branches, so he climbed up to the highest canopy and checked the countryside.

He sighed in relief when he realized he wasn't that far away from where he got separated from his father's scouting party.

He could navigate much better from up here in the trees. He applied more leaf paste to his injuries, but at least his head didn't hurt as much anymore.

He took the time to make himself another dose of Gooji juice just in case he needed it. Then he moved on.

He balanced through the treetops and the sun rose before he found the place where Shadow told him to do what he thought was best. The Godless weren't here anymore.

Shadow would keep traveling until he made it back to the long camp. That was his objective—to warn the band and to evacuate the women and children before the Renegade Clan got too close.

Hangman followed the line of tracks toward the east, but he lost the trail after only an hour. It vanished into thin air. He searched for another hour before he gave up. He couldn't find a single track of any Godless.

That didn't matter because he knew where the long camp was. He would just go back there and meet up with his relatives. They would almost certainly already get there before him.

Chapter 7

Mora looked up from her work when she heard a commotion outside her house. It sounded louder than usual. Then she heard some of the women saying the names of men in Shadow's scouting party. The men must be coming back.

She smiled to herself when she walked outside. Her smile evaporated when the men limped into camp. Every single one of them had suffered serious injuries. They collapsed into the arms of their mothers, wives, sisters, and cousins.

Women helped the men to their houses......and left Mora standing there alone. Shadow hobbled over to Katha and she got under his arm to help him. Cross went off to his own house.

Mora gulped. She didn't want to ask, but she had to. "Where's......where's Hangman?"

Shadow stopped and turned around to make eye contact with her. "He got separated from us in the confusion. He's still out there one way or the other."

He didn't say another word before he turned his back on her and went into his house.

He left her standing there really alone this time. The camp completely emptied. She was the last and only person standing outside.

She cast a desperate glance from one house to the next, but Hangman didn't come out of any of them.

She looked toward the jungle path where the men returned to the camp. He didn't come from there, either. Was he dead out there? Shadow didn't outright say Hangman was dead, but Shadow didn't give her any extra hope, either.

She couldn't stay out here alone. The camp looked too desolate without Hangman.

He and the scouting party had been gone for four months since the night she first found out she was pregnant with her first child. What would she do if Hangman didn't return?

She stumbled back into the house and slumped next to the fire pit. She had been living here alone all this time without him.

She should be able to keep doing the same thing. Nothing changed between now and a few minutes ago—and yet everything changed.

She let herself depend on Hangman as her husband. He wasn't perfect, but he turned out to be a lot better than she hoped.

She stared down at her hands. She didn't know he was dead. He might return. He went off on his own all the time. This wouldn't be any different. She would just have to keep going.....

She tried to keep busy and finish her chores in the house. She came out of the house at sunset and joined the other women.

Some of the men had gone hunting. The women divided the meat and gave her a share to keep her going. They went through the same procedure every day.

She stayed by the fires talking to the women until she heard the men talking in a nearby shelter.

This was the three-sided shelter the Kral used to hold meetings with his warriors. Butcher used it while he lived. Now Shadow sat inside it with his brother on his left side and his nephews around him.

She crept closer to listen to their conversation.

"We'll need to send out scouts to see where the Renegades are," he began. "Don't engage them. Just monitor their progress and see how close they come. Then we'll know where they are if we want to launch an attack of our own."

"How do you want to prepare the women and children to evacuate?" Viking asked.

"We can start to prepare extra dried meat and gather extra Gooji sap for the journey," Shadow replied. "We won't know how urgently we should evacuate until we know where the Renegades are and what forces they're bringing against us. We'll keep packs of food and supplies wrapped up and ready to go at a moment's notice."

"What will you do about Hangman's wife?" Devil asked. "You should give her to one of the single men, now that Hangman is gone."

"We don't even know if Hangman is dead," Alien snapped. "He's been gone longer than this before."

"He would have caught up with us by now if he was still alive," Breaker added. "He was gone for over a week before we made it back here. He should have gotten rid of those Renegades and met back up with us."

"You're only saying that because you don't have a wife," Viking interrupted. "You want to take another man's wife before you even know he's dead."

"And you're only saying that because you do have a wife," Devil countered. "It's easy for you to sit back and tell us to wait when you already have a wife of your own. It's against the law to keep a healthy woman from the men who might make her a husband. You're all holding out false hope that Hangman is still alive because he's the Kral's son."

"Who would you have me give her to?" Shadow interrupted. "By my count, there are more than eleven single men in this camp. Cross is underage, but he'll grow up pretty soon and he'll need a wife, too. How do you propose to decide who should take Mora as a wife? Something tells me you won't be so eager to let one of your brothers take her, Devil."

Devil lowered his eyes. "That will be for you to decide. You're the Kral, not me."

Mora spun away and took off running back to the fires. These men were not talking about giving her to another man. She couldn't stand that.

She hunted high and low through the camp until she found Katha. Katha was on her way down to the stream to fill her water gourds.

"The men are over there talking about giving me to another man," Mora blurted out.

"I'm not surprised," Katha replied over her shoulder. "Hangman has been gone for over a week. The single men are bound to get agitated."

"Aren't you going to do anything about this?!" Mora insisted.

"What do you want me to do? I can't stop the men from talking."

Mora dove in front of her. "Come on! You have to help me!"

"How, exactly?"

"You're the Kral's wife. Can't you talk to him?"

Katha compressed her lips. "I shouldn't. I could get into a lot of trouble with Shadow, but I'll help you this once."

She turned around and strode back to the camp. Mora had to hustle to keep up with Katha's long strides. Katha marched right over to the Kral's shelter. The men were still arguing about the same topic.

"We should have a test of strength to see who marriers her," Feather suggested.

"That would be the same as a challenge and could lead to deaths," Banjo pointed out. "We don't want to lose good men fighting over a woman."

"We should give her to the youngest man over the age of gathering," Breaker interjected. "That's Grizzly. He would be scheduled to return to the gathering again this year anyway."

"If you're going to make that argument, then Mora should return to the gathering this year, too," Viking pointed out. "Why should any of you get a second chance at her when the younger men haven't gone to the gathering at all? Keeping her back means one of them has to go home empty-handed."

"Excuse me!" Katha raised her voice extra loud so the men could hear her over their conversation.

Shadow looked up and saw her and Mora standing there side by side. The other men had to turn around to see who had the nerve to interrupt them.

"Is something wrong?" Shadow asked. "We're in the middle of a discussion here."

"You're discussing giving Mora to another man," Katha replied. "I thought you would all like to know that she's pregnant with Hangman's child. You can't give her to anyone until after the child is born."

Shadow frowned. "That does complicate things."

The other men wilted in dejection. "How long will that take?" Devil asked.

"We found her to be carrying the child just before you all went on this scouting party," Katha replied. "Give it six months. Then you can decide who to give her to." Katha turned to Mora. "There. Are you satisfied?"

Katha walked off heading for the stream again. All the men stared up at Mora. She squirmed under their direct gaze and bolted away.

She raced up behind Katha. "That wasn't the help I was hoping for!"

"What did you expect me to do?" Katha snapped over her shoulder. "Those men are all facing a lifetime alone. You can't expect them not to start getting ideas the minute Hangman disappears."

"This doesn't solve my problem at all! I'll only be facing the same problem six months from now! How is this supposed to help me?!"

"No, you won't." Katha squatted down by the stream, took out her blade, and set it near her while she filled her water gourds. "Hangman isn't dead. He's still alive out there."

Mora stopped in her tracks. "He is? How can you be certain?"

Katha snorted. "I know my sons, little rabbit. He's too tough. I don't know what happened to delay him. Shadow says he got badly injured before he got separated from the party. Maybe that's what's wrong, but he's still out there and still trying to get back to us. He'll return before this child is born. Then you won't have to marry anyone else."

Mora winced. "I sure hope you're right."

"So do I, but even if I'm not, six months is enough time for you to finally accept that he isn't coming back. Then you'll be ready to marry someone else. These men have been waiting all their lives. They can wait a little longer."

Chapter 8

Mora squatted in the center of the long camp helping Rila and Nagana finish butchering a fully grown Gurlg the men killed earlier that day.

The creature took five men to bring it down. The women had been working all day to cut up the meat and smoke it for the evacuation supplies.

Everyone had been working in a fever of agitation ever since Shadow announced his plan to move the band deeper into Godless territory. He was only waiting for Bantam, Cross, and Feather to return with news before Shadow decided when to move everyone out.

The remaining men had been hunting more and more to bring in meat to cure. The underage boys had been searching for any supplies of Gooji sap they could find.

Mora wiped her sweaty forehead across her shoulder, sliced the last hunk of meat off the bone, and handed the meat to Estia to put on the fire.

Estia had deteriorated rapidly since the deaths of her two sons. She aged overnight and continued to decline with every passing day.

She talked openly about staying behind when the band evacuated. She didn't want to go through the ordeal of traveling. Her presence would only slow the band down and make it harder for the men to defend everyone.

No one argued with her or begged or insisted that she should come. She no longer had a single living member of her immediate family left alive. She had come to the Godless from the Whisperers. She had no other blood relatives in this band.

Mora didn't get involved in convincing Estia to come. Mora would have been the only person even to suggest it.

No one in the Followers would ever dream of leaving someone behind, not even someone old, weak, and frail. The family band would simply find a way to make it work. A person's life was too valuable.

Mora knew better than to tell the Godless that, but listening to Estia talk about staying behind made Mora sick to her stomach.

She usually had to leave the area so she wouldn't hear Estia, and even worse, so Mora wouldn't hear what the others didn't say to contradict Estia's decision.

Mora had enough on her mind. She straightened up, stretched her stiff back, and headed down to the stream to wash the blood off her arms, body, face, and blade.

She lashed the blade to a pole and set it next to her before she approached the water's edge. She knew better now, especially when she saw Dushags arching their spines in the middle of the channel.

She cupped the water, splashed and rubbed it on her face, and scooped more of it onto her shoulders to wash down her arms.

She started to cup the water over her head to wash her hair next. She poured one scoop over her head and bent over to get another one when someone squatted down on the bank next to her.

She jolted and spun around. She stared in confusion when she saw Breaker squatting next to her. Devil was the oldest of Cosmos's sons, but Breaker was taller and bigger in the shoulders.

Devil had a compact, feral, dangerous quality like he would just as soon kill someone as look at them. Breaker acted softer and more easygoing.

Bantam came in somewhere between Devil and Breaker on the height scale, but he didn't grow as bulky or as chunky as either of his older brothers.

Their younger brother Grizzly grew almost as tall and big as Breaker, but Grizzly had a slow, almost dull-witted way of staring out at the world. He went along with everything, rarely expressed any opinion, and didn't seem to have a single original thought in his head.

Breaker smiled at Mora. "Be careful of the Dushags."

Mora went back to washing her hair. "I am."

"Don't worry. I'll protect you from them."

"I don't need you to. You can go back to the camp."

"You could bring home a Dushag all by yourself, couldn't you? Then everyone would know what a mighty warrior you are even though you're a Follower."

She glared at him. "What do you want?" She already had a pretty good idea.

"What would your family say if they saw what a Godless heathen you've become?"

Mora looked away to pour another handful of water over her head. "I'm sure they would be very proud of me. Both my parents told me before I left to make myself an asset to this Clan and not to give anyone any reason to shame me or my family. That's what I'm doing."

"Does it bother you to kill?" he asked.

She snorted, picked up her blade, and moved to a safe distance from the water before she untied the blade from the branch. "I think you better go back to the Kral and your brothers."

He followed her back toward the camp. "Why are you so hostile toward men? You know you're going to marry one of us eventually."

"You better discuss that with the Kral and your brothers, too," she replied over her shoulder. "The odds are heavily stacked against the Kral choosing you as my new husband."

He sprang forward, grabbed her elbow, and turned her around to face him. "He would choose me if you told him you loved me and wanted to marry me." He sidled closer to her. "We could spend the next six months getting to know each other.....and I could get to know you......" He dragged his eyes down to her body. "Then you wouldn't have to go to a stranger."

She tried to walk away, but he crossed the last few inches of space and put his arm around her.

He was a lot bigger, stronger, and more intimidating than Hangman. Mora would probably have found Breaker attractive if he wasn't trying to horn in on Hangman when the band didn't even know if Hangman was dead.

Hangman might be ugly, but he did have one thing going for him that none of these other single men had. She respected him.

She could think of dozens of incidents that made her respect him. She had no reason to respect any of these other single men—except maybe Alien.

He didn't argue that he should be able to marry Mora within a week of Hangman's disappearance. Alien actually spoke in favor of Mora marrying anyone.

Mora would have vastly preferred to marry Alien than Breaker or any of Cosmos's sons. She actually liked Alien.

She shoved Breaker away with all her might. He could have restrained her, but he let her go.

"Leave me alone and don't ever touch me again," she snapped. "I'm not your wife. If you ever touch me again, I'll inform the Kral and he'll feed you to the ants. You're nothing until he does give me to you as your wife. Until then, you better treat me as belonging to another man—because I do."

She stormed off back to the camp, but she couldn't return to her work or go to her own house. She walked into the camp just in time to see Katha ducking into her own house. Shadow and the others sat around under his shelter.

She hustled over to Katha's house and ducked inside without knocking. Katha looked up in surprise. "What are you doing here?" she snapped.

"I need your help! You gotta help me!"

Katha groaned. "Not again!"

"Breaker just made a move on me down by the stream! He tried to...." Mora broke off. "He said we could get close to each other in the next six months and then I could tell Shadow that I wanted to marry Breaker."

Katha's features hardened. "That's illegal. He shouldn't be touching a woman who isn't his wife."

"Don't you see?!" Mora wailed. "I can't keep doing this for the next six months. I have to go out there and see if I can find Hangman. You said yourself he might be injured. He could be right out there! He might need help! I have to at least go try to find him."

Katha pinched her lips and went back to whatever she had been doing just a few minutes ago. "All right. If that's the way you feel, I better go with you."

Mora opened her mouth to protest—and stopped. "You mean it?"

"I can't let you go alone." Katha cast an appraising look at Mora's blades. Mora always wore them everywhere she went. "Are you ready to go?"

Mora's jaw dropped. "You mean....now?!"

"Why not? We still have a few hours of daylight left. If you're right about Hangman being injured, then we should find him immediately—or as soon as possible. Let's go."

Mora was still standing there with her mouth open when Katha walked out of the house without a backward glance.

Mora had to shake herself to race after her. The men stood around talking to each other instead of sitting under Shadow's shelter.

Katha went over to her husband, said a few words to him, and rejoined Mora. "Let's go," Katha repeated and set off for the path leading into the jungle.

Chapter 9

H angman staggered between trees trying to keep one step ahead of another Krakelow coming after him. The creature coiled from branch to branch to catch up with him.

Only Hangman's constant evasions and direction changes slowed the creature down. It collided with trees mere seconds after he diverted in a different direction.

He held both his kukris in his hands, but he didn't dare to get into a fight against this creature—not with both his arms injured.

The Krakelow could move too fast and he already felt himself getting tired. He would have to stop one of these times—unless the Krakelow took him down first.

He cast a desperate glance in all directions. He had to find some way to stop this creature from chasing him. He kept hearing different creatures in the jungle, but none of them was big enough to occupy the Krakelow long enough for Hangman to get away.

He also had to make sure that the creature he chose didn't attack him first. That complicated the problem.

He missed his footing and staggered again. His exhaustion was starting to get the better of him. He came within inches of colliding with a tree. That would really have slowed him down.

He corrected in time just as the Krakelow landed on a tree less than five feet away. Hangman didn't try at all to keep his footsteps quiet. Staying alive was a much higher priority right now. He hoped the noise would bring out some larger predators.

It worked. He dodged the Krakelow three more times before he blundered into a mob of four Demonex.

The cats turned around when they heard the noise, saw a helpless human stumbling through the jungle way too chaotically, and they all came after him.

Hangman almost sobbed in relief when he saw the Demonex closing on him. He charged straight for them, but running in a straight line left him unprotected from the Krakelow.

The Demonex picked up speed to close the distance with him. They didn't see the Krakelow. He didn't dare to change his course now, so he fell flat on his face.

The Krakelow sailed straight over his head and collided with the biggest male Demonex in the lead. The other Demonex realized their mistake and tried to get away in time, but the Krakelow divided and hurled three parts of itself at the other Demonex.

They all went down scrapping and fighting to free themselves. Hangman scrambled to his feet and turned away to flee with his life before any of the combatants came after him.

He barely got fifteen feet away from the creatures when the telltale thump of Crusher footsteps vibrated the ground under his feet.

He looked up and saw three of them stomping through the canopy heading for him. The bellows and shrieks coming from the Demonex must have attracted the Crushers.

They looked straight down at the battle scene with Hangman standing right there. Crushers were one of the very few creatures that preyed on Krakelows and Demonex. The Crushers didn't care what a creature was. If it moved, it was food.

The Crushers eyed Hangman with their beady, unrelenting gaze. He wouldn't make more than a mouthful to a Crusher—and maybe not even that. Now he stood alone between them and a meal that might actually satisfy them for a few minutes. He had to get out of here.

He wanted to lead them toward the Krakelow-Demonex battle, so he ran backward and around the fight. The Krakelow released a few of its sections to grab him, but he dodged and kept on running.

He collapsed a hundred yards from the fight. He needed more than anything to get back to the long camp, but he couldn't go another step.

All this constant fighting against creatures and struggling through dangers aggravated his injuries. He had to use his arms for everything, so his injuries never had a chance to heal.

He really needed to lie down somewhere for a few weeks and do nothing, but that wouldn't happen even after he made it back to the long camp.

Shadow would need Hangman and all the able-bodied men to help with the evacuation. No way would Hangman let his relatives carry him out of the camp on a stretcher. That would be unthinkable.

He couldn't even summon the energy to climb into the branches even though he knew he should. Staying on the ground was too dangerous.

He passed out and woke up hours later when an Abnormit bit him on the leg. It started chewing at his shin and made him strike out in a rage. He staggered to his feet and spotted four more Abnormits coming toward him. He had to get off the ground.

The idea of using his arms to pull himself up into the branches made him want to puke. He couldn't do that again.

He struck out at the creatures with his kukris, backed away, and found some branches and twisted trunks low enough that he could walk up them without using his arms as much. He still had to use them to balance.

He only climbed thirty feet off the ground and slumped on a branch. He allowed himself to whimper in misery, now that he was alone and no one could see or hear him.

He should have climbed into the canopy to check his route to the long camp, but he just couldn't face it right now.

He should have given himself another dose of Gooji juice. He should have done a lot of things, but he only shut his eyes, tilted his head back against the trunk, and let himself drift off into a semi-conscious stupor.

He just couldn't stay awake for more than a few hours at a time before exhaustion overtook him. He couldn't remember ever feeling this exhausted before in his life.

He didn't even really care if another Krakelow found him here. At least his ordeal would finally come to an end.

The idea of death seemed so sweet in that moment. He wouldn't even try to fight back. He would just try to stay asleep for the whole attack until it ended.

He must be really spiraling if he thought like that. His mind kept slipping into different thoughts, memories, sensations, emotions, and jumbled ideas. He couldn't stay focused on more than one thing.

Different images kept morphing in front of his eyes. He saw the long camp again with all the relatives he knew walking around, talking, and doing things. He saw the Ashtaw Valley and Mora standing down there feeding the young ones Fogpo leaves.

Then he saw the Renegade Clan's encampment in the Jagged Points. They built their sturdy houses of thicker branches lashed together. He relived the moment of hiding in the bushes and listening to them talk. Their conversation filtered into his fuzzy dream state.

"As soon as we cross that ridge, we'll spread out to surround the camp," their burly leader ordered. "Kill as many Godless men and boys as you can, but make sure the women and girls don't escape. Surrounding the camp and keeping everyone inside will be the most important thing, even if we trap fighting men inside. We can eliminate them, but we need to take the women and girls alive."

Hangman floundered out of his dream. He never heard those words when he eavesdropped on the Renegades in the mountains.

They never talked about surrounding anyone. They didn't know the Godless were there before—and the Godless didn't have a camp in those mountains.

He looked around trying to figure it out—and heard more voices coming from directly below him. A war party of twenty men stood on the ground at the base of this tree.

"The old people will be just as dangerous," another man remarked. "The Godless don't get less dangerous when they grow old."

"Did you just hear what I said?!" the first guy snapped. "I said surround the camp, drive everyone inside, including the fighting men and anyone else who comes out against us. We have to take advantage of our numbers to trap them inside. We can worry about who to eliminate after we capture everyone."

"We won't be able to eliminate anyone if we trap the fighting men inside," a third man pointed out. "The Godless get ferocious when they have to defend their families."

The first man threw up his hands. "This isn't up for debate. I just told you what to do. Now go do it and don't waste any more of my time. We have to meet up with the other parties so we have enough men. Come on."

He led the way into the jungle. They headed east—toward the long camp.

So the Renegades really were going after the long camp. They brought in multiple war parties to surround the camp, wipe out the fighting men, and capture the women and girls.

Hangman's first thought was to hurry ahead of the Renegades and warn his father and cousins about this.

Hangman would never get there in time. He couldn't travel the way he used to. He had to come up with a different solution.

Almost as if his own thoughts made it happen, he heard another Krakelow coming toward him. It came from the east. Perfect.

He struggled to stand up. He had to grit his teeth against pain to balance himself with his arms, but at least he wouldn't have to fight either the Krakelow or the Renegades.

He had to reduce the Renegade numbers. Their advantage was in their numbers and the element of surprise. Hangman could take away one of those advantages, at least.

He tried to hurry along the branches getting closer to the Krakelow. He got close enough to attract its attention. It picked up speed to follow him.

He went into another similar race to keep out of its way. He had to be extra careful not to lose his footing in the branches so he didn't plummet to his death.

He led the Krakelow around in front of the Renegades. He chose his spot with care, stopped, and turned around to face the Krakelow.

He moved his hands to his kukris like he wanted to make his stand and fight the creature, but he had no intention of doing anything like that. He couldn't.

The creature uncoiled its body from the branches and spun over and over itself coming straight for him. He leapt off his own branch and dropped straight down into the party of Renegades.

They all jumped when they saw him—and then they all pounced on him to drag him to the ground. Half of them raised their fists to punch him—right up until the Krakelow fell on top of them.

He cringed into a ball under all their bodies. Their screams and yells rang in his ears. He had to get out from under them. They reared upright, pulled their weapon, and wrenched themselves around to fight the creature.

Hangman hurled himself sideways, bumped into some of their ankles, and knocked a few of them over before he dragged himself out from under the pile.

Half the Renegades got away and ran for it. Some got away and turned back to help their friends. Three of them saw Hangman making a break for freedom and came after him. One of the Renegades went down when a Krakelow segment attacked him from behind.

That left two Renegades coming after Hangman. He had to come up with some way to eliminate them next.

He didn't know how many more Renegades survived the Krakelow attack. However many remained, they would meet up with others of their kind to continue their campaign against the Godless.

He pulled his kukris on the run, but he couldn't fight the Renegades. He couldn't fight even one of them. He had to reduce their numbers, too. He had to kill them one at a time by some method other than fighting them hand to hand.

This was the coward's way, but his injuries left him no choice. He ran until he couldn't run anymore, ducked behind a tree, flattened his back against it, and waited for the Renegades to catch up with him.

They slowed their advance when they saw him hiding there. He didn't even try to conceal his presence. They already knew he was here.

He held his breath counting down the seconds until they separated. They surrounded the tree from both sides so he couldn't get away. They both raised their blades to strike him down, but he struck first.

He waited just long enough for both of them to step into view before he stabbed one kukri into his lefthand opponent's neck and took off running again.

The second Renegade swung his blade. The sharp edge embedded in the trunk where Hangman had just been hiding, but he was already gone. He ran for his life to get away from his last Renegade pursuer.

The guy got the jump on Hangman, though. He closed the gap in seconds and his fingers brushed in Hangman's hair when the guy stretched out his arm to grab Hangman.

Hangman went into another panic trying to decide what to do. He saw a blank piece of sandy ground ahead and headed for it.

He checked all around for some way to save himself and noticed a cluster of low-hanging branches directly over the Cursed Sand. He would have to use his arms, but he didn't have a choice about that, either.

He stuck his kukris back into his waistband, burst through a curtain of undergrowth surrounding the Cursed Sand, and launched himself in a flying leap over the circle of sand.

He grabbed the branches and swung himself out over the circle within inches of touching the surface. He barely pulled his legs up in time before the last Renegade blundered through the undergrowth and ran straight into the sand.

The cone collapsed underneath him. He scrambled to crawl out of it, but his own speed carried him too far toward the center.

All the sand spiraled down toward the hole at the bottom. The guy tried again and again to climb out, but he eventually fell screaming into the hole where the creature dragged him under.

Hangman's shoulders screamed in pain. He might have screamed a few times, too—each time his momentum made him swing from the branches. He eventually stopped swinging—and there he hung without the strength to pull himself up to safety.

He didn't dare to let go, but he only felt himself weakening more and more the longer this went on. He had to do something.

He looked around for some way to get himself out of this. He even heard more Renegades coming closer. They must have followed their comrades to find out what happened to them.

Hangman tried again and again to pull himself up, but he always collapsed gasping and reeling in pain. He had to stop trying or he would fall into the pit himself.

He was still hanging there when the Renegades found him. They glared at him. Then they laughed at him. Then they put their heads together and discussed how they could capture him.

They took a long, long time to decide what to do. The Cursed Sand creature kicked all its sand out of its hole and smoothed out the surface to lay its trap again. These Renegades knew better than to set foot on it.

They eventually decided to send three of their men to climb into the trees, balance along the branches until they got directly above Hangman, and try to pull him up that way.

The branch from which he hung turned out to be too thin to support all four men's weight. Two of them tried to come out before they changed their minds.

Their burly leader must have fallen under the Krakelow because a different guy gave them orders this time. "Climb up to that branch above him," the guy ordered. "Make a noose and loop it around his wrists."

"Just lower me a noose and I'll grab onto it," Hangman called over. "I don't want to hang here anymore."

"Shut up," one of the men above him told him.

Hangman didn't interject again. The idea of these men pulling him up by his wrists sounded like his idea of pure Hell, but anything was better than falling into the Cursed Sand.

At least he stood a chance of escaping if they captured him. They would probably torture him for information about the Godless position, but he could survive that.

Or maybe he couldn't. He might not be able to survive more injuries than he already sustained.

He didn't have much choice about much of anything right now. He just had to concentrate the last of his strength on holding on until these men got hold of him.

They took an even longer time braiding a rope and finding the right position to hook him with their noose.

First they tried to loop it around his legs. He considered grabbing the loop and holding onto it, but he absolutely could not bring himself to unclamp his fingers from the branch. He didn't trust himself not to lose his grip on the rope, too.

In the end, they finally listened to his continued assurances that he wanted them to capture him and get him the hell out of here.

They widened their loop and lowered it as far as his feet. He used his feet to grab the loop, hook it around one leg, and then maneuver the noose up his waist.

The Renegades cinched the noose around his waist and started to haul him up. The rope bit into his sides, but at least it didn't break.

They hauled him up to their branch where all three men grabbed him and held him down to tie him up. He didn't fight back. He relaxed into the inevitable. He didn't want to move anyway.

Chapter 10

The Renegades threw Hangman onto the ground next to a roaring bonfire somewhere deep in the jungle. At least forty Renegades camped here.

Hangman had never seen the Renegades spend any time in the trees, not even to rest or to keep away from dangerous creatures. They always camped on the ground.

They didn't appear to be in the slightest bit concerned about these fires attracting unwanted attention from creatures or other humans.

The Godless would never make a blunder like that, but then again, the Godless wouldn't get up a war party this big to attack a camp full of women and children—not even enemy women and children. The Godless didn't do that.

Hangman lay where the Renegades put him. He didn't struggle or try to move. He didn't have the energy for that and every move of his arms made his shoulders hurt.

The Renegades talked to each other about a bunch of people, things, and locations that Hangman didn't understand. He half-tried and half didn't try to follow their conversation. He already knew enough about their plans.

The only real question was what they wanted to know about him. They must already know enough about the Godless and Shadow's long camp. The Renegades didn't need any new information to carry out this attack.

The Renegades settled down to eat and relax for a long time before they paid any attention to him. They passed around their food and water. They even joked with each other.

They told a lot of rude, disgusting jokes about their own women. The Godless wouldn't have done that, either. Godless men didn't talk about their women to other men.

Too many single men lived alone their entire lives. Talking about a woman in front of them would have been considered cruel and offensive to everyone, including the woman in question.

The Renegades didn't have the same scruples, especially about discussing their women in front of Hangman. He truly hoped he never met any of these women in person. That would have been awful.

He rested his head in the dirt and waited. He expected them to go straight to the torture. He could only feel grateful for every blissful second that passed before it happened.

One of the Renegades knelt down in the middle of their conversation and held a piece of dried meat in front of Hangman's face. "Are you hungry, little brother? Here. Eat this."

He moved the meat close to Hangman's mouth. He opened his mouth and the guy angled the meat to put it into Hangman's mouth, but the guy pulled it away before Hangman could bite down on it.

The others exploded in crude laughter. Hangman only smiled at them. He didn't resent them for playing games with him. The Godless didn't do that, either, but not everyone was Godless.

The same guy bent down a second time. He couldn't stop laughing when he held out the meat again. "No, really," he told Hangman. "Open your mouth."

Hangman didn't move. The other men fell over themselves laughing.

"He's onto you now, Upro," one skinny guy observed.

Upro sat back down and bit into the meat himself. Hangman watched the guy chew. Hangman had been unable to hunt while he was injured. He had been getting steadily hungrier, but he wouldn't tell the Renegades that.

He stared into the fire instead and waited for the inevitable. The Renegades actually all went to sleep and left him lying there tied up.

Now would have been the perfect time if he wanted to escape and had been able to do so. The Renegades didn't take his kukris away from him, but he couldn't get to them with his hands tied.

Lying here with his hands tied never posed a problem for him before. Now it presented an insurmountable obstacle.

He eventually fell into an exhausted sleep. Any creatures who came would attack the Renegades first before the creatures got to him. Maybe he would find a way to escape then.

He woke up when someone kicked him in the back. He jolted out of a sound sleep and that movement made him howl in pain when he yanked his arms against the ropes binding him.

"Wake up, Godless scum," one of the Renegades snapped.

Hangman wilted onto the ground again. He really hoped they would hurry up and get to the torture or beating or whatever they planned to do with him. Anything would be better than waiting.

The guy kicked him five more times in the ribs and kidneys. Hangman concentrated hard on not moving his arms. He wouldn't be able to escape unless someone actually put a knife in his hand.

The coals of last night's fire still smoldered in front of his face. Smoke curled up through the camp as the other Renegades sat up, scratched themselves, and stumbled to their feet.

The guy got tired of kicking Hangman and went off somewhere. Everyone ignored him, so at least he got a few more seconds of rest.

He snapped wide awake again when another party of Renegades came out of the undergrowth—and then another party of Renegades showed up. Renegades converged from all sides. Hundreds of them gathered here. This was not good at all.

His mind went into a tailspin about what to do about this. Did Shadow order the evacuation yet? Did he even realize the Renegades brought this many men into the area?

The Godless would be sitting ducks if Shadow didn't realize or if he didn't already order the evacuation. Hangman didn't have time to warn them now. He couldn't think of anything to overcome this many men......except the ants.

They had a force strong enough to defeat the Renegades. He couldn't think of any other creature with enough members and enough organization to come against a body of men this big.

That plan would take time, too. He would have to escape, find the ants, and then lure them somewhere they could intercept the Renegades. How would he accomplish that?

First he had to get out of here, but even that looked impossible with so many enemy warriors standing around. Breaking or cutting these ropes would only get him killed quicker.

He made sure not to move while he thought it over. He wouldn't have been able to defeat all these Renegades even if he had been perfectly strong and healthy. One man couldn't do anything against a force this size.

He found out soon enough why they left him alone overnight. The Renegades stood around talking. Their conversation blended into a tide of voices. He couldn't hear any of what they were saying.

They all fell silent when a completely different guy shouldered his way through the crowd. He wasn't the biggest Renegade here—not by a long shot. In fact, he was one of the shortest, but he still carried a hefty load of muscle.

His carriage and facial expression said it all. He had to be one of the Renegade Clan's leaders if not *the* leader.

Four enormous warriors surrounded him in a guarding posture. No one could get near him. No one shoved or jostled him. Everyone pulled back to let him through.

He stopped and narrowed his eyes at Hangman. "Who are you?" the guy asked. "Where do you come from and which band do you belong to?"

Hangman cleared his throat. "My name is Hangman, son of Shadow, the Kral of the long camp your men plan to attack. That's my home family band."

Murmurs went through the party of Renegades standing around listening. Their noise didn't tell Hangman whether they believed him or not.

"Were you the one who killed my men?" the guy asked.

Hangman twisted his head upward so he could look the guy straight in the eye. "Yes, I was the one and I will continue to kill as many of your men as long as I'm still alive. I won't stop."

The short guy compressed his lips and sniffed to dismiss that. "How many more men do you have running around out here pulling ambushes on us?"

"None," Hangman replied. "I'm the last one."

The short guy narrowed his eyes. "I don't believe you."

"I don't care if you believe me or not." Hangman nodded toward his left shoulder—the one with the round wound hole going through it. "Your men injured me with those exploding weapons of yours. I got separated from my father's scouting party. They left me for dead. They don't know I'm still alive. I'm alone out here. I would have rejoined them a long time ago if I could have."

The short guy dipped one nod to the beefy bodyguard on his right. The bodyguard squatted down next to Hangman. Here it came.

Hangman panicked again when the bodyguard raised his hands to take hold of Hangman. He lacked the strength even to struggle when the guy clamped his muscular hand on Hangman's shoulder and drilled his thick fingers into the flesh surrounding the hole wound.

Hangman screamed and then roared and bellowed in the throes of brutal agony. The guy screwed his fingers into the swollen, bruised flesh. Just when the pain started to subside, he moved his fingers a fraction of an inch and did the same thing in another place.

Hangman collapsed screaming and howling on the ground. All the Renegades stood around watching until the bodyguard stopped.

Hangman slumped in a puddle of misery, but at least he was finally going through it now. It would end, either with the Renegades stopping this torment or they would kill him.

"I'll ask you again," the short guy went on. "How many other people are out here with you? How many are waiting to ambush us between here and the camp?"

"I'm alone!" Hangman wailed. "I'm alone! I've been trying to get home.....for a week......or maybe more.....I just want to go home....."

The short guy nodded to his bodyguard again. Hangman couldn't deal with this a second longer, but he had to.

The bodyguard did the same thing. He twisted his finger into the wounded flesh of Hangman's shoulder, and when he finished that, the Renegades flipped Hangman over so the bodyguard could do the same thing to the blade cut on Hangman's neck.

The bodyguard only tormented that shoulder for a few minutes before Hangman passed out completely. He woke up lying in the same place with his arms and legs still tied. He didn't try to move. The Renegades still stood around him—or some of them did.

It became obvious with every passing second that the attack party was organizing to move out. The short guy went from group to group giving orders to everyone. Hangman couldn't pick up anything he didn't already know.

Each party left the area as soon as the short guy finished talking to them. The area emptied more and more as the Renegade leader worked his way through the crowd.

Hangman only listened for a few seconds before one of the other men came over and cut the rope around Hangman's ankles. Three Renegades pulled him to his feet so he could walk on his own.

Two men flanked him on either side. They held onto his arms and made his shoulders hurt, but at least he could stand up now.

His recent torture drained his energy more than ever. Every particle of his being trembled. He barely held himself together. He had never felt more fragile in his life.

The Renegades kept filing out of the area, but they didn't all leave in the same direction. They all headed east, but some headed so far northeast that they couldn't hope to meet up with those heading southeast.

The men escorting Hangman headed due east on a straight course for the long camp. Did the Renegades plan to use him as a hostage to threaten Shadow's band?

Hangman would have liked to believe that Shadow would be strong enough not to negotiate with the Renegades for Hangman's life.

No one in the Godless Clan had ever gotten themselves into this situation before—not that Hangman ever heard of. It certainly never happened in Hangman's lifetime.

He didn't actually know if Shadow would let the Renegades kill Hangman rather than negotiate. Shadow valued Hangman. Hangman knew that. No one had to explain it to him. Shadow respected Hangman as much as anyone—and even more than some.

Hangman would be humiliated if the Renegades used his life to extort concessions from the Godless. He dreaded the moment when his relatives saw him as a helpless captive.

The Renegades probably wanted the Godless to hand over their women and then leave the territory so the Renegades could take over this country.

Hangman would have been even more catastrophically humiliated if his father conceded something like that. Which women would Shadow hand over—Mora? Or Katha?

Hangman couldn't let that happen, but he was powerless to prevent it. That was the real truth.

This was the first time in his life when he had ever been truly powerless to do anything. He lacked strength when he was young, but he never lacked his wits and the will to use them.

What he lacked in strength, he made up for with ingenuity and resourcefulness. He could accomplish almost anything as long as he thought it over and came up with some other way of doing things—other ways that didn't require strength.

He should do the same thing now. The creatures of the surrounding jungle offered him an unlimited array of options. The only question was how to get them involved in the right way without Hangman getting killed in the process.

Chapter 11

T he short Renegade leader took charge of the party heading due east. He, his bodyguards, and the rest of his men surrounded Hangman. Breaking or cutting the rope around his wrists wouldn't save him from these enemies.

The party traveled for an hour before the leader called everyone to a halt. He sent one of his men into the canopy to check their direction.

Hangman took the time to look around for a way to attract a creature to the party. The ants would be the best choice, but he didn't have time for that.

The man came down and directed the party a few degrees to the left so they would stay in line with the long camp.

Everyone set off again. Hangman's legs went numb. He wouldn't be able to walk much further. Then the Renegades would either carry him to the long camp or kill him as an inconvenience.

His vision started to blur when the party emerged from the trees. They had to cross a twenty-foot-wide rock flat before they entered another path leading down to the long camp.

No trees or any other vegetation grew on the rock flat. Hangman knew this rock flat well. The party was less than five miles away from the long camp.

The short leader stepped out of the trees first along with his bodyguards. Hangman's escort pulled him forward even though he had been cooperating with everything.

His feet didn't want to obey him and he stumbled again. He caught his own balance so his guards didn't have to tug his arms to keep him going.

He straightened up, and at that moment, a flock of Boultars dropped out of the sky. They landed right on the rock flat and took down a dozen Renegades in a split second.

The Boultars took down two of the short leader's bodyguards, including the man who tortured Hangman. The Boultars stabbed their long beaks into the men to impale them. More Boultars went after the rest of the party.

The Renegades sprang forward, drew their weapons, and fought back. Hangman's escorts did the same thing. They rushed forward to defend their leader.

The escorts left Hangman unguarded, but only for a minute before another Boultar attacked from the left. The creature flanked Hangman and came after him. He couldn't defend himself with his hands tied.

He backed away to put distance between him and the creature. The Boultar flexed its wings and screeched in his face. His escorts noticed him moving around. They must have thought he was trying to escape—which he was.

They backstepped and moved in to position themselves between him and the Boultar. The escorts maneuvered Hangman behind them—and right then, three Ridgebeaks dropped at the same time.

One of the Ridgebeaks slammed down on top of the Boultar that wanted to attack Hangman. The Ridgebeak grasped the Boultar in its claws, but the Boultar struggled so hard that the Ridgebeak had to pump its wings to keep its balance.

The bird didn't even realize when its wings knocked the two Renegades aside. They both crashed down on the stone.

Hangman turned and ran for it. He would never get a better chance than this. He charged into the undergrowth heading straight west. All his fatigue vanished in a blur of adrenaline.

He didn't try to untie his wrists—not yet. He really hoped the Renegades followed him away from the long camp.

Maybe he should have run east instead so he could get to the long camp and warn his father in time. Hangman's mind didn't seem to be working right, but he could only think about getting away from the Renegades right now before they recovered enough to come after him.

He dove under branches, dodged trees, leapt fallen logs, and almost ran into a trail of ants marching from north to south. He had to hurdle them so he didn't run straight through them. He didn't want them to follow him or come after him.

He kept on running until his knees gave out at the base of a tree somewhere. He wheezed for air and fought to keep his eyes open. He couldn't pass out right now. He had to stay awake and keep moving no matter what.

He forced himself onto his knees and hunted around until he found a fallen tree with some sharp splinters sticking out of the shattered trunk.

He allowed himself to sob in pain when he moved his arms up and down to saw the rope loose. Then he buckled in the dirt in a delirium of agony and relief.

He couldn't stay here, though. He had to think. He had to come up with the best strategy—either to lure the Renegades away from the camp or to warn his father. Hangman couldn't do both.

The separate attack parties must have spread themselves out too far by now. They would line up around the long camp. They would recapture him if he tried to get through. Luring them away looked like the better option right now.

He pushed himself up and finally stumbled to his feet, but he could barely move his arms at all now. That one bodyguard inflicted more damage on the tissue around his wounds and made them even more swollen and painful than before.

The swelling got into the joints and made them stiff. Hangman couldn't even draw his kukris.

He went through the same sequence of thought processes. He didn't have strength. He needed something else to fight the Renegades.

He eventually came to the same conclusion—the ants. He just passed a trail of them a few minutes ago. They had been going from north to south. All he had to do was lure them where he wanted them to go.

He made a snap decision and set off stumbling through the jungle. He kept an eye open for the pollen trees the ants favored. He would need a lot of pollen to cover all that territory—or maybe he wouldn't.

He would need the use of his arms. Climbing the pollen trees required his arms.

He found a tree loaded with pollen, but the clusters hung a hundred feet above his head. He would have to carry all that pollen even if he collected it.

He stood there thinking it over when he heard branches crashing to the east and voices yelling back and forth. The same two Renegades came after him. They survived the Boultar attack.

Hangman didn't stick around long enough to find out if the short leader and his men would come after Hangman next.

He jumped up and pulled himself into the branches. He sat right out in plain view and grabbed some nearby vines to use as a rope. He twisted them as quickly as he dared and settled himself down to wait.

He didn't have to wait long. The two Renegades spotted him the way he hoped they would. They hustled over to the tree and yelled back and forth about climbing up to recapture him.

They either didn't notice him holding his vine rope or they didn't think of it. One of them approached the trunk and walked too close under Hangman's position.

He dropped the rope on top of the guy's head, cinched a noose around his neck, and pulled. Hangman had looped the rope over another sturdy limb above him, wrapped the rope around his own waist, and sat down to use his own weight to heft the guy off the ground.

The Renegade dropped his weapon, grabbed the rope trying to get it off, and kicked out his legs to free himself, but he only yanked the rope tighter. Hangman hoisted the rope another length to lift his victim far enough off the ground.

The Renegade's comrade rushed over to help his friend. The stricken man kicked too hard, spun on the rope at the same time, and accidentally kicked his friend over.

That gave Hangman a few more seconds to hoist his victim just high enough. The second Renegade couldn't do anything but stand there and watch his friend strangle.

"You bastard!" the second Renegade roared. "I'll kill you for this! I'll make you pay, you Godless scum!"

The man ran around down there watching until his friend stopped twitching. The guy started to climb the tree, changed his mind, and ran off toward the rock shelf. He yelled plenty of threats until he vanished into the undergrowth.

Hangman didn't wait around. He lowered his victim to the ground, jumped down, unwound the rope from the guy's neck, and then Hangman used the rope to form a harness around his own chest.

He looped the other end of the rope to the corpse's wrists. Hangman could drag the dead man like this without putting any pressure on his injured shoulders.

He set off, but he had already wasted too much time. He didn't know how far south the ants might have already gotten.

He hustled through the jungle, bumped the body over rocks and fallen trunks, and finally heard the ants scuffling farther east.

Hangman had to run to get in front of them. He used his kukris to hack the dead Renegade's feet to bloody pulp. Then Hangman positioned the body right in the ants' path.

They fell right into his trap. The frontmost ants found the body and started chewing into the guy's feet. Hangman turned around and started walking. He had to march fast—much faster than he wanted to. He just had to keep going.

He hiked for half an hour before he spotted a different group of Renegades moving in on the long camp.

He didn't hear all of the short leader's instructions, but he must have ordered them to assemble in the right position and wait for all the other groups to take their places. Then they would all attack at once.

This group wasn't doing anything except standing around under the trees and waiting. They spotted Hangman first, of course, and they all turned around to confront him.

He walked right into their midst and the ants attacked.

Hangman waited until the ants took down the first Renegades. Then he took off running and dragging his dead Renegade with him.

He stopped there out of range, waited for the ants to take down all the Renegades, and then positioned the dead body close enough for the ants to find it.

They started chewing at it and he took off walking again. He led them to the second group of Renegades and the same thing happened. He could do this all day.

Chapter 12

K atha stopped and looked around at the ground under her feet. "This is where they stopped."

"Who?" Mora asked.

"Shadow and the other men. This is where Hangman parted from them."

"How can you tell?" Mora asked.

Katha pointed to the ground. "I recognize their footprints. Shadow was leading the others on their way east. They followed this path all the way to the long camp, but Hangman wasn't with them."

Mora gulped. "Where was he?"

"He was in the trees, but he jumped down right here. He and Shadow had a conversation and then Hangman left."

"What does that mean?" Mora shut her eyes. "Don't answer that."

"Shadow probably sent Hangman off to do something. Maybe the Renegades threatened them or just followed them. Shadow probably sent Hangman to get rid of them."

"Does Shadow do that a lot?"

"All the time. He would have been quicker to send Hangman than anyone. Hangman is the most capable."

"So how do we find him if he's in the trees?"

"If he's in the trees, he'll be out of danger. We won't need to find him."

"Oh, come on!" Mora countered. "He would have come back to the long camp by now if he possibly could have. You know this as well as I do. Something went wrong."

Katha compressed her lips. "Let's keep moving. We'll follow their trail back toward the west. If the Renegades did follow the men, Hangman would have gone that way to intercept the Renegades."

Katha set off. Mora stayed behind her and didn't break the silence. Mora really needed to learn more tracking skills, but now obviously wasn't the time.

They traveled for ten minutes before Katha stopped in her tracks to listen. Mora didn't have to ask what the problem was. Crusher roars echoed through the trees from the right.

Katha waved Mora away. The two women retreated and then Katha motioned for Mora to climb up into the branches.

The women crouched in hiding for ten minutes before three Crushers stomped into their path. Blood stained the Crushers' jaws and bodies. They didn't notice the women.

The Crushers passed on. Katha waited a while before she signaled to Mora that it was safe to climb down.

Katha didn't head in the same direction to follow the men's trail. She motioned for Mora to follow her farther south. This was out of their way, but Mora didn't know enough to argue.

The women came upon a scene of carnage the Crushers must just have left. A dozen dismembered Demonex lay on the ground. The Abnormits were already moving in to finish off the scraps.

Katha and Mora backed away. Katha hustled back to the scouting party's trail and the two women pressed on farther west.

Mora fell into the thoughtful silence. At least she didn't have to wait around to find out what happened to Hangman. Katha's skill gave Mora hope that they would find him one way or the other.

Gorlock screeches startled her back to her senses. She stiffened when she heard that sound and almost stopped walking while she looked around trying to find the creatures.

"Don't worry. They aren't close enough," Katha remarked over her shoulder. "Just keep moving."

"Um......Katha.....?" Mora stammered.

Katha looked up and she stiffened, too. Two Gorlock heads stuck up over the canopy. The heads bobbed on a sea of foliage as the creatures crashed and barged their way straight for the women.

Katha started to back away again. Mora went with her, but the Gorlocks came too fast. They ran at their top speed—faster than a person could run.

The women ran a hundred yards, but the Gorlocks only gained. Katha pulled her axes and spun around to make her stand. The Gorlocks towered over her and Mora.

Mora drew her blades and stood in line next to her mother-in-law, but Mora would have much preferred to cower behind Katha and let the older woman do the fighting.

The Gorlocks closed, eyed the two women with beady intent, and screeched. That sound sent a shiver up Mora's spine. She wouldn't survive a fight against two of these creatures.

At that second, a person soared out of nowhere and tackled both women to the ground. Mora had a split second to realize it was Hangman before he flattened both women and all three of them rolled a dozen yards backward.

He flew off and landed hard on the ground, but he only jumped to his feet, grabbed both women, and dragged them to their feet. "Come on!" he yelled. "Run for it!"

Mora glanced over her shoulder. Her stomach turned when she saw an absolutely massive swarm of ants enveloping the Gorlocks.

The ants attacked with terrifying speed, rushed up the Gorlocks' legs, and started devouring the creatures alive.

The Gorlocks screeched, bellowed, thrashed, and beat their wings, but they couldn't free themselves. Hangman grabbed Mora's hand and pulled both women away. The three companions took off running into the jungle and left the ants behind.

Katha and Mora could have run a lot further, but Hangman collapsed first. His knees failed and he pitched face first onto the ground.

The two women attacked him, turned him over—and that was the moment when Mora fully realized what terrible shape he was in.

He looked skeletal and pale with multiple wounds all over his body. He could barely keep his eyes open. Mora couldn't tell if he even recognized where he was or who he was with.

A length of rope wound around his torso. The other end hung off to one side with nothing attached to it.

"My God!" Katha breathed. "This is awful!"

Mora touched his shoulder. "He's been shot."

"What does that mean?" Katha tried to touch the round wound there.

Hangman reared off the ground roaring in pain. The flesh around the wound throbbed with black, hot, infected blood.

"He's in bad shape," Mora murmured. "He needs Gooji juice—a lot of it."

"I'll get it. You take care of him." Katha stood up and walked away into the jungle.

Mora looked around at the surroundings. She didn't know how much danger Hangman would be in on the ground, but she had no way of carrying him into the branches.

She supposed they could have used a rope to haul him up there, but she would have to make the Gooji juice on the ground.

She decided to wait for Katha to come back. The two of them would have better success if they worked together to lift him into the branches.

She examined the wound on Hangman's head and then the cut on his other shoulder. The wound on his head didn't look too bad. It wasn't deep enough to cause any problems. The leaf paste took care of it and he might even have given himself a dose of Gooji juice already.

The blade cut on his neck looked as bad as the gunshot wound. Both had become infected and the tissue around them pulverized by some force. Both wounds wept puss that did nothing to improve their condition.

She built a fire and found some stones to heat to boil water. She rummaged in Hangman's bags and found a bowl of leaf paste just as Katha came back with the Gooji sap.

"Give me the paste," Katha told her. "I'll put it on."

"We can't. We need to clean out the wounds first. They're already suppurating."

"I don't know what that word means," Katha muttered.

Mora pointed to Hangman's shoulder where the gunshot wound went all the way through. "Something happened to this wound. A gunshot wound shouldn't look like this. The tissue around it should be undamaged, but it isn't. This is much worse than a normal gunshot wound."

"I didn't understand half of what you just said," Katha countered. "How do you know so much about this?"

"The Followers study medicine. We favor medical books and anything that tells us about ailments and how to treat them. We always take those books when we find them in the ancient cities. Follower bands always train people in medicine to treat wounds and medical problems."

Katha made a face. "Don't start telling me how great the Followers are. I don't need to hear that."

"You asked. I'm telling you. We need to clean these wounds before we re-apply the paste or the Gooji juice. We need to clean out whatever is causing the infection."

"What do you think is causing it?"

"I don't know. I can't tell. It looks like something dirty got into the wounds—both of them—but that shouldn't be possible. Hangman put the leaf paste on them already. See the dried layers? You know what he's like. He would have been very careful to keep the wounds clean and keep them covered in paste."

"Then how did this happen?"

"I don't know, but cleaning these will be painful. The procedure will probably wake him up. I'll need you to help me hold him down while I clean his wounds."

Katha swallowed hard. "I don't know if I can hold him down. He's stronger than I am. He might be stronger than both of us."

"He's weak. Look at him. He could barely stand before. Come on. He might die if we don't do this now. Just do your best. I'll try to explain it to him if he wakes up enough to listen to me."

Katha gulped again. Mora wasn't looking forward to the procedure, either, but she had to do it. She took out one of her blades, inhaled a deep breath, and scraped the blade across the swollen, puss-filled tissue of the blade cut.

Hangman burst to life with a frightful roar and tried to lunge off the ground. Katha lay across his chest and used all her weight to hold him down.

Mora turned out to be right about his weakened condition. He fought as hard as he could to break free, but he couldn't overcome his mother's strength.

"We have to clean the wounds, Hangman!" Mora yelled in his ear while she worked. "We have to get rid of the infection! I know it hurts! It will be over soon!"

She did her best to block his roars and screams out of her mind. She kept scraping and even cut away some of the flaps of skin until the wound bled freely. Then she blotted it with a ball of fluff, pressed on it to make it stop bleeding, and sealed it with paste.

Then she had to deal with the gunshot wound. She took Katha's hunting knife for that, screwed it into the hole as deep as she could go, and scraped away as much of the infected tissue as possible.

She had to get Katha to roll Hangman onto his side so Mora could scrape away at the exit wound on the back of his shoulder.

He screamed and bellowed right up until she drilled the knife into the exit wound. Then he passed out.

She went through the procedure as thoroughly as possible before she helped Katha lay him out flat on the ground. "We should cover him up," Mora remarked. "We need to keep him warm."

"It's already hot enough out here," Katha pointed out.

"Not out here. I'm talking about in him. He won't be able to keep himself warm. We need a hide or something to cover him."

"Wait here. I'll get one."

Katha left. Mora didn't know where her mother-in-law would find a random creature's hide out here.

Mora spent the time making Gooji juice and set it aside to cool by the time Katha came back. She brought the hide of a fully grown male Demonex with her.

"Where did you get that?" Mora asked.

Katha jerked her thumb over her shoulder. "The Abnormits left it behind. They were fighting over the skeleton and organs. The hide got pushed to the side."

Mora cleaned the inside of the hide as much as she could, but in the end, she just left it bloody and draped it over Hangman.

He fell into a deep unconscious sleep and didn't revive. "How long should we wait before we give him the Gooji juice?" Katha asked.

"Let's wait until sundown," Mora replied. "He needs to be at least awake enough to swallow it or else he might choke on it."

Chapter 13

Katha left again and came back with the carcass of an adolescent Gurlg chick. It stood as tall as a man at its head. She worked for a few hours to butcher it and put the meat over the fire to cook. "Thank you," Mora told her.

Katha shot her a look. "You were right about him. He wouldn't have survived if we didn't come out here and find him." She grimaced at her unconscious son. "I never thought I would see him this bad."

"Did you know the Renegade Clan had firearms?" Mora asked.

"I don't know what that is. Whatever happened to him out here must have been bad. He's come home injured before, but never like this. He didn't even make it home this time."

Katha sat down next to Mora and started cutting the cooked meat off the hunk on the spit.

"I guess I got used to him always being able to handle anything out here," Katha murmured to herself. "I never thought he was dead when Devil and the others started talking about giving you to someone else. I never would have thought to come out here looking for him. I didn't think he needed me to."

"I probably would have thought the same thing. I wouldn't have decided to come out here if Breaker hadn't pushed me to it."

Katha looked deep into the flames. "When you first came to the Godless, I thought it was the worst thing that could happen to our Clan. I cursed the day he married you, but now I think you're the best woman for him. I'm glad he married you and not some other woman."

Mora didn't trust herself to speak. She and Katha had come a long way together—and not just by traveling through the jungle.

Mora would have liked to tell Katha how grateful she was for all of Katha's guidance, support, and help. Mora couldn't bring herself to say that. Those words would have dishonored the moment and spoiled it somehow.

Katha handed her a bowl full of meat shavings. Mora at them in silence and so did Katha. They kept watch over Hangman while he slept.

He went into a fevered delirium, tossed and turned, whimpered, and even yelled out in fear without waking up.

"What's wrong with him?" Katha whispered.

"The infection might be getting into his brain." Mora picked up the basin of Gooji Juice. "Let's see if we can give him the first dose."

"What if he can't swallow it?"

"We have to try." Mora shook Hangman by the shoulder. "Wake up, Hangman! Wake up! You need to drink this Gooji juice!"

He startled out of his trance, but he didn't open his eyes completely. He didn't focus on anything. He mumbled, "Huh?"

"Help me sit him up," Mora ordered.

She and Katha lifted him into a sitting position. Mora held the basin to his lips and tipped the liquid into his mouth. He started gulping as soon as he tasted it. He drank a lot of it. He must have sensed that he needed it.

She let him drink as much as he wanted before she and Katha put him down. He groaned in what sounded like relief and his eyes slipped shut. The two women covered him up and tucked him in.

"Do we have enough Gooji juice for another dose?" Katha asked.

"Something tells me he'll need more than one more dose. He might need a lot more doses. We should make some more."

Katha only nodded. "I'll go get it."

Mora went through the same procedure to make another batch of Gooji juice. She found herself searching the area while she gathered firewood and waited for the stones to heat up.

Night was coming on. She and Katha would have to take turns defending Hangman until he got strong enough to travel back to the long camp.

He startled her by rasping in his sleep, "Renegades......"

She turned around fast and looked down at him. He kept struggling to open his eyes.

She bent over him and got in his face. "Hangman! What about the Renegades? Are they the ones who did this to you?"

"Renegades...." he husked. "Surrounding.....the long camp.....eva cuate......"

Mora froze. Her veins turned to ice at those words. Was he hallucinating again or was he trying to warn his family about a real, credible danger?

Katha came back just as he made a few more indistinct noises. They sounded like he was trying to talk.

She squatted down and opened a piece of hide holding another pile of Gooji sap—a bigger pile this time. "What did he say?" Katha asked. "Is he still unconscious?"

"He said......" Mora floundered to clear her head. "He said.....the Renegades.....were surrounding the long camp. He said we needed to evacuate. Then he passed out again."

Katha's head shot up. She stared at Mora with such ferocious intensity that Mora trembled.

Katha launched to her feet. "Stay here—and guard him," she snapped. "Don't let anything happen to him."

Katha took off running through the jungle. Mora watched her out of sight and then stared into the flames. Katha would take the news back to the long camp. Mora had her own responsibility to attend to.

She settled in for a long night, but at least Katha left her with plenty of food. Mora started to cut herself another bowl of meat when Hangman rasped in his sleep again.

She glanced at him in time to see him start to open his eyes. He actually focused on her this time. "More......" he whispered. "I need .....more....."

"More what?!" She had to stop herself from yelling at him. "Tell me what you need. Are you hungry? I have some food here."

"Juice.....more juice.....I need more....."

She grabbed the basin, helped him sit up, and poured the rest of it down his throat.

"I'm making another batch now. I'll give you some more later."

He sank back on the ground sighing in relief. "Thank you."

She rested her hand on his chest. His heart pounded through his sternum, but at least he was still here.

She touched his face, but just then, Katha came running back through the trees. She squatted down by the fire still breathing heavily.

"Shadow knows," she panted. "I told him."

She froze when she saw her son awake. He stared up at her with perfectly clear dark eyes.

She gulped. "Are you.....can you hear me?"

"I can hear you just fine, Mother," he breathed. "I'm not dead."

"You almost were," Mora told him. "What happened?"

"The Renegades.....they have a new weapon.....it explodes someh ow....."

"They're firearms," Mora told him.

His head shot up and he stared at her. "You know what they are?"

"Some people call them guns. There's a cylinder with a projectile inside it. The weapon sets off a kind of exploding dust. The burst sends the projectile out to strike the target."

"Yes!" Hangman whispered. "That's exactly what happened."

"The ancients developed them. They used the weapons all the time. They were common for fighting in ancient times—even more common than blades."

"Where do you think they got them?" Katha asked. "How could the Renegade Clan have a weapon none of us have ever even heard of?"

"The Renegades could have all kinds of resources in their territories," Mora remarked. "Maybe that's why they want to encroach to take the Godless' territory. The Renegades want to find out if we have resources they don't have."

"We don't have anything." Katha turned back to Hangman. "Mora says the weapons shouldn't have injured you like this. She says something else happened to make them worse."

He snorted and turned to look straight up at the canopy. "You could say that."

"Are the Renegades bringing firearms against the long camp?" Mora asked. "The men won't be able to fight that."

"Shadow already knows about the weapons," Hangman replied. "We all fought the Renegades when they brought out the weapons. We stole the weapons from dead Renegades, but the weapons didn't work for us. The weapons worked when we used them against creatures, but the weapons failed when we tried to defend ourselves against the Renegades. Maybe the men are right and the Renegades are using some kind of witchcraft."

"It isn't witchcraft," Mora told him. "The weapons probably just ran out of ammunition."

"What does that mean?" Katha asked.

"The projectiles the weapons use." Mora held up her fingers. "The weapons use a small package like this. It contains the projectile and the exploding dust. The weapon triggers the dust and sends out the projectile. The whole package is called ammunition. The person has to load the weapon with ammunition or it won't work—and then the weapon won't work again after the person uses up all the ammunition."

"Then the Renegades must have ammunition," Hangman pointed out.

She nodded. "They have more than ammunition. They must have found a large supply of ammunition somewhere in their territory. They would need a lot of ammunition to learn how to use the weapons well enough to bring them on a campaign like this. The Renegades wouldn't have brought the weapons at all if they weren't certain they had enough ammunition to finish the invasion."

Hangman frowned in thought. "You're right. I didn't think of that."

Mora turned to Katha. "Is Shadow evacuating the long camp? We should take Hangman back there before everyone leaves."

"I didn't stay long enough to find out what he plans to do. I think he still wants to find out how many Renegades are in the area."

Mora glanced at Hangman. "Do you know how many Renegades are still in the area?"

"No, I don't. I got rid of as many as I could the way he told me to, but I might have missed a few. I wasn't thinking as clearly as I might have been—and it wasn't like I could move around very well."

His words reminded her of something. "How did you get the ants to attack the Gorlocks like that?"

He looked away. "Never mind."

Now her curiosity really got the better of her, but she let it go and decided not to push it. "Are you hungry? You look like you haven't eaten in a while."

"I haven't. I don't think I've eaten in a week."

She cut him a bowl of meat and held it out to him before she remembered.

He kept his hands and arms under the Demonex hide. He probably couldn't move them very well with those injuries.

She picked up one of the meat shavings, held it out to him, and he opened his mouth so she could feed it to him.

He held eye contact while he wrapped his lips around her fingers and sucked the juice into his mouth. She felt her cheeks burning when the sensation rushed up her arm.

She looked down at the bowl to pick up the second piece, but she had to look at him when she put the second piece into his mouth.

He curled his tongue around her fingers this time. That satin wetness shot straight into her guts. He really was giving her a sexual suggestion right here in front of his mother.

Of course Katha already knew about Hangman and Mora doing it. How else could Mora get pregnant?

Right then, as if on cue, Katha leaned over, curled up on the ground with her back to the fire, folded her arm under her head, and didn't move again. She turned her back to Mora and Hangman.

Mora's cheeks burned again when she saw her mother-in-law lying over there. Katha wouldn't just sit there staring at Mora and Hangman together.

Hangman broke in on her thoughts by murmuring under his breath, "I missed you."

She swallowed hard and turned back, but that left her no choice but to feed him another piece of meat. "I missed you, too. I feared the worst when you didn't come back."

"What are you and Katha doing out here?" he asked. "The whole country is crawling with Renegades. It isn't safe out here for you, not even if you're with her."

She tried to shake that out of her head, but putting another piece of meat into his mouth only reminded her of her encounter with Breaker.

"I had to find you. Some of the other men....." She broke off. "They started talking when you didn't come back. They started to say......Well, let's just say they started talking about what they would do if you never came back. I had to find you. That's all."

"I'm surprised Katha came with you. She should have told you that I would come back eventually."

"She did say that—but what if you didn't? When would you have come back? What if you couldn't?" She shook her head again. "It doesn't matter because we found you—or you found us—one or the other."

He cocked his head to study her. She couldn't meet his eye. Did he know? Did he sense what she didn't say about the other men?

He understood a lot more about his family band than she did. Maybe he already knew about Breaker's designs on other men's wives.

Chapter 14

H angman watched Mora prepare another batch of Gooji juice. He needed it. He felt that in every fiber of his being.

He couldn't move at all. He just had to lie here and let her do everything for him, but he already felt the juice working.

She did something to his wounds while he was unconscious. He didn't remember her doing anything. Whatever it was made them hurt more, but they already started to feel better. He still needed more Gooji juice. Then he would be able to really start healing.

He found himself admiring her beauty and goodness when she wasn't looking at him. She took good care of him. She fed him. She covered him. She tended his wounds.

She felt more like his wife now than before. He wanted her, but he wouldn't be able to do that now while he was so weak.

He would just have to wait. He didn't want to do anything with her in front of Katha anyway. He would get a chance when they went home to the long camp.

He really hoped his father took the warning seriously and evacuated everyone. Hangman couldn't be sure how many Renegades he fed to the ants. He might have slowed the attack down. He definitely didn't stop it.

His gaze migrated down to her body. She hadn't started to swell up with pregnancy yet—not in the belly at least.

Her breasts looked bigger and her waist, hips, and thighs looked more curvaceous. The idea of her being pregnant turned him on. He wanted to do it with her again while she was pregnant even though he didn't need to.

He forced himself to look away. She kept working and set the new pan of Gooji juice aside to cool.

She immediately started making a third batch, heated the stones, left to fetch a basin of water, and scooped the last of the sap dust into it.

"Three batches should be enough," she told him without looking up.

"Kiss me, Mora," he told her.

She spun around to stare at him for a second, but only for a second. She threw back her hair, bent over him, and kissed him deep, slow, and succulent for a long time.

He sank into that feeling. She was here. They were together again, thank all the Heavens. He made it.

She pulled away, stretched out next to him, and put her arms around him. "Thank God you're back," she murmured.

He kissed her hair. "I'm sorry I couldn't come back sooner. I tried. I really did."

"I know you did," she murmured. "I know you did everything."

He couldn't answer. He shut his eyes and fell into another exhausted sleep. This one felt much more natural and not so delirious and fevered. He actually slept this time.

He wouldn't have woken up at all, but Mora woke him up in the middle of the night to give him another massive dose of juice. He drank as much as he could possibly hold before she laid him down and let him pass out again.

He woke up in the morning, stared at the sky, and listened to all the creatures around. A snap of twigs startled him out of his skin. He tried to sit up—and saw Katha standing over him.

She gave him a hard look before her eyes darted sideways to Mora asleep on the ground. She had curled up next to Hangman.

"She saved your life last night," Katha murmured. "She knows more about wounds than anyone I've ever met."

Hangman couldn't look away from Mora's sleeping face. A light glowed out of her features. It made her unimaginably beautiful, but of course he didn't tell his mother that.

Mora was pregnant. He was going to become a father.

He needed to be more cautious out here in the jungle. He couldn't take the kinds of risks he took in the past. He had to take better care that he always came home from every trip.

At the same time, his impending fatherhood made him want to take even more risks—wilder risks, more reckless risks. He wanted to do more to eliminate all his enemies—both his human and non-human enemies.

He *would* take a lot more risks. He would become a thousand times deadlier, stealthier, and more fearless.

He would hazard anything to protect Mora and their children. He would make certain his children grew to the age of gathering and married their own spouses. The Godless Clan would continue no matter what. He would make certain of it.

He saw all of that in her face. It radiated out of her pregnant body. She meant something more to him than just a body for him to sleep with and satisfy himself with.

His progeny would come from her. She would be their mother the way Katha was his mother.

He married the right woman. She might not be fully Godless yet. She might never become fully Godless.

That didn't matter because she was his wife, the mother of his children, the keeper of his house, the foundation of every generation that would come after him.

He didn't tell Katha any of that. She probably already understood it. Of course she did.

He contented himself by simply saying, "She knows more about a lot of things than anyone I've ever met."

Katha squatted by the fire and started cutting up the last of the meat that hung on the spit. "How do you feel this morning, my son? We should take you back to the long camp as soon as you're able to travel."

"I can travel," he replied. "I can still walk. Moving my arms and using my weapons might be more challenging, but I can walk as far as the camp—as long as we don't get into any fights along the way."

Katha snorted. "You should know better than to say something like that."

Their conversation roused Mora. She sighed, stretched, sat up, and scowled at everyone. "What's happening?"

"We're going back to the long camp this morning," Katha announced. "We've been sitting here on the ground for too long as it is. Hangman can rest there."

"Unless Shadow calls the evacuation," Hangman corrected.

"We have to go back either way," Katha told him. "Eat something so we can go. I don't want to stay out here if there's a chance the Renegades could come between us and the camp."

She walked over to him, pulled the Demonex hide off him, and handed him a bowl of cut-up meat.

Mora helped him sit up so he didn't have to use his arms, but he didn't want her to treat him like an invalid anymore.

He was the one who should protect his wife and his mother—not the other way around. He might be injured, but he still had a job to do.

He used his fingers to put his own food into his mouth. Mora sat next to him and ate the food Katha gave her. Mora didn't offer to help him, but he felt her watching him and waiting for a chance to do something—anything.

Her attention and care meant the world, but he knew what he had to do now. He finished eating, drank another dose of Gooji juice by lifting the basin himself, and floundered to stand up.

His legs and knees still felt weak and watery, but at least he could stand. He leaned against a tree while he waited for the women to finish packing up the camp.

Katha left the Demonex hide where it was, wrapped up the last scraps of meat in a small piece of hide, and the three companions set off heading east.

Hangman kept a much closer watch on the surrounding countryside on the way there. He could focus his vision and hear much better like this. He picked up sounds and details he didn't notice in the last few days.

The country sounded quiet. He paused more than once to search everywhere for signs of Renegades near the long camp.

The party stopped at the halfway mark so Katha could climb into the canopy and check the surroundings. She didn't see anything, either, but Hangman didn't want to trust that.

The three companions crossed the last few miles and entered the long camp toward dusk. A surge of commotion broke out when

Hangman returned. Everyone rushed him, hugged him, and far too many people patted and squeezed his shoulders.

He tolerated it all, told them all how much he missed them all, and did his best to smile at everyone. It sure was nice to be appreciated.

He had to push his way through the crowd to get to his house. His relatives fell behind. He spotted his father and brothers standing off to one side. Shadow beamed at him glowing with pride. Shadow wouldn't stop smiling and his eyes glistened with emotion.

Hangman smiled and wound up blushing. He always came home, but he wasn't so sure this time if he would really make it.

He wouldn't have without Mora. Katha was right about that. Even if Hangman made it home injured this badly, his injuries would have killed him without her help.

He stopped in the middle of the camp and looked around. He planned to tell his relatives that he was fine and to send them all home to their own houses.

He stopped himself when he spotted Devil, Breaker, and Bantam standing off to one side by themselves. None of them came forward to welcome Hangman home. None of the three cousins smiled. They scowled at him.

Mora's words made sense in that moment. Not everyone was happy to see Hangman come home alive. One of the single men would have taken Mora for his wife if Hangman never returned.

Did something happen? It must have. Something must have scared her enough to make her leave the camp and come out to find him.

Whatever it was must have been serious enough to convince Katha to come with her. Hangman didn't have to think too hard to realize what the inciting incident must have been.

He didn't do or say anything to indicate that he understood. He just made up his mind to keep an eye on Mora.

He turned back to his relatives. "I'm fine, Auntie," he murmured. "Really. You go home. I'll be fine. I'll talk to you soon. Good night."

He walked away, but not before his father intercepted him. Shadow met up with him and the two men strolled over to Shadow's shelter. No one else came with them.

Hangman's younger brothers vanished into the woodwork. The other initiated men returned to their own houses. Mora went inside the house she shared with Hangman. Katha returned to the house she shared with Shadow.

"What's out there, my son?" Shadow breathed. "Tell me what you saw."

"The Renegade Clan is bringing in a huge war party," Hangman replied under his breath. "They plan to surround the camp, trap everyone inside, kill all the fighting men and boys, and carry off the women and girls."

Shadow nodded. "That's nothing we didn't already expect."

"No, you don't understand, Father," Hangman insisted. "This war party—it's hundreds of men—or it was."

"What do you mean—it was?"

Hangman shrugged. "I reduced them, but I don't know by how much. I don't know how many men are out there. They might bring in even more." He rubbed his eyes. "I wasn't thinking clearly at the end."

His father scowled at him. "You should go rest, my son. You look terrible."

Hangman snorted. "You should have seen me when Katha and Mora found me."

Shadow laughed, but he did it quietly. He patted Hangman on the back instead of the shoulder. "Go lie down, my son, before you fall over. I'll talk to the others about scouting the country....."

"You should evacuate anyway," Hangman insisted. "You should evacuate right now—tonight if possible. Don't delay. I mean it, Father. You have to listen to me."

"I am listening to you, my son, but we would be walking through the jungle in the dark if we left now. Go home to your wife. I'll send you word when we make a decision."

Hangman had to accept that. He didn't really want to go trekking off through the jungle again right now anyway.

He hobbled to his house, went inside, and collapsed on his bed with a groan. Mora smiled at him and handed him another bowl of food. "You'll be able to sleep here."

He hauled his eyes open, pushed the bowl away, and took hold of her arm to pull her toward him. "I don't want to sleep and I don't want to eat. Come here."

He pulled her down on top of him. He simply couldn't resist the urge to use his arms to touch her.

He shut his eyes and let all the bad memories of the past two weeks evaporate out of his mind. He just wanted to forget all about the dangers—just for one night.

He pulled his kukris out of his waistband while he kissed her. She lowered her weight on top of him.

Her body felt as full and ripe as he imagined. She had put on weight since she came from the Followers. She filled out with muscle. Now her pregnancy added roundness and firmness everywhere he touched and squeezed.

She sank into his mouth and her hair fell over his face. She smelled succulent and inviting—and then a scream and a crash split the stillness outside.

Chapter 15

M ora jerked off Hangman with a gasp. They stared into each other's eyes for a second until another crash sent vibrations through the ground.

Mora scrambled to stand up fast enough. Hangman took longer. He grabbed his kukris, but before he could move, a catastrophic force smashed through the wall on his left.

Branches and broken wood splinters whirled in his face. He couldn't see anything for a second. Then he heard Mora screaming.

He whirled to the right just in time to see three enormous Renegades storm through the shattered walls of his house. One of them snatched Mora around the waist, lifted her completely off the ground, and backed away with her.

She burst into a fit of kicking, screaming, and struggling. She tried again and again to grab her blades, but the guy pinned her arms down to stop her from striking him.

Hangman sprang forward to intervene only to meet up with another three Renegades invading through the lefthand wall. Four more Renegades moved in front of the invader to block Hangman from going after Mora.

He couldn't have fought this many men even if he had been in the prime of his strength. He had no choice but to back away.

The attack on his house destroyed enough of the structure to compromise the back wall, too. It crumbled behind him and left him clear to leap out into the open camp.

The Renegades didn't surround the camp—or maybe they surrounded the camp and sent men in to attack at the same time.

He couldn't see much in the mayhem. He turned around to see Renegades smashing their way into every single house.

The Renegades sent at least eight men against each house—more than enough to hold the Godless warriors at bay while the Renegades made off with the women.

More screams echoed from out of sight. Hangman couldn't tell from here, but most of those screams sounded like women struggling to break free of their captors.

Godless warriors battled Renegades everywhere Hangman turned. He took a split second to decide what to do before he saw the Renegades break back through the destroyed walls.

They left his house going the same direction through which they entered it. He dodged away, raced around his house to the other side, and attacked the Renegades from behind.

He took a flying leap, raised one of his kukris, and impaled Mora's captor through the back of the skull. The body crumpled on the spot and Mora struggled out of the guy's grip.

She landed on her feet, spun around, and raced over to join Hangman with both her blades drawn.

He barely noticed. He dove from one man to the next stabbing, slashing, chopping, and hacking every Renegade in sight.

He still couldn't see a single one of his cousins or other male relatives fighting in the confusion. He didn't get a chance to look before the remaining Renegades realized he was there.

He thought he killed enough to eliminate the men who invaded his house. The Renegades must have brought a lot more men than he realized.

They surrounded him, but he didn't recognize any of these men. None of them belonged to the parties he saw in the jungle nor did they belong to the party that invaded his house.

Was there no end to the numbers the Renegades could bring against the Godless? Did they bring an unlimited number of men to flood the territory and drive the Godless out?

The Renegades didn't want to drive the Godless out. The Renegades wanted to kill all the men and take all the women. The Godless Clan would cease to exist. The women would become Renegade women. No one else would remain.

A dozen Renegades closed around Hangman. He looked around in wild desperation for any way to stop what was about to happen.

In that one moment when he looked behind him, he saw Mora wielding her blades against another posse of Renegades at a distance from him. The Renegades had cut her away from him. He couldn't get to her without fighting his way through all these other enemies surrounding him.

She swiped her blades at four of her attackers, but the minute she made her first strike, another two rushed her from behind. They caught her around the arms again, pinned her weapons down, and started hauling her away.

She screamed and roared in fury, but she couldn't do anything to stop them. They overpowered her with their strength. More Renegades followed. She kicked out at them, but they stayed out of range.

Hangman had to pay attention when the Renegades charged him. He barely dodged out of the way to avoid two of them slashing their blades at him.

He saw the writing on the wall and backed away. The Renegades were already trying to surround him. In fact, they did surround him.

They all moved in to attack. He had to get away from them—and he had to get out of the camp before the larger Renegade force surrounded it completely.

He had to get Mora back. His mind fixated on that one thought and nothing else.

He dove under the arm of the next Renegade who lunged for him. Hangman broke out of the circle, hacked the same guy across the back, and broke away.

He had to swerve in all directions to avoid getting pulled into other fights all over the camp. The Renegades were already withdrawing with all the captured women.

The Godless men got trapped in skirmishes, but most saw what was happening and escaped in time to race for the safety of the jungle.

Hangman kept running until he couldn't hear the screams and crashes anymore. He wilted against a tree trunk to catch his breath, but he didn't dare to sit down. He might never be able to get up if he did.

He had to meet up with his relatives—any of them who survived to escape the camp. He definitely saw Alien, Viking, and Cross running for the trees. Hangman didn't see anyone else.

He set off at a walk and made sure to avoid the retreating Renegades. If he had been stronger, he would have climbed into the canopy to check the situation in the camp.

He decided not to. He skirted the camp in a wide loop and eventually met up with his brother and his two beefy cousins.

"Did anyone else make it out?" Hangman asked.

Alien sneered at him. "Do you mean anyone besides the women? *They* all made it out."

"You know what I mean," Hangman countered. "Did you see Shadow anywhere?"

Viking jerked his thumb over his shoulder. "I saw him with your younger brothers over there. I think Breaker, Bantam, and Grizzly were with him."

Hangman waved to the others. "Let's go. We can't stay here."

"What are you going to do?" Alien asked on the way.

"I'm going to meet back up with as many of our men as we can find. Then I'm going to get my wife back."

"Not even you can fight that many Renegades, little brother," Viking told him. "You aren't in the greatest shape, you know."

Hangman spun around. "Are you really saying you would leave Nagana in Renegade hands? Don't even talk to me like that."

"I'm not saying I would leave her in their hands. I'm saying I wouldn't be able to rescue her if I was dead or……" Viking dragged his eyes down to Hangman's body. "Or injured."

Hangman turned on his heel and stormed off. "It doesn't matter. We just have to meet back up with Shadow."

He didn't say the rest. If anything happened to Shadow, Hangman would become Kral. Then any surviving Godless would have to do what he told them to do.

He didn't plan to leave Mora in Renegade hands, injuries or no injuries. He accomplished a lot in the last few days. He felt better now than he did then. He would damn sure go after them now.

Using his ingenuity and resourcefulness to attack them and take them out en masse worked so well. He was starting to get addicted to this way of fighting. He could kill so many more Renegades this way.

He would have to come up with some especially devious method to kill them so he wouldn't put the women in danger. The women would distract the Renegades. That would leave the enemy vulnerable to unforeseen attacks.

The Renegades didn't strike him as very creative thinkers when it came to fighting the Godless. The Renegades relied on their numbers and their firearms.

Hangman stopped in his tracks when he remembered. The Renegades didn't use firearms in this assault. Did that mean something? Did it mean they ran out of ammunition before the assault?

Maybe they just didn't want to put the women in danger. That made more sense.

Viking came up behind him. "Is something wrong, little brother?"

Hangman shook himself back to reality. "No. I was just thinking."

They kept walking and found Shadow and the others a few minutes later. All the men were here along with Hangman's and Cross's two younger brothers, Landus and Jerun, and a bunch of other underage boys.

"What's the plan?" Hangman asked.

"We're falling back to the east," Shadow replied. "We don't have enough men to go after them."

Hangman clamped his mouth shut. "You go. I'm staying behind to go rescue Mora."

"You can't do that, my son," Shadow replied. "You can barely hold a weapon."

"Falling back now would be cowardly. Do you really plan to leave my mother to those fiends?"

Now Shadow was the one who clamped his mouth shut. "Did you just call me a coward?"

Hangman waved that away. He probably wasn't thinking clearly now, either. "I'm saying I would be a coward if I left. I'm going back to get my wife and any other women I can free from those animals. Any of you men who want to come with me are welcome to stay behind, too."

"I am the Kral here, my son—not you," Shadow snarled. "I will be the one who decides who stays behind and who doesn't."

"I'll stay behind nonetheless. I won't leave my wife a captive. I may be injured, but all of you together won't be able to stop me. I got away from the Renegades more than once already. I can get away from you."

Hangman tried not to glare at his father, but Hangman was in no mood to be nice to anyone, especially not anyone who stood between him and Mora. He didn't come this far and start caring about her to let all of that go now.

His visions of last night came rushing back. She was the foundation of everything he would build for the future. He had no choice but to get her back.

He would lose his whole future if he lost her. He simply could not let that happen. He would rather lose his life fighting the Renegades than face it.

Alien spoke up first. "I'm with you, little brother. I'm coming with you."

"So am I," Viking added. "What's the point of falling back to safe territory without our women?"

"I'm going, too," Cross chimed in.

Shadow jerked back and forth glaring at everyone. He was too smart not to bow to the inevitable. "Very well, my son," he finally growled. "You may take your cousins and your brother to see about getting the women back. I will take these boys and any of our remaining people to safe territory before I come back to rejoin you."

Hangman nodded. He didn't call his father a coward—or even mean to imply that Shadow was a coward. Hangman knew he wasn't.

Shadow did have a responsibility to these people. He couldn't just abandon underage boys nor could he allow them to participate in any campaign against the Renegade Clan. Shadow had to take the boys to safety. That left Hangman in charge of the raiding party.

Hangman looked at the men around him. Alien. Viking. Cross. They were the only men who stood with him.

Hangman waved to his companions. They backed away. Shadow and the others retreated toward the east.

Hangman felt a stab of despair that so few men stood with him, but he hardened himself against that feeling. It didn't matter in the end. He just had to get the job done.

The two parties moved farther apart, but right then, a woman's voice yelled out in the distance. It sounded half like a scream and half like a broken cry. It came from south of the men's party. Everyone spun around to stare and then took off running.

They found the women and girls huddled under some trees all clinging to each other and struggling not to cry out loud.

Their terrified eyes darted in every direction. "What happened?!" Shadow grabbed Katha. "What happened?! Where are the Renegades?"

"I don't know!" She wrestled her features in the closest thing to hysteria that Hangman had ever seen. "They're back there!"

"What happened?!" he demanded again. "How did you get away from them?"

"They were carrying us off!" she practically shrieked. "A huge swarm of Blitzwords attacked them! I've never seen anything like it! The Renegades dropped us and we ran for it! We barely got away!"

Hangman's eye skipped over the women and girls. Most of them suffered Blitzword bites and stings. The women's faces and arms were already starting to swell up.

He only asked one question. "Where's Mora?"

Katha's cheek spasmed and she looked away. "I don't know. We all got separated. We rejoined in the jungle. We looked, but we couldn't find her."

Hangman turned on his heel and strode off into the jungle heading west. He didn't know or care if any of his male relatives came with him.

Shadow would be even more reluctant to send anyone with Hangman, now that Shadow had to guard the women and girls, too.

Shadow couldn't take the time to go after one woman—not when the rest of the band needed help more than Mora did.

Chapter 16

A lien caught up with Hangman. "Slow down, little brother," Alien breathed in his ear. "You're heading too far west. We need to cut south to intercept the raiding party. They might not even have Mora at all. She could have gotten away. We should scout them and check."

Hangman stopped in his tracks when he realized Alien was right. Hangman's one thought was to get to Renegade territory as quickly as possible.

Of course the Renegades wouldn't have gotten there yet. He didn't even know if Mora was still their prisoner or if she got away when the other women did.

Viking and Cross caught up with him a few seconds later. They all followed Hangman this far. He would have liked to thank them for supporting him, but he didn't want to waste time on formalities.

"You should go home to your wife," Hangman told Viking. "She needs you right now."

"How do you think you'll get Mora back with only the three of you?" Viking replied. "I'm going with you. Don't say another word about it."

Hangman shut his mouth and struck off to the southwest. He didn't feel right about going straight south in case he missed the Renegades.

"We should get into the branches," Alien suggested after another hour of travel. "We'll be able to see and hear more there."

Hangman nodded. His arms still hurt and he still felt weak, but his drive to get Mora back erased every other consideration.

He had to gasp and groan a lot when he pulled himself into the branches, but he already felt stronger than before Mora found him. He just had to push through this and heal on the way. That was all there was to it.

The cousins traveled much faster in the branches and stopped another five miles farther southwest. The sun was starting to go down. Hangman strained his ears and picked up the sound of human voices at a distance. None of them sounded female.

He and his cousins sat listening for a while. Whoever was talking sounded a long way off, but the voices definitely came from the west and they were all male.

He couldn't tell from here if they were Renegades. It was too late and he felt too tired to find out tonight. His cousins didn't push it. They stayed where they were, shared some food Viking took out of his bag, and then fell asleep.

Hangman woke up first. He used the time while he waited for his cousins to wake up to put another layer of leaf paste on his shoulder wounds. They already felt better after just a few days since Mora's treatment.

Cross woke up next, pulled some dried meat out of his bag, and handed it to Hangman. "Thank you for coming with me," Hangman murmured under his breath. "You didn't have to."

"You would have come with me if our positions were reversed," Cross replied between mouthfuls. "Maybe one day I'll get a wife and I'll need you to help me rescue her if she gets captured."

Hangman looked away. "Let's hope not."

"You've killed more Renegades than anyone I know, brother," Cross told him. "You're the reason the Renegades didn't attack the long camp a long time ago. Now all the women are back with Shadow and the others. I think we can spare a few men to go after your wife."

Hangman didn't get a chance to answer before Alien and Viking woke up. They sniffed and cleared their throats while they surveyed the jungle around them.

"Have you heard anything?" Alien growled.

"Nothing," Hangman replied. "It's all quiet."

"We should track back to where the Blitzwords attacked," Viking suggested. "We can trace Mora from there. There's no point going after the Renegades when we don't know for certain if she's with them."

Hangman bowed to the logic of this suggestion. He wanted to catch and kill Renegades right now, not screw around tracking footprints on the ground.

He remained silent when the four cousins set off toward the place Katha seemed to indicate the women escaped from the Renegades.

Hangman sensed Mora getting farther and farther away from him. His gut told him he wouldn't find her wandering around out here in the jungle by herself. The Renegades still had her. His gut told him that. They wouldn't let her go once they got her.

He couldn't explain why he thought she was so valuable to them—more valuable than the other women. Katha made it sound like the other women scattered when they escaped from the Renegades. Mora would have done the same thing.

Maybe she escaped to the west and they just blundered onto her. It didn't matter because they still held her as a prisoner—and they took her with them to the west. Hangman was never more certain of anything.

The cousins stayed in the branches. This way of traveling required Hangman to use his arms more than traveling along the ground.

The pain in his shoulders morphed into murderous rage. He better not catch the men who took her—or anyone else who attacked the long camp.

He had already developed a history of attacking and killing Renegades on a mass scale. Taking Mora away from him would be their last and worst mistake.

The cousins returned to the Renegades' track leading away from the long camp. The four cousins descended to the ground and followed the Renegades' footprints.

The Renegades carried the Godless women and girls seven miles into the jungle before the Blitzwords attacked. The women's tracks scattered in all directions. The cousins tracked each one down until they met up with Shadow's party.

The cousins then had to hunt high and low before they found out what happened to Mora. She ran south and bumped into a different party of Renegades. They were the ones who carried her off.

They never let her set foot on the ground after that. They must have tied her up and carried her out of the territory. Only two Renegades survived the Blitzword attack. They met up with the party that captured Mora, but both men died within a day.

Hangman and his comrades found the bodies abandoned by the side of the trail. The cousins followed the Renegades to the place where they spent that first night.

Hangman squatted down by a tree to one side of their camp. "They tied her up here. They left her here for the night."

"At least we know they're keeping her alive," Viking remarked. "They wouldn't sacrifice such a valuable woman."

Hangman didn't answer. He kept following the same track until it got too dark for him to see. He and his cousins retreated into the branches and ate the last of whatever food the four of them happened to be carrying in their bags.

"We'll have to hunt tomorrow," Alien remarked.

"That will mean building a fire," Cross pointed out. "The Renegades will detect it."

"We can't build a fire," Hangman interrupted. "We're crossing into Renegade territory. We have to be more careful and use stealth."

"What do you want to do about the.....?" Viking broke off when the cousins heard voices in the distance again. They were male voices.

Hangman sprang up, said a quick, "Stay here," to his brother and his cousins, balanced through the branches as fast as he could go, and homed in the sound of those voices.

The jungle was already getting dark by the time he crouched in the crook of two sturdy limbs and looked down on a party of Renegades talking on the ground.

They didn't take any pains to hide themselves or stop anyone from knowing they were here. They had built a big fire—much bigger than any Godless would have built.

The Renegades talked fast and pointed in different directions. They talked about different people, parties, and maneuvers they were making in the area.

Hangman's intense gaze scanned the clearing for any sign of Mora. She wasn't there. He watched until the Renegades parted and went off in different directions.

He raced back through the branches. This mission took over his mind. He no longer even noticed the pain in his shoulders unless he chose to concentrate on it.

He ran back to the place where he and his cousins left off tracking Mora's captors. He found the spot where he last knew they still had her. He strained his eyes in the dark and eventually came to a point where her captors met up with a second group of Renegades.

One group left toward the west. That must have been the party of Renegades the cousins just observed. The second group left toward the southwest and took Mora with them. Those men Hangman and his cousins just observed no longer had her if they ever did.

He returned to his cousins. Cross was already asleep.

"What did you find, little brother?" Alien asked.

"A different party of Renegades took her to the southwest," Hangman replied. "They either transferred her to another group or they changed direction. This party doesn't matter anymore."

Alien only nodded and he went to sleep, too. Only Viking stayed awake. He didn't act like Hangman's behavior was anything unusual.

Hangman gazed at his cousin and Viking gazed back. Neither man spoke the obvious truth between them. Viking gave up protecting his own family to help Hangman get Mora back. Hangman couldn't even begin to express his gratitude for that.

His bloodthirsty rage against the Renegades obliterated even his gratitude. The world would pay for this.

His rage almost stopped him from going to sleep. Viking drifted off first and left Hangman awake to brood, but he eventually succumbed to his own exhaustion anyway.

Chapter 17

Hangman woke to find his brother and cousins already awake and waiting for him to wake up. "Why didn't you wake me?" he asked. "We could have left a long time ago."

"We don't know where to go," Viking replied. "We need you to show us the track to follow."

"Not yet," Hangman told him. "We can shorten this process. Follow me."

He led the way through the branches. The Renegades took much less care to conceal their presence and their direction of travel, now that they were inside their own territory.

They broke more branches and left more obvious trail signs. Hangman and the others could track the Renegades without going down to the ground at all.

They caught up with the second group of Renegades—the one that split off northwest after yesterday's conversation.

This group consisted of five men. None of them was as big as Viking and Alien. None of these Renegades had as much reason to kill someone as Hangman did.

He used hand signals to direct his cousins to surround the Renegades. Viking and Alien followed the enemy. Cross flanked the Renegades on the south side.

Hangman used his speed and cunning to race ahead of the party. He wasn't as strong as his big cousins, now or in the past. He didn't need to be.

He jumped down and landed in the Renegades' path. He didn't even have to draw his kukris. He only had to show himself to them. They stopped dead in their tracks and stared at him. Then their hands flew to their own weapons.

That signal triggered Viking, Alien, and Cross to attack from three sides and behind the Renegades. The three cousins hacked three Renegades to the ground instantly.

The other two spun around to face their attackers, but the Renegades didn't react fast enough. Alien took down one of them by cleaving the guy's head in half with another massive stroke of Alien's much larger kukris.

The last man wheeled to confront Cross. He was the smallest man here. Viking struck from behind, embedded his axe in the Renegade's thigh, and the guy howled in agony, but he still didn't fall.

He raised his blade to strike Cross. Alien lashed out a third time and embedded his kukri in the Renegade's arm just above the elbow. Alien's weapon stuck in the bone. It cracked when Alien yanked the blade out.

The Renegade shrieked in pain again, but Hangman wasn't playing games anymore He caught the guy by the back of the shirt. These Renegades wore too many clothes for their own good.

Hangman yanked the man onto his back on the ground and drove his kukri to the hilt into the Renegade's abdomen right next to the hip.

The man wailed out loud and Hangman fed his own sadistic rage by twisting the blade until blood puddled around the handle.

"Where's the woman you took from the Godless?!" Hangman bellowed over the man's ongoing screams. "Where are your friends taking her?"

The man collapsed back on the ground thrashing and screeching.

"Shut him up, Hangman!" Viking yelled. "He's making too much noise!"

Cross sprang forward and clamped his hand over the man's mouth. "We can't let him go and we can't kill him. He's too valuable for the information he could give us." Cross nodded at Hangman. "Go on."

Those words released the beast in Hangman's heart. He pulled out his kukri, chose his next target with care, and placed the tip of his weapon at the notch in the Renegade's shoulder.

No one knew better than Hangman how much a wound in that part of the shoulder hurt. He had been living with it all this time. He twisted the blade extra slowly until the guy roared and fought behind Cross's hand.

Hangman planted his foot on his victim's chest and screwed his blade an inch into the guy's shoulder before he stopped. He left the blade embedded there until the man slumped sobbing and whimpering on the ground.

Cross removed his hand.

"I'm going to keep going and asking until you give me an answer," Hangman told him. "Where are they taking the woman? You transferred her to another party of Renegades heading southwest. Where are they going?"

The man actually did start sobbing. "They'll kill me!....They'll kill me if I tell you.....!"

"I'm going to kill you anyway," Hangman replied. "If you don't tell me, I'll keep you alive until you do. Tell me what I want to know and

I might kill you quickly instead of cutting you into small pieces and leaving you alive with only a few scraps attached to your bones."

"The camp.....the camp.....it was only the first target......."

Alien frowned. "It's the only camp. It's the farthest camp to the east."

"Larth gave orders......" the Renegade gasped. "To track the survivors....."

"Is Larth the short man who ordered all of you to spread out west of the camp?" Hangman asked.

The man raised his eyes to meet Hangman's. "I'm sorry.....I'm sorry......I didn't....I wasn't ......I didn't....."

"You weren't what?" Hangman snapped. "Say it."

"I wasn't the one who hurt you......"

Hangman overreacted. He didn't think those words would cause such an overpowering swell of fury in his soul.

He slammed his foot against the guy's chest, grabbed his kukri, and drilled it in another inch. He twisted much harder this time.

Cross barely got there in time to silence the guy.

"Do you think I give a crap about that?!" Hangman snarled. "That woman is my wife—and you *were* one of the bastards who attacked our camp and carried off all our women! My mother was in that group! This man's wife was in that group! Now your rotten kin are holding my wife as a captive! Now stop telling me about Larth's orders and tell me where they took her! This is your last chance!"

The guy screamed a lot longer this time. Hangman realized too late that he was still twisting the blade to torment the guy. Hangman had to stop so the guy could wilt in a sobbing heap of agony. Hangman really wanted to hurt the guy now.

Hangman could wait until he got his answer. Then he didn't know what he would do. It wouldn't be anything nice, though.

"Now spit it out and make it quick," Hangman muttered. "You don't have long to live either way. Where are they taking her?"

"Xano...." The guy panted between sobs. "Xano......"

"What is that?" Alien demanded. "We don't know your language."

"It's a village....southwest....." The prisoner's eyes darted to the mountains behind him. "Behind the Jagged Points.....Behind the Gapewell Pass.....you'll find it....."

Hangman straightened up, pulled out his kukri, and wiped the blood on a bunch of foliage hanging nearby.

"You said....you said you would kill me.....quickly......if I told you ....." the guy whimpered.

"I'm going to. You're useless to us now and you're too vile to disgrace this country anymore."

Hangman grabbed the guy by the clothes and yanked the man to his feet so violently that Hangman accidentally bumped into Cross by mistake.

The prisoner couldn't support himself. He kept crying out every time Hangman jerked him forward.

Hangman half-marched, half-dragged the prisoner back down the path to an Abnormit mound he'd seen earlier. The dribbled mud formed a cone sticking out of the ground.

The guy started to struggle when he saw it. "No!" he squealed. "No—you promised!"

"I said I would kill you quickly. Don't worry. It will be quick."

Hangman marched to within six feet of the mound and flung the guy into the mud walls of the cone. He couldn't stop himself from falling straight into them.

They cracked under his weight and hundreds of Abnormits swarmed out from inside the nest. They enveloped the guy and he screamed when they started devouring him.

Hangman darted away and rejoined his cousins and his brother at a safe distance from the ever-widening circle of Abnormits. They covered the guy in seconds. His screams escalated, spiked, and then died away as the creatures ate him down to the bone.

Hangman turned away first and swung himself up into the branches. His cousins and his brother joined him a second later. "We can move faster in the branches. We'll have to stay concealed when we cross the Gapewell Pass."

"We'll have to stay concealed long before that," Cross pointed out. "We're already inside their territory. Things will only get more treacherous the farther we go."

"All the more reason for us to stay in the branches," Hangman replied. "We'll have to go down onto the ground once we venture into the mountains. We don't need to do it here."

"We'll need food, little brother," Viking pointed out. "If you really want to cross the Jagged Pins into Renegade territory, we should withdraw to our own country, hunt, and prepare the food for travel before we leave. We don't need to track anyone now. We can use our speed, but we won't be able to hunt or prepare food once we get that deep inside Renegade country."

Hangman only nodded. Viking was right. None of the cousins had any food left. They didn't dare to start a fire here. They had already traveled too far west.

Chapter 18

The cousins retreated as far as they dared. Hangman searched in the trees until he located a Gorlock feeding on an ancient Crusher carcass.

Viking and Alien positioned themselves in the trees above the Gorlock. Then Viking dropped in front of the creature and confronted it with his axe raised. Alien dropped behind the Gorlock and hacked one of its legs while its back was turned.

The creature spun around and had to lower its head to snap its jaws at Alien. Viking leapt forward, chopped his axe into the back of the creature's skull, and brought it down.

Hangman stayed in the canopy and kept watch over the surrounding country while his brother and cousins lit a fire, cooked the Gorlock meat, and smoked as much of it as they could.

They talked while they worked. He stayed out of it. He wasn't good company for them right now.

The four men took the work in shifts all night long to keep the fire going and continuously move the meat around so it would dry. Hangman heard them laughing with their mouths full while they ate as much of the food as they could hold.

Hangman took the time to rest his arms. He really didn't care anymore if his arms hurt. Every passing minute only made him more determined than ever to get payback on the people who did this to him and his family.

He stiffened when Cross climbed up to the canopy, perched on a nearby branch, and held out a small square of hide with a hunk of roasted meat in it. "You should eat, Hangman."

Hangman took the food from him. "Thank you, little brother. I'm grateful."

Cross didn't leave. "What is it like—being married?"

Hangman snorted and used his teeth to tear off a piece of meat. "You can see what it's like."

"Not that!" Cross exclaimed. "The other part."

"What other part? I don't know what you're asking."

"You and Mora....you aren't like the others. You actually talk to her and listen to her. You took her to consult with Butcher. None of the others do that."

"That's because Mora knows things we don't. I would be stupid not to listen to her about those things. She knew what those weapons were. She's the only one who knew—and she knew how they work. She told us things we never could have found out any other way."

"No, it isn't that," Cross insisted. "It's something else."

"Then I don't know what you're talking about."

"You and Mora....you're like Mother and Father. They trust each other, but they've been married for so many years. You hated Mora at first....."

"There was plenty to hate then."

"And now you trust her the way Father trusts Mother. You and Mora—no one acts like you do."

Hangman looked away. He hoped he could pretend he didn't know what Cross was talking about, but Hangman did know what Cross was talking about.

"I don't know how to answer you, little brother," Hangman muttered under his breath. "I couldn't say exactly if I trust Mora or not. I barely know her, but she isn't the defenseless little rabbit we thought she was. She isn't Godless. I don't think she ever will be Godless. She's something else. She's a foreigner. She always will be a foreigner and a Follower, but she's here now. I see no reason to continue to treat her like a cowardly little rabbit when she could be useful to us instead."

Cross studied him too closely. Maybe Cross picked up on what Hangman didn't say. Maybe Cross didn't pick up on it.

Hangman wasn't sure anymore what Mora was or what she wasn't. He only knew one thing. She was his wife. Cross already knew that. He just didn't know what it meant.

Hangman didn't know what it meant before he got married. He didn't know what it meant even after he got married. He didn't fully understand what it meant to say she was his wife until after she got pregnant. That's when things changed in Hangman's mind.

He might never fully understand it himself. In fact, he probably never would. He couldn't explain it to Cross, though. Cross already knew everything Hangman could say about having children and raising the next generation.

A man couldn't have children and raise the next generation without a wife. Cross knew that as well as everyone else knew it.

Hangman understood it so much better now that it was actually happening to him. He couldn't explain that to anyone—not without sounding like a fool. He would only be repeating what everyone already knew.

He didn't understand before how much it meant. Maybe that was it. He thought before he married Mora that he would have been perfectly satisfied to live his life alone, childless, and dedicate himself to defending his band.

He wanted a woman for himself. He didn't fully grasp what it would mean to him—how much he would actually become bound and invested in it—if he actually faced the possibility of having children—who might then have children of his own.

The initiation process changed him, but it didn't make him a man. He didn't become a man—not really—not until that night when he found Mora was pregnant.

He couldn't tell his brother that. Hangman would never say those words out loud—especially not to an unmarried man. That would have been the ultimate insult—if Hangman implied that an unmarried man wasn't really a man yet because he wasn't becoming a father.

Hangman believed it in his heart, though. It was definitely true for him.

He was never a man before. He never really became a man until that morning when he saw a vision of his progeny spreading through the generations. That was the moment when he truly became a man.

Mora was all those things. She was the vessel carrying all of that inside her right now. She and their unborn children meant more than the world. They meant everything.

He would hazard any risk to protect that. His life meant nothing without that.

He and Cross sat in silence while Hangman ate. Alien called up the tree in a little while for Cross to come down and take his shift on the fire so Alien could get some sleep.

Cross climbed down and left Hangman alone. He ate as much as he dared, put the rest of the food in his bag, and went back to listening for sounds of any approaching enemy.

This was all just another delay, but Viking was right about one other thing. The Renegades wouldn't harm Mora. Every man in the whole country understood the importance of a woman her age.

The Renegades went to a lot of trouble to capture Godless women. They carried off one. They would guard her and make sure nothing happened to her.

This village of Xano that Hangman's prisoner mentioned—it sat behind the Jagged Pins—deep enough in Renegade Territory.

None of the Renegade Clan's enemies penetrated the territory to put the village in danger. Mora would be safe there—from everyone other than the Renegades themselves. Her presence would cause a stir among the single men. They would all vie for possession of her.

The presence of a young, single, unattached woman could even lead to violence. One of the men might decide to kill her rather than see her go to another man. It wouldn't be the first time.

The Godless were one of the very few Clans in which that kind of thing didn't happen—not unless something went disastrously wrong and someone completely violated the Clan's code of conduct.

Other Clans didn't hold such rules. Some operated on the might-makes-right principle. If a man wanted another man's wife, the first man could kill the second man and take the woman with no questions asked.

Other Clans used challenges to settle disputes. Every Clan used its own system or no system at all.

Hangman didn't know or care what the Renegades' rules were or if the particular Renegade bands in this area held to different rules from every other Renegade band.

They attacked their enemies and carried off women by force. That on its own made the Renegades the scum of the Earth as far as Hangman was concerned.

They had no propriety. Why not attack each other to steal another man's wife? Why follow any rules at all?

His rage and impatience kept him up all night. He didn't sleep, so he had no trouble staying awake until dawn when his brother and cousins started packing up the food for their journey.

Chapter 19

Mora's heart sank when the Renegades carried her over a rocky mountain pass and headed down many crooked pathways to a village in the distance.

The Renegades kept her tied up the whole way here. One of the biggest members of their party carried her slung over his shoulder.

His shoulder bone stabbed her in the stomach every time he took a step. Her stomach ached from the constant pressure. Would this endless mistreatment harm her child?

She tried to comfort herself by telling herself that the bruising cut into her abdomen well above the growing knot of solid flesh farther down—closer to her pubic bone.

The journey didn't do her any favors, but she couldn't look forward to what would happen to her when these men carried her into their village.

This village resembled nothing she'd ever seen before. The Renegades built the small houses out of solid logs—at least some of them. Twenty of these houses dotted the village with tents scattered between them.

These tents came in different sizes. Some were enormous. Others looked barely big enough to hold two people.

The Renegades dressed differently from other Clans. The men all wore the same combination of pants, shirts, vests, and boots.

The women wore a bizarre combination of any kind of clothes imaginable. Some wore almost nothing but a few flimsy scraps to cover their breasts and their privates. Others dressed the same as the men.

A few women wore extremely short skirts hardly bigger than the Godless' loincloths. These women usually wore skimpy tops cut short across the upper ribs with sleeves that only covered the sides of the shoulders.

Mora also saw plenty of people completely wrapped from the neck down to the ankles in what looked like miles and miles of torn rags. The Followers wrapped their dead that way for burial. These people's clothing—if she could call it that—made them look like corpses.

Their faces and bodies looked like corpses, too. These people were all far paler, bonier, and more sunken than anyone else in the village. Most of these people looked barely alive.

Their clothing, wasted appearance, and dead, sunken eyes made it nearly impossible to tell which of them were male and which were female. They all looked like something beyond human—or maybe less than human.

She didn't see any difference between any of the rest of these people—apart from their clothes, that is.

She tried to look around from her precarious position to see what these people were really like. She didn't get a chance to before her captor threw her on the ground in the middle of the village.

She tried not to notice that falling like this exposed too much of her body to the enemy, but she had to notice it when a bunch of men gathered around and crowded one against the other to stare at her.

"She's young, isn't she?" one of them remarked.

"She's a breeder." A different man kicked her in the hip with his boot. "She's choice. She'll make a perfect broodmare."

The man who had been carrying her all the way here tried to push away those closest to him. "Don't touch her. We have to wait to hear what Ulmeo says about her."

"Why should we?" another asked. "We can decide for ourselves who to give her to."

"How would we decide that?" another asked. "The only way to decide is to fight over her. We would lose half the men in the village doing it that way."

"No one will decide anything until Ulmeo gets here," Mora's captor snapped. "All of you back off. You can bet he won't give her to any of you."

"You better shut up, Rorus," another snarled. "I'm sure you had your way with her a dozen times on the way here."

"I did not!" Rorus countered. "I didn't touch her! None of us did and neither will you—not unless Ulmeo gives her to you. Now back off, all of you! Go on! Get out of here! Leave her alone!"

He dove in and tried to grab her—probably to get her away from these guys. The two men who had been arguing over her jumped in and knocked Rorus away. Both of them swiveled between her and Rorus, but more men surged inward just as fast.

Some attacked Rorus from behind. Someone hit him over the head with something and he buckled on the spot. Another five men went after the two who blocked him from Mora.

A massive brawl broke out right there on top of her. Different men charged her and tried to dive on top of her only to get dragged off and mauled by other combatants.

She curled onto her side for some small protection, but she couldn't move with these ropes tied around her wrists and ankles.

Different assailants kept pulling her onto her back and jumping on top of her. Her weight crushed her hands and arms underneath her. Each assailant's body made the problem worse. One man actually managed to force her knees apart and shoved his hips between her thighs.

She stared up at the sky fearing the worst before another Renegade appeared out of nowhere, swung a massive battle axe through the air, and buried the weapon straight into the assailant's back.

Another combatant took that man's head off with one stroke of a blade. Every man who attacked Mora wound up getting dragged off into the mayhem and slaughtered in brutal fury.

She lay stunned and cringing on the ground. She had to get out of here—but how? All of these men would see her if she somehow managed to untie her ankles and run for the jungle.

She was too far away from Godless territory to get back there on her own. She had dropped her blades during the assault on the long camp. She wouldn't have been able to get to them even if she still had her weapons tied and sheathed at her sides.

A deep gong sounded through the village right then. The fight stopped instantly. All the combatants stopped brawling and straightened up—all the combatants who were still alive, that is.

Rorus got to his feet still bleeding from the scalp, pulled his blade, stormed over to Mora, and planted himself there to defend her—as if that would make any difference at all.

The other Renegades milled around standing next to each other as though it never crossed their minds to fight each other.

Mora huddled on the ground waiting for the end. It came when a different Renegade man strode into the village—or maybe he strode out of it. Mora couldn't be sure whether he was already inside the village before this moment.

He stalked into view glaring at everyone. He looked like he might be about Shadow's age or maybe even older. This must be Ulmeo, the person who passed for a leader among the Renegades—the person who would decide what happened to Mora.

He shot death stares at the surviving combatants and all the dead bodies on the ground. Then he spotted Mora and shot her a death stare, too.

"What is the meaning of this?!" he demanded of the crowd at large.

"This is one of the Godless women from Larth's campaign," Rorus mumbled. "We just brought her in. The men wanted to decide who would take her."

"One of the women from Larth's campaign!" Ulmeo snapped. "We sent almost a thousand men into Godless territory and you came back with one woman?! Just one?!"

Rorus shuffled his feet. "You don't understand. They defended themselves."

"What does that mean?!" Ulmeo barked. "How could a bunch of Godless scum defend themselves against those numbers?"

Rorus tried to shrug and wound up squirming. "They....they attacked us before we got to their camp. They.....they sent out......"

"Spit it out!" Ulmeo snapped. "They sent out what?"

Rorus opened his mouth more than once before he finally worked up the courage to say, "You won't believe me if I tell you."

"You better tell me!" Ulmeo countered. "Tell me what they sent out that stopped so many men from carrying out their mission to bring back more women for us."

"They sent out.....well.....it was only one man.....and he was injured. Larth....he captured the man.....but not before this man killed dozens of ours. Larth tortured him, but the guy only came back. He killed hundreds, I would say. I don't exactly know how many it was. He was all over the country."

"He couldn't have been *all* over the country!" Ulmeo sneered. "How did he do it if he was so injured?"

"He used the ants," Rorus replied in a tiny voice.

Mora's brain switched gears. Hangman. He used the ants against that Gorlock. He had been injured to the point of death.

Rorus's story about Larth torturing Hangman—it all made sense now. The damage to his shoulders—the bruising and crushed tissue around Hangman's injuries.....Larth must have done that.

"He's my husband," she blurted out. "The man you're talking about is my husband. He'll come after you. He'll kill you all. He'll never rest until he feeds all of you to the ants."

Everyone turned around to stare at her. Rorus's face went as white as chalk. A whisper of anxiety went through the crowd.

Ulmeo didn't react the same way. He snorted in her face, lunged for her, and grabbed her by one arm. "Come with me, you stupid piece of meat."

He yanked her off the ground, but she couldn't walk with her ankles tied. She screamed out, but in the end, she stopped trying to struggle and just let him drag her across the ground.

He dragged her through the crowd, through the village, and away from all the people standing around staring at her. He stormed to a small house barely bigger than the shelter where she lived with Hangman.

Ulmeo pushed open the door and dragged her inside. The house itself was totally empty from one wall to the other.

He flung her down extra hard near one wall, yanked and muscled her into a sitting position, untied her wrists, wrapped the rope around one of the house's support posts, and re-tied her wrists behind her back.

"Stay there," he snapped. "Don't move and don't try to escape. Every man in the village will be after you. You'll be much safer in here."

"What if one of them comes in here?" she asked. "I won't be able to protect myself."

He kicked her in the leg again. "Shut up and stay here! You're already causing enough trouble just by being here."

He stormed out, slammed the door behind him, and she heard something scrape against the door. He must have been barricading her in—like that would keep any of the men out if they really wanted to get to her.

She relaxed at last—as much as she could while she was still tied up like this. She would have liked to check her stomach to make sure her child was still okay. She would have liked it even better if she could have asked Katha to check.

Katha wasn't here. Mora was on her own with these animals.

Right then, she felt a tiny squirming sensation in her lower belly for the first time. It felt like a very small fish moving around in there. She wilted in relief when she felt her child moving around. The journey here must not have harmed the child.

She couldn't be so sure about the future. She would just have to do her best to deal with whatever happened. She tried to think and come up with a plan to escape.

She didn't have any weapons. She would need those and a way to free her hands so she could use weapons when she found them.

The more she thought, the more her fatigue and distress overwhelmed her. She fell into an exhausted sleep and slumped right there still leaning against the post.

Chapter 20

Mora startled wide awake when she heard a scrape and a thump right outside the house in which Ulmeo confined her. She strained her ears. Someone was removing the barricade to get inside this house.

She stiffened for another attack by one or more of the single men in this camp. The Renegades must have been truly desperate if they rallied a thousand men to invade Godless territory to steal women.

Another thump hit the wall and the door opened. Mora gasped in relief when an old woman entered, shut the door behind her, and gave Mora a toothless grin.

"Well, well, well, dearier-oh," the woman sang. "Look who's wide awake and ready for anything."

"What do you want?" Mora demanded.

The woman held up what looked like a crock made out of pottery. "I brought you some food—but don't thank me. I'm only here because Ulmeo told me to come."

Mora had to look away. "I'm sorry. Thank you. I guess....I'm just agitated."

The woman cackled with fiendish laughter. "Oh, you don't have to tell me about it! Be thankful you're in here."

"That's what Ulmeo said."

"You don't know the half of it." The woman sat down next to Mora and put the pot between them. "The whole village is boiling over with tension. The single men are all ready to explode. They keep getting into more fights even though Ulmeo expressly forbade it."

The old woman took a piece of cooked meat out of the pot and held it out to Mora. The woman moved the meat close to Mora's mouth.

Mora had a flashback of feeding Hangman—was it only a few nights ago? He couldn't use his arms so she put the food into his mouth.

She opened her mouth and the woman put the food in for her. Mora made certain not to use her lips in any kind of suggestive way with this woman.

"Thank you," Mora mumbled with her mouth full. "I'm really grateful to you for bringing me this."

The woman grinned and held up another piece. "Enjoy this time of peace and quiet while it lasts. Ulmeo won't be able to keep you here for much longer."

Mora's head shot up. "What do you mean? Where would he send me if he didn't keep me here?"

"Oh, I couldn't tell you that. Who can understand a man's ways, right?" The woman cackled again. "Something will happen sooner or later. You won't stay in here forever."

The woman tried to put another piece of meat in Mora's mouth. "Wait a minute," Mora countered. "Are you saying he plans to send me somewhere else or give me to one of the men here?"

The woman smirked at her. "You'll go to a man either way. That's the one thing certain. Whether it's here or somewhere else—what difference does it make? It comes to the same thing in the end."

The woman touched the food to Mora's lips to prompt her to open her mouth. Mora thought fast while she chewed.

"Listen....I'm so sorry," Mora exclaimed. "I forgot to ask your name."

The woman smiled more broadly. "I'm Zeslea, dearie. Thanks for asking."

"Listen to me, Zeslea. I need you to do something for me."

Zeslea cackled with insane glee. "I can't untie you, dearie! Ulmeo would kill me!"

"It isn't that. Listen to me. I'm pregnant. I've been pregnant for four months—maybe five. You have to tell Ulmeo."

Zeslea's insane grin evaporated exactly the way Mora thought it would. Zeslea frowned. "Oh. That changes things, doesn't it?"

"You have to tell Ulmeo—before he gives me to someone else."

Zeslea scowled at her so intently that Mora couldn't tell if Zeslea even heard anything else. She finally snapped out of her trance, put the pot aside, and pressed her hands into Mora's abdomen.

Zeslea probed lower and lower until she found the mass of solid tissue buried right there at the top bone of Mora's pelvis. Zeslea's features turned even stonier when she felt it.

She shot to her feet and charged out of the house without looking back. She barely remembered to shut the door. She didn't remember to barricade it.

Mora glanced at the crock of food. She would have liked to eat more of it, but that didn't look likely to happen. She should have waited until after Zeslea finished feeding her and then told Zeslea the truth.

Mora sat there for a long time in the silence thinking things over. The Godless refused to hand Mora over to another man until after she gave birth to Hangman's child.

She only hoped the Renegade Clan had a similar rule. She wouldn't be able to get pregnant from another man until after she gave birth.

That wouldn't stop anyone and everyone from taking advantage of her in the meantime. Breaker didn't seem to have a problem with that.

The thin cracks between the logs in the walls turned dark. The house fell into darkness, too. She started to drift off when Zeslea came back with five huge men.

Two of them held onto her arms while a third untied her wrists. They pulled her to her feet, re-tied her, and dragged her out of the house. These men made more of an effort to carry her off the ground instead of dragging her over it the way Ulmeo did.

She found out as soon as she got outside what Zeslea meant about the single men. They all stopped what they were doing and stared at her as she passed.

The whole village throbbed with tension, but it felt more like sexual tension than outright hostility—not toward her. Maybe the village went back to throbbing with hostility as soon as anyone took her out of these men's sight.

They dragged her to a different house, pushed the door open, and entered. This house was not an empty little shack. Furnishings filled the place.

Couches, dressers, tables, chairs, display cases with pieces of decorative china behind glass windows, and even bookshelves full of books lined all the walls and filled every inch of the floor.

The house even had carpets on the floors. Mora recognized most of this stuff from the ancient cities or pictures she'd seen of ancient life.

She also saw right away that the Renegades didn't understand any of this stuff. They must have just collected it for its own sake.

All the books sat on the shelves with their lettering going in different directions. None of the Renegades could read. They probably didn't even know what books were.

The Renegades displayed some of the other furnishings and objects incorrectly, too. One of the painted china plates had been displayed with its beautiful country landscape scene turned almost completely upside down.

One of the oil paintings hung sideways on the wall with the person's head pointing to the left. Ulmeo sat on a large pile of cushions on the floor. Maybe he didn't understand what a couch or a chair were supposed to be used for.

He waved to the men who brought Mora in. "Put her over there. Tie her up so she doesn't run off."

The men sat her against one of the enormous wooden display cases. They tied her wrists to its foot so she wouldn't be able to escape by overturning the case. They left her sitting there. Ulmeo completely ignored her while he ate out of another crock.

Zeslea showed up with the original pot she brought to the shack, sat down, and started feeding Mora without a word. Zeslea smiled as much as ever, but her eyes sparked with warning to tell Mora not to break the silence.

Mora ate what the woman put in her mouth. Zeslea finally delivered the last piece of meat, grinned again, and padded silently out of the house.

Mora collapsed against the dresser to wait. She couldn't get away—not like this. Every man in the village would be watching and waiting to see if she tried anything. She eventually fell asleep there with her chin resting on her chest.

Men's voices started her awake. The Renegades' houses didn't have windows—not the kind with glass that Mora had seen in the cities.

The Renegades used shutters that let in light and air. Dim, grey, early morning daylight streamed into the room. Another day was dawning outside.

Ulmeo, Rorus, and ten other Renegades occupied the room talking.

"We'll take her over Castle Keep," Ulmeo was saying. "Send out your scouts to Ceon to let Thomion know we're coming. He'll want to take precautions. The rest of you pack up and get ready to go. We'll leave in ten minutes. You come with me, Rorus."

All the men left except Ulmeo and Rorus. They walked over to Mora and Ulmeo frowned when he saw her awake.

"What's going on?" she asked. "Where are you taking me?"

"We're transporting you over the mountains to your section leader. He's in command of the Renegade Clan in this area. He'll decide what to do with you."

"Can't you decide what to do with me?" she asked.

"Not the way things are. He has to make the decision."

He didn't have to explain it any further. Ulmeo might have been able to give her to one of his own men—assuming Ulmeo could decide which one to give her to. He couldn't make that decision while she was pregnant. That required a different level of authority.

Rorus used a knife to cut the ropes on Mora's wrists and ankles. She rubbed the pain out of her wrists while Ulmeo pulled her to her feet. He waved to Rorus who took hold of Mora's elbow to lead her outside.

"I'm going to leave you untied for the journey, but you'll be under heavy guard the whole time," he told her on the way. "Do yourself a favor and don't do anything stupid like try to escape. The men will have orders to do anything to subdue you. Don't give them a reason to do anything or to fight amongst themselves where you're concerned. If you try anything, they'll restrain you again—and that's not the worst thing that could happen."

Mora could think of a lot of things worse that could happen besides getting restrained and packed off deeper inside Renegade territory.

She doubted more and more with every passing minute that Hangman or anyone else would come to help her. Hangman might be dead. All the Godless might be dead.

At least her pregnancy made the Renegades pause. Maybe it would be enough to make Thomion pause, too. Maybe it would stop him from giving her to someone—at least until after she gave birth.

That would come sooner rather than later, but maybe she would find another way to escape before then. She would just have to keep her eyes open.

She would be escaping into deepest, darkest Renegade country if she did that. She might escape from whatever place they took her, but she wouldn't escape from the entire territory—not without the Renegades finding and recapturing her.

All her ideas about escape went straight out of her head when Rorus led her outside. Forty men stood around waiting for her. They all came armed and they stared at her with a mixture of furious hatred and insane, predatory hunger.

She lowered her eyes and refused to look at any of them again. She stayed near Rorus. He was the one man in this whole village who actually tried to protect her.

He kept his hand on his weapon and shot death glares at his comrades. They shot death glares back at him. No one could shoot death glares like the Renegade Clan.

The party stood around for five minutes before Ulmeo ordered the Renegades to move out. They formed a single-file line heading west—the same direction Rorus followed to bring Mora here.

At least the Renegades let her walk by herself, but the same pulse of barely suppressed tension vibrated through the party every step of the way. Mora kept her head down and watched her feet moving over the ground in front of her. She didn't dare to look up.

She didn't have to. Rorus and Ulmeo showed no interest in getting her for themselves. Every other eye in the group remained riveted on her alone.

Zeslea followed at the far end of the line. She didn't engage with any of the men and they all ignored her.

Mora found out why Zeslea came with them when the men made camp that night. They tied Mora hand and foot to a tree, camped on the ground, built big bonfires, and the men lounged around cooking whatever creatures they hunted for their food.

They talked and laughed loudly. None of them took pains to conceal their whereabouts the way the Godless did.

Zeslea came over to Mora, sat down next to Mora, and fed her the same as always. Then Zeslea held a water gourd to Mora's lips. That was all.

Zeslea never said a word to Mora and Zeslea vanished into the darkness as soon as she finished feeding Mora.

Mora didn't try to engage with the men, either. They only cared about her as a piece of meat and a breeding cow. Why should she try to engage with them?

They appeared so crude, so ruthless, and so much more barbaric than the Godless. She hated the Godless when she first went to live with them. Now she saw them differently. They actually had some manners. They actually talked to her even when they hated her.

She represented everything they looked down on, but at least they talked to her. They never treated her like a piece of meat.

Hangman never would have done it with her at all if she hadn't made the first move. He never would have forced himself on her. He respected himself too much.

Katha actually tried to help Mora back then. Mora winced when she remembered their interaction during those first couple of days.

Mora would give just about anything to see Katha right now. They started out despising everything about each other. Now they respected and even liked each other.

The men took it in shifts to keep watch. She fell asleep long before that. She woke up at dawn on the second day. The men untied her and started on another long, dreary march heading deeper into the mountains to the west.

Chapter 21

M ora staggered into another, much larger village somewhere deep inside Renegade territory. She long ago gave up any hope after four days of grueling travel that anyone would find her, let alone rescue her.

She barely saw anything in front of her anymore. She concentrated all her attention on keeping going. Nothing else mattered.

No one talked to her. She opened her mouth in blind obedience when Zeslea fed her. Nothing else interrupted the endless monotony of walking and more walking.

The Renegades met up with another band of men coming from the party's destination. The Renegades called this larger village Ceon. It looked exactly the same as Xano except for its size.

Mora paid no attention to anything else. Ulmeo's party accompanied the men from Ceon as far as the village. Then Ulmeo and all his people turned on their heels and walked away without even saying goodbye.

They left Mora with the men from Ceon. At least the men from Ceon acted more self-controlled than the men from Xano. No one got into any fights over her. No one seethed with barely disguised sexual fury ready to break through the surface at a moment's notice.

The men of Ceon barely looked at her. They marched her to the village and took her straight to one of the largest tents. The same combination of furniture and mismatched trinkets from the ancient cities decorated the tent walls. Carpets covered the floor.

This stuff didn't look so out of place in Ulmeo's crude house. The stuff looked even more like a jackdaw's hoard in a tent.

Thomion turned out to be an older man about Ulmeo's age. Thomion barely looked at her, too. He waved to one side. "Put her over there where she won't cause any trouble."

The men lead her to a corner, wrapped a rope around her wrists in the front this time, and tied that to one of the tent posts. They left a longer leash so she didn't have to lean right up against the post.

She slumped on the ground and looked around. The men who brought her here didn't leave. They turned their backs on Mora and gathered around Thomion.

The men dwarfed him in size. She couldn't see what he was doing, but she heard his voice directing them and giving them orders.

"We'll have to retreat to the Stone Flats before we make another push," Thomion began. "We can't continue without fresh supplies."

"The Stone Flats supply is getting low, too," one of the men pointed out. "We'll have to fall back all the way to Jeweled River to get more. We have plenty there."

"Even the supply at Jeweled River won't last forever," another added. "Then we would lose all our advantage and wind up back where we started. We should explore the countryside to find another supply."

Mora pricked up her ears. These Renegades had to be talking about their ammunition supply. That was the only thing that gave them any decisive advantage over their enemies.

Wherever the Jeweled River supply was, it must be attached to some ancient military store. That was the only reason the Renegades would say they had plenty of ammunition there.

No one else in the ancient world hoarded ammunition like the military. The Followers had seen military bases in books and pictures. Their supplies and stories of vehicles, supplies, and weapons bordered on the insane.

"We'll clean out the Stone Flats for the rest of this campaign," Thomion decided. "After that, we'll just have to do what we can with the Jeweled River supply for as long as it lasts. Maybe we'll find something else in Godless territory or somewhere else."

"The Godless might have already found it," a third man corrected.

"They would have used the weapons against us by now if they did find it," the first man argued.

"Not necessarily. They might not understand the weapons or they might not realize that the weapons need ammunition."

"We aren't here to talk about that," Thomion snapped. "You heard what I said. Mendio, you'll get up the next campaign. Take whatever you need from the Stone Flats supply. I have to deal with this disaster first, so you men will have to handle it on your own."

A different man said, "Yes, Sir."

"Get out of here and go do your jobs," Thomion growled. "Let me know when you have something to report."

Half the men left. Mora kept waiting for the others to leave, but they stayed behind.

They sat around on cushions on the floor the way Ulmeo did. None of the men used the couches or chairs to sit off the floor. Did they even understand what couches and chairs were for?

"What do you want us to do, Father?" one of the men asked.

Thomion jerked his thumb toward Mora. "Just keep an eye on her. Make sure none of the single men get to her before we have a chance to hand her over to Dixor. He'll want to give her to one of his sons."

"Why not just keep her?" another asked. "Dixor never has to find out she was here."

"The longer we keep her here, the more likely that something will go wrong," Thomion muttered. "She's a disaster waiting to happen. One of these single men will attack her or steal her or they'll fight each other for her. We'll be better off if we pass her on and get her out of here."

The younger men didn't talk about it any further, but Mora caught them stealing glances at her behind their father's back. The tension radiating off these men became palpable. It was just as bad right here in Thomion's tent as it ever was in Xano.

Thomion didn't notice. He puttered around the tent and picked up some paper sheets of maps off the floor. He must have been showing his men the terrain on those maps while he gave them their instructions.

Mora would have traded almost anything for a look at those maps, but Thomion never gave her a chance. He rolled them up, stuffed them among all the books and trinkets on his shelves, and slumped on his cushions.

His sons did the same thing. They must all be his sons. Why else would he keep them in his tent while he sent out all the rest of the village men on some campaign?

If Thomion did decide to give Mora to someone in this village, he would certainly give her to one of his own sons the way Zeslea said he would.

Maybe that's why his sons kept looking at her. They expected their father to give her to one of them. They probably thought she was theirs by right.

They pretended not to watch her even when they did. Their eyes kept skimming down her body every time they glanced in her direction.

Just then, a young woman entered the tent from somewhere. She had a graceful figure and wore a short blue skirt and a pink cropped top. She sat down in the middle of the floor, placed another crock of food in front of the men, and retreated to sit next to Thomion.

She didn't look old enough to be in any kind of relationship with him, but maybe the Renegades had different marriage customs than the other Clans.

The men leaned forward to help themselves to the food. Thomion jerked his thumb toward Mora. "Give her something to eat, my dear. We can't have her going hungry."

"Who is she, Father?" the young woman asked.

"She's a Godless captive," one of the young men replied. "Father is handing her over to Dixor to give to one of his sons."

"Why not keep her here?" the young woman asked. "We have plenty of single men who need wives. All your own sons need wives."

"This one will only cause trouble," Thomion repeated. "We have to send her on."

"What trouble can she cause?" one of the sons asked. "She can breed like any other. What else do we need to know?"

"She's already bred," Thomion mutters. "Whoever takes her has to wait until she gives birth first. Every minute she stays in this village is another step closer to a full-scale battle against our own kind. She's dangerous the way she is. Let Dixor deal with her. He can wait until she births, kill the child, and hand her on to one of his sons to marry. Then we can all forget about her."

"It's sad for her that her child has to be killed," the young woman remarked.

Thomion snorted. "Not as sad as for the child, I'm sure."

The young woman stood up, picked up the crock, carried it over to Mora, and set it on the floor in front of her. "Are you hungry?" the young woman asked. "I'm Rosta. What's your name?"

Mora glared at her. "Don't pretend to be kind to me. Your father told you to feed me—nothing more. Don't talk to me. Don't even look at me."

The girl only smiled. "Let me untie you."

She held out her hands to Mora's wrists, but Thomion snapped, "Don't! Leave her where she is!"

Rosta dropped her hands, but she didn't leave. She squatted on her heels, moved the crock closer to Mora, and left it there. "Eat something. You must be hungry and tired."

Mora kept a close eye on everyone in the tent. She didn't take her eyes off anyone while she took a piece of meat out of the crock and put it in her mouth. She had to move both her bound hands at the same time, but at least she could move around.

She could get to a weapon like this. She spotted quite a few extra Renegade weapons lying around in the rest of Thomion's junk hoard. He and his men didn't seem to be aware of that—or maybe they didn't think they had to worry about it as long as they kept her tied up.

She would be able to use one of the weapons to free herself if she could just get to it. Some of them sat on the bookshelf near her head.

She might have been able to get to one if she stood up at the end of this leash—but then the leash itself would stop her from moving her hands over to pick up the weapon.

She wouldn't be able to do any of that with all of the men sitting around watching her. Thomion kept saying they had to keep an eye on her. That would make it much more difficult to escape.

Too many Renegades occupied this village and even this very tent. Then she would have to travel across countless miles of Renegade-infested territory before she made it back to Godless country.

Rosta sat there right in front of Mora and smiled at her in beaming delight while Mora ate. The girl's presence got on Mora's nerves, but she made a strategic decision not to mention it—or anything else.

"What is it like in the Godless?" Rosta finally blurted out.

"Leave her alone!" Thomion snapped. "What do you care what it's like in the Godless?"

"I'm curious," Rosta replied over her shoulder and turned back to Mora. "Is it like it is here?"

"Of course it isn't like it is here," one of her brothers told her. "The Godless don't live in houses and tents."

"Yes, they do," another brother interjected. "They make their houses out of branches."

"They sleep on the ground," another pointed out.

"Not all the time," a third corrected. "They only sleep on the ground when they travel."

"Is that true?" Rosta asked again. "We hear the Godless eat human flesh."

"No, they don't," Thomion barked. "You're talking nonsense."

"I'm not likely to learn anywhere else," Rosta pointed out. "I might never see another Godless again."

"You won't if I have anything to say about it," her father snarled. "Stop questioning her or I'll send you out of the tent."

Rosta ignored the threat. "How do the Godless raise their children? What did your parents do with you when you were small?"

Mora opened her mouth to say that she didn't grow up with the Godless, but one of the brothers interjected again before she had a chance to say anything.

"You'll have to come on one of our raiding expeditions. Then you can see Godless camps for yourself."

"So I can see you raze them and kill women and children?" Rosta snapped. "No, thank you."

"Then go over the Jagged Points and look for yourself," another brother suggested. "The country is crawling with Godless over there."

"You know I couldn't go by myself." Rosta turned back to Mora. "How old are your children?"

"Keep quiet," Thomion snapped. "She doesn't have any children. You can see that for yourself."

"How?" Rosta asked. "I can't tell. She looks like any woman to me."

"Look at her stomach. She doesn't have any stretch marks. She's too young. She's bred with her first right now."

"She is?" Rosta frowned at Mora's body. "How can you tell? She isn't swollen."

"One of Ulmeo's women told him and he told us," one of her brothers informed her.

"Let me see." Rosta put out her hands to touch Mora's stomach.

Mora overacted and slapped the young woman's hands away. Mora stopped herself from grabbing a weapon right then and there, but she wanted to.

She sat tense and watchful on the floor. She didn't want to fight these people, but she wouldn't sit here and let them poke and prod at her like a piece of livestock.

Rosta's eyes popped out of their sockets. "I wasn't going to hurt you! I'm just curious."

"Stay away from me," Mora snarled. "You keep your hands off me—all of you!"

Thomion snorted. "I told you so. Back off and leave her alone, girl."

Rosta humphed under her breath, got to her feet, and flounced back to sit next to her father.

At least she left the crock there so Mora could keep eating. She didn't regret lashing out. She would do the same to anyone who came near her—until the inevitable moment came when she couldn't stop them anymore.

Chapter 22

Mora woke up in the middle of the night. She couldn't tell exactly what made her wake up, but something did. The hair on the back of her neck stood on end when she heard men breathing nearby. She wasn't in the jungle with the Godless anymore.

She recognized Thomion's tent. She didn't recognize the sound of any of those men breathing.

She didn't have to sit up to know who was over there on the other side of the room. Thomion, Rosta, and Thomion's sons all fell asleep on the floor. Not even Thomion thought to use the couch as a bed.

Mora fell asleep after them. She didn't dare to shut her eyes as long as any of the men stayed awake. They never stopped stealing glances at her—not until they closed their eyes for the night.

Now she heard them all breathing deeply and even snoring in their sleep, but something woke her up. Something didn't feel right.

She found out why when one of Thomion's sons stood up. He must not have been asleep at all. Maybe he pretended or maybe his brothers' breathing covered up the fact that he wasn't breathing heavily in sleep.

He stood there in the darkness for a minute and looked down at his sleeping father and brothers. Very faint starlight shone through the tent and set off the guy's outline. Mora couldn't tell which brother it was. She wouldn't have been able to tell them apart anyway.

She tensed when the guy stepped over his brothers with extreme care and walked around the couch. He stopped in front of Mora and stared down at her the same way.

She stared up at him hardly daring to breathe. He could only be here for one reason. She measured how she would deal with him when the moment came for him to attack her. She had to get to a weapon at all costs—before he attacked her.

The attack would wake up the others. They would stop her from escaping, but maybe she could save herself from the guy this once.

Thomion lived in oblivion about what his sons might be capable of. It obviously never crossed his mind that one of his own sons would do what he suspected the other single men of planning to do.

The guy lowered himself onto his knees and slumped there as though this whole process cost him all his strength. His head bobbed in pathetic resignation of what he was about to do.

Mora's fear turned to rage. How dare he feel sorry for himself?

She lashed out sooner than she planned—but she didn't really plan anything.

She kicked out, hit him in the chin hard enough to snap his head back, and then spun around and kicked the bookshelf with all her might.

A bunch of stuff fell off, including some of the weapons closest to the edge. One of the long, square Renegade blades bounced off the carpet right next to her. She knew how to use that.

She snatched it and spun around to face the guy, but he retaliated too fast. He dove on top of her and pinned her under his weight. He weighed a lot and overpowered her easily. He held her arms down and drove his body into her hips.

She flew into a panic, squirmed onto her side to buy herself just a few inches of space, and used the pocket between her side and his chest to bring her knee up.

She flipped over on her back, wedged her knee between his body and herself, and kicked out again. She only moved him a few inches, but those few inches were enough.

She used all the strength in both her arms to whip her blade across her chest and slashed him from shoulder to shoulder.

He roared in pain and rage, jolted upright onto his knees to get away from her blade, and she hacked down hard into his arm. The blade stuck in the bone until she yanked it free and ripped a long gash down the side of his elbow.

He staggered back on his knees and collapsed on his seat bellowing and clutching his arm. The noise roused everyone the way she expected to. Thomion, Rosta, and Thomion's other sons all sprang up and rushed over.

"Get a light!" Thomion thundered. "Get a light now!"

One of his sons charged outside and came back with a flaming torch. Then everyone saw Mora sitting up holding her blood-stained weapon and the attacker sprawled there bleeding from his wounds.

"What the hell are you doing?!" Thomion roared.

Mora bared her teeth and brandished her weapon at everyone, including Rosta. "I told you to leave me alone!" she snarled. "Come near me again and I swear I'll kill you."

Thomion stared at her and then at his injured son. Mora didn't move except to rasp for air between her bared teeth.

Her fevered brain didn't register anything but the need to kill anyone who messed with her. She might not be able to stop them from selling her to another man, but she had no plans to cooperate.

Thomion recovered himself, took a step forward, and kicked her across the side of the head so fast that she never saw it coming. She flipped backward onto the floor in a daze.

He kicked her one more time and tore her blade out of her hands before he rounded on his sons. "Get out of here—all of you! Everybody out! I told you to leave her alone and you didn't! Get out! OUT!!"

He waved his sons away, and when they didn't move fast enough to satisfy him, he actually swung Mora's blade at them. The wounded attacker didn't get up quickly enough. His brothers had to pick him up and drag him out of the room.

Rosta hesitated and her father struck her across the face to make her leave. She screamed and ran for it until only Thomion remained. The sons took the torch with them and plunged the tent back into darkness.

"I knew you were going to be trouble," Thomion muttered under his breath. "You'll keep causing trouble as long as you're here. You'll be gone soon enough and then things will settle down."

He went around the tent gathering all the weapons off the floor. He took them to the other side of the tent, well out of her reach, and piled them in the corner.

He finally returned to his place on the floor, sighed and cursed to himself a few more times, and went back to sleep. Mora stayed awake for a long time. She didn't trust one of the other single men not to sneak into this tent while Thomion slept.

Now she was unarmed. She wouldn't be able to protect herself from one of them if they did come, especially if they came armed. They might kill Thomion and then another battle would break out with everyone fighting over her.

Chapter 23

Hangman peered through the foliage at the village in the distance. Then he checked behind him. "This is it. This is the village behind Gapewell Pass. Mora must be in there somewhere."

"How do we find out where she is?" Cross asked.

"We just have to go in there," Alien pointed out. "We should wait until nightfall. We can search the village without anyone seeing us."

"Not so fast." "We have to deal with *them* first." Hangman pointed to his right. The cousins observed parties of Renegades patrolling the surrounding jungle. They all returned to the village, met up with other groups, and divided. "It's the same routine we saw at the other place."

"Then we deal with them the same way," Viking suggested.

Hangman nodded. "It's too early now. We'll withdraw into the canopy and wait until dusk before we go in."

The cousins climbed the nearest trees and found a place to settle down. Hangman rested his shoulders. The journey here made them ache, but he no longer let it bother him.

They might ache for the rest of his life. He could live with pain. He couldn't live with not being able to move around.

Viking and Alien ate while they waited. The cousins kept working their way through their food supplies every day they spent traveling here, but the supply held out. The cousins didn't need to hunt anytime soon.

Hangman counted down the hours until sundown. All this waiting annoyed him, but he only used it as fuel. He became more ferociously determined to hurt someone when he finally caught up with whoever was holding Mora right now.

Alien dozed off. Hangman worked on his kukris while he waited. Cross had developed a disconcerting habit of staring at Hangman during these downtimes. Hangman pretended not to notice his brother watching his every move.

At least Cross didn't question Hangman anymore—about anything. Hangman didn't want to talk. He wanted to kill.

His murderous intent gave him all the patience he needed to wait until dusk. He roused his cousins and the four men separated to different parts of the jungle.

Dusk made the Renegades more complacent about keeping an eye on things. The men on patrol talked to each other more and even laughed.

They walked through jungle miles behind their territorial boundary. They must have patrolled this terrain every day for years and never seen a single enemy.

Their attitude made them perfect targets. Hangman didn't even try to use stealth. He dropped onto the ground at a distance and charged them. They fought back, but they didn't rally fast enough or with sufficient strength to overcome his bloodlust.

If any of them started to get the better of him, he took off into the gathering darkness, attacked another group, and came back for the stragglers.

The sounds of conflict brought more men out of the village. Hangman saw them coming, darted away into the undergrowth, and skirted the village to its other side.

Viking and Alien made a lot of noise and attracted most of the Renegade fighters. They came out of tents and houses carrying their weapons and converged on the two cousins.

The commotion escalated as darkness fell over the village and surrounding mountains. The Renegades' metal blades clanged extra loudly on the cousin's weapons.

That sound acted as a homing beacon to tell Hangman exactly where his cousins were. He could track his cousins' position by their noise alone.

The village emptied as more and more fighting men left the village. Hangman didn't see where Cross was. Hangman couldn't wait any longer.

He strode into the village, threw back the flap on a tent, took one look around to make sure Mora wasn't there, and stormed to the next house. He kicked in the door and startled a woman feeding her three children. Mora wasn't there, either.

He went from house to house and still didn't find her. He even broke open an empty little shed with nothing in it at all. He kept going until he came to the biggest tent. He threw back the flap and an older man looked up at him.

The guy's expression went through a few rapid changes before he relaxed his shoulders and sighed. "Ah. You must be the husband."

"Where is she?" Hangman snarled. "You had her here. I know you did."

The guy jerked his thumb over his shoulder. "Our men took her farther west—to another village. You can't get her back."

"Where is the village?" Hangman demanded. "How do I find it?"

The guy opened his mouth to answer, but at that moment, something struck Hangman across the back of the head and knocked him out. He woke up tied hand and foot on the ground. Two dozen enormous Renegades surrounded him.

His brother Cross lay on the ground next to him. Cross gave him a knowing look. Cross didn't look or act scared at all. He nodded once. Did he get himself caught to help Hangman?

"This is the man." One of the Renegades pointed to the wound on Hangman's shoulder. "See that? That's where Larth tortured him."

"I hear you killed many of our warriors," the older Renegade Hangman. "Is that true?"

"Not enough," Hangman muttered. "I'll kill plenty more before I stop."

The guy snorted. "You will never find your wife. She's gone. Go get yourself another woman."

Hangman didn't answer at all. He twisted his head around to search the Renegades and their village. He didn't see Viking or Alien anywhere. They must have gotten away—assuming the Renegades didn't kill the cousins already.

Hangman did see one of the nearby Renegades holding his kukris. The man held both weapons lightly in one hand while the guy watched the interaction between Hangman and the man he assumed must be the leader of this village.

"Tell me where your other men are hiding—the men who attacked our patrols earlier," the leader ordered.

"I don't know where they are," Hangman muttered. "They must have escaped into the jungle, but I wouldn't tell you even if I knew."

"Would you tell me if I killed this young one?" the guy went down on one knee, yanked Cross back by the hair, and held a knife to Cross's throat.

Cross kept his steadfast eyes locked on Hangman. Cross still didn't act scared.

"I would tell you to save his life, but I don't know," Hangman replied. "I separated from them when we attacked the patrols. I left them so I could enter the village to find my wife."

The guy let go of Cross and straightened up. "I believe you would save him. You look similar. Is he your brother or your cousin? It doesn't matter. Your friends will come back to get you. Then we'll capture them, too, and none of you will bother us anymore."

He motioned to his men. They picked up Cross and Hangman, dragged them to the center of the village, and tied both brothers to posts facing outward toward the eastern jungle. If Viking and Alien were out there, they would come from that direction.

The Renegade leader walked back and forth in front of the two brothers, raised his voice, and bellowed out into the open jungle. "I know you're out there!! I know you can hear me!! We have your friends as our prisoners!! Show yourselves and give yourselves up!! We'll inflict damage on them until you come!!"

The guy spun around at those words and drove his knife into Cross's leg. Cross thrashed against the ropes and roared in pain, but no one helped him.

The guy pulled the knife out, left Cross hanging there bleeding, and went back to pacing. "You see how it is!!" he roared. "The longer you wait, the more damage we will inflict!! There won't be much left if you don't hurry up!!"

The guy spun around a second time and stabbed Hangman right in the shoulder—right into the hole injury the Renegades inflicted on him the first time.

He erupted in excruciating bellows, but the guy only pulled the knife out and walked away. Hangman wilted against the ropes still roaring in agony, but he couldn't do anything but hang here.

His chin sank onto his chest. Cold sweat broke out all over him. He couldn't go through all of that again. He went through enough the first time. He couldn't let the guy stab him or Cross a second time.

Ten Renegades stayed behind to guard the brothers. One of these Renegades was the one holding Hangman's kukris.

His pain and desperation morphed back into rage and murderous determination. The Renegades made another crucial blunder by keeping his kukris near him where he could see them.

All these Renegades carried weapons, but they didn't inspire him the way his own kukris did. He didn't want just any weapon. He wanted *those* weapons, and by God, he would get them back.

He hated that man for even touching the weapons that Hangman crafted with his own hands. He would kill that man first and then kill all the rest of these filthy creatures with the same weapons.

He had to get free from these ropes first and he didn't have a blade to do it. He did have his fingernails, though.

The ropes had been woven from braided vines. All the Clans made rope the same way.

He grimaced in pain when he wrenched his shoulders around so he could grasp just one strand of the rope braid.

The pain fogged his brain with battle fury. His pain and rage blocked out everything else. His pain became the energy to fuel his strength and determination.

He used his fingernails to claw through that one strand—and then the next. The process took forever, but he kept his eyes locked on his kukris at all costs. His hands itched to close around his weapons one more time.

The Renegades paid more attention to the jungle than they did to the two prisoners. The Renegades cast occasional glances at the brothers before the guards went back to scanning the surroundings.

The whole scene replayed the same sequence of events that occurred when the Renegades captured Butcher's band. These Renegades must have all gotten the same training and the same orders on how to deal with this.

Full dark fell over the area. The guards built bonfires around the captured brothers. The fires only blinded the Renegades to anything moving in the shadowy jungle beyond the edge of the village.

Cross gasped and whimpered on the post next to Hangman. "Hangman...." Cross husked. "Hangman....help me....."

Hangman glanced at his brother. Cross stared back at Hangman with huge, frightened eyes—the huge, frightened eyes Hangman expected to see before now—but he didn't see them before now.

The surrounding Renegades also looked up to see Cross staring at Hangman with huge, frightened eyes. The Renegades relaxed when they saw how terrified and pathetic Cross looked.

That was the moment when Hangman saw his brother's hands moving. Cross twisted his hands in knots to work his fingernails into the rope.

Cross held Hangman's gaze until Hangman looked away. Hangman let his chin fall back on his chest and let out a shaky sigh.

It was a genuine sigh of desperate agony and near-hopeless resignation to an impossible situation. He couldn't overcome his enemies like this.

He only let his desperate agony get to nearly hopeless resignation. He didn't let it go all the way.

He could overcome his enemies just as soon as he worked his way through these ropes. Just one more strand.....

He didn't let himself think about what he would do or how he would do it. That didn't matter. Something would come up. It always did. He just had to keep going....keep pushing through this pain.....

His shoulder stopped hurting and went numb. So much the better. The rest of him started to get cold and numb, too. He welcomed it. The less he felt, the better.

He welcomed it when the Renegade leader came back and started pacing up and down in front of the brothers again.

The guy stopped in front of the man holding Hangman's kukris. Hangman's attention zeroed to a pinprick when the Renegade leader took the kukris into his own hands, turned them over, and raised his eyebrows at their workmanship.

He turned back the other way and started pacing again. "You still haven't shown yourselves!!" he yelled out into the jungle. "Do you really want to hide in the darkness like the cowards you are and watch them bleed?!"

He stopped in front of Hangman and raised one of the kukris to stab Hangman again. Hangman let his fury off its leash. His kukri hovered right there in front of his delirious eyes.

His fingernail snipped the last strand of the rope, and at that moment, Viking and Alien charged the village from the shadows. They hacked three Renegades to the ground before the alarm went up.

More Renegades emerged from houses and tents all over the village. The Renegade fighters closed on the two Godless. The Renegade leader glanced over his shoulder with the kukri still raised in his hand.

Hangman yanked the ropes the rest of the way apart and dove for the guy. Cross broke free at exactly the same moment and pounced on a Renegade who happened to be running past with a weapon in his hand.

Hangman lost sight of everything else but his own weapons. He grabbed the Renegade leader by the hair with one hand and by the wrist with the other.

Hangman wrenched the guy's head around and drilled the kukri straight through the man's cheekbone all the way into the back of his skull.

Hangman gave a cruel twist, cracked the skull in half, and plucked the two kukris out of his victim's hands as the body crumpled at his feet.

Hangman turned on the Renegades closest to him. Viking and Alien only stayed in the village long enough to see Cross and Hangman break free.

Viking shot Hangman a single glance through the mayhem. Renegades broke away from fighting Viking and Alien to come after Cross and Hangman instead. The cousins couldn't stay here.

Hangman cast a similar glance at his brother. All four of the cousins read the situation for what it was.

Hangman struck out at the Renegades closest to him, and at an unspoken signal, all four cousins turned away and bolted in opposite directions.

Hangman plunged out of the village heading off to the left. Cross broke away to the right. Cross ran well and sprinted for the trees even on his injured leg. Viking and Alien split apart and took off in opposite directions from each other. They didn't stick together.

The Renegades had to divide into four different parties to come after the cousins. Hangman drove himself to his top speed to put as much distance as possible between himself and his enemies.

He made it fifty yards into the dense, pitch-dark jungle before he leapt into the branches. He didn't feel a thing in his injured shoulder.

He scaled as high into the canopy as he could get, put his weapons into his waistband, found a hollow between two branches, tucked himself into it, and settled down to wait.

He forced himself to quiet his breathing, closed his eyes, and went perfectly, unnaturally still.

He didn't have to wait long before the Renegades came along carrying torches. They ruined their night vision by using artificial light to see something that wasn't there.

They never climbed into the branches. They couldn't see this high into the canopy from so far down on the ground. They searched everywhere, found the last of Hangman's tracks, and followed the trail to the point where Hangman left the ground.

The Renegades couldn't follow him anywhere else. They hunted around for hours before they gave up and went back to their village.

Chapter 24

Hangman woke up in the clear grey light of dawn. The pain in his shoulder was back with a vengeance, but at least the wound didn't bleed anymore.

The blood all over his chest and shoulder dried overnight. His shoulder hurt like crazy when he moved it, but he really just didn't care anymore.

He dragged himself out of the hollow between the branches, stood up, and balanced through the canopy until he came in sight of the Renegade Clan village not far away.

The remaining fighters had gathered all their dead in rows in the middle of the village. Their glorious leader lay there with them like the rotten, useless corpse he was. Good riddance.

A different man walked around giving orders to everyone. Hangman didn't try to hear what he said to his men. Sure enough, the guy ordered one of his men out of line and pointed toward the west. The guy nodded and left at a jog in that direction.

Hangman stayed in the canopy and worked his way around the village to the south. Cross ran away in that direction.

Hangman came upon Viking and Alien sitting together in the branches on the way there. "You're hurt again, little brother," Viking remarked.

"Not at all," Hangman replied. "The Renegades just sent a messenger to warn the other village."

"What other village?" Alien asked.

"The village to the west where they're keeping Mora. They sent her farther inland. The messenger is on his way there to warn them that we're coming. Come on. We have to go."

"Go?" Viking asked. "Go where? How can we find Mora if we don't know where this other village is?"

"We find her by following the messenger, you big dolt. Now come on. We have to hurry before he gets too far ahead of us."

"Why are you heading south if the village is to the west?" Alien asked.

"We have to find Cross first. He probably needs our help."

The cousins followed Hangman through the canopy. It didn't take long for them to find Cross.

He made it easy for them because he wasn't in the canopy. He had descended to the ground during the night, put leaf paste on his wounded leg, and had already brewed himself a dose of Gooji juice.

He had constructed his fire between two big stands of rock to conceal the light. The darkness must have concealed the smoke.

Hangman had to admire his brother's grit and resourcefulness. The whole procedure worked amazingly well. Now the basin of Gooji juice sat there cooling on the ground.

Cross eyed Hangman's shoulder. "It looks like you need this more than I do, brother," Cross remarked.

"You made it. You drink it," Hangman told him. "I'll be fine."

Cross snorted. "That's what worries me. I'll drink half of it and you can drink the other half."

Cross tipped up the basin, gulped down half the juice, and handed the basin to Hangman.

Hangman didn't dare to turn down his brother's generosity, so Hangman swallowed the remaining juice.

"How is your leg?" Hangman asked after he finished. "Can you travel?"

"I can travel as well as you can with your shoulder like that," Cross returned. "Are we going?"

Hangman let the subject drop. The cousins stayed in the canopy for several miles back toward the north, circled the village at a distance, and came to the edge of the trees even more miles out of sight of the village.

The jungle ended there. Rocky terrain crossed the mountains to steeper valleys on the other side. Hangman, Cross, and their cousins dropped to the ground and stepped out into the open without a word of discussion.

They set off running up the mountain to catch up with the Renegades' messenger. Cross kept up with the others. He showed no sign that his wound distressed him at all.

Hangman was really starting to admire his brother's fortitude. Cross was becoming more of a man than Hangman ever thought possible.

The cousins made it to a narrow, treacherous mountain pass by the next evening. Hangman spotted a tiny speck of movement farther down the other side of the mountain.

None of the cousins stopped. They kept running and even picked up speed on the downhill side. They closed the gap to overtake the messenger.

He must not have realized someone was following him. He stopped at dusk and lit a fire that led the cousins straight to him.

Hangman and his cousins hid in the rocks at a distance and observed the man at his leisure. He ate, lounged in comfort, and then fell asleep totally unprotected. He left his fire blazing for all the world to see.

Hangman would have liked to kill the guy, but then the messenger wouldn't be able to lead Hangman to Mora's location.

Hangman and his companions shared their food supplies as night fell over the mountains. The rocks protected the cousins from the wind.

Hangman would have stayed awake to keep watch over his enemy, but Viking told him to go to sleep while Viking and Alien kept watch. Hangman didn't argue.

He woke up when Viking shook him. "He's moving out," Viking murmured low. "It's time to go."

The cousins advanced much more slowly today. The messenger didn't run or even jog. He walked. The cousins had to dodge behind hidden places, wait for the guy to cover some distance, and then run to catch up with him. The process dragged on for an eternity.

The messenger didn't enter the second village until later on the third day. The cousins took up another protected, hidden vantage point in the rocks and watched the Renegades lead Mora into one of the larger tents.

Fights broke out among the men as soon as soon as the others took her inside. Men punched, ganged up on each other, and even stabbed each other.

The fights escalated into major battles until another older Renegade man stepped out of the same tent and bellowed at them all to stop.

"They have a lot more women here," Alien observed. "I wonder if they plan to keep her here."

"I doubt it," Viking replied. "Look how much conflict her presence is causing. Giving her to any one man would only make the problem worse."

"I'm going down there," Hangman decided.

"Are you insane?!" Viking hissed. "This village is even bigger than the last. They have more men—and you and Cross are both injured."

"It's the only way to find Mora. You don't have to come. Take Cross back up into the mountains. I'll get myself captured....."

All three men exploded in protests, including Cross. He had never protested anything Hangman said before.

"They'll kill you, Hangman!" Cross insisted.

"It's the only way to get into the village," Hangman replied. "They'll take me to see Mora. I'll find out where she is."

"They'll take you to her so they can kill you right in front of her," Alien snapped. "You came all this way to save her, not to see her."

"I can't save her if I don't enter the village," Hangman countered. "There is no other way to get in there. Go on, Alien. Go up into those mountains. I'll come back with Mora and we'll return to our own territory."

"You won't come back," Alien snarled. "You aren't invincible, little brother, even though you like to pretend you are."

Hangman smiled at his brother and his cousins. "I will come back. I know it."

He turned back to the village. He didn't want to think about or worry about Cross and his cousins anymore. He knew where Mora was. Seeing her even from a distance snapped the rest of his resolve. He had to go down there no matter what it took.

He started to stand up when a different group of twenty Renegades came over the hill behind the four cousins. The Renegades saw the four Godless hiding behind the rocks.

Hangman froze—and then he and his comrades relaxed. They couldn't get away. There was no point in fighting back.

The Renegades surrounded the cousins, disarmed them, and marched them the rest of the way down the mountain to the village. At least Hangman was getting what he wanted now.

The Renegades walked straight past the tent where Hangman had seen them take Mora. She never found out Hangman was even here.

The Renegades pushed the cousins into another empty house. This one was bigger than the shack Hangman saw in the first village.

Five Renegades entered first. Then the prisoners entered and another six Renegades followed. Hangman wasn't even surprised when the Renegades fell on all four cousins, beat them to the ground, and kept beating and kicking them into unconsciousness.

Chapter 25

Hangman swam back to semi-consciousness when someone touched his swollen face. He jolted from the pain, but he couldn't move anything except his head.

More ropes cut into his wrists and ankles. He tried to work his arms around so he could tear through the ropes, but he couldn't move well enough while he lay on his side.

He looked all around him and dragged his vision into focus on a woman squatting in front of him. She wore a long dress buttoned up to her neck, buttoned around the wrists, and trailing all the way to the ground.

It reminded Hangman of the full dresses the Followers wore, but he couldn't be sure if she really was a Follower. She didn't wear her hair up the way Follower women did. She wore it down in long black tresses past her shoulders.

She dabbed his face with something soft, cool, and wet. "Drink some water," she murmured. "It will make you feel better."

"Who are you?" he husked.

"My name is Cheina," she breathed. "I'm here to take care of you and your men. Drink this."

She angled a water gourd onto its side and maneuvered the mouth to his swollen, cracked, puffy lips.

She poured water into his mouth and waited each time while he swallowed it. He collapsed back into the dirt with a shaky sigh of relief. "Thank you."

"Are you hungry? I brought you some food."

"My mouth hurts," he rasped. "I don't want to eat."

She cast a glance behind her. Viking, Alien, and Cross all lay sprawled and bound on the floor nearby. "Your men are all right. They'll all recover."

"Thank you. What do the Renegades plan to do with us?"

"I couldn't tell you that, but they'll take you to see Thomion soon. I'm sure he'll tell you."

"The woman....the Godless woman they're holding as a prisoner .....is she all right? Did they hurt her?"

She winced and looked down at her hands cleaning the blood off his face. She didn't answer to tell him about Mora.

"At least tell me she's still in this village," Hangman insisted. "At least tell me they didn't move her."

"She is here, but not for long. They plan to send her farther west. I don't know when."

"Do you see her?" Hangman insisted. "She's my wife. Please tell her I'm here to save her. Tell her I won't stop until I take her home."

"I don't see her," Cheina murmured. "No one sees her except Rosta. Thomion won't let anyone else go near the woman."

"Who is Rosta?"

"She's Thomion's daughter. She's the only woman Thomion trusts to look after the woman." Cheina cast a terrified glance around. "You mustn't talk about her anymore. A messenger already came to tell Thomion that the woman's husband was in the country. He'll kill you as soon as he realizes why you're here."

Hangman fell silent while she finished cleaning his face. He tried not to flinch when she put leaf paste on his injuries.

He couldn't fathom why the Renegades wanted to heal him or take care of him—unless they planned to torture him again. He had to act fast. The question was what he could do in this situation.

Cheina moved on and cleaned up the other three, too. Alien groaned a lot. Cross woke up when she started working on him.

He twisted onto his back and looked up at her while she worked. Then he exchanged glances with Hangman.

She was just finishing with Viking when a bunch of the Renegades came back. They cut the ropes on the prisoners' feet and walked them back to the leader's tent. Hangman counted down the seconds until he saw Mora, but when he walked in, she wasn't there.

The middle-aged leader sat on the floor with three other men. This must be the famous Thomion.

He must have moved Mora to another tent or house when he heard his men had captured her husband. Thomion got a flash of wild triumph in his eyes when Hangman looked around at the tent full of furnishings.

A young woman sat to one side watching the whole affair. Thomion got to his feet. His men stayed seated. "So this is the husband we've been hearing so much about," Thomion began. "Welcome. You finally made it. Well done."

"I don't know what you're talking about," Hangman replied. "I'm not married. None of us are."

Thomion made a face and then frowned. Did Hangman dare to believe this might actually work?

Thomion tried to shrug it off. "You don't have to play coy with me. We know you came for your wife. You've been killing Renegades halfway across the country."

"I told you I don't have a wife. I don't know who you mean. Maybe she's someone else's wife and you have me confused with someone else."

Thomion glared at him. "If you didn't come to rescue your wife, why are you so far out of your territory?"

"Out of our territory? This is Godless territory," Hangman replied. "You stole it from us—but you're apparently too arrogant to realize that we can just as easily steal it back from you. You sit back here in comfort. You only defend your forward boundary. You leave the rest of the country unprotected. You're weak. All we have to do is break across your boundary, kill all your men, and we'll retake this territory for ourselves."

Thomion's eyes popped. "You're here to retake our territory?!"

"*Our* territory," Hangman corrected. "You will never hold this territory against a force as strong as ours."

Thomion narrowed his eyes and glared at Hangman. "I don't believe you. You're making it up to stop me from knowing you are the woman's husband."

Hangman only shrugged. "Believe what you want. By all means, continue to believe I'm this woman's husband—whoever she is. You'll only make yourselves weaker than you already are—messing around with other men's wives. You have your heads so far between your women's legs that you don't even bother to defend the country. Your men are out there right now fighting over a single woman. They never knew we were here until we got within line of sight of this village. What does that tell you about what the Godless attack force will be able to do?"

Thomion waved to the men behind the prisoners. "Take them back. My sons will interrogate the prisoners. Get them out of here."

The Renegades moved in and yanked Hangman and his comrades out of the tent. Hangman cast one last glance through the flap before it closed.

Mora wasn't in there. Was she still in this village? He would have to escape immediately if she wasn't. He had to catch up with her before the Renegades moved her too far away.

The Renegades took the four men back to the same empty building structure. The Renegades turned the prisoners around to sit them down on the floor. The Renegades brought in more lengths of rope and tied the prisoners' feet together again.

Six Renegades stayed inside the room to guard the prisoners. Hangman caught his cousins' eyes and started working his way through the ropes again. He had to strike back once Thomion's sons came to interrogate the prisoners.

The guards let their vigilance lapse here, too. They leaned against the walls and looked around at everything other than the prisoners.

Hangman lay on his side with his hands behind him. He positioned himself so his body blocked the guards from seeing what he was doing. Cross and the cousins did the same thing. They all faced the guards while the four men tore the ropes apart as fast as they dared.

The guards saw the prisoners lying there helpless and unmoving. The guards didn't pay attention to anything else. Hangman strained his ears to listen for any sound of people coming closer. He heard a lot of different sounds outside.

He heard women and children interacting. He heard what sounded like men and he also heard what sounded like teenage boys and girls all jumbled together.

He wished now that he'd questioned Cheina more about the people in this village. He'd never seen the Renegades this close up before. He knew nothing about their social structure—not that he cared.

She might have told him something useful—something he could have used against these people. Now it was too late.

He made it halfway through the rope before heavy footsteps approached from outside. Shadows crossed the line of daylight coming from under the bottom logs of the opposite wall.

Someone stopped by the door, opened it from the outside, and the three younger men from Thomion's tent entered. They waved the guards away. These three certainly acted over-confident.

They shut the door behind them. Two of the brothers stood back while one of them approached Hangman. This must have been Thomion's oldest son and the bigshot of them all.

Hangman braced himself and broke out in a cold sweat when he expected the guy to dig his fingers into Hangman's shoulder wound again. He didn't. He just squatted down and got in Hangman's face.

"You're going to tell us all about this Godless force invading our territory," the guy snarled under his breath. "I could bring the little woman here and violate her in front of you. Would you like that? Or I could cut on her with my knife for a while. You could watch her bleed while she cries out to you for help. You'll tell me either way."

Hangman glared at the guy and clamped his mouth shut to stop himself from answering. Hangman used his fury to tear another strand of the rope.

Every minute this bastard paid attention to Hangman was another minute the three idiots didn't pay attention to Viking, Alien, and Cross. Thomion's sons really were too brainless to live.

All three came armed. Each of them came carrying two of the Renegades' long square blades like the ones Mora carried. The Renegades used similar sheaths tied to each man's outer legs.

Hangman actually got the idea and modeled her sheaths after theirs, but they used thicker leather that held the blades more securely.

The sheaths left the blades ripe for the picking. Then, in the most delicious stroke of iron yet, one son strolled over to his brother and the second man handed over Hangman's kukris.

Hangman couldn't believe his good fortune when the oldest son came back and waved the kukris in Hangman's face. He couldn't ask for a better incentive to kick these morons into next week.

The oldest son pointed the weapons in Hangman's face and then moved over to Cross.

Hangman couldn't tell from here how far Cross and the others were getting toward freeing themselves. Hangman couldn't see Cross's or his cousins' hands. Their bodies blocked him from seeing.

The oldest son grabbed Cross by the hair, stuck one of Hangman's kukris in Cross's face, and scratched the tip down Cross's cheek.

"Maybe you would like it better if I cut on this one instead," the oldest son drawled. "He's so young. Maybe you feel like protecting him if the woman isn't yours."

"All right! All right!" Hangman yelled. "I'll tell you! Just....just don't hurt him!"

The oldest son snorted. These guys must never have heard of deception or guile.

The oldest son stood up, kicked Cross once in the ribs, and sauntered back over to stand above Hangman. "Well? So tell me. Where are they? How many are the Godless bringing? What are their plans? Tell me everything."

"They're bringing.....they're bringing....." Hangman snapped another strand of the rope. Almost there..... "They're bringing five hundred....from the east....."

"Five hundred?! That's all?" The oldest son snorted. "That's nothing. We can handle that easily."

"That's only from the east," Hangman went on. "They're bringing another thousand from the south—around the Jagged Points."

The oldest son scowled at him. *"Around* the Jagged Points....from the south.....?"

Hangman nodded fast and snapped the last strand. The rope parted in his hands, but he didn't react right away.

He savored the sight of this dupe falling straight into Hangman's trap. No sane person would take a force of a thousand men around the Jagged Points, a mountain range hundreds of miles long, to attack the Renegade Clan from the south. That was just stupid.

Hangman watched the wheels grinding in the guy's head. The oldest son furrowed his brow in deep thought trying to understand all of this. It never once occurred to him that Hangman might be making it all up.

He decided to throw the oldest son a curve ball he would never see coming. "There's another force of a thousand coming from the north," Hangman added. "They're going around the Jagged Points from the other side."

That did it. The oldest son turned to his brothers and took a few steps in their direction to consult with them.

Alien exploded out of his position at that moment, launched to his feet, and attacked the oldest son from behind.

The younger two brothers saw Alien first. Their hands flew to their weapons, but their brother blocked them from getting to Alien. The oldest son tried to turn around to defend himself, but Alien grabbed him first.

Alien dwarfed the guy in size and strength, threw an arm around the oldest son's arms to knock them down, and snatched one of the oldest son's blades from his side.

Alien kept his grip on the oldest son even against the man's best efforts to struggle free. Alien pinned the oldest son against his body and used the guy as a shield when the younger two tried to attack.

Alien struck out with the blade just as Viking, Cross, and Hangman sprang to their feet. Viking rushed in to help Alien.

Viking snatched the oldest son's other blade and left the guy defenseless. That left Cross and Hangman to get their weapons from the other two brothers.

Hangman rushed the oldest son and stripped the kukris out of the guy's hands. Hangman unleashed his berserk rage on all these men, drove his kukri into the oldest son's temple, and the man folded at the knees.

Alien still didn't let him go. The oldest son's body offered the best protection against Thomion's other two sons.

Hangman pivoted around the cluster and went after the last two brothers from the side. Viking rushed them from the opposite direction and hacked at the lefthand brother to hit him in the head.

Both brothers got their weapons unsheathed just fine. They met Viking and Hangman in a flurry of whirling blades. The four men locked together.

Hangman's opponent turned to confront him. The man overpowered Hangman in size and strength. The guy fought well with two blades much bigger than Hangman's.

The brother chopped down both his blades to cleave Hangman's head in half. Hangman crossed his kukris to block both blades above his head, but he already felt his arms weakening, especially his injured shoulder.

Alien lunged out of position at that moment and stabbed the brother under the arm. Alien's blade punctured the man's ribs and he winced over onto his side.

Hangman struck out with his kukri and chopped into the side of the guy's skull. The brother went down. That left Viking against the third brother.

Cross dove for the guy before Hangman and Alien had a chance to turn around. Cross tackled the third brother flat on the floor and Viking dove in to stab the helpless brother through the eye socket.

Chapter 26

A breathless silence fell over the room while Viking helped Cross to his feet. The cousins had weapons now. Hangman had his kukris back.

Viking, Alien, and Cross divided up the weapons taken from Thomion's sons. "I sure would like to get my kukris back," Alien muttered.

"And my axe," Viking added.

"We'll find them," Hangman told them. "We have to search the village until we find Mora. Your weapons must be somewhere near Thomion's tent and so is she—if they aren't actually in it."

"It would be nice if we could create a diversion like we did last time," Cross suggested.

"We don't have time," Hangman decided. "We're already inside the village. We need to find her and get her out. We can't mess around going out and coming in multiple times."

"How do you want to search for her?" Viking asked. "Without arousing the Renegades' suspicions."

Hangman eased over to the door, pulled it open, and peeked out. "The sun is going down. Everyone will be going into their houses for the night. We may go undetected if we go silently."

His cousins exchanged doubtful glances, but he couldn't wait anymore. He eased the door open a second time and peered outside.

No Renegades stood guard. The few he saw still walking around the village headed for different houses and tents. None of them noticed anything strange about the sounds coming from this building.

Hangman slipped through the door and headed straight for Thomion's tent. Any sense of caution Hangman might have left evaporated on the way there.

He made up his mind to kill the bastard one way or the other. Hangman didn't even want to wait long enough for Thomion to tell him where Mora was. Hangman would just find her on his own.

He threw back the tent flap. Thomion wasn't in there. Neither was Mora. Hangman did see Alien's enormous kukris, Viking's axe, and Cross's blades in one corner of the tent.

Rosta sat on the carpet and looked up in confusion when Hangman stopped on the threshold. "Where's the Godless woman your father held as a captive?" Hangman demanded.

She opened her mouth to answer, but a blood-curdling bellow startled him into spinning around.

He came face to face with a mob of Renegades circling the cousins. One of the Renegades must have surprised Alien and hacked a blade into Alien's upper arm before he could turn around and defend himself.

Alien spun around with the blade still lodged in his arm, swung the blade he stole from Thomion's sons, and cleaved his attacker's skull off the top.

The other Renegades moved in. Hangman didn't have a chance to retrieve his cousins' weapons. He charged outside and joined his cousins to defend them.

The noise brought more Renegades out of their houses. They gathered by the dozen and boxed the four cousins in. Hangman and his companions couldn't escape. All four of them looked around for a way to retreat, but Thomion's tent blocked their way to the rear.

Hangman snatched the tent covering and yanked it with all his strength. The tent toppled with Rosta still trapped inside.

She screamed and scrambled out as all the posts and the covering tilted away and fell to one side. The tent left Thomion's hoard and the cousins' weapons exposed.

Hangman and his cousins backed away. He snatched up the weapons and tossed them to his cousins and his brother, but the Renegades advanced to follow the party.

The four cousins drew level with the first house. Hangman couldn't lower his weapons to open the door, so he kicked out one of the corner posts. That house collapsed and the people inside yelled and floundered to get out of the wreckage. Mora wasn't in there.

Another two dozen Renegades closed from behind the four cousins. Viking and Alien pivoted to their left trying to angle their way out of the village, but the Renegades cut them off everywhere the cousins turned.

Hangman kicked over house after house and tore down tent after tent. He didn't find Mora anywhere. Did Thomion send her away after all?

"We have to fall back," Alien snarled. "We have to look for her another way."

Hangman didn't want to accept that. He didn't want to accept that he couldn't fight his way through so many enemies. Right at that moment, he heard a woman scream across the village. He recognized Mora's voice instantly.

He charged into the thickest crowd of Renegades hacking and slashing in lunatic fury. He didn't care if they killed him. He only cared about getting to her.

He hit the first man and turned to the others as countless Renegades moved in to destroy him. His brother and cousins attacked at the same time.

Only the smallest, darkest, most forgotten corner of Hangman's mind realized how hopeless it was. All four of them together couldn't defeat the whole village.

He turned to the second man, and at that moment, something struck the Renegade from behind. He raised his kukri to stab and slash—only for the body to fall in front of him. He found himself staring at Cheina standing in front of him.

Shrieks, screams, and crashes resounded through the village—but not from the Renegades taking down the four cousins.

Hangman didn't want to believe the evidence of his senses when women, children, and teenagers of both sexes and all ages closed in an even bigger mob outside the Renegades.

Each of those people carried a different weapon. Some brought kitchen utensils or wood axes. Others used stakes cut out of tree limbs.

Women, children, young men, and young girls attacked the Renegades in even greater numbers. The women, children, and teenagers outnumbered the Renegades easily and overpowered them.

Most of the Renegades died from blows and axe chops from behind. Only some of the Renegades even realized who it was who killed them.

The Renegades toppled in droves and left all the women, children, and teenagers standing there holding their weapons dripping in blood.

Hangman, Alien, Viking, and Cross stood stock still and stared around them in wordless astonishment. Hangman didn't know what to do or say. What was there to do or say?

Cheina startled him by striding up to him extra fast. "We're captives!" she choked. "We're all captives! Take us with you! None of us wants to stay here! We want to go with you! Take us out of here!"

Just then, Mora screamed again. He charged away toward the sound, but he had to dodge all the women and children.

She didn't stop screaming this time. Her voice led him to a different house across the village.

He kicked in the door and saw a man straddling Mora's abdomen while she lay on the floor. She flailed and thrashed trying to punch and kick him. He fought to grab her wrists and restrain her.

Hangman burst in and buried his kukri in the back of the man's skull. The attacker slumped off to one side. Hangman grabbed Mora off the ground. She sprang at him, grabbed him around the neck, and burst into tears.

He patted her on the back. "It's all right," he croaked. "It's all right. We're going home. Come on."

He had to use force to unwrap her arms from around him so he could lead her outside. She kept sniffling all the way, but she looked unharmed—apart from a few bruises.

She stopped sniffing when they stepped out of the house. Women, children, and teenagers packed the village. No one moved. Alien, Viking, and Cross stood in the same places.

Hangman slowed and eventually stopped where he was to look around. There must have been a hundred people here including small boys and girls as young as five or six.

Some of the women held babies in their arms. All the children and teenagers carried bloody weapons. All those children and young people killed Renegades today.

Hangman led Mora over to his cousins. He wanted to take her and get the hell out of here, but he couldn't deny Cheina's plea. He and his cousins were alive right now because of these people. Mora was alive right now because of these people.

Cheina sealed the deal by striding up to him a second time. A young boy about ten years old stood near her. The boy held a battle axe many times too big for him. Blood and a few pieces of hair and skin clung to the blade.

"Take us with you," Cheina insisted. "We can help you get through Renegade territory. You won't make it alone. We can go with you. We can fight for you."

"Did you come from the Followers?" He studied her clothes and noticed that she was holding one of the Renegades' metal weapons, too. Blood stained that blade, too. "You fight. You aren't a Follower."

"I came from the Followers, but that was many years ago. The Renegade Clan took me as a captive and brought me here. Most of us have been looking for a way out for years. Let us come with you."

"We're going back to Godless territory," Hangman told her. "We won't be able to return all of you to your families."

"Then make us Godless," one of the teenage boys exclaimed. "The Godless is an honorable Clan. We would rather join them than stay here."

"Bring them, little brother," Viking interjected. "The woman is right. We can't make it through Renegade territory alone."

"All right," Hangman agreed. "Pack up whatever you want to bring and let's go. Don't linger."

He didn't even need to say it. The women, children, and young people bolted at his word. They didn't want to linger.

They returned to their houses and tents and reassembled much faster than he expected. They talked excitedly as they gathered in the center of the village carrying bundles and even more weapons.

Hangman started to notice a pattern in their clothes. Some definitely wore Follower attire. Others still wore the distinctive clothing of their original Clans.

Others wore a curious mixture of Renegade clothing, but these people all brought weapons. Even Cheina and the other former Followers brought weapons.

Mora turned to Hangman while they waited for everyone to come back. "You're hurt," she croaked. "You re-injured your shoulder."

"Forget it," he murmured out the side of his mouth. "You can take care of it after we get out of here."

She slipped her hand into his and squeezed. "Thank you," she husked. "I was so scared."

He didn't look at her when he squeezed her hand back. "Hush," he murmured. "I wouldn't leave you here. I'm going to take you home."

She sniffed again. She didn't say anything else as all those people came back. Mora didn't say anything about Hangman's pulverized face, either.

"Let's go!" Hangman called to everyone. "Follow us to the east! We'll take refuge in the mountains!"

He led the way up the hills along the route the four cousins used to get here. Mora broke away immediately. "Do you have any leaf paste? Alien is hurt."

Hangman had completely forgotten about Alien's arm. Mora raced up to him. The blade still stuck out of his arm.

He roared when she pulled it out. She snatched a handful of dry grass from the ground, pressed it into the wound to stop the bleeding, and then smeared it with leaf paste.

"We need Gooji juice," she remarked. "We won't find it on these rocky mountaintops."

"We'll have to get it in the jungle down there," Hangman decided. "We can't change our course now."

Chapter 27

Hangman slumped on the ground, rested his back against a rock, and shut his eyes. Alien didn't even get that far. His knees gave out and he sprawled on the rocky ground.

The party that escaped Ceon barely found a place protected by rock outcroppings before the men's strength failed.

Mora took one look at Hangman's shoulder. This was definitely not a firearms wound. Someone had stabbed a blade through the same hole.

The wound wasn't bleeding anymore, but he looked pale. He didn't open his eyes even to acknowledge her.

She didn't dare to disturb Alien. She straightened up and faced all the freed captives from Ceon. "Right. We need to build some fires. I need some of you to go over the mountain and collect Gooji sap." She pointed out three teenage boys. "You, you, and you can go."

A tall boy said, "Yes, Ma'am," and led the others away.

She picked out three younger boys and two younger girls. "You all go around and gather any firewood you can find. You might need to go down into the jungle, too."

"What about going back to the village?" one boy asked. "There was plenty of wood there."

"Anyone coming to the village from somewhere else will see all the dead Renegades," she told him. "You don't want to be there for that. You'll be able to find enough in the jungle. Go on. We need to stay away from Renegade villages from now on."

Viking got to his feet. "I'm going hunting. These people will need to eat. Come on, Cross."

"He's hurt, Viking," Mora countered. "He can't go."

"I'll go," Cross interjected. "I'm okay. You take care of these two, Mora. We'll be back soon."

She didn't argue and Cross and Viking left. Cross only limped very slightly on his injured leg. He didn't look back and he kept up with Viking just fine on their way over the hilltop to the jungle on the other side.

Mora satisfied herself with that. She wouldn't have been able to stop Cross from going.

One of the boys brought a handful of twigs and dropped them near her. She squatted down and started to build a fire.

The woman who spoke to Hangman earlier happened to be sitting nearby. Mora caught the woman looking at her. "I came from the Followers, too," Mora told her. "You have nothing to worry about. These are good men. They won't hurt you." She held out her hand. "I'm Mora. What's your name?"

"Cheina." The woman shook. "This is Aliva, Choma, and Hicia."

She indicated three of the women nearest her. None of them wore Follower attire.

One wore the rags wrapped around her from the neck down. The other two wore a combination of Renegade clothes.

"Which band of Followers did you come from?" Mora asked. "My family's territory is south of Portland."

Cheina looked down at her hands. "My family territory is far to the north—near a place called Prince George. You've probably never heard of it."

Mora gasped in horror. "That far! They brought you all the way here?!"

Cheina's lips twisted in a grimace of pure misery. "I was younger than the age of gathering."

Mora shut her mouth and forced herself to pay attention to lighting the fire. "I'm so sorry. I don't know how you could ever get home again."

"I will never go home again," Cheina husked. "Kalo is right. We'll be better off joining the Godless."

Mora found herself smiling at the woman. "I'm sure you would all make good Godless. You already understand the need to fight and defend yourselves. That's more than I had when I came to them."

Cheina's eyes darted toward Hangman. "He's so ugly—but so brave...."

"He's a good man," Mora replied. "He came all this way and endured all of this to save me. Who cares what he looks like?"

Cheina smiled at her with tears in her eyes. "You're lucky. I envy you."

Mora used the sticks to light the fire the way Katha and the other women taught her. She pretended not to notice Cheina taking care of her ten-year-old son and what looked like an eight-year-old daughter.

The woman could only have gotten them one way. The Renegade Clan captured her when she was too young even to go to the gathering. One of the Renegades must have taken her as his wife and gotten her pregnant with these children by force.

Mora let the subject drop. All these women must have gone through exactly the same thing. All of these children must have been born in captivity.

She got off easy by comparison. No one had to tell her how lucky she was that Hangman got to her when he did.

She only had to look at him and his cousins and brother to see what they must have gone through.

She built up the fire with wood the younger children collected. Cross and Viking came back with a good-sized Dushag, butchered it, and gave it to Mora to cook.

She sent the teenage girls to hunt around these mountaintops for rocks she could use to boil the Gooji juice. She put the stones on the coals to heat just as the older boys came back with a large ball of Gooji sap.

"This is perfect!" she exclaimed. "We can take it with us for the journey."

"How far is it to Godless territory?" one of the older boys asked. This was the one Cheina called Kalo.

"About two weeks' travel," Viking exclaimed. "It might take us less than that if we don't meet any resistance."

"Did you meet with a lot of resistance on the way here?" Kalo asked.

Viking nodded down into the flames. "We had to stop along the way and find out where Mora was. A few different conflicts slowed us down."

He didn't explain any further. Mora checked all the preparations and left the fire in the care of one of the teenage girls.

Mora squatted down next to Hangman and touched his hand. "Hangman....I need to take a look at your shoulder now. I'm sorry if I hurt you."

He didn't open his eyes. "Do what you have to do," he rasped. "I'm ready. I won't fight back."

She smiled at him even though he wasn't looking at her. She started to dab some wet fluff on his shoulder to clean away the dried blood.

"I'm making you some Gooji juice," she told him. "You'll need to drink that before you go to sleep."

"I'm not asleep," he growled.

She glanced around. No one was watching or listening to her. "I need to tell you something—something about the Renegade's weapons—the ammunition I told you about."

His eyes snapped open and he glared at her extra hard. "What about it?"

"They have a store of ammunition somewhere called Jeweled River. I don't know where that is. I could find it if I saw one of Thomion's maps. He showed his men on the maps where they had to go to get more ammunition. It might be connected to a military installation or something like that—but that's where the Renegades are getting it."

Hangman shut his eyes and rested his head back against the rock. "That's very good. Thank you. That's very useful information to have."

"But you don't know where Jeweled River is. You won't be able to stop the Renegade Clan from resupplying there."

"We'll be able to stop them by destroying their supply," Hangman muttered still without opening his eyes.

"How will you do that if you can't find it?"

"You're going to help us."

"Me?!" she countered. "I can't find it!"

"You just said you could find it on a map."

"I don't have a map!"

"You said Thomion had a map."

"You can't get to it! It's back there in Ceon."

Hangman shifted his position and winced in pain. "We'll find it. Then we have to destroy the ammunition supply. We can't let the Renegades use these weapons against us."

She didn't question him any further. She cleaned his shoulder and put leaf paste on the wound, but the penetration site had already become so completely blocked up with dried blood that she didn't dare to do anything else to it.

She turned her attention to Alien. She had to get Viking to help her turn Alien over. The paste she put on his arm earlier stopped the bleeding, but the wound still sagged open with bone exposed.

"We need to tie it closed." Mora looked around. "One of you Follower women tear a strip off your dress and give it to me to use as a bandage."

"You can take this." Cheina stood up, grabbed her dress, and pulled it off over her head.

Mora gaped at the woman when Cheina held it out. "What are you doing?!" Mora gasped.

Cheina shrugged and started taking off her white linen underwear. "I don't want to wear it anymore. I kept it on to hide myself from the Renegades. We're becoming Godless now. I don't need it."

Mora became aware of everyone else in their party watching the exchange, including Viking and Cross. Hangman had his eyes open and listening with rapt fascination.

Mora stared in stark disbelief when Cheina ripped her underwear off mid-thigh to make loose-fitting shorts. She tore her shift bodice off at the waist, tore off the sleeves to make a sleeveless top, and let her hair down.

Her clothes covered more than Godless clothing. Cheina looked a lot less like a Follower this way. She didn't look like a Follower at all.

The other women and girls exchanged glances. Then three more Follower women stood up and did exactly the same thing. They took off their dresses, ripped their underwear to make the closest thing possible to Godless clothing, and unwound their hair to let it hang free.

The women gave all their old garments to Mora. She stared at the woman and then at the dresses in her hands. She didn't need all of this to use as bandages, but it served the purpose.

She mumbled, "Thank you," to the women and got busy tearing the dresses and fragments of underwear into pieces.

The women went straight back to what they were doing before. They didn't act like they were any different from everyone else in their group.

Mora put fresh paste on Alien's arm and wrapped the bandages around it to close the wound. The pain woke up Alien when she cinched the bandage tight. He bellowed and struggled to knock her away.

Viking and Hangman both scrambled over to restrain him. "She's trying to help you, brother!" Hangman yelled in his ear. "Sit still while she takes care of your arm! Be quiet, Alien!"

Alien didn't be quiet. He kept roaring in agony when she tightened the bandages around his upper arm, but at least he didn't fight back again.

He finally sank back against the rock next to Hangman after she finished. He slumped there panting hard and sweating heavily.

"Drink some Gooji juice, Alien," Mora told him. "You'll be okay."

"Thank you, little sister," he husked. "I'm sorry I went after you before."

"I don't blame you. Can you move your arm without pain apart from the cut itself? Is the bone broken?"

"It isn't broken."

She turned to Cross. "Do you want me to take a look at your leg or are you taking care of it yourself?"

"I'm fine, Mora," he replied. "Give the Gooji juice to Hangman and Alien. I don't need it."

She sneered at him. "You better drink it, too, just to be safe."

Kalo interrupted just then. "How old are you?"

Everyone looked up to find him staring at Cross. Cross took one look at the boy and looked away. "I'm fourteen."

"How is it you come on an expedition like this when you're so young?" Kalo insisted. "Why didn't they bring an older, bigger, stronger man?"

"I am a man," Cross returned. "I'm as much a man as they are even if I'm young."

"Did they choose you?" Kalo demanded. "You must be a great warrior."

"I'm not a great warrior—not as great as they are," Cross murmured. "I came to help my brother get his wife back. None of the other men of our band could come. They had to stay and protect their wives and children. So I came instead."

"How do you say you're a man when you're so young?" Kalo asked. "When do the Godless call a boy a man."

"We initiate them," Hangman interrupted. "A boy initiates when he's fourteen. If he passes the test, he becomes a man the same as everyone else. His age doesn't matter after that—until he goes to the gathering. He holds all the rights of a man in every other area." Hangman cocked his head and narrowed his eyes. "How old are you?"

"Fourteen," Kalo replied. "I want to initiate into the Godless."

Viking snorted. "You have some ground to cover first, boy."

"Why?" Kalo demanded. "What do I have to do besides pass the test?"

"Nothing," Alien replied. "That's all you have to do."

"What *is* the test?" Kalo asked. "How hard is it?"

"It's as hard as you make it for yourself," Hangman replied. "You choose a creature to fight and you fight it. If you defeat the creature, you become a man and we rename you. Your old self dies and no one calls you by that name again."

"What was your name before?" Kalo asked.

Hangman snorted. "Using that name is a serious insult. My name is Hangman. Don't call me anything else. This is Alien. This is Viking and this is Cross. If you initiate, no one will ever call you Kalo again."

"So all I have to do is fight a creature? That's easy."

"Not just any creature," Cross interjected. "If you choose one that's easy to defeat, we'll all know you're a coward and we'll treat you as such."

Kalo frowned. "Oh. I see."

The men laughed at him. "What you choose will depend on you and what you think you can defeat," Hangman went on.

"Don't listen to anything Hangman says about which creature to choose," Viking teased.

The others laughed some more. "You may need to take some time to hone your fighting skills," Alien told the boy. "Take your time and make sure you survive the initiation. Godless boys grow up fighting. They prepare all their lives for initiation. It might take you longer."

Kalo frowned again. "I see that now. The Renegades didn't train us."

Mora turned aside to take the stones off the fire. "You men come and eat," she told them. "You all need rest and food to regain your strength."

She put the hot rocks into the basin of Gooji juice and then cut up meat for the men. The other women helped her cook the Dushag meat on different fires and distribute the food to all the children and teenagers.

The camp settled down for the night—all except Kalo. "The boys and I will stand guard tonight. We'll take watches to make sure no one comes."

"Stay out of the firelight," Hangman told him. "Stick to the shadows so no one sees you."

Kalo said, "Yes, Sir," and took six other teenage boys with him out of the rock outcroppings.

"He seems a good boy," Alien remarked.

"He is," Cheina interrupted. "He always tries to do the right thing for everyone."

"Is he your son?" Mora asked.

Cheina smiled and nodded. "He's my oldest. This is Aster and this is Lonion." She indicated her young daughter and son. They sat close to her.

"How does Kalo know so much about the Godless?" Mora asked.

"He listens to everything the Renegades say about the Godless. He understands more than the Renegades realize. He decided a long time ago he wanted to become Godless. He just didn't know how."

"How well does he know how to fight?" Alien asked.

Cheina grimaced. "Not well. The Renegades don't train the children of captives. The Renegades don't trust captives not to rebel and break free."

Alien snorted. "Of course not."

"They attacked the Renegades just fine in the village," Hangman remarked. "I think these young ones will do just fine once they get used to it and get some training." He turned to Mora. "Maybe you could take responsibility for training the women."

"I'm hardly qualified to train them."

"We won't have time to do it," he pointed out. "The four of us are the only grown men here. We'll have a hard enough time keeping the Renegades at bay. We need these people ready to fight as soon as possible. Just do what you can. Anything will be better than nothing."

Chapter 28

A pattering of stones woke Hangman out of a deep sleep. He tried to look around and felt the pain in his shoulder.

He stayed where he was while he assessed his surroundings in the hard grey light of early morning. All the freed captives lay asleep around their smoldering fires or these people were just waking up.

Mora sat by one of the fires cutting up what was left of the Dushag meat.

"We'll need to hunt again," he told her.

She looked up, smiled at him, and handed him a bowl full of the meat. "I don't suppose you'll agree to keeping your arm immobilized until your shoulder heals."

"How would I do that when I have to defend these people? I have to move my arm—and so does Alien. It isn't even a question."

She only nodded at him. "I thought so."

Alien woke up just then, stumbled behind the rocks to relieve himself, and the growing noise of everyone changing position woke up everyone else.

Hangman finished eating and got to his feet. "Where did you find the Dushag?" he asked Viking.

Viking jerked his thumb over his shoulder toward the east. "There's a stream down there in the jungle. We should get off these mountaintops and under cover as soon as possible."

"Everyone finish eating, pack up your things, and get ready to move!" Hangman called to the group. "We won't stay in one place for long."

"We should train them to stay in the trees and move through the canopy," Cross suggested. "This many people won't be safe on the ground anywhere—especially not all these children."

Hangman winced. "These people have a lot to learn about everything."

"What do you mean about staying in the trees?" Kalo interrupted.

"Didn't you learn anything from listening to the Renegades?" Alien asked. "Didn't they talk about the Godless attacking from the trees?"

Kalo frowned. "Oh, yeah. They did, but I didn't understand it."

"The trees are the safest place from the creatures," Hangman told him.

"What about Krakelows?" Kalo asked.

"You can hear them coming," Hangman replied. "Now move out."

The group didn't take long to do as he said. The cousins' conversation motivated everyone to keep moving.

They paused at the top when everyone looked down at the village of Xano in the distance. "We went that way." Viking pointed to the south. "We should stay out of sight from them."

Hangman nodded and directed everyone that way. Kalo went in front with his core group of boys his own age. None of them appeared older than fifteen.

Hangman set off to follow them, but Viking held him back. "Wait, little brother."

Hangman turned around to find his cousins and his brother standing there. "What's wrong? We can't leave them alone in the jungle. They aren't going to be as helpful to us as we will be to them."

"We need to decide which of us will take over as Kral of this group," Viking told him. "We don't know how long we'll be out here. We need a definite Kral who makes decisions for all of us."

"That's simple, brother," Hangman replied. "You're the oldest. You should be Kral."

"That's ridiculous," Alien interjected. "You're already Kral."

Hangman glanced behind him to make sure he didn't misunderstand. "Me?! Are you joking?! I'm younger and weaker than both of you. I can't be Kral. If it came to a challenge, either of you would flatten me."

"It won't come to a challenge because we both support you," Viking went on. "You're Shadow's oldest son, but we would support you either way. You're already in charge of this band, Hangman. You have been since we left Godless territory."

"This is hardly a band, brothers. Look around you," Hangman insisted. "These are nothing but a bunch of women, children, and underage boys. The four of us are the only Godless men here."

"Then you're the same Kral you were when we parted from Shadow," Cross pointed out. "If it's between the four of us, we choose you."

"I can't be Kral!" Hangman insisted. "You all call me little brother! I'm half your size, Viking! Stop talking like that."

Viking clamped his lips shut. "You are Kral whether you call yourself that or not."

Hangman glanced at Alien and then at Cross. They all insisted.

The worst part was that Viking was right. Hangman had been making decisions and telling his brother and cousins what to do since they first separated from Shadow. He didn't think of himself as Kral then. He only did it because they were going after Mora.

Viking and a few others had been dropping hints in Hangman's ears all his life that he would become Kral one day. He always knew his cousins would support him if it came to that.

It never came to that because Hangman never would have challenged Butcher or Shadow. Shadow needed Hangman's support even more than Butcher needed Shadow's support.

Who else would become Kral now if Hangman refused? Whoever became Kral would still wind up deferring to Hangman's judgment. They would always take his opinion and turn it into their own decision exactly the way Butcher did with Shadow.

Butcher only served as Kral in name. Shadow had always been the real power behind Butcher. Everyone knew it. Hangman didn't want to become that. He also didn't want to make one of his cousins appear too weak to rule as Kral in his own right.

Hangman would resent either of his cousins for becoming Kral. Some secret part of Hangman's heart and soul would always know he was better qualified for the job.

Viking read his mind, clapped him on his less-injured shoulder, and murmured, "Let's go," as he passed Hangman on the way down the hill.

Alien and then Cross followed Viking away. Hangman stayed behind. That was it. He was Kral of this band now—for as long as it lasted.

These people might not survive a single day in the jungle. It was his responsibility to make sure they survived as long as possible. They saved his life. Now he owed them the same consideration.

He set off down the hill and jogged to catch up with his brother and cousins. That was the end of the discussion.

The entered the trees and found Mora standing amongst all the freed captives. "You need to climb up into the tree branches and all the way up to the top canopy." She pointed above her. "We'll be safer from creatures and Renegades there."

"How will we travel if we're in the trees?" Kalo asked.

"We'll show you," Hangman told him and swung himself up.

The freed captives took different approaches to climbing that high or even climbing at all. The youngest children managed it the easiest. They scrambled into the branches and kept scaling until they caught up with Hangman and his cousins.

The teenagers took more time. The women had the most difficult time. Some had to find low branches just to get off the ground.

They ran into more difficulty once they started climbing. Some made it thirty feet off the ground and lost heart when they saw how high they were. Some froze and got stuck. They couldn't summon the courage to grasp the next limb right in front of them.

"The Renegades will come looking for you soon!" Hangman called down. "The closer you are to the ground, the more likely they will be to see you and recapture you."

That got a few of them moving. Others absolutely refused to go any higher.

"Maybe this was a bad idea," Alien muttered.

"What's the alternative?" Hangman asked. "We would be sitting ducks if we traveled along the ground. The Renegades stick to the ground—and that isn't even counting creatures."

"How long do we have to stay here?" Aster asked.

Kalo stroked her hair. "We'll leave soon. Don't worry."

Hangman watched the women and some of the younger girls struggle through the branches for a little longer. "Kalo, you and your boys stay here and guard the women and children."

"Where are you going?" Kalo asked.

"There's something I have to do. Some of you younger children should go down there and coach your mothers on how to climb. Don't go anywhere. Just stay here and let them get used to climbing through the branches. Don't travel or leave the area until all of you can climb well, fast, and without fear."

"What if we get hungry or thirsty?" Lonion asked.

Hangman gestured over his shoulder. "Some of you can go over to the stream and get water. Then come straight back here. You can share what's left of the food until the men and I get back."

Mora looked up. "Do you want me to come with you?"

Hangman turned away. "That would be great."

Chapter 29

Mora lowered herself to the ground with Hangman, Viking, Alien, and Cross. All the freed captives talked and climbed through the branches high above the jungle floor.

"Will they be all right here by themselves?" Mora asked.

"They'll be as all right as they're ever going to be," Hangman replied. "Let's go. We have to move fast."

The four men set off at a dead run back up the mountain. Mora had to struggle to keep up with them. They slowed down to keep pace with her and they stopped a lot more often than they otherwise would have.

They stopped once at the mountain peak, hid in the rocks, and studied what was left of the village of Ceon in the distance.

"There are still plenty of people there," she remarked.

"I don't see any fighting men," Cross added. "They all came out to attack us and fell to the captives. Only women and children are left."

"Let's get in, get out, and get back to the jungle." Hangman stepped out of the rocks. "If anything goes wrong, you go to Thomion's tent and find that map. We'll give you any cover we can before we pull the plug and run for it."

Mora nodded and the party set off. They descended from the mountain at a brisk walk this time. The men kept their hands on their weapons, but none of the men drew them. Mora didn't have her blades anymore, but she knew where to get new ones in Thomion's tent.

Someone had put the tent back up since the Godless escaped with all those captives. Mora saw Rosta going into and out of her father's tent.

Mora didn't see Thomion anywhere. "Thomion is still here somewhere," she murmured on their way down the hill. "Unless one of you killed him."

"We didn't kill him," Hangman replied.

"We did kill his pig sons, though," Alien snarled.

The friends stopped talking when they entered the village. Everyone else stopped what they were doing to stare at the Godless.

The surviving Renegades had removed all the dead bodies. The village had a desolate, ravaged atmosphere, now that so few people lived here. These were the only real Renegades in the village. The captives made up the bulk of the population.

Hangman dipped his chin to Mora in one quick nod. He, Cross, and the two cousins turned their backs to the flap of Thomion's tent and stood guard.

Mora barged right in. Rosta sat in her usual place on the floor next to the couch. She looked up in surprised shock when Mora walked in.

Mora looked around and spotted a stack of rolled papers on the bookshelf opposite her. She didn't know which of them was the map she needed, but it had to be one of them.

Rosta got to her feet and squared her shoulders. "What are you doing here? My father will recapture you. You won't get away."

Mora ignored her, walked around the couch, and took two square Renegade blades from the pile in the corner. She turned around and pointed one of the weapons at Rosta. "Sit down where you were."

Rosta moved her mouth a few different times before she sank back onto the carpet.

Mora sheathed both her blades, strode over to the bookshelf, and scooped up the whole pile of maps. She didn't have time to go through them now.

"What are you doing?!" Rosta exclaimed. "Those aren't yours! Put them back!"

Mora walked straight past her and left the tent. She only nodded to the men before they all took off up the mountain. They started out walking, sped up to a jog, and then sprinted as far as the rocks before they stopped.

"Are you sure one of these is the one we need?" Hangman asked.

"I don't know!....." Mora gasped. "I don't know.....I just took......all the maps he had.....We'll figure it out....later....."

The men waited for her to catch her breath. She took the time to unroll the maps, fold them into flat squares, and make them into a stack that she stashed in one of Hangman's shoulder bags. She really needed to get some of those for herself.

The party took off up the mountain and didn't stop until they rejoined the freed captives in the trees. Everyone scaled to the highest canopy. Even the women acted much more comfortable and confident up here.

Viking took Kalo and the other teenage boys hunting. Mora opened Hangman's bag and took out the maps.

She went over them one after another. "Do you know this territory, Mora?" Cross asked.

"I don't know it, but I have seen it on maps before. I should be able to recognize some of these mountains and rivers. The Renegades didn't blindfold me on the way here. Just give me some time....."

"Can you find Jeweled River?" Hangman asked.

"I'm trying to. The problem is that the Renegades could only have gotten these maps from the ancients. The Renegades may have renamed certain things."

"How do you know the Renegades got the maps from the ancients?" Alien asked. "Maybe the Renegades made the maps themselves."

"The Renegades don't read. I don't know where Thomion got these maps. He may have stolen them from another Clan."

She stopped what she was doing and stared into space for a minute.

"What's wrong?" Hangman asked. "Can't you find it?"

"The Renegades captured Followers. The Renegades must have taken these maps from the Followers—and then gotten the female captives to explain the maps to them." She shot one glance toward the freed captives and bent over the maps again.

"So how will you find Jeweled River if the map uses a different name?" Viking asked.

"Just a minute...." Mora searched the maps one after the other. "Yeah, see? I was right. There it is."

"What is it?" Hangman asked.

She turned the map around and pointed. "Do you see that grey square?"

"It doesn't tell me anything."

"That's the installation I told you about. Military installations usually have a lot of concrete. Sometimes they're attached to airfields and runways and tarmacs and stuff."

"What does that mean?" Alien asked. "I've never heard of any of those things."

"There's a creek next to the airfield," she mumbled to herself. "The map calls it Jeweled River. The ammunition store must be near there."

"If we get close enough, we can track the Renegades," Hangman replied. "They'll lead us to it."

Mora checked three other maps. "We're here as far as I can tell." She shuffled the maps one after the other. "We'll need to keep all of these. They show the territory between here and there. We'll have to keep checking to make sure we're going the right way."

"So which way do we have to go to get to Jeweled River?" Hangman asked.

"Southwest," Mora replied.

Viking, Alien, Cross, and Hangman all groaned loudly. "No!!" Cross whimpered.

She smiled at all four of them. "Sorry. We can go after this ammunition supply or we can go back to Godless territory. We can't do both."

"What are you talking about?" Kalo interrupted. "What's Jeweled River?"

Hangman looked up at him. No one else answered. Then Hangman turned to all the other freed captives.

Cross broke the uncomfortable silence. "At least we won't have to teach them to travel through the canopy if we go southwest. We won't be traveling through the jungle then."

"There is a swath of jungle farther south." Mora rifled her maps again. "We could go due south through this jungle and connect up with another stretch heading west. It wouldn't be the most direct route, but we would be better hidden."

"I guess that's better than traveling out in the open," Alien remarked.

"Why would we go southwest?" Kalo asked. "Godless territory is to the east."

Hangman raised his voice. "All of you come over here and gather around. We need to talk."

The freed captives climbed through the branches to gather around the four Godless men. The women climbed slowly, but they got more confident with every passing minute.

"You may have noticed the Renegades using firearms," Hangman began. "The Renegade Clan uses these weapons against other Clans and overpowers them, steals their territory, and carries off their women and girls. The Renegade Clan may have used firearms against your peoples to take you captive."

A bunch of the women nodded.

"These weapons need ammunition to work," Hangman went on. "The Renegade Clan is using firearms against the Godless, too. If we go back to Godless territory now, we'll face more Renegade forces armed with firearms. They could do exactly the same thing to you, to us, and to our women and girls. The only way to stop them is to cut off their supply of ammunition. We know where it is and we're going after it, but it means we have to delay our journey to Godless territory. We have to travel deeper inside Renegade country, overcome them, and find a way to destroy this supply. If you don't want to come, you can set off for the east now, but we have to defend our Clan the best way we know how and this is it."

He let that silence linger for a long time. The women and children exchanged glances. No one spoke up to contradict him.

Mora refolded her maps. She knew enough now. She didn't have to look at them again—not for a while.

Chapter 30

H angman pulled his kukris when he dropped down onto the ground. The freed captives stayed in the branches.

The party had been traveling south for two days. The freed captives traveled slowly at first while they got the hang of balancing from branch to branch.

They picked up speed with every passing day. They also got more adept at fighting off tree creatures. All the freed captives had enough weaponry to last them for a long time. They just didn't have the skill to use them—not as effectively as they might.

Mora had been giving the women and children tips during their moments of rest, but none of them had time to practice. Everyone had to learn on the move.

Viking, Alien, Cross, Kalo, and three of his boys dropped out of the trees behind Hangman.

Kalo and his fellow teenagers were becoming a unified fighting force all their own. They always stayed together and they didn't ask permission to join the men in whatever Hangman and his men did.

Hangman didn't correct the boys or tell them not to come. The boys wouldn't have been allowed to come on any expedition if this had been a real Godless band.

It wasn't a real Godless band. Hangman came to accept that more and more with every passing hour.

All the rules of the past disappeared or at least became so blurred that they might as well have disappeared. Mora sat in on the men's conferences, gave them information, and made suggestions on where to go and what to do.

Hangman came to accept her input as much as if she was one of his most trusted cousins or brothers. He didn't have a choice but to take her recommendations. She knew way too much about the territory and all the surrounding features of the landscape.

She tried to explain what she meant about airfields, military installations, tarmacs, airplanes, and all the other bizarre ancient words she used.

Hangman and his men only understood a handful of the words she used to explain, which didn't help at all.

He became more and more lax about the women doing things usually reserved only for Godless men. The women hunted more and so did the children. The group simply didn't have enough men to do everything, not even with Kalo and his boys helping out.

Most of the time, Hangman needed to boys too much to help defend the party. None of them could spend the time hunting or making camp in those rare times when the group camped on the ground.

He waved above his head and the women, children, and teenagers advanced through the canopy heading south. The party still hadn't turned west yet. Mora kept telling Hangman they were still too far north.

She tried to explain the maps to him, but he found it impossible because he couldn't read them the way she could. They made no sense to him.

Hangman stopped where he was and waited for the women and children to pass farther south and farther to the west. They moved silently through the canopy. No one talked or even rustled the leaves.

Hangman had to give these freed captives credit. They certainly learned quickly. No one had to explain the danger to them. No one knew better than they did what would happen if the Renegade Clan retook them all.

Mora went with them. Cheina and three other women had joined Mora in taking charge of the freed captives.

Aliva and Choma both had young children. Choma had a baby she carried in a piece of fabric tied into a pouch across her chest.

She nursed the child on the move and supported the pouch with one hand while she climbed and balanced with the other.

Hicia was an older woman with three teenage sons, all of whom belonged to Kalo's group. Two of these boys were twins. Their names were Hitro and Ethio. Their younger brother was named Carro.

They spent almost no time with their mother. None of Kalo's boys spent time with their mothers. They spent all their time with each other. Hangman never would have known which boys belonged to which mothers if Mora hadn't told him.

Kalo's group became an insulted little band all its own with Kalo as their Kral, but Hangman didn't mention or protest against this, either. The boys were too valuable the way they were.

Kalo and his boys had been the first to harvest the hides of animals they hunted, clean them up, and fashion them into loincloths to make themselves look Godless.

The boys then did the same thing for their mothers and younger siblings. Less than half of the original party still wore Renegade clothing. The rest looked as Godless as Hangman and his men.

He had to admit that they acted more Godless by the day, too. All of these people threw themselves into it with all their energy. They did everything in their power to do everything the Godless way.

He couldn't argue with that. It just startled him to see them change so fast. None of them tried to stick to the ways of their original Clans.

The women who had originally been Followers changed the fastest. They discarded every trace of their clothing, killed, defended their children, and maintained their weapons with the best of them.

These women became indistinguishable from originally born Godless. Even Mora remarked on the amazing transformation.

Hangman watched the band retreat into the canopy until he lost sight of them. He had to strain his ears to hear any trace of their movements.

He didn't worry about them being able to protect themselves from anything up there, even Krakelows. He had to worry more about himself and his men on the ground.

He waited a lot longer than he needed to before he advanced. He and his men crept through the undergrowth. He signaled Kalo to take his boys to the left.

Kalo split his boys into pairs and used hand gestures to direct them to different positions. Viking, Alien, and Cross spread themselves out to the right.

The men inched forward, pushed the foliage aside, and peered into another Renegade camp. This wasn't a regular village with houses made from logs. It resembled the camps the Godless had seen with stronger temporary shelters made out of tree branches.

Every person in the camp was a man—an armed man. These Renegades must have been either a scouting party or a defensive patrol. They didn't bring any women with them, not even captive women.

Hangman watched the Renegades for a while. Some of them gathered in the center of their camp, discussed a few things, pointed in different directions, and separated.

Some left the camp to patrol the area. A party of four left heading farther south. They headed directly into the path of Kalo and his boys.

Another Renegade party came toward Hangman and his cousins. The third Renegade party left heading east—away from the Godless men.

Hangman waved his cousins away. They retreated further into the jungle and met up with Kalo and the boys. The party rejoined and pulled even farther back and farther east—beyond the Renegades' line of travel heading that way.

Hangman collected his men under the trees, counted down the breathless moments until he heard footsteps coming through the jungle, and pulled his kukris.

His men all drew their weapons, too. Kalo and the boys used Renegade weapons. Kalo himself had gotten into the habit of sitting near Hangman when they rested in the evenings.

Kalo spent hours bombarding Hangman with questions about how he did everything from making his weapons, ambushing his enemies, and killing creatures.

Alien had spilled the whole story about how Hangman got his name. Kalo and the other boys simply would not leave Hangman alone after that.

Kalo had already decided to make himself some stone weapons exactly like Hangman's kukris. Hangman couldn't help but be impressed by this young man. Hangman no longer doubted that Kalo would accomplish everything he set out to do.

The boys flanked the Godless men on the left. Hangman no longer bothered to give these boys specific orders about how to do anything.

They just handled themselves and never gave him any cause to complain about how they did it.

They put some distance between themselves on one side and the Godless men on the other. The boys automatically arranged it so they worked together in their own band.

The two groups set forward and then burst into a rush of speed. They overtook the first party of Renegades and overwhelmed them. Kalo's boys charged the Renegades from one side. Hangman and his men closed opposite and pincered the Renegades in a heartbeat.

The four Renegades rotated outward to defend themselves. The two flanks of Godless split apart. The Renegades couldn't even face everyone at the same time, much less fight them.

Hangman and his men cut the Renegades down, kept on running, and overtook the next party of Renegades.

The Godless men moved fast and sure from one enemy patrol to the next, worked their way around the Renegade camp in a curved route, and cleared the area without anyone inside the camp knowing the Godless were there.

Hangman pulled up short at the far end of the curve. He had to hold his breath to listen for the slightest sound. Men's voices came from the camp. Everything sounded peaceful and relaxed over there. None of the Renegades raised their voices in alarm.

He signaled his men to withdraw. The friends backed away into the undergrowth—only to run into a swarm of Abnormits.

Hangman and the men sprang up into the branches to get out of the creatures' way. The Abnormits headed for the dead Renegades the friends left lying dead on the ground.

"I have an idea," Hangman murmured.

"Don't even think about it," Alien growled.

"I'm already thinking about it, brother," Hangman countered.

"What is it?" Kalo asked.

"Isn't it obvious?" Viking interjected. "He wants to use the bodies to lure the Abnormits to the Renegade camp."

Kalo furrowed his brow. "Can you do that?"

"He always does this kind of thing," Alien snapped. "He can't resist the urge to kill them all. Some is never enough for this bloodthirsty monster."

Hangman laughed, but he did it quietly. "Can you blame me? Who can pass up an opportunity like this?"

"I'm sure you can pass it up if you really try," Alien replied.

"Isn't that dangerous?" Kalo asked. "You might make a mistake and the Abnormits would get you, too."

"Of course it's dangerous!" Alien fired back. "That's exactly why he does it. He does all kinds of things no one else is stupid or reckless enough to do."

"Is it stupid and reckless if it works?" Hangman asked.

"You can't do this, little brother," Viking interrupted. "You're Kral now. Your band needs you. You already killed enough Renegades for today. You got your band to safety. That was your objective. Now you should withdraw and make sure they get to their destination. Your people would suffer if anything happened to you."

Hangman looked away. He didn't want that responsibility, especially not with such a tempting chance in front of him.

He gave it up and ordered his men to withdraw. They had to fight a few different creatures in the canopy before they made it back to the women and children.

Chapter 31

Hangman's band had traveled a long way from where they separated from the men by the time the raiding party caught up with the women and children. The men found everyone on the ground near a steep cliff with a stone overhang to protect everyone from above.

This cliff reminded Hangman of the overhang where he escaped from the Ridgebeak. A small stream curved back and forth along a gravel bed a dozen yards from the overhang.

Jungle trees protected this stream from the air. No one had to go out into the open to get water.

He found Mora and the other women cooking the cut-up remains of an adult Gurlg. He didn't ask which of their party killed the creature.

He and his men settled down under the overhang with the others. Cheina came over, squatted down next to Alien, put her arm around his shoulder, and rested her head against his.

Hangman pretended not to notice. He also pretended not to notice Cross getting closer to one of the young teenage girls.

Her name was Sema and she wasn't the daughter of any of the women in the party. Hangman didn't ask where she came from. She might have gotten captured from another Clan, too.

She was very pretty and extremely sweet. She doted on Cross and he obviously returned her affections.

They weren't the only ones. Hangman would have had to be blind not to notice Kalo getting closer to a girl named Vina. Two of his boys were getting overly friendly with teenage girls their own age.

None of these young people tried to hide what they were doing. They didn't get outright intimate with each other in front of anyone. They never kissed nor did they engage in any kind of sexual contact—not that Hangman saw.

They could have been fooling around with each other out in the jungle away from prying eyes—except that almost no one in the band ever separated from the others. Everyone made an effort to stick together.

All the travelers stayed within line of sight of each other all day long while they traveled. They only separated in the evenings when they made camp—and only then during those rare times when the party camped on the ground.

Then the girls and the boys went off in opposite directions from each other. The couples didn't meet up. They were too busy gathering firewood, hunting, and doing other camp chores.

Everyone stayed together when they camped in the trees. None of the lovebirds could have gone off alone together then.

Alien and Cheina were both far above the age of gathering. Alien shouldn't technically have been allowed to get together with any woman of any age after he missed his chance at the gathering.

By rights, a band's Kral should be the one to decide who a woman married once she became single and available again.

Hangman's men selected him to be their Kral, so the decision should have fallen to him. Viking was the only other man above the age of gathering and he was already married. That left Alien.

Alien blurred the lines again by not asking Hangman's permission to cozy up to Cheina. They just did it.

Cross and the others his age were a completely different story. None of them would reach the age of gathering for another four years. They shouldn't have been cozying up to anyone of any age.

None of the young people asked for Hangman's permission to pair off, either. Then again, they didn't need to ask to get close to each other and start caring for each other.

They hadn't technically violated any rules—not unless they did start getting intimate with each other.

It wasn't completely outside the law or even outside the norm for a couple to get together in early adolescence or even to get attached to each other in their young childhood. It wouldn't be the first time.

They could care about each other, commit to each other, and even decide to marry—as long as they didn't do anything. They weren't allowed to do anything until they both went to the gathering.

They didn't have to choose anyone else at the gathering. They could choose each other and sit straight down right there in their own family band. No one could argue with that as long as they weren't related by blood.

They did still need to go to the gathering, though. That was the one rule. These young people couldn't get together with each other before that.

Hangman made up his mind not to say anything to Alien at all. Hangman's party might never make it to the gathering—not that Alien would ever go back to the gathering. He was too old.

Hangman couldn't resent his cousin for finding a woman at this point in his life. The party already included too many single women and not enough single men. Alien could take his pick.

He clearly loved Cheina and her children. He showed as much affection to Aster and Lonion as he did to her. Kalo admired all four of Hangman's men. Kalo treated Cross with a level of respect and even reverence far beyond Cross's age.

Kalo listened and obeyed every word Cross said to him even though they couldn't be more than a few months apart in age.

Kalo treated Hangman, Viking, and Alien with a kind of awe. He bombarded all of them with questions, picked their brains about how they did everything and everything they thought about everything that, and sat in on their conferences to drink in every scrap of wisdom he could get from them.

His boys did the same thing, but they didn't bombard the Godless men with questions. The boys hardly dared to speak around the four men.

Hangman surveyed his band while he squatted under the overhang. He found himself evaluating each person, their health, their energy levels, their appearance, and their general demeanor.

The responsibility for all these lives weighed heavily on his shoulders. He was finally learning what it meant to be Kral of his own band. He didn't shy away from the task. He just discovered new dimensions of care within himself.

These people had been strangers just a few short days ago. Now he knew all their names, all their interrelationships, and every detail of their physical ailments, challenges, and complaints.

Mora squatted down next to him and handed him a bowl of food and a gourd of water. "Thank you," he murmured.

"We can start heading west tomorrow," she told him. "We're far enough south now."

"It's too bad the maps don't show us where the Renegade camps are," he remarked. "That would be more helpful than knowing where the ammunition store is."

She smiled at him. "That would be hard considering that the Renegades move around all the time and they don't read or write. They might write down where their camps *were,* but they would have to use messengers for that."

He looked up. "What do you mean?"

"In ancient times, the leaders would use messengers to send information back and forth to and from different parts of their army. When one band moved position, they would send word back to their commander so the commander knew where all the different bands were on the battlefield."

He frowned at her. "That's a little overcomplicated, isn't it?"

She shrugged. "Think about it. If you organized multiple bands of Godless to fight multiple bands of Renegades, you would need to know where all those bands of Godless were, what maneuvers they were making, and where they were setting up positions. You would need to keep that information current so you knew what moves to make yourself. Then you would send the messenger back to each band with your orders about where to move and where to attack next."

He looked down at the food in his hand. He never thought of things the way she described.

Shadow and Butcher never combined their fighting men with any other Godless band. Neither of those Krals ever seemed to think they might use multiple bands of Godless to fight multiple bands of Renegades.

"What's on your mind?" she asked.

"The Renegades sent multiple bands after us—multiple patrols and war parties. I didn't see....." He trailed off.

"You didn't see what? Were you going to say you didn't see messengers—or did you?"

"The only messenger I saw was the one who left Xano to tell Thomion that I attacked Ulmeo. I didn't see Larth using messengers. He had to gather all his parties in one place so he could give orders to everyone at the same time."

She made a face. "That's primitive."

He frowned to himself. He didn't know what this meant, but he couldn't do anything about it now. "Are you absolutely certain the Renegades don't read and write?" he asked.

She nodded. "I'm certain. Both Ulmeo and Thomion had stacks of books in their houses, but none of the Renegades ever read those books. All the books were jumbled in no particular order and they were covered in dust. The Renegades just collect stuff from the ancient cities. The Renegades don't even use couches and chairs."

Hangman frowned. "What is that?"

She blushed and grinned at him. "Those stuffed, cushiony things you saw in Thomion's tent. You're supposed to sit or lie on them, but both Ulmeo and Thomion sat and slept on the floor. The couches and chairs were covered in dust, too. No one ever used them. I don't think the Renegades ever even opened a book. They could have looked at the pictures and seen what that stuff was for. Why do you ask?"

"I want to make sure they aren't using these maps for something else—like organizing against us."

"I would be very surprised if the Renegades organize much of anything."

"You didn't see Larth. He was very organized."

"Ulmeo and Thomion weren't. Maybe that's because they were so far inside Renegade territory. They didn't need to be as organized as a leader who actually ventured into another Clan's land to capture their women and drive them out."

"How do you think the Renegades found out about the weapons, then? How do you think they learned how to use them—and how to use the ammunition and everything?"

"Isn't it obvious? These women must have shown them—or some other captive women must have shown them. It would have been much easier for the Renegades to learn from someone showing them than to learn from reading a book or even following a picture in a book."

Hangman looked away. He couldn't argue with the sense of what she said. She always made sense.

Right then, Lonion entered the overhang, crossed the floor, and sat down on Alien's other side. Alien rumpled the boy's hair and started talking to him. Lonion laughed at something Alien said.

Then Alien and the boy got up, left Cheina there, and went outside. Alien used his kukris to cut a long staff and then chopped it in half to make two smaller ones.

He gave the sticks to Lonion and started coaching him on how to fight. Alien held up his kukris and Lonion attacked to try to disarm Alien.

They kept at it for an hour before the boy's arms gave out. Alien mussed up the boy's hair and gave him a quick hug around the neck before he sent the boy back inside to get something to eat.

Hangman watched his cousin from a distance while Alien squatted down by the stream out there. Hangman's experience with the Ridge-beak made him suspicious and watchful every time someone went down to the stream, but nothing ever happened.

Alien was still down there when Kalo and his boys returned from somewhere. They usually went off by themselves without explaining or asking permission first.

Hangman never questioned them about where they went or why they needed to go. No one knew better than he did why they needed to go.

He wouldn't even have minded if they formed their own separate band with Kalo as their Kral. Why shouldn't they? They already had their own little hierarchy between themselves.

None of them ever challenged Hangman. They wouldn't dare. The day might come, though. Hangman had to prepare himself for that.

Alien stood up and held a conversation with the boys down by the water's edge. Kalo pointed in different directions and got Alien's input on whatever they were talking about. Then all the boys climbed up to the overhang while Kalo and Alien stayed behind.

They went off to the side, sat down next to each other, and held a long conversation by themselves. Alien occasionally gripped the back of Kalo's neck and gave him affectionate shakes to make his point.

Hangman suffered a pang of longing for his father and his other cousins. He loved Viking, Alien, and Cross, but he missed the rest of his band.

Hangman tore his eyes away from Kalo and Alien. Hangman found his gaze migrating toward Viking. He never showed even the slightest inkling of interest toward any of these single women.

He might never see his wife and children again, but he always kept strictly to himself. Hangman saw plenty of the single women trying to be nice to Viking. He treated them politely, but he held them at a distance and occasionally told them straight out that he was already married.

Chapter 32

"Do we really have to leave?" Aliva asked the next morning. "This overhang is so much more comfortable than traveling all the time. Can't we stay here—at least for a little while?"

"*You* don't have to leave," Hangman told her. "You and the other women and children can stay here. We'll go to the ammunition store. Then we'll come back for you on our way to Godless territory."

"Just remember that you're inside Renegade territory here," Mora added. "They could follow us here and then they would find you unprotected."

Aliva's face fell. "Oh, of course. I forgot about that."

"We only have a few more days' travel before we get to Jeweled River," Hangman told her. "We'll camp at a distance from the site. You and the other women can stay in one place while the men and I scout the terrain and decide how to attack the store."

"Let's get moving," Mora suggested. "The sooner we get there, the sooner we can make camp and then leave."

The party took longer to leave the overhang than they normally did. Just spending a single night here definitely made everyone more complacent and more reluctant to move.

Hangman would have to correct that, but he also sensed a growing problem as the party got closer to their destination.

He absolutely refused to take children into any kind of battle against the Renegades. Taking Kalo and the others didn't bother him so much even though they were still technically uninitiated boys. They could handle themselves.

The children—no way. He wouldn't take the women, either—especially not the mothers with young children. He made up his mind long before he got near Jeweled River to find a sheltered place to leave them.

He wouldn't be able to spare any of the men to stay behind and defend the women and children. They would just have to defend themselves and each other if it came to that.

The party avoided contact with creatures and Renegade patrols. The Renegades became more common the closer the Godless band got to Jeweled River. Then, for some reason Hangman couldn't understand, the patrols died out completely.

The band camped in the trees on the second night while Mora consulted the maps by moonlight. "The Renegades might be trying to divert attention away from the store. They might think surrounding the place with armed men would draw too much attention."

"They're right," Alien grunted. "Surrounding the place with armed men would show us exactly where it is."

"We'll have to expect any armed men we do meet to be armed with these weapons," Hangman pointed out. "We'll have to be extra careful."

"How do you want to do this?" Viking asked. "It's impossible to plan our approach when we don't know where the store is or what the terrain looks like or what position the store is in."

"We'll have to infiltrate the country, locate the store first, and then fall back to decide on our plan of attack."

Mora interjected. "I know it isn't the Godless way, but you'll have better luck if you find a way to destroy the ammunition without the Renegades ever knowing you're there."

"How would we do that?" Cross asked.

"The explosive powder in the ammunition—you could detonate it and blow up the whole store."

"How would we get near enough to do that without the Renegades finding out?" Alien demanded. "They would attack us and our surprise would be spoiled."

"That's what I'm saying. Depending on how many Renegades are around, you might find the store unguarded."

Viking snorted. "That's impossible. They wouldn't leave such a valuable resource unguarded."

"They would if they wanted to avoid attracting attention to it," she pointed out. "Why do you think we kept running into all those patrols and then they suddenly vanished? They're patrolling the area from a distance. They want to stop anyone from infiltrating the country without actually showing any invaders where the store is."

"But if you're right that the store is attached to a military installation, then shouldn't its location be obvious to anyone who goes looking for it?" Cross asked.

"No," she told him. "These installations can be dozens of miles across or even bigger. Anyway, the Renegades might have moved the store somewhere away from the installation."

"Then how do we find it?" Alien asked. "I think we should sneak in and observe the Renegades. They'll go back to the store eventually to reload and restock their weapons. The process might take longer, but at least we won't tip them off that we're here."

"That is definitely not the Godless way," Viking growled.

"There are only four of you plus Kalo's boys," Mora pointed out. "You need to change up your methods or all four of you will get killed long before you get anywhere near the store."

"That doesn't explain how we blow up the store once we find it," Hangman went on.

"You'll have to wait for night or sometime when the Renegades aren't there. If I'm right that they're patrolling from a distance, they'll take their restocks and retreat away from the store. Then you can get in, leave a trail of gunpowder, and ignite the store that way."

"How do we do that?" Cross asked. "We would get blown up in the process."

She compressed her lips in the first show of impatience. She never lost her patience with the men, but she occasionally let slip tiny little displays of frustration when they didn't understand her explanations for things.

"I think I better come with you," she muttered. "You men find the store and then come and get me when you know where it is. It will be easier that way."

No one argued with her. Hangman believed her. She kept dropping words and phrases none of the others understood. Having her blow up the store would be far quicker and easier than having her explain it to any of them.

He didn't like taking his pregnant wife into danger like that, but if she was right, the Renegades would have all retreated by then anyway. They wouldn't be around to put her in danger.

He, his men, and Kalo and the boys left the camp at the first light of dawn the next morning. Half the women and children were still asleep.

The men and boys darted silently away and put as much distance between themselves and the band as possible. Hangman didn't want his actions to draw attention to them, either.

He had given Mora strict instructions last night not to take the women and children away from that spot. They had enough food and water to survive in the canopy for a few days. They shouldn't need to come down for any reason.

The men traveled straight west until they came to a high ridge overlooking a valley. Mora had also given Hangman strict instructions on how to approach the installation with the ammunition store—or where the band though the ammunition store was.

Hangman would really never know where the ammunition store was until the Renegades led him to it. That would be extremely dangerous, especially if the store was actually on the installation somewhere.

He stopped on the ridge. He and his men retreated deeper into the branches where they could observe the installation from a safe distance.

Mora turned out to be right—as if he ever doubted her. The installation consisted of a vast expanse of smooth, flat stone—what she called tarmac. Hangman and his men had seen this in the pictures of the much larger weapons, but he didn't tell Mora that.

He didn't tell her about the larger weapons at all, but she must have already known about them. She just didn't know the Godless were searching for the weapons. Would he find them here? This wouldn't be the same installation, but this one might have similar weapons.

He wouldn't be able to take the time to look for them. He had to stay focused on the store. That was more important than finding weapons he didn't even know how to use.

Not a single tree grew on the tarmac. A few ancient buildings dotted the installation, but other than that, the place offered no cover for the Godless to go out there without the Renegades seeing them.

He scanned the countryside until he spotted three different Renegade patrols in the distance. They were all far away from each other, but they all headed in the same direction. They looked like they were converging on the same point.

He signaled his men. They traveled through the canopy, but they didn't overtake the patrols. Hangman hung off at a distance and stayed that distance. He came close to one patrol and slowed enough to follow the men hiking along the ground.

The Godless traveled silently from branch to branch. Hangman surveyed the terrain ahead. The other two patrols came in sight. They spotted the Renegades Hangman had been following.

The Renegades greeted each other. They all acted relaxed and casual. They had no idea a group of Godless warriors was following them.

The three patrols turned in the same direction. They would merge any second now. Hangman looked in that direction to see if he could locate the store from up here. He froze when he saw another group of Godless squatting in the branches.

He stopped right there and let the Renegades pass out of sight. He didn't recognize any of these unknown Godless. They were all young men over the age of gathering. They must have been about nineteen or twenty and there were twelve of them—all the same age.

They spotted him and his men at the same time. The two parties eyes each other across the canopy. Neither made any move toward or away from the other.

The Renegades talked to each other down on the ground. Some of them even laughed. None of the Godless moved a muscle. Hangman didn't dare to continue on his journey, not even to find out where the store was.

He would just have to track a different patrol and find the store another time. He couldn't pass up the opportunity to talk to these Godless men—whoever they were.

It looked pretty obvious what they were doing here. They had to be staking out the ammunition store, too. Why else would they travel so deep inside Renegade territory?

They took one hell of a risk coming here. They risked their lives and possibly torture and life-long captivity.

The same motive must have driven them here that drove Hangman and his men. This ammunition was the key to the Renegades' power. None of the Clans could stand against the Renegades as long as this ammunition existed.

The Renegades messed around over there for a long time. They didn't hurry to restock their weapons, but they eventually wandered off. They left in three different directions following the same routes they used to get here.

The sound of their voices dwindled into silence. Hangman and his men stayed where they were for another eternity after that. The strangers finally came forward first. They balanced, squatted, and crouched on the branches the same as all Godless.

Everything about them stuck Hangman as painfully familiar. They all wore shoulder bags across their bodies in both directions. They wore a combination of decorations and plaits in their hair.

Three of their party were as big as Viking, but obviously much younger. Another two were barely as big as Cross, but the strangers' features gave them away as being older.

One tall, wiry young man squatted on a branch nearby and eyed Hangman closely. The guy kept tilting his head from side to side and studying Hangman with fascinated interest.

It took Hangman a minute to understand that this young man was studying Hangman's scars. Maybe the guy had never seen someone as heavily scarred as Hangman.

"I am Red," the guy finally blurted out.

"I am Hangman," Hangman replied. "Are you the Kral of this band?"

"We have no Kral," Red replied. "We travel alone as brothers in our own hunting party. Our Kral and our band are all back on in our home country where they belong."

"Where is your home country?" Hangman asked. "Our territory is east of the Jagged Points. I've never seen you before."

"Ah, you belong to Butcher's band. He is my father's distant cousin."

"Butcher is dead," Alien interjected. "His brother Shadow is Kral of the band now."

"He is Kral of the band beyond the Jagged Points," Viking added. "Hangman is our Kral now."

Red raised his eyebrows. "You are too young to be Kral."

"No man is too young to be Kral as long as he's initiated," Viking growled. "Hangman is our Kral and that is the way it will stay."

"This is Viking, Alien, and Cross," Hangman went on. "Viking and Alien are my cousins—Butcher's nephews. Cross is my younger brother."

Red went around the group and introduced his men—at least, Hangman assumed Red was the closest thing to a leader these men had.

The three big ones were Rapid, Legend, and Burn. The two short ones were brothers named Baron and Carnage.

Carnage looked like the more mild-mannered of the two. Hangman didn't ask how he got his name. Hangman really didn't want to find out.

Hangman only caught four other names: Jolt, Wildling, Prodigy, and Butch. He didn't pick up the others fast enough.

Then Hangman introduced Kalo and his comrades. "These boys are not yet initiated."

"How do uninitiated boys come to join your hunting party?" Red asked.

Hangman shrugged. "We came over the Jagged Points to rescue my wife after the Renegades took her captive. Other captive women helped us escape and they joined us along with some of their children. These boys were in the party. They joined us, too. We have too few men, so they help us whenever they can until they initiate."

"You came to the ammunition store, didn't you?" Red asked. "You wouldn't be here for anything else."

"How do you know about that?" Kalo asked.

"They wouldn't be here for anything else, either." Hangman turned back to Red. "Please excuse him. He's eager to learn and initiate into the Godless Clan. He's full of questions."

Red nodded. "It is good to learn from those who know what you wish to know."

"We came today to find the store," Hangman went on. Then he frowned to himself. "How long have you men been in this country?"

"We have been traveling here for more than three months," Red replied. "We just got here three days ago. We've been staking out the store so we can find the best time to attack it."

"Do you know where it is?!" Hangman exclaimed.

"Of course. It's in a cave right over there." Red jerked his thumb over his shoulder.

Hangman glanced in that direction. He couldn't see anything but trees. He made a strategic decision not to go over there and hunt around to find the store himself. He might not need to.

He cast one more look around at the men in front of him. They were all strong, straight, and clear-eyed.

"If you're trying to destroy the ammunition store and we're trying to destroy the ammunition store, we should join together," Hangman told them. "We can help each other."

Red only nodded. "We're happy to serve any Kral of the Godless Clan. We don't know how to destroy the store anyway. That's what we were trying to decide. We don't know enough about these weapons."

"Show me where the store is. Then we'll decide."

Chapter 33

M ora snapped alert when she heard rustling in the canopy nearby. She spun around expecting to see a Krakelow coming after the freed captive women and children.

She relaxed when Hangman returned with his men. Then she stiffened all over when she saw a bunch of strangers coming with him. They were all young Godless men. They didn't look dangerous except that she didn't know them.

She stood up on her branch, held onto another to balance herself, and prepared to meet the strangers. She made a quick mental calculation of the band's food and water supplies.

Their supplies would run low much quicker if they had to provide for twelve additional fully grown men. Maybe they would be reasonable enough to hunt for themselves or at least help the band secure food and water.

The newcomers' ever-alert eyes darted around the group. Hangman didn't introduce Mora or any of the other women. He and the men settled on a series of branches to one side.

"How much have you seen of the Renegade patrols approaching the store?" Hangman asked one of the young men. "You must have learned a lot from watching them for three whole days."

"We saw a lot of them. We didn't pick up any pattern in their movements. They seem to come and go randomly. We didn't see the same patrol returning more than once before they disappeared into the jungle."

"Did you see them take the supplies out of the store?"

The young man nodded. "They take everything out in boxes." He held up the thumbs and forefingers of both hands to make a square. "They carry the boxes in pockets in their clothes."

"So you didn't see the ammunition itself?"

The young man shook his head.

"How did you find out about the ammunition?" Viking asked. "How do you know what it is?"

"A man of another Clan blundered into my cousin's territory. He was half dead from hunger and injuries. He collapsed in our camp and begged us to help him. We nursed him back to health and found out that he came from the Followers originally. He got taken captive by the Bounty Hunters. He escaped and had to travel through Renegade country before he got to us. He came to live with us and eventually initiated into our Clan. He was with us when the Renegades attacked. He told us what the weapons were and how they worked." The young man cocked his head. "How did you find out?"

Cross waved at Mora. "Mora here came to us from the Followers when she married Hangman. She told us."

Almost all the young men in the group turned around to stare at Mora. She realized too late that she probably shouldn't have been listening in on their conversation.

She tried to deflect their attention by pulling out a large chunk of Gorlock meat from her bag. She held it out to the young man. "Are you hungry? You're welcome to what we have."

He took it from her. "Thank you," he exclaimed. "You're very kind."

"Any Godless are welcome here."

"This is Red, Legend, and Carnage." Hangman waved to the young strangers and then turned back to Red. "Mora helped us find this place. She knows a way to destroy the store. She suggested that we do it at night or when no Renegade patrols are around. We understand it isn't the Godless way, but it seemed to make sense when we only had four men to carry out the attack."

Red raised his eyebrows. "I didn't think of that. As I said, we were still trying to decide what to do when you found us."

The men kept talking about the ammunition stores, their respective family bands, and the journey both parties took to get here.

Red used his teeth to tear off a strip of the Gorlock meat. He chewed it and passed the rest of the hunk to his men. It only lasted long enough to make it through seven of their number before it ran out.

Mora went through the women in her party, held whispered conversations with each of them, and scrounged up enough to feed the rest of Red's men.

"That's all the food we have left," Choma whispered. "Where are we going to get more?"

"I don't know, but we have to give these young men hospitality," Mora pointed out. "We can't let them go hungry. It looks like Hangman and the others want to work with them."

Red interrupted just then. "We have some food of our own, but we should hunt for you if we're going to join your band."

"I'll go with you," Viking offered.

"The boys and I will come, too," Kalo chimed in.

Hangman nodded. "Excellent. Make it back here by dark. Then we'll decide how to proceed."

The men dropped to the ground and set off into the jungle. Mora went over to sit next to Hangman. "Who are they?"

"They're just young men from another band. They want to join us. We found them standing watch over the ammunition store. They want to destroy it, but they don't know how. They can help us. We need all the Godless men we can get and they seem strong and solid."

"I wonder who the Follower man was who joined their band. Maybe he's someone I know."

"I don't think so," Hangman replied. "Their band is far to the northeast—far beyond my father's territory. Whoever that man is, he didn't come from the south. You wouldn't have met him."

She slumped. "Oh. I didn't realize."

"These men may not be willing to carry out an attack on the ammunition store when the Renegades aren't there. These men don't understand your ways. They may think it's cowardly not to fight the Renegades in the open in order to defeat them."

She didn't look up. She already knew this. Hangman, Viking, Alien, and Cross had let the rules slide more and more the longer their party stayed isolated from other Godless.

Hangman especially had become more agreeable to doing things differently. She couldn't assign all of that to his interactions with her.

He seemed to be tempering his reckless behavior as he got older and took more responsibility for the safety of others.

He seemed much more inclined to use his wits, the element of surprise, and any other strategy besides a full, frontal assault to accomplish the same thing.

He used the ants to kill hundreds of Renegades. Maybe that's when it started—when he got too weak and injured to use his strength.

She should have expected him to go back to the Godless way as soon as he met up with others of his Clan. She did expect it. She didn't argue against it now.

She only lowered her voice so Cross and Alien wouldn't hear her. "I'll only tell you this much. This way I know to blow up the ammunition store—it will take time. I won't be able to do it quickly or under attack from Renegades. If you fight your way in, you and the men will have to kill all the Renegades around so I can lay the gunpowder trail far enough away from the store that none of us gets killed when we blow it up."

"I don't understand how you plan to blow it up," he told her. "I'm leaving that up to you. If you tell me you need time to do it carefully when the Renegades aren't around, then that's what we'll do. I don't care how we do it as long as we get it done."

She looked up at him. The understanding between them gave her courage—now that they could finally talk quietly and alone together like this. "There is another possibility."

"What is it?" he asked. "Tell me anything you know so I can make the best decision."

"You could show me where the ammunition store is and I could go alone. I could sneak in and blow it up. I'm not Godless. No one can accuse me of being a coward if I sneak around and hide while I wait for my enemies to leave."

He actually laughed. "You are Godless, Mora. You are as Godless as the rest of us if not more so."

"But that works against us here, don't you see? I could do it the Follower way. You and the men wouldn't have to go near the place."

"Then some would call us cowards. That would never work."

She thought fast. "Then you could create a diversion. You could attack one of the patrols. You have enough men now. The commotion would draw any other patrols away from the store while I go in and do the job."

His eyes twinkled and his cheeks flushed with pleasure when he smiled at her. "You are definitely not a coward. I'm proud of you."

"So do you want me to do it?"

"Wait a little while. I need to talk to the men and think about it first. Conditions might change between now and then."

She looked around. "I'm sorry I don't have any food to give you. I gave it all to the men and now we don't have any left."

"Forget about it. They'll bring some back. These young men are going to be an asset to us. Now I need you to explain this to me."

"Explain what?"

"About how you plan to blow up the store."

"You said you wanted me to do it. Why do you need to know?"

"I need to know in case something happens to you or our plans go catastrophically wrong—which they very well may. I need to understand this in case I need to come up with an alternate plan. How does it work? What is the stuff you're calling gunpowder?"

"It's the explosive dust I told you about inside the ammunition."

"So how would you do it?"

"You could do it a couple of different ways. One way is that you use one of the firearms and shoot into the store, but I wasn't planning to do that since we don't have a weapon."

"How were you planning to do it?"

"Each piece of ammunition has a tube with the projectile at the top—like this." She formed a cylinder with one hand and made a fist at the top with the other to show him what she meant.

"You explained all of this to me," he told her.

"You can pry off the projectile and pour out the dust. If you use enough of them, you can form a trail of gunpowder along the ground, touch a live coal to the powder, and it will spark and ignite along the trail back to the ammunition store. The fire will blow up the rest of the ammunition."

He frowned to himself and rubbed his chin. "I see."

"So what do you want to do?"

"I would rather not send you to the store at all if I don't have to. You're a woman, you're pregnant, and you're my wife. You should stay in the rear. One of us should carry out the plan."

"But don't you need all the men to fight the Renegades?"

"Yes, exactly. That's exactly why I would send you. I just want to make sure we do it in a way that keeps you safe."

"It would be safe if I went when no Renegades are around. I don't see why it's cowardly to do it the smart way. I told you before you could blow this store without the Renegades ever finding out that we're here."

He nodded to himself. "I understand and I actually agree with you. Even one of us going alone would be better than losing some of our men in a fight."

She didn't press her advantage by saying anything else. Hangman saying he agreed with her was a huge step. He'd never gone as far as that before, especially not when it came to something that directly contradicted the Godless way.

He had never outright agreed that the Followers' way of doing something was the better strategy. She didn't want to shatter the moment by pushing him too far.

They sat in silence for a while. Cross and Alien left to refill the party's water gourds. They returned and handed out the water to everyone. Viking and Kalo's boys returned a little while later.

Kalo came carrying a large pot made out of clay surrounded in a thick mat of dry grass.

"What is that?" Alien demanded.

"Red explained it to me," Kalo replied. "Look. His men built a fire in the pot. They cook the meat like this. They can cook in the treetops without building a fire on the ground. No one can see the flames. It's genius!"

The others gathered around to see an enormous slab of Stalkion meat sizzling on a bed of coals inside the pot.

The boys balanced it between two branches and left it there. They turned the meat every now and then until they took it out, carved off pieces, and served it to everyone.

Viking and Red's party didn't return for a long time. Carnage and Baron went back and forth between the band in the treetops and wherever it was that Viking and the others killed the Stalkion.

The two brothers brought one slab of meat after another—enough to feed the whole band. Kalo and his boys stood guard over the pot and supervised both the cooking and the serving to make sure everyone got their share.

At last, Carnage and Baron delivered the last section of meat and stayed with the band to wait for their turn.

"When are Viking and the others coming back?" Hangman asked them.

"Viking said to tell you he, Red, and the others will stay over there to smoke the meat at a distance so the fire doesn't bring the Renegades near your people," Baron replied. "He said to tell you they'll come back with the food in the morning."

Hangman didn't argue with that. This band was growing much faster than he realized.

Baron and Carnage didn't talk at all for the rest of the night. Mora couldn't tell why, but none of these young men talked. Red did all their talking for them.

Did they have some rule against that? Mora would probably never know—not until she got to know them better.

Chapter 34

Hangman followed the trail of smoke to a distant camp many miles from where he left the women and children. He found Viking, Red, and the rest of Red's men tending half a dozen fires, each with a tripod of meat strips smoking on the rails.

Hangman only had to take a look at five of Red's men asleep on the ground to understand exactly what these men had been doing all night. They must have been working in shifts to cure as much food for the band as possible.

Red, Wildling, and Legend all stood up when Hangman arrived with Cross, Carnage, and Baron. "How close are you to being done?" Hangman asked.

"Maybe another hour," Viking replied. "We should deliver all of this back to the band before we go anywhere."

"They won't need to eat again for a month after last night," Cross chimed in.

Some of Red's men laughed.

"Do you need us sooner than that?" Viking asked. "We could probably cut it short."

"You don't have to. I came out here to talk to you all about our strategy going into the store." He turned to Red and the others. "We've been doing things differently since we got stranded out here with only four men. We have to get creative and use our brains instead of strength. How important is it to you that you fight your way to the store? Are you comfortable using stealth and surprise—and maybe not fighting at all?"

"You're Kral here," Red pointed out. "It's a good idea. We couldn't think of any way to accomplish it even with fighting. If you think we can destroy the store this way, we'll follow you."

"Why aren't you Kral of your band?" Hangman asked. "Why haven't you all chosen a Kral for yourselves?"

"We aren't a band," Red pointed out. "We're just a hunting party—maybe a scouting party. We don't have wives and children and camps to defend. We didn't think we needed a Kral for this. We're only brothers on a mission together."

Hangman let that go. "In that case, we're going to send Mora in to blow up the store. If it works out, she'll go alone....."

"She can't go alone," Viking interjected. "She's a woman and she's pregnant. It's too dangerous."

"I don't mean she would go all the way there and do the job alone. We would stand guard and watch to make sure no Renegades come while she goes to the store. She knows the best what to do, but she needs time and protection. If any Renegades come, we'll attack them at a distance from the store to distract them and draw any others away until she blows it."

"How much time does she need?" Cross asked.

"I have no idea. That's why I'm leaving it to her. She explained what she plans to do last night, but I still didn't understand it well. I might be able to pull it off, but she's still our best option. I don't like sending her in any more than you do, but we didn't come all this way to fail in our mission." Hangman turned back to Red. "Are you comfortable with that?"

Red nodded. "Yes. It's a good plan."

Hangman turned to leave. "Excellent. We'll wait for all of you to come back to the band. Then we'll take Mora out to the canopy over the store and keep watch until it's clear. We may have to wait until nightfall. I'll see you all back at the camp."

He started to leave until Red stopped him. "Hangman—wait."

Hangman turned around. "What's wrong? If you have a problem with this plan, tell me now."

"We don't have a problem with this plan. I need to ask you....if we join your band.....I mean.....if we join for good—after this....."

"Yes?" Hangman asked. "What about it? I don't see how you wouldn't join us. You're all good men. You hunted for us and stayed out here to provide for us. You're helping us carry out this mission. We need you a lot more than you need us."

"It's your women," Red blurted out. "You have so many of them and so few men. Viking told me last night he left his wife back in your home territory. Alien already has a wife in your band and Cross is too young—but we're all over the age of gathering."

"Oh, I see what you mean," Hangman interrupted. "If you join us and you prove yourselves as dedicated as I think you will, then all of you would have my permission to marry any of those women that you choose and who choose you in return. That would be my only requirement—that they choose you willingly. Apart from that, I don't see any barrier to all of you marrying."

Red's men burst into excited jumping up and down, squirming, grinning, and grabbing each other's arms.

"And I would remind all of you that none of these women are Godless—not originally," Hangman went on. "They all came from other Clans. Some of them are Followers. Some of them are Whisperers. I don't know which Clans half of them came from. You won't be able to expect them to act like true-born Godless women—but they learn fast and they're willing and enthusiastic. Be patient with them and let them learn. That's all you have to do."

Hangman took his leave. So these men wanted to marry into his band. He saw no problem with that, but it gave him a lot to think about.

Red's comments about what it took to be Kral of a band like this gnawed at Hangman's mind. He didn't think of this group as a band—not when it only had four initiated men and a whole slew of unattached women and children.

It would be a band if twelve Godless men married these women. They would have more children. They would have to organize to hunt more. They would also need protected places to camp—places outside Renegade territory.

He made it back to the camp in the trees, but he didn't climb up there. Carnage and Baron stayed behind with Red and the others.

Hangman stopped Cross under the branches. "Go up there, tell Kalo and his boys that I want to see them down here, and you come down with them."

Cross shimmied up the trees. Hangman had to stop himself from pacing while he waited for the boys to come back. They jumped down, landed in front of and around him, and straightened up to face him. Cross came with them.

"Where are Viking and the others?" Kalo asked. "Is anything wrong?"

"Nothing is wrong. They're preparing food for the band. I want to talk to all of you before we leave to go to the ammunition store."

"Are you angry with us?" Kalo asked. "Did we do something wrong?"

"That depends on what you did and what you didn't do. All of you have been getting closer to these girls we rescued from the Renegades, but it falls to me as your Kral to remind you all that you're all underage. None of you is old enough to take a wife. I hope all of you are remembering that when you're gazing into these girls' eyes and holding their hands."

A wave of uncomfortable tension went through the group. "Yes, of course we remember that, Hangman," Kalo murmured.

"Are you sure?" Hangman turned to each member of the group and finally locked eyes on his brother. "If any of you has broken the law, I need to know right now. Tell the truth or the consequences could be far, far worse."

"I haven't, Hangman. I swear it," Cross replied. "I would never take a woman I wasn't legally married to."

Hangman measured his brother's response and finally nodded. "All right. I believe you. What about the rest of you? Tell me the truth. Your futures in this band depend more on you telling the truth than on what you may or may not actually have done."

"I haven't," Kalo choked. "I....I wanted to.....but I want to be Godless more."

"It's critical that all of you wait until you come of age," Hangman went on. "If you break the law, I might have to decide that you could never marry. If any of you are serious about marrying these girls and raising families with them, it's imperative that you don't do anything with them intimately until all of you come of age. Is that clear?"

The boys nodded.

"Now each of you tell me the truth about whether you have or you haven't done it yet. Have any of you done it? If I find out later that you lied to me, I may have to take drastic action to punish you. Tell the truth now and I'll consider it on account of none of you being officially Godless yet."

The boys glanced at each other. A few said, "I haven't." Others just shook their heads.

Hangman didn't know them well enough to tell if they were telling the truth or not. They might just have been so petrified of him that he couldn't read their expressions.

He leveled each of them with a hard glare. Cross was the only man here that Hangman had absolutely no doubt told the truth. Cross grew up Godless. He knew the rules better than anyone. He wouldn't break them.

Hangman felt pretty certain about Kalo, too. None of the boys wanted to be Godless more than Kalo. He admitted that he actually stopped himself from doing it because his desire to be Godless over-rode his body's needs. That counted for a lot, especially at his age.

Hangman just had to take the rest of them at their word.

"If I find out later that any of you lied to me, it won't go well at all," he repeated. "If any of you wants to be Godless, your first law is fealty to your Kral. That starts now. Betraying and disobeying your Kral is an offense punishable by feeding you to the ants if I judge it necessary. I'm warning you all right now. If you don't feel comfortable telling me the truth in front of your friends, you can come to me privately, but don't keep it a secret. The other possibility is that we would all go on as a band of the Godless Clan and the liar will go out alone into the jungle and fend for himself. I'm sure none of you wants that. Become Godless right now, follow the rules, and you can marry these girls in a few years when you all get old enough. Remember that and be patient. Every married man has waited many years to marry. You can do the same thing. It isn't that hard if you dedicate yourself to your family band and your Clan. That's all I'll say about it, but I'll be keeping an eye on all of you. Don't let me down. Now get up into the trees and go back to defending your mothers and sisters. We'll be leaving soon to go back to the ammunition store."

Kalo and the boys sprang up into the trees and climbed back up to rejoin their families. Cross stayed behind.

"I'm sorry I did anything to make you doubt me, Hangman," Cross murmured once they were alone. "I won't do it again. I see my error now."

"Just tell her to wait a few years," Hangman replied. "If it's real, you can marry when you're eighteen. It isn't that long to wait."

"I see that now. I should have been more careful. I'm sorry."

"You can stop saying that. We corrected the problem and you didn't break the law. You have nothing to worry about. You can care for each other, love each other, and plan your future together without doing it. Then you'll be ready when the time comes."

Cross nodded. "Thank you. You're forgiving. You're a good Kral."

Hangman snorted. "I'm doing the best I can. Now get up there."

The brothers climbed up to the branches. None of the boys talked about the recent confrontation.

He did see some of the young couples exchanging worried glances with each other. They would all have to have a conversation later about how serious they were about going the distance with each other.

Hangman did his best to put the matter out of his mind. Kalo and the boys would come with the men on this expedition to the ammunition store.

Some of these boys might not even make it back alive. The question of them marrying or even initiating into the Godless Clan wouldn't even be relevant anymore.

Hangman couldn't do a thing about that. Some of Red's men might not make it, either. They wouldn't marry anyone or get a second chance after getting passed over at the gathering.

Chapter 35

H angman stood up on his branch. Viking, Red, and the other newcomers were just in the process of distributing a massive load of dried meat to all the women and children of the band.

Everyone was too full from last night to be interested in food or water right now, but Mora found herself assessing the band's supplies anyway. They once again had enough to keep the women and children going for a few days.

Cross, Kalo, and his boys stood apart from the group talking privately with whatever girl the boy had been getting interested in. Hangman narrowed his eyes at each of them in turn, but he didn't give anything away about what might be going on.

Mora read his mind. She had been wondering when he would step in and intervene between all these budding underage couples.

He must have laid the hammer down because all those couples held hands, but they didn't kiss. Cross and Hicia's sons, Hitro and Ethio, all hugged the girls, but that was it.

Mora tried to stop herself from watching. The boys finally broke away. Two of the girls burst into tears when the boys joined up with Hangman and the other men.

Hangman locked eyes with Mora, said, "Let's go," and took off through the branches.

Mora had to struggle to keep pace with them. She had been starting to feel heavy and sluggish these last few weeks on the journey. She couldn't climb and keep up with the men the way she used to.

Hangman noticed. He slowed down to stay with her. The others copied him until the whole group surrounded her. She hated slowing them down, but she couldn't help that she was pregnant.

The party entered a part of the canopy she had never seen before. They kept going until they came to a high patch of branches overlooking a valley in the distance.

She spotted the military installation she recognized from Thomion's maps, but the men didn't go that way. They turned off and kept traveling for another two miles before they stopped.

She buckled in the branches and gasped to catch her breath. The men pretended not to notice her so exhausted and dripping with sweat. She felt herself shaking, but fortunately, none of the men moved or did anything for a while.

They stayed in one place long enough for her to settle down and rest. The men stayed in that one place for a long time—much longer than she expected.

She shot Hangman a questioning glance. She knew better than to ask him anything out loud. He pointed toward a different patch of leaves behind Red's men.

The men lounged. They didn't pay attention to very much. Some of Red's party who had been out all night actually put their heads down and shut their eyes in total relaxation.

Hangman jolted alert first. The others responded at the same time. They all sat up and strained their ears toward the south.

Mora didn't hear anything, but all the men did. Some moved their hands to their weapons. Some who had been relaxing got up and squatted on the branches instead.

Mora froze where she was and didn't move. She didn't want to find out what happened after whatever it was got close enough for her to see.

She found out when a Renegade patrol strolled out of the jungle. They appeared as relaxed as the Godless men just had been.

The Renegades didn't even look around to check the area. They definitely didn't look up. They engaged in a lively conversation and joked back and forth while they walked through the trees. None of them kept their hands on their weapons.

Mora had seen enough of Hangman's attacks on Renegades. He and his men could easily drop out of the canopy and slaughter these men right here, but the Godless didn't attack.

They let the Renegades pass unmolested. The Renegades broke through another curtain of undergrowth over there—where Hangman said the ammunition store was.

The Renegades kept talking in the same easy, casual, joking manner. Their voices bubbled up from the jungle floor and filled the whole area.

Anyone would have been able to tell exactly where these men were. They made no effort at all to hide their location even though this ammunition store was supposed to be so secret.

They stayed a long time—long enough for a second patrol to show up and do the same thing. The two parties joined at the store and stood there talking even longer.

They both eventually left heading in opposite directions from which they came. They left the area silent and all the Godless still sitting up and holding their breath to listen for the slightest sound.

Mora's chest ached from both holding her breath and straining to breathe quietly enough so the Renegades wouldn't hear her.

She probably didn't have to worry about that. They made so much noise they wouldn't have been able to hear anything anyway, but she didn't want to be the reason the Renegades discovered the Godless were even in this country.

Both bands of Godless stayed concealed until now. No one wanted more than Mora to keep it that way.

The silence went on and on. No more Renegades came. The men eventually settled down, but they never let their guard down entirely. They always stayed watchful even in those silent times between Renegade patrols.

The second patrol didn't talk or joke around. They held themselves on high alert the entire time—coming, resupplying, and leaving. They never stopped searching the jungle in all directions for any sign of trouble.

A few of them did look up, but the canopy hid the Godless' presence from view.

The quiet became oppressive after the second group left. The sun was starting to go down by the time the third group arrived.

Mora stole a glance at Hangman. Did he want her to wait until nightfall to go to the ammunition store? She might not be able to see what she was doing well enough to carry out their plan.

The third Renegade patrol didn't laugh and joke, but they didn't pay as much attention as the second group. The third group strolled casually on their way and didn't check much of anything other than where they put their feet.

They disappeared behind the curtain of foliage, resupplied pretty soon, and left. Hangman waited until their footsteps died away in the distance. All sound of their movements through the undergrowth faded out of the jungle.

"Go now, Mora," he whispered. "Lay your gunpowder trail, make a live coal, and destroy the store if you can."

"You and the men will need to move away from it before I blow it up," she whispered back. "You're too close here. You might get caught in the blast."

"What about you? Make sure you get far enough away."

"I will, but you and the men won't know where I am."

"We'll keep an eye on you," he whispered. "We'll follow you so we can intervene if anyone comes."

"If that happens, you'll need to draw them away from the store."

"Wouldn't it work better if we drew them into the store? Then they would get caught in the blast."

"You would get caught in the blast along with them. You have to lead them away. Besides, you might intervene when I'm in the middle of laying the trail. You bringing them there would stop me from doing that. You said you would create a distraction to draw any additional patrols away."

He nodded. "Yes. I remember. All right. We'll do it that way. Go now before anyone comes. If they do come, the men and I will drop down and intercept them before they get to you."

Mora nodded back. She understood what she had to do. That didn't help her do it.

She climbed down to the ground fighting nerves. She definitely had never done anything like this before.

She only found out from books that someone *could* create a gunpowder trail and use it to blow up a supply of ammunition. She had never tried it before. She had never even seen a supply of ammunition big enough to blow up with a gunpowder trail.

She had never seen firearms or any other kind of ammunition before the Renegades started using them. She never thought she would ever have to see them. The Followers avoided that kind of thing.

She paused there on the ground to look around. Now her chest really hurt. Her heart pounded so badly that her head ached.

She scanned the surrounding undergrowth. Everything sounded quiet. She couldn't delay anymore.

She turned toward the curtain of leaves that hid the ammunition store. She pushed through and found herself in a ten-foot clearing in front of a fifteen-foot-tall cave.

She didn't know how deep the cave ran, but the ammunition stores blocked the whole round front entrance.

Wooden crates, metal boxes, plastic totes, and steel lockers lay stacked one on top of the other. Some of the wooden crates sat on wooden pallets against the righthand wall.

Spraypainted letters and numbers marked the outside of each container. The markings didn't tell her anything. They were just identification or serial numbers.

She crossed the clearing and stopped there trying to decide what to do first. Rustling in the canopy above her head made her look up.

Hangman and the others moved through the branches to reposition themselves at a distance from her. They could see her and keep watch on the surrounding terrain.

The men stayed much more alert and tense while she worked—or while she stood here trying to figure out what to do first.

She took one more step and opened one of the wooden crates. It was full of large, pointed metal cartridges laid out in rows grey of foam cushioning.

She picked up one of the cartridges. The long, brass casing stretched as long as her thumb. The crimped edge of the casing clasped around the bullet at the end.

Her mind kicked into high gear. This casing must contain a lot of gunpowder—much more than she would be able to get from a smaller caliber casing.

She thought fast, clamped her molars around the bullet, and twisted. She had to be careful when it came away from the casing.

She kept it upright, spat the bullet out, and peered into the casing. The gunpowder lay inside in a tiny, grey pool filling the casing two-thirds of the way to the top.

She dumped the gunpowder there in a pile on the floor right under the pallet holding the wooden crates. They would be the most flammable and the easiest to set alight.

Once she started, her anxiety about getting out of her faster kicked her energy into high gear. She had to get this done before any more Renegade patrols showed up.

She snatched a big double fistful of the cartridges out of the crate and worked her fastest to twist the bullets off.

She made a hefty little pile of gunpowder there under the pallet. This thing would make one hell of a blast if she did ignite it.

Her heart threatened to pound straight through her ribs. The process took forever. She really needed some other kind of tool to take these cartridges apart, but finding one would only cost her extra time.

She finally created a pile she judged big enough to ignite the rest of the store. She used one cartridge after another to pour gunpowder across the floor in a thin trail leading to the entrance.

She didn't hear anything going on outside. She almost wished she did hear something. Then she could have done something about it—like run away before someone caught her in the act.

She laid her gunpowder trail as far as the cave entrance. She had to work with her back to the surroundings, but she still didn't hear anything. She twisted off one more cartridge. Just a few inches further and she would make it outside.

She decided to lead the trail to the left. She could hide there in the undergrowth so no one would see her there.

She would have to come back multiple times to get more cartridges. It would take a lot of cartridges to make a gunpowder trail long enough for her to get to a safe distance. She didn't even know what a safe distance was.

She would just have to ignite the trail and run for it. She would have to put as much distance as possible between herself and the blast. Then she just had to hope for the best. At least the ammunition would get destroyed. The rest would take care of itself—she hoped.

She put another cartridge in her mouth, twisted, and bent over to run the trail outside. She froze in place when she heard voices coming closer. They sounded conversational. They were close to the ground. Renegades.

She snatched up as many of the spare cartridges and empty casings as she could carry. She had already been thinking about hiding all the evidence of what she was doing—all except the gunpowder itself.

She shut the crate each time she took cartridges out of it. She always took the empty casings with her.

She whirled away and dove into the undergrowth to hide. Movement in the branches overhead drew her eye upward.

Hangman and the other men shot away into the canopy. They passed out of sight, and the next minute, blood-curdling roars, screams, and the clash of weapons echoed through the jungle.

Mora stayed rooted to the spot for a minute while the truth sank into her head. The Godless must have attacked the Renegade patrol.

The Godless were carrying out their plan to distract the Renegades from her presence.

She left all the empty casings there in the bushes, dove outside, and rushed back to the gunpowder trail. She had to steady her shaking hands so she would dump the gunpowder in a straight line.

She worked ten times faster, but the sounds of battle and men screaming and raging out of sight racked her nerves to the breaking point.

She opened cartridge after cartridge and curved the trail to the left. She was nowhere even close to crossing the clearing. This was taking too long.

The battle surged from one direction to another. She couldn't tell if the Godless were overcoming the Renegades. She might not find out until the Renegades burst through those trees and discovered her here. Then what would she do?

She just had to keep going and pray to High Heaven that she got there before disaster struck.

Chapter 36

H angman hacked his kukris one way, met a Renegade swinging at his head, and deflected the stroke before he spun around to block another attack from someone else.

The battle kept escalating. Brief snatches of quiet in between attacks brought the sounds of more Renegades rushing in to help their friends.

Hangman's men fought all over the jungle floor and got separated in the confusion. Some of the Renegades got trapped between Kalo and the boys on the north side while Hangman and the rest of the men got stuck over here.

Kalo and the boys retreated from the Renegades. Kalo didn't realize he was leading the Renegades back toward the ammunition store. Hangman couldn't let the Renegades find Mora.

He took a chance, parried another Renegade attack, and dove between his enemies to join up with Kalo's group. "This way!" Hangman yelled and diverted to the west.

He would rather have led the Renegades south, but that would have made it too obvious that he was trying to get away from the ammunition store.

The foliage concealing the cave ended in a stand of trees on the west side. He would have to make the Renegades think the Godless were trying to skirt around the undergrowth and get to the store that way.

Kalo and the boys fell in with him. Viking, Red, and some of the new guys didn't get the message in time until Alien plowed his way over there and got their attention.

The men laid into the Renegades twice as hard and forced the enemy back toward Hangman and the boys.

The two flanks of Godless pincered the Renegades there for a minute. The Godless outnumbered the Renegades, but the noise would draw more patrols pretty soon. The Godless would lose their advantage.

Hangman couldn't see Mora through the undergrowth. How close was she to blowing the ammunition store? He tried again and again to steer the battle away from there to put more distance between her and the Renegades.

Hangman and his men were too close to the store. They would all die if she blew it up now. He glanced that way again and again, but no amount of looking would show him anything through that curtain of leaves.

Shouts echoed from farther east when another patrol rushed out of the surrounding jungle to back up their comrades.

Viking, Alien, Red, and the other new guys glanced behind them, saw the enemy closing in, and Viking yelled something to the others.

The Godless men charged around their enemies in what Viking must have hoped looked like one last act of terrified desperation.

Viking and the others joined up with Hangman and the boys so they all stood on one side of the battle and the Renegades all stood on the other.

The maneuver shifted the bulk of the Godless ranks farther south and the incoming Renegades toward the north—closer to the ammunition store.

Only a thin layer of undergrowth separated the Renegades from Mora. She would have been totally defenseless if they realized she was there.

They fought with their backs to the bushes. The Godless assaulted their enemies even harder to occupy the Renegades and keep them paying attention to the Godless over anything else.

The new patrol balanced the Godless and Renegade numbers, but the Godless proved the stronger side. Hangman and the others had to continually pull back and slacken their efforts to stop themselves from pushing the Renegades too far back.

Kalo and the boys didn't realize what was happening. They fought their hardest no matter what. Hangman and the men had to fall back even more to compensate for the boys' efforts.

Viking and Alien eventually had to stop fighting entirely. They looked around and made eye contact with Hangman.

He was just making up his mind how to withdraw completely without making it too obvious that he was trying to lead the Renegades away from the ammunition store.

He looked behind him toward the south. The Renegades must realize by now that the Godless could have broken through the Renegades' barricade to get to the store. Two or three Godless not fighting at all must have given it away.

Fortunately, a third Renegade patrol showed up right then and gave Hangman the perfect excuse to call his men back. Viking and Alien had to rejoin the fight.

The Godless backed off. They could have fought harder and maybe even overcome this number of Renegades, but the Godless allowed the Renegades to push them farther south. This was perfect.

Hangman took the time in between deflecting Renegade attacks to measure how far he should lead the Renegades to give Mora the space and time she needed. Too many unknowns made it impossible for him to tell.

He glanced behind him one last time. The jungle got thicker just there. Fighting the Renegades would be harder once the Godless got there.

He decided to stop at the fringe of trees and let the Renegades think they trapped the Godless there. That should be far enough away to distract the Renegades.

It wouldn't be far enough to escape the blast when it happened. He really needed a better way to communicate with Mora so she could tell him when she was ready to set off the explosion.

The Godless pulled up in front of the trees. Hangman and his men couldn't retreat any further without breaking and running for it.

That might have worked to draw the Renegades away, but he wasn't ready to give up so easily—not while he and his men still stood their ground.

The clang of weapons and the bellows of attackers on both sides drowned out every other sound in the jungle. Hangman caught sight of two other patrols converging on the battle.

The Godless would definitely have to flee once the Renegades got here. The Renegades would definitely understand that.

Hangman went back to fighting the Renegades in front of him, but at that moment, a huge male Stalkion charged out of the undergrowth coming from the north.

The creature cut around the hill with the ammunition store buried underneath it, swerved southward, and stampeded one of the patrols moving in on the battle.

The creature's arrival startled Hangman so much that he forgot to fight. He stopped in his tracks and stared as another ten Stalkions followed that first big male.

The creatures thundered around the hill in a pack, trampled the patrol into the ground, and kept right on plowing straight for the battle.

The rest of Hangman's men also froze with their weapons still raised. Every eye fell out of the Godless' heads in stunned shock as the Stalkions bore down on the two sides locked in mortal combat.

The other approaching patrol stopped in time not to get to the battlefield at all. The patrols already on the field didn't turn around in time.

The Stalkions got within twenty feet of the Renegades before the combatants turned around and saw these massive creatures barreling down on them at top speed.

The Renegades screamed. Some of them bolted out of the way. Others hesitated just a fraction of an instant too long.

The Stalkions lowered their heads and impaled their tusks into a bunch of Renegades, trampled others, and carried the bodies away with them when the Stalkions kept right on running.

Everyone else broke and ran for it. The second incoming patrol got off the easiest. Half the Renegades fell on the field.

Hangman took off into the jungle. He only ran a dozen yards before he vaulted into the branches and kept on climbing. More Godless swarmed the canopy all around him to get as far as possible out of the Stalkions' way.

Kalo and the boys didn't think to climb. They kept running and only later remembered to get off the ground. The Godless rejoined in the canopy and listened to the Stalkions bellowing and rumbling in the distance as they hunted down any Renegades left alive.

Hangman listened to them for a while, but the sounds didn't tell him anything. He tiptoed along the branches, returned to the ammunition store, and looked down. Mora wasn't there.

Chapter 37

Mora dove into the undergrowth and fell against some spiky brambles to get out of the way of three enraged Stalkions charging through the clearing.

She dropped her remaining cartridges all over the ground when she ran away from them. She only got her gunpowder trail half a dozen yards away from the cave before she had to take cover.

She cowered in the bushes trying to hear something over the incessant hammering of her own pulse in her ears.

She heard plenty of Stalkions stampeding around in the distant jungle. She also heard plenty of men yelling, screaming, and deadly crashes shaking the ground and trees out there.

She stayed where she was for a lot longer than she should have. She kept waiting for someone or something else to come along and interrupt her—or attack her—or capture her.

She swatted a Blitzword away, but all this constant interference only proved the point. She had to get this done and fast.

Any random Renegade who showed up at the ammunition store would see the trail of gunpowder. They might not realize what it meant, but they couldn't fail to realize that someone was here messing with their precious resources.

She measured the clearing again and again even though she could already see there was no one there.

She decided to change her strategy. She twisted the slugs off all her remaining cartridges and balanced them upright in one hand. She did all of that without coming out of hiding.

Then she broke cover, went out there, and poured them all one after another into a line to extend her trail. Each one only stretched the line a few inches before that cartridge ran out.

She hid the empty casings, loaded up with another collection of cartridges, and took them all into the bushes to open them before she went out there again. At least she could stay hidden some of the time.

She did this again and again and finally, finally got the trail to the bushes. Now she didn't have to worry about hiding the casings. She could just throw them on the ground. The undergrowth would hide them.

She could stay hidden all the time except when she went to collect more cartridges. She changed her strategy again and loaded her shoulder bag with as many cartridges as it would hold. Then she retreated to the bushes and stayed there.

She extended her line again and again. She retreated a long way before she determined that she was far enough away.

She sank onto the ground under the cover of a thick knot of branches and vines. She took a second to just sit there and catch her breath before she did anything else.

She needed a live coal. She didn't need to build a fire. Just one coal would set off the trail.

She picked up her head and looked around. She didn't see any branches here that would be dry enough to rub together to make a coal. She would have to leave this little shelter to find the right combination of sticks and tinder.

She pushed herself off the ground, but she stopped dead when she heard men shouting again. These were definitely not yelling about any attacking Stalkions.

None of these voices belonged to the Godless men or even Kalo's boys. These had to be Renegades—and they were coming straight for her.

She listened just to make absolutely sure she wasn't fooling herself. Then she stuck her head up through the leaves and looked.

She saw the Renegades before they saw her. They strode through the jungle calling instructions to each other and pointing at the ground. They were following the trail of gunpowder straight to her.

She held her breath there for a second—and then the frontmost men looked up and saw her sitting right there less than thirty feet away from them. They yelled even louder to their friends that they found her. She had to get out of here.

She tore out of the thicket, took off running, and hurled herself into the branches. She climbed as never before, but they followed her every step of the way.

The Renegades didn't climb the way the Godless did. The Renegades ran along the ground and pointed up into the branches to tell each other where she was. She had to lose them before she went back and ignited the gunpowder.

She climbed all the way up to the highest canopy, but they could still see her here. She clambered all the way up on top of the tallest trees so the leaves hid her from the ground.

She lay down flat on her stomach and swam across the dense mat of foliage until she got far enough away.

She stayed lying down like that and peeked through. The Renegades kept walking around, pointing up, and trying to spot her, but they concentrated on the place where they lost sight of her.

They didn't recognize the signs of movement in the leaves. They didn't follow her to her new hiding spot.

She collapsed there on her stomach, shut her eyes, and concentrated on just breathing. She would just have to wait until the Renegades left.

It was already starting to get dark. They wouldn't be able to see her, but she wouldn't be able to see, either. She wasn't even sure if she would be able to find her way back to the gunpowder trail.

A million doubts plagued her mind. What if the Renegades did understand it? What if they understood enough to either break the trail or sweep it up to stop her from igniting it?

She would have to go through all of that again—and the Renegades already knew she was out here.

If they did understand the meaning behind the trail, they would already have put the pieces together about what she was trying to do. They would probably post a guard over the ammunition store to stop her from doing it again.

The Renegades knew the Godless were here and attacking the store. The Renegades would be stupid not to post guards on the store now.

She tried to use the time to come up with an alternate strategy to blow up the store. She might have been able to find some artillery at the military installation and shoot a larger shell into the store to blow it up.

That would take too long. It would be much simpler to just wait until daylight, create a live coal, and carry it back to the store—assuming the gunpowder trail was still there.

A screech overhead snapped her back to her senses. She flipped onto her back just in time to see a Ridgebeak drop out of the sky heading straight for her.

The bird didn't start out heading straight for her. She only realized now that she was lying too close to the Ridgebeak's nest.

The bird had been on its way back there. It didn't see her in the gathering darkness until it got close enough. Then it diverted to pounce on her.

She rolled sideways just in time, plummeted through the branches so the canopy would protect her, and crashed down on another branch below her.

She might have fallen all the way down to the jungle floor, but she caught herself just in time and held on for dear life. She didn't dare to let go. She even wrapped her arms around the branch to hold herself up.

The Renegades' voices kept moving around in the jungle at a distance from her. They never came any closer and they never found her.

She stayed like that for what felt like hours. Deep, dense night settled over the jungle. The Renegades wouldn't have been able to see her even if they looked right at her. Their voices eventually faded and they left the area.

She would have stayed in that position all night, but her arms and legs got too tired. She waited until they started to tremble from the effort of holding on so tightly. She couldn't stay here.

She slowly, carefully, painstakingly lowered herself onto the next branch below her, perched on it, and once again allowed herself a few precious moments to gather herself and quiet down.

She was safe here for now. No one knew where she was. The Renegades couldn't find her.

Hangman and the others didn't know where she was, either. They wouldn't come looking for her until morning at the earliest.

She scooted along the branch, found a nook in the main trunk, and settled down for the night, but she couldn't fall asleep.

Night would be the most ideal time to go back to the ammunition store. The Renegades wouldn't be there now. They wouldn't be able to see as well even if they were there and they posted guards right outside the cave mouth.

She wouldn't have to go back to the cave mouth or even enter the clearing. She only had to find the gunpowder trail and follow it to its end—without the Renegades catching her.

She would have to be extra careful and extra quiet. She would have to move slowly—but even that would be quicker than waiting until morning.

The Godless wouldn't be anywhere near the ammunition store before morning, either. Hangman would have withdrawn when he lost track of her. He wouldn't risk his men to come looking for her—unless he did it alone.

Everything about this situation would be better if she blew the store before morning. She couldn't think of any better option than that.

She would also be better able to hide from any Renegades who came after her after the fact. She would be able to blend into the shadowy jungle and maybe even wait until morning before she tried to rejoin Hangman's band.

She experienced one moment of wild panic when she thought about how she would rejoin the rest of the band. How would she find them—even in broad daylight? Hangman might have ordered the band to leave the area.

He would come back for her. He would follow her. He followed her all the way into Renegade territory. He would come back for her here.

She had to keep believing that at all costs even if it wasn't true. She would drive herself crazy if she let herself think like that.

She tried again and again to put her head down and go to sleep, but her mind kept spinning out of control thinking all these thoughts again and again.

She raised her head and stared into the darkness while she thought it all over. She watched jungle creatures moving around in the canopy. Checking to make sure they didn't put her in danger didn't take her mind off all the possible scenarios and courses of action.

In the end, she gave it up and inched toward the ground. She could at least get closer to the gunpowder trail. That would save her some time tomorrow morning.

Her feet touched the ground. She stopped where she was and looked all around her. She took a risk coming down to the ground. She might as well make it pay off.

She was far enough away from the ammunition store here. She could create the live coal without the Renegades seeing or hearing her—or she hoped so.

She would only increase the risk if she waited until she got closer, so she got to work. She gathered sticks, pieces of wood, and tinder by moonlight.

She also spent some time hollowing out a large stick to fashion a small bowl to carry the coal once she made it. She would have to keep it alive until the time came to use it.

Then she got busy sawing one of her sticks into another to create the coal. This didn't take her long. She squinted when the smoke got into her eyes. The end of the stick started to glow and then flared when she blew on it.

She dropped the coal into a bed of tinder and blew on it to make a small flame. It glowed inside the hollowed-out bowl.

She kept the flame small and then blew it out so the coal smoldered in the bottom of the bowl. The coal started to eat into the wood. That would keep it going long enough for her to find the gunpowder trail.

Chapter 38

M ora crept through the jungle from one bush to another, hid in
the dense undergrowth, and kept going, but she never moved
very fast.

She placed each foot or hand extra carefully to make sure she moved
silently each time she moved at all. She never rustled the leaves or
stepped on anything that made any noise.

She hid in the undergrowth each time before she advanced another
few feet. It took her almost all night to get back to the ammunition
store in the cave. She still couldn't even see it, but at least she was
almost there.

She paused at each hiding place to check the live coal in her wooden
bowl. The coal ate further down inside the thick log she used to carry
the coal here.

The bowl got deeper and deeper with every passing hour, but its
depth only worked in Mora's favor to hide the coal from the outside
world.

She looked down into the bowl just long enough to make sure the
coal was still going. Then she strained her ears for any sight or sound
of the Renegades ahead.

Pale grey dawn light streamed through the canopy by the time she
made it back to the ammunition store. She could see everything now,

but only what was right in front of her. The surrounding jungle cut off her line of sight to everything else.

She heard the Renegades well enough. Their voices led her to the cave. She would have been able to find it even if she came here in pitch darkness. They stood guard over the cave. She made out at least seven different men over there.

The only question was whether the gunpowder trail was still there. She didn't see how it possibly could be with seven men standing around. They must have seen it.

She couldn't imagine how she would ever be able to recreate the trail a second time with all those men standing guard. She might not be able to do it at all.

She might have to withdraw and somehow meet up with Hangman and the others. He would have to decide what to do.

She continued her slow, painstaking creep through the jungle, but she skirted to one side and angled her approach around the hill behind the cave.

The sun climbed higher into the trees by the time she worked her way around to the same side where she laid the gunpowder trail.

She found the trail. She had laid it a long way out into the trees—a lot farther than here. Nothing disturbed the trail out here.

The only question was whether the Renegades would have disturbed the trail leading right out of the cave—and the heap of gunpowder directly under the stores themselves. Those would be the more crucial factors in whether the store blew up.

She checked her coal again, tucked the stick bowl into her bag, and climbed into the branches. She had to do everything slowly and take extreme care with every move she made.

She scaled all the way into the canopy and stopped there to make sure the Renegades didn't spot her. Staying hidden and out of sight was more important than blowing the store.

Her childhood experience of hiding and staying hidden paid off. She always knew how to hide and stay hidden. It came naturally to her. Going out into the open and putting herself in dangerous situations—that was the hard part.

She took a long time to work up the courage to advance further toward the cave. She finally snuck beyond the curtain of foliage so she could look down at the cave from above.

She perched in the same branches where Hangman and his men watched her lay the trail in the first place.

The Renegades stood guard and paced back and forth in the clearing, but they didn't walk near the gunpowder trail. In fact, none of them even went near the cave.

They patrolled the clearing at a distance from it. The Renegades paid more attention scanning the surrounding jungle for any sign of another Godless attack.

This vantage point gave her the perfect position to see and hear anything else going on around her in the nearby jungle. More Renegade patrols circled the outer areas searching for Godless who might be out there making a move on the ammunition store.

All the Renegades faced outward toward the surrounding jungle. None of them seemed to consider that a single Godless might be sneaking up on the cave by stealth or that one of them might get this close.

The gunpowder trail was still there. She didn't see any break in the trail at all. That made sense. The Renegades didn't understand gunpowder or firearms well enough to know a person *could* lay a gunpowder trail to blow up the store.

If she was right, the Renegades learned about firearms from captive Followers and other educated Clans. These captives would have explained the firearms and the ammunition.

It probably never occurred to the captives to explain how a gunpowder trail worked. The subject probably never would have come up. The Renegades wouldn't need a gunpowder trail to blow up their own stores.

Mora couldn't think of any other explanation for why the Renegades would leave a heap of exposed gunpowder lying right there underneath their stores with a clear trail of gunpowder leading out of the cave into the jungle.

The Renegades even knew the Godless were nearby and trying to attack the store. The Renegades just didn't put the puzzle pieces together.

She actually felt sorry for them. They couldn't fight this war without all the crucial information they needed. They fought with a glaring disadvantage.

No Followers ever signed up to join the Godless. The Godless only found out about these weapons by sheer chance.

The Godless found out the information they needed to tip the scales. The Godless found out the one critical piece of the puzzle they needed to swing this war in their favor.

They found that out by being kind to the Followers who did join them. The Godless might not be the softest people in the world, but they took Mora in. They protected her, taught her, and made her one of their own.

They made her want to help them in return by telling them what she knew. The man who joined Red's band must have done the same thing. He initiated into their Clan and told them what they needed to know to fight their enemies.

The Renegade captives wouldn't have done that. They wouldn't volunteer anything the Renegades didn't force the captives to tell. The Renegades probably never even thought to learn from their Follower captives.

The Renegades could have been smart and gotten their Follower captives to teach the Renegades to read. That would have been really helpful. Then the Renegades would have been able to read their own maps

Mora shook those thoughts out of her head. She could see the gunpowder trail clearly from here. It lay uninterrupted from the cave to the trees where it disappeared.

She retreated far out of sight before she dared to climb down. She listened for any sign of a patrol coming, but the Renegades' voices made it hard to hear anything else.

She took a long time before she returned to the cave and picked up the gunpowder trail. It looked intact here, too. The Renegades didn't disturb it when they followed it to track her down.

She hardly dared to believe her luck when she followed the trail back toward its farthest end. She went through this whole process slowly, hid plenty of times, checked her coal, and also checked every inch of the trail to make sure nothing broke or disturbed it.

A thousand doubts plagued her on the way. They got worse and more agonizing the closer she came to the end of the trail.

She really wished now that she had made the trail thicker. What if something happened after she ignited the trail? What if it didn't burn all the way to the end and this whole exercise came to nothing?

She followed the trail into another clump of bushes. She bent over the wooden bowl and added a few more pinches of twigs to the coal to keep it alive.

The outside part of the stick was starting to warm up. She needed to drop the coal and ignite the trail pretty soon before the coal ate all the way through the bowl. She could always make a new bowl, but why waste time when she already had this one?

She put it away and scanned the trail ahead to decide where to go and what to do next. That was the moment when she heard movement in the jungle nearby.

She didn't hear any voices, but she definitely heard human footsteps crossing from her left to her right. The patrols must be searching for the Godless.

She froze and cowered in place to hide. She held her breath and stared as five Renegades strode out of the trees.

They crossed from her left to her right, but they paid more atten-tion to the gunpowder trail than any other Renegades she'd seen so far.

They changed their direction when they came near the trail, paced away to follow it deeper into the jungle, and then turned around to walk straight toward her.

The trail disappeared under these bushes. The Renegades didn't see her right away, but they would as soon as they got close enough.

Her mind went into a tailspin. She couldn't run the risk of them capturing her—not without blowing the trail. She came too far and went through too much to get here.

She scrambled to pull the bowl out of her bag again. She fumbled it in her haste and almost dropped it.

Her sudden movement alerted the Renegades. "Hey!!" one of them yelled to his friends. "I found one! It's a female! She's under that bush! There's a Godless over here!"

Chapter 39

The Renegades came running. Mora didn't dare to look up to see what they were doing. She snagged the stick bowl on the edge of her bag, steadied it just in time, and tipped the coal toward the gunpowder trail.

The Renegades charged in to grab her. Two of them burst through the undergrowth and tackled her just as the coal fell out of the bowl.

It dropped toward the gunpowder trail just as both Renegades collided with her. The coal tumbled sideways and lay smoldering there on the ground two feet away.

She screamed and tried to grab it even though she couldn't touch it with her bare hands. The Renegades slammed her down on the ground and knocked the stick bowl out of her hands, but she didn't need it anymore.

She kicked and thrashed under the weight of the first two men. Then another two showed up to help their friends subdue her. She screamed, roared, and fought with all her might, but she couldn't free herself. She couldn't even see the coal from here.

They pinned her face down and one of them threw a length of rope around her wrists to restrain her.

"Tie her legs up, too, Abuno!" one of them yelled over the noise.

"We can't!" his friend called. "We have to walk her back to the cave."

"Forget it," a third chimed in. "She's small enough to carry and we can't risk her escaping."

That decided it. The men flipped her onto her back. One of them turned aside to grab some vines from the nearby undergrowth. The others straightened up to look down at her.

She floundered to sit up, but she didn't dare to run for it with all these much bigger men around. They would catch her before she even got to her feet.

She glanced around in panicked desperation and spotted the coal. It lay to one side still smoldering away. How long would it last outside the bowl?

The Renegades didn't see it, or if they did, they didn't understand why she needed it. They stood in a ring around her glaring down at her.

That one guy came back with his vines and bent over to lash them around her ankles. She couldn't let him do that. She had to get to that coal and ignite the gunpowder trail. Nothing else mattered.

She kicked out at the guy and even tried to kick him in the face. He reared back to get out of range. Two other men moved in to hold her legs down, but right then, another five Renegades showed up.

These men didn't belong to one of the outer perimeter patrols. These men had been standing guard over the cave until just a few minutes ago.

"What's going on here?" One of the men narrowed his eyes at Mora. "Where are the Godless warriors who attacked us yesterday?"

She curled her lip at him and bared her teeth. "I don't know what you're talking about," she snarled.

"You must have traveled here with them. A woman wouldn't be out here alone. You must belong to the same band. You may as well tell us where they are. We'll only hold you as a captive until they come to save you. Then we'll find the band anyway."

"I don't know where they are, okay?" she snapped. "I would be with them now if I knew where they were."

"Why did you come with them?" he demanded. "Why did the Godless bring one of their women on a war party like this?"

"Do you think I wanted to come?!" she fired back. "I hate you!"

She looked away in the other direction. She really didn't want him asking her these questions. She didn't trust herself not to give something away.

He snorted, looked away, too, and waved to his men. "Bring her back to the cave. The Godless will come looking for her. They won't be able to leave one of their women behind. They'll come inside our patrols and we'll kill them then. Let's go."

Two of his men moved in to take hold of Mora's arms. The third man bent over her feet to tie up her ankles. She saw herself about to become a captive again. Anything would be better than that.

She kicked out and struggled a lot harder this time. The man with the vine had to move his head out of the way of her kicks, but he didn't back off a second time.

More Renegades closed around her to hold her down and subdue her. She couldn't fight this many. She wouldn't have been able to fight them even if she somehow got her hands free.

They overpowered her, turned her onto her stomach, and held her down. Two others leaned on her legs to stop her from kicking so the third man could bind her ankles.

A crash and a roar interrupted the operation. She didn't know what caused that sound until she turned her head and saw five Godless men attacking the Renegades from one side.

All these men belonged to Red's band. They overran the Renegades in seconds—and then Viking and Alien materialized out of nowhere from the opposite line of undergrowth.

The sudden attack made all the Renegades spring away from Mora. She didn't see Hangman anywhere, but she couldn't waste time looking for him.

She floundered onto her knees, fell over, and flip-flopped across the ground toward the coal. She made it halfway there before two combatants fell on top of her from somewhere.

She didn't even see who they were. They slammed her down on the ground and rolled off before she saw that one of the combatants was Prodigy.

He grappled tooth and nail with a Renegade man as big and strong as himself. Prodigy got the upper hand. Then the Renegade flipped him and slammed Prodigy onto his back before he reversed their positions and overcame his enemy.

Prodigy seized his opponent by the shirt, lifted him off the ground, and slammed him down hard.

The Renegade stabbed out at Prodigy with a large blade. Prodigy seized the man's wrist and pinned that down, too, but neither of the men could overpower the other completely.

Prodigy had to keep one hand on his opponent's wrist to control that weapon. Mora saw her chance and kicked out.

She knocked the weapon out of the guy's hand and then blundered over there to pick it up herself.

She had to turn backward and lie all the way down onto her back so she could get her hands on the weapon. The battle raged all around her, but she couldn't do anything without her hands.

She swiveled the blade around and started sawing her way through the ropes binding her wrists. The process took way too long.

The Godless and Renegades hacked, slashed, wrestled, and stabbed each other all over the place. Some of them tripped over her and a few Renegades even tried to attack her before the Godless intervened and saved her life.

Lying like this on her back gave her a clear view of the battle. Hangman wasn't here. Did the Renegades kill him yesterday? She couldn't think of any other reason why he wouldn't come to rescue her.

The coal. She had to get the coal and ignite the gunpowder trail. She didn't even know if it would work.

The rope separated and she scrambled onto her knees. She didn't take the time to get to her feet. She scuttled across the bare ground and used the blade to scoop up the coal. She had to balance it there so she wouldn't drop it.

She hustled back between more deadly fights to carry the coal to the powder trail, but at that moment, another three combatants crashed into her from behind.

They toppled her and the coal went flying again. She landed hard and then had to whip over onto her back when one of the Renegades attacked her.

He raised two blades to hack her to pieces. This one small weapon in her hand wouldn't help her.

She rolled out of the way just in time. His blades stuck in the dirt, but he came after her in seconds. She pushed herself onto her hands and knees to run for it. She didn't see the coal anywhere.

She glanced behind her in time to see the same guy raising both his blades for a second attack, but Viking charged in and saved Mora at the last second. The guy didn't see Viking until it was too late. The Renegade fixed his furious eyes on Mora alone.

Viking swung his axe upward, smashed it against the guy's blades just as the Renegade brought them down for the killing stroke, and drove the Renegade away from Mora.

She sprang up on her hands and knees searching everywhere for the coal and spotted it under some bushes. She no longer trusted using her blade to pick it up. She couldn't waste any more time trying to find another way to carry it.

More Renegades converged on the battle from every direction—or it sure looked that way.

She lunged for the coal, and in her last act of desperation, she grabbed it with her bare hand. She screamed when it burned her, but panic and hopeless despair drove her past her limit.

Some of the incoming Renegades saw her. They diverted from the main battle to come after her instead. It was now or never.

She dove sideways just as they caught hold of her. They slammed her down on the ground under their weight again, but this time, they knocked her down within arm's reach of the powder trail.

She bellowed in wordless rage and pain. The coal seared her hand beyond endurance, but she held on just long enough to slam the coal down right on top of the powder trail.

She pressed the coal into it with all her strength even as the Renegades grappled to gain control of her arm. They pulled her away like they wanted to tie her wrists together again.

The powder ignited under her hand. Sparks flared and she screamed again when the heat scorched around her hand, but the Renegades pulled her hand away before the powder could burn her any worse.

It was too late. The powder flared and sparks and tiny licks of fire spluttered and fizzed down the trail heading toward the ammunition store.

Enraged yells and bellows echoed all around her. She couldn't even tell what was happening with the battle anymore. The Renegades seized her by the arms and yanked her off the ground. She barely paid attention.

The sparks traveled over the trail and vanished into the trees. She lost sight of it. She would probably never find out if it worked or not.

The Renegades jerked her almost off her feet to pull her away from the battle. More Godless rushed in. They were all Red's men. They attacked the Renegades who captured Mora and another battle broke out right there on top of her.

She cradled her injured hand and cowered behind armed fighting men on both sides. She could have drawn one of her blades to join the battle, but she could barely tell one side from the other.

The men jostled and bumped her in their fury to attack each other. She went down on one knee with armed Renegades and Godless hacking, slashing, and killing each other all around her.

More Renegades came after her. They might not be trying to kill her. They might just have been trying to stop the Godless from retaking her.

She only saw armed men standing over her with their weapons raised the same way that other Renegade tried to kill her. She shrank from them and her left hand moved toward her blade.

At that moment, something dropped out of the canopy moving too fast to see. It rocketed out of nowhere, plunged into the battle, and snatched Mora away.

An impossible force yanked her straight up off her feet and sailed away with her into the high trees.

She barely noticed anything else before Hangman grabbed her around the waist and took off running through the branches somewhere far away from here.

He barely made it a dozen yards before a catastrophic boom went off somewhere in the distance. The hillside behind the battle detonated in a massive earthquake that ruptured the jungle for miles around.

The shockwave uprooted trees and sent a wave of destruction through the surrounding jungle. The impact threw Hangman off balance.

Mora screamed again when they both fell off their branches and plummeted through the trees toward the ground.

She instinctively threw her arms around his neck for dear life, but he caught his balance and took off running again to put more distance between him and the explosion.

Chapter 40

Hangman balanced in the branches with one arm. He kept the other wrapped around Mora's waist.

She clung to his neck so tightly that she choked him, but he didn't tell her to loosen her grip. He didn't want her to.

He hardly dared to believe that she actually did it. She blew up the Renegade Clan's ammunition store.

He didn't let himself believe last night that she would do it or that he would get her back, but he did. He couldn't let her go again. She was too valuable.

He kept going for another few miles before he let himself stop. He lowered her into the crook of some branches, but she wouldn't let go of his neck.

She hung onto him shaking like a leaf. She panted and gasped and moaned in his ear.

He patted her on the back and even stroked her hair. "It's all right," he murmured. "You're all right. You did it. It's over." He had to use force to pry her arms off. "Let me see your hand."

She wouldn't stop shaking when she sank back into the hollow. Her features spasmed all over the place. She looked awful, but at least she wasn't crying.

Her body quaked and she sat hunched over clutching her hand close to her stomach. He had to pull and twist her wrist to make her hold out her hand.

The burn covered all of her palm and the inside surface of her fingers. Blisters surrounded her hand and curled up onto the back of her knuckles.

"It isn't as bad as I thought it would be." He kept his hold on her wrist while he pulled the leaf paste out of his bag.

She barely looked at him when he spread the paste on the burn. He needed to cover it up with something, but he didn't have anything.

Then he remembered the cloth bandages she took from the captive women's clothing. She still carried a supply of the bandages in her bag.

He had to force her to hold her hand out while he dug into her bag, pulled out the bandages, and wrapped them around her hand.

He kept catching her eye while he did it. She flinched each time she looked at him—not in pain at him handling her injury, but from the strain of everything she must have gone through last night.

He decided not to say anything to her about it or ask her what happened. It didn't matter because she accomplished their objective. She destroyed the ammunition store.

He finally tucked in the bandage. She immediately pulled her hand back, hid it behind her other arm, and cowered there squirming and trembling with buried agitation.

He couldn't stand to see her like this—not at the moment of her greatest victory so far. He stroked his fingertips down the side of her hair, but she hardly recognized that he was sitting here in front of her.

"I'm going to take you back to the women and children," he murmured. "Kalo and the boys are there. They'll defend you. You can rest while I go out and find the other men. They'll be out here in the jungle somewhere. Will you be okay there?"

She nodded in wordless shock. How much of what he said even penetrated her head?

"Come here," he murmured and pulled her toward him.

He steered her arms around his neck so he would be able to carry her through the canopy, but this also gave him a perfect opportunity to put his arms around her and comfort her.

He would have offered her food and water if he thought she could wake up enough to eat and drink. He held her for a minute and let her tremble and gasp in his arms to help her calm down.

She fell apart even more when she tightened her hold on him. She huddled in his arms and buried her face in his neck so she could quake and whimper as much as she needed to.

He waited. He could wait all day and maybe even all night if he had to. She needed protection and care right now. He was too proud of her to rush her. She deserved a lot more than this for her accomplishment, but it almost meant more to say nothing.

She made it. She survived it. Now he had to take her home—wherever that was.

He didn't make her loosen her arms from his neck. He stood up with her still clutching at him, wrapped his arm around her waist, and picked her up.

He set off through the canopy, but he didn't travel as quickly as he could have. He didn't want to rush the moment when he got her back to the band and then had to leave again.

That moment eventually came. He slowed when he spotted the women and children ahead. Kalo and the boys stood or perched fully armed on their branches. The boys straightened up when they saw someone approaching.

Cross, Red, and Red's men all made it back, too. Viking and Alien weren't here. They must still be out there somewhere. They might be injured or even dead. Hangman had to find out.

The men didn't slacken their posture when they saw who was coming. They surrounded Hangman, shot death glares out at the jungle, and closed around him while he lowered Mora onto the branches with the other women.

He didn't stop himself from petting her cheeks and combing his fingers through her hair one last time. "Stay here. The women will give you something to eat and water to drink. Try to rest. I have to go back out. I'll see you when I come back. Okay?"

She didn't look up at all when she nodded down at her injured hand. He kissed her on the forehead, petted her hair one last time, and straightened up. All the men, women, and children stood around staring at her. No one made a sound.

Hangman made eye contact with Kalo and most of Red's men. They would protect Mora until Hangman came back.

He couldn't wait any longer, so he took off into the trees following the same route as before. He didn't know where to go to find Viking and Alien. He didn't see what happened to them when the ammunition store blew up.

He slowed when he got near the spot. The landscape didn't look the same. He didn't see the hillside at all.

He had to use landmarks in the treetops until he made it all the way back there. He found Viking and Alien sitting next to each other in the trees near where the ammunition store used to be—in the last remaining trees that were still intact.

Hangman settled down next to his cousins and looked down at the flattened hillside. The blast had leveled all the trees for five hundred yards in every direction.

A huge, flat, perfectly round circle surrounded where the hillside used to be. The trees had crushed a dozen Renegade bodies under their weight when the trees toppled.

"Are any Renegades still alive?" Hangman finally asked.

"They're alive, but they aren't alive in this area," Alien told him. "They all evacuated the area when they realized the ammunition was gone."

"How's your wife?" Viking asked.

Hangman nodded down at the ground. He didn't look up to make eye contact with his cousins. "She's fine. She burned her hand, but that's all—and she's in shock. She's exhausted and emotional, but she'll recover."

"She's a good woman," Alien remarked. "You got a good one there."

Hangman didn't look up nor did he respond. Never in a million years would he have suspected Mora would be capable of accomplishing something like this—especially not considering everything that happened to her this morning.

She got captured and attacked by Renegades—and she still pulled it off. She might have permanently injured her hand, but she did it anyway. She did it for the Clan.

That made her Godless if anything did. She did more for the Clan than some Godless men Hangman could name.

"Why are you waiting here if there are no more Renegades around?" he finally asked his cousins.

"I don't know," Alien murmured. "It seemed like someone should wait here and keep watch—just to see it."

"Did the others make it back?" Viking asked. "I thought we should stay in case someone got lost and came back here to find us."

"They're all back at the camp," Hangman replied. "You two are the only two still out here."

"And you," Alien pointed out.

"I came to find you two." Hangman stood up. "Come on. We should withdraw to our own country now."

His cousins followed him back to the camp, but the three men traveled slowly.

Hangman had to think about where to go and what to do after this. He had spent so much time and mental energy just getting here. Now he had to change his strategy.

He returned to the camp in the trees by sunset. No one went down to the ground. The band gathered in the treetops.

Hangman sat down next to Mora. She sat with her knees drawn up to her chest and her head resting on her arms. She didn't look up when people started talking.

"You men should go back to your own band," Hangman told Red. "We accomplished what we set out to accomplish."

Red glanced around at the women and children listening. "We would rather stay with you if you don't mind."

Hangman shrugged. "It's up to you. You could take your wives home with you."

"We'll stay with you," Red repeated. "This is a good band and you're a good Kral. We would survive better by fighting with you. We have a better chance of getting out of Renegade territory and returning to our own country where we can live with other Godless."

Hangman looked away. "It's up to you if you stay or go."

"Then we'll stay. You're a good Kral."

"Do you need to consult the maps to find out where to go?" Viking asked.

"I don't think so," Hangman replied. "We should be able to get back to Godless country by heading straight east from here and then north to rendezvous with Shadow's band." He glanced at Mora, but she still didn't look up. "We'll start by heading east. Mora can check the maps for us when she's ready."

"We traveled farther south than we were before," Alien pointed out. "We should cross those mountains somewhere in her home Clan's territory. She probably knows that country well enough to take us home."

"Shadow's band won't be in the same country," Cross chimed in. "He said he would evacuate the band. He won't stay there when the Renegades already threatened the long camp."

"Then we'll retreat farther east," Hangman decided. "We'll leave Renegade country either way. We can't stay here and the quickest way to leave it is by striking out due east."

The conversation ended there. The women handed out what was left of the party's food supplies.

Hangman tried not to notice the single men and women getting closer to each other. Cheina and Alien no longer made any effort to hide their relationship. Red and his men paired off with different women. That didn't take long at all.

Hangman gave up pretending it wasn't happening. What difference did it make in the end? Men and women pairing off was only natural. None of these people were young enough to attend the gathering a second time if they ever attended in the first place.

He did keep an eye on Kalo and the boys. They and Cross talked to their girls, but Hangman didn't see any of them doing anything inappropriate.

All of them kept it civil and respectful. Each couple sat together, ate together, and some of them held hands. That was all.

They would have been allowed to kiss, but they didn't. They spent the evening together and then separated when the time came to go to sleep. None of those young couples left together. They stayed in plain view of everyone else.

Mora kept her head down all evening. Hangman had to fight the urge to put his arms around her and get close to her.

She only roused once, shook back her hair, and squinted at everyone settling down to sleep. She scooted along the branch, curled up in the crook of the trunk, and buried her head in her arms before she passed out again.

Hangman watched her and gave it up. She needed rest more than anything. He wouldn't disturb that.

Thinking about her kept him awake for a long time. He didn't regret taking her advice and letting her give him direction on how to carry out this mission. He wouldn't regret consulting her about getting back to Godless country, either.

He did regret putting her in danger. He shouldn't have let her do all of that last night. He should have done it himself. He might not have been able to, but at least she would have been safe. She wouldn't be nursing an injured hand right now.

He couldn't make up his mind if blowing the ammunition store had been worth the effort that went into the project, but it definitely wasn't worth her safety. He had to be more careful with her in the future. She was carrying his child. He had to protect both of them.

He might not get another chance like this. The next time might be something much more serious than burning her hand. She might lose the child and never be able to have another one—or he might lose her along with the child.

Nothing was worth that. He wouldn't be any kind of husband if he let that happen.

Chapter 41

M ora crouched in the bushes to hide. All the members of Hangman's band hid in bushes up and down the line of hills on her right and left.

No one showed themselves. No one had to show any part of themselves. Everyone could see a large crowd of Renegade warriors passing the hills in front of the party.

These hills led up into the mountains to the east. Thomion's maps revealed that this was a different mountain range than the Jagged Points that bordered Shadow's territory.

Hangman's band had traveled a lot farther south than any of them realized. The map called these mountains the Kettle Range. Mora recognized them on the map.

The Followers called them the Gorlock's Spine because the line of ridgetops arched in a downward curve like a Gorlock's spine.

None of the Godless could get near the mountains with all these Renegades blocking the way. Hundreds of them marched past. Their own single-minded determination stopped them from seeing the Godless hiding so close to the Renegades' route.

They all headed north. None of them turned aside to go back toward the military installation.

None of the Godless got out of their hiding places even to retreat. The Renegades would attack if they realized so many Godless were within weapons range of attacking the Renegades first.

The party hid in breathless silence for more than two hours until the last Renegades passed by. They kept marching north and filed out of sight around the nearest hills.

Hangman waited even longer before he signaled the party to advance. All the men kept their weapons up, out, and ready and every nerve alert on the way up the hill.

Red and his men waited for their women and children to advance before the men escorted their new families up the hill.

The party had been traveling for over a week to get to these hills. The party still wasn't even close to crossing the Gorlock's Spine.

Red's men had settled into the band. Everyone treated the new couples as the old couples now. Hangman didn't have to reprimand any of the young people for their behavior. Everyone behaved themselves perfectly.

Mora took extra long to stand up. Her pregnancy still hadn't advanced far enough to interfere with her movements, but she felt a lot bigger and heavier than she should have.

She had to be careful about moving and she couldn't do anything quickly. Being pregnant sapped her strength and energy. She never would have been able to blow up the ammunition store now.

She didn't think a week would make that much difference, but it did. Her nausea went away and this heaviness took its place.

She had to stop there and help some of the younger children get out of the bushes. Cheina and four other women who married Red's men were also showing signs of pregnancy, but it was too early for anyone to be certain.

Mora tried to help the other women with her children, but she found it more and more difficult with every passing day to do anything.

Hangman hung back to help her. She finally straightened up, pushed the children in front of her, and advanced up the hill to follow the others.

The hills leading up to the Gorlock's Spine turned out to be taller, steeper, and more treacherous than she realized. The hills weren't low swells the party could cross easily. It would take days just to cross these hills. Then the party had to cross the mountains themselves.

Mora didn't let herself think about how she would cross the Gorlock's Spine. She would lose her nerve if she thought that. She just had to keep going as well as she could. At least she wasn't the only woman slowing the party down.

The men took extra pains to protect and help all the women and children, even the women and children who weren't theirs. The band became more cohesive by the day, but that didn't make the journey any easier.

Mora got winded within a few minutes of climbing the hills. She couldn't help anyone. She had to stop every few steps, prop her hands on her knees, and catch her breath.

Other women stopped with her. Kalo and the boys forged ahead with the women and children who could move faster.

Viking, Alien, Hangman, and half of Red's men stayed behind to stand guard over Mora and the other women.

Mora tried again and again to get moving, but she only made it a few dozen yards before she had to stop again.

Some of the younger children hung back to stay near their mothers. No one argued or told these children to move on. Kalo and the others passed beyond the first hilltop and vanished down the other side.

The sight of the rest of the band getting farther away made Mora stand up. She really wished she could push herself harder. What would Katha say if she saw Mora now?

Mora already knew what Katha would say. Katha would probably say that the same thing happened to her when she was pregnant with Hangman—or something equally encouraging.

Knowing that didn't make Mora feel better. She put her arm around a little boy near her to steer him up the hill.

She startled when all the men raised their weapons and sprang together on the left side of the group. Mora spun around and her stomach dropped when another group of Renegades came over the hills from the south.

They came from the same place and headed in the same direction as all the other Renegades the Godless had been trying to avoid. These men must have gotten delayed and separated from the others.

"Get out of here!" Alien snapped over his shoulder. "Get over those hills—NOW!!"

Mora and Cheina charged forward. The other women tried to follow. They started out by running, but the women only lasted a few seconds before most of them had to slow down and walk.

Mora staggered up the hill pushing three children in front of her. They could run just fine, but they always slowed down to wait for their mothers.

The men stayed behind and turned in one body to confront the Renegades. The Renegades recognized immediately what they were seeing and started forward to intercept the party.

Mora hardly dared to look over her shoulder. She didn't want to see. She tried again and again to get the others moving faster—and to get herself moving faster. If the Renegades overcame the men.....

A clash of metal clanged across the countryside behind her. She made the mistake of glancing behind her, saw the men locked in battle against the Renegades, and took off running as fast as she could up the hill.

Her lungs burned and her legs gave out at almost every step. Some of the other women leaned on their children for support.

Lonion practically dragged Cheina up the hill. His face spasmed in panic and he cried out in terror every time he took a step, but he kept going.

The women drifted too slowly to the top of the hill. The sounds of battle escalated. Blood-curdling roars split through the air behind the women. Mora didn't give herself the option to look back a second time.

She nearly collapsed at the top and collided full tilt with Kalo coming up from the other side. Mora didn't see any of the other women or children.

"What's happening?!" he bellowed in her face.

She couldn't breathe well enough to say a word. She waved behind her.

He shot a terrible glance down the hill and took off running to join up with the other men. All his boys ran after him.

They left Mora and the other women to go on alone. They staggered down the hill and joined up with the rest of the band in a gulley at the bottom.

All the women and children had scrambled into the treetops for protection, but nothing could protect them from the sounds of battle coming from the other side of the hills.

Mora stopped under the canopy. She couldn't climb up there. She didn't even want to try.

"We can't stay here!" she called up. "The Renegades know we came this way. We have to keep going. Come on down."

She only waited long enough for the women and children to climb down from their hiding place. None of the men remained. She motioned everyone to keep climbing and then had an idea. The band could move faster by following the gulley.

The Renegades would expect the Godless to keep traveling east—to cross the Gorlock's Spine to Godless country on the other side.

None of the other women questioned when Mora headed up the gulley and around multiple corners. Her strategy worked. She and the pregnant women could travel faster this way with fewer stops and stumbles.

No one talked. The gulley entered a thicker, denser jungle than the band traveled through before. The trees offered more cover here.

She kept going until the sun started to set. The lighter day of traveling gave the women enough energy to climb up into the branches and hide themselves in the dense undergrowth.

"How much food do we have left?" she asked once everyone settled down with something to eat.

"Probably enough for one more day," Hicia replied. "Someone will have to go hunting soon."

"I'll go," Lonion offered. "I can move faster than any of you."

"We'll need to hunt something bigger than you can kill yourself," Mora pointed out. "We should all go."

"How will we do that?" Aliva asked. "We can't hunt well enough to kill something that big."

"We'll set up an ambush," Mora replied. "That's the way we did it in the Followers."

"We aren't Followers," Lonion cut in. "We're Godless."

"We'll be dead if we don't kill something to feed ourselves," Mora pointed out. "We'll also be dead if we try to fight something too big or too strong for us. Would you rather be Godless and dead or a Follower and alive?"

The boy looked away. Mora prepared herself to deal with more protests, but the sound of footsteps coming through the jungle cut off the conversation.

The party fell silent until they saw the men staggering down the gulley. Hangman supported Viking on his shoulder. Blood flowed from a deep cut across the side of Viking's face. He held one bloody arm across his stomach and he barely held up his own weight on both blood-stained legs.

Red and his men half-dragged, half-carried their wounded comrades down the gulley. Hangman looked up, made one moment of eye contact with Mora, and lowered Viking to the ground at the base of the trees.

The others stopped there and put their wounded down, too. Rapid and Legend got busy building a fire.

Hangman leapt up into the trees and swung himself all the way to the top canopy where the women watched in horror. "Where's Kalo?!" Cheina blurted out. "Where are the rest of the boys?"

"They went hunting." Hangman looked around at the women and children sheltering in the branches. "This is as good a place as any for us to make camp. All of you stay up here. Don't risk yourselves by going down to the ground. We'll stay down there and take care of our injured brothers. All of you stay up here. Do you have enough food?"

"For now," Mora replied.

He nodded. "The boys will bring back enough for the next part of our journey."

Mora opened her mouth to suggest that the band not travel straight east to cross the Gorlock's Spine, but she stopped herself from saying anything. The band wouldn't be going anywhere until the injured men got better.

Hangman waited for her to say something. She shut her mouth and shook her head. She would just have to tell him later.

He climbed down and got to work cleaning up Viking's wounds. Hangman and the others went from man to man applying leaf paste, grinding more of it, and preparing the fire to make Gooji juice.

Mora and the women settled down for the night. The fire blazed down there on the ground. The light didn't make it this far into the canopy.

The men were still working on their friends when Mora's exhaustion overcame her. She curled up in the branches and went to sleep.

Chapter 42

Hangman and Alien worked together to heave Viking into a sitting position. Alien supported Viking's head while Hangman used a stick to pry his cousin's mouth open and dumped a dose of Gooji juice down Viking's throat.

Viking woke up enough to swallow it before he collapsed again.

Hangman returned to the fire, got a second basin of juice, and he and Alien went around the circle dosing all the other injured men with Gooji juice, too.

The two cousins worked until they ran out of juice. They gave the more seriously injured more than one dose before the two cousins used up all their available juice.

"You should get some sleep," Alien told Hangman when the two men sat down by the fire again. They were the last two awake.

"*You* should get some sleep," Hangman returned. "You've been working as hard as I have."

"We have some more Gooji sap," Alien pointed out. "We should make a few more batches for when the men wake up."

Hangman nodded. "I can do that while you're asleep."

Alien made a face. "I can do it while *you're* asleep."

"How about I make juice from half the sap and you make juice from the other half of the sap?"

Alien burst out laughing. "But which of us will go to sleep first?"

"Neither," Hangman replied. "We'll make the juice first. Then we'll sleep while it cools."

Alien snorted. "I think it would be better if we had a contest to see who could go the longest before he passes out from exhaustion."

"I think it would be better if we *didn't* have a contest to see who could go the longest before he passes out from exhaustion. I think it would be better if we made the remaining sap into juice and then we both went to sleep at the same time. Then neither of us could declare himself the winner."

Alien beamed at him. "You're the Kral. I have to do it your way."

Hangman rolled his eyes to heaven. "Please, brother. I'll never be your Kral."

Alien's smile evaporated. "You've always been my Kral, little brother, even when Butcher was alive. Didn't you know that?"

Hangman looked away. He didn't want to think about that—mainly because he already knew it was true. Men like Viking and Alien always treated Hangman as their Kral.

Hangman picked up the stones he and Alien used to boil water to make the juice. He used two sticks to lower the stones into the coals.

Hangman cast one look around the group of sleeping men. Some of Red's men made it back uninjured from the battle against the Renegades.

These few uninjured men would guard their wounded comrades for a few minutes until Hangman and Alien came back.

Hangman took a few extra seconds to check on Viking. He fought harder and suffered more injuries than anyone else. Hangman still didn't know if Viking would make it.

"Grab your basin and let's get the water." Hangman picked up his basin and he and Alien set off up the gulley. They found a trickle of water coming out of the hillside. Hangman filled his basin first and waited for Alien to fill his.

"Now I understand why Butcher and Shadow stayed in the long camp for so long," Alien remarked on their way back. "Traveling with women and children is a lot more dangerous and complicated than it seems."

"I don't know about that," Hangman replied. "It has some advantages."

"Like what? They can't run or hide or climb or fight the way they used to. The stakes are higher—now that so many of our men are married and our women are pregnant."

"The Renegades aren't looking for us here," Hangman pointed out. "They don't know we're here at all—not after we killed those men who saw us. We're better hidden here. The Renegades spent months planning that assault on the long camp. They never would have been able to ambush us if we lived wild in the jungle. Take this band here for example. The Renegades would never be able to wage a campaign like that against us. We never stay in one place for very long. It will take the Renegades a lot longer to find us, and when they do, we will have already moved on. I think this is a better way to live."

Alien shrugged. "You may be right, but I don't like to see Cheina in danger. Having a wife makes life and danger mean something different."

Hangman nodded. "I understand and I agree with you, but think about it, brother. The Godless must have started this way. We started out as wandering bands fighting for survival. We never stayed in one place for long. It's our natural state. The long camp is the lazy man's way. It might be easier for women and children, but it also puts them in more danger. Everyone knows they're there. Anyone or anything that wants to kill them can always go and find them there in the same place." He looked away and shook his head. "I like this way better."

"That's because you're you," Alien pointed out. "You always want to travel faster and stay less in one place. That's you. You would get Mora and your children to live like that if you could possibly convince them."

Hangman laughed. "You got me there. You're right. I'll always want to move around."

The two cousins returned to their comrades, put their basins next to the fire, and Hangman sprinkled half the Gooji dust into his hand and half into Alien's hand.

The two cousins narrowed their eyes at each other and then laughed as they both sprinkled the sap into the water at exactly the same time.

Hangman lifted his heated rock out of the coals, lowered it into the water to bring it to a boil, and handed over the sticks. Alien laughed when he took them and used them to lift out the second rock.

The two cousins couldn't stop laughing at the joke when they both stretched out on the ground at the same time. They faced each other and laughed again when neither of them went to sleep.

"Go to sleep, Alien," Hangman ordered.

"*You* go to sleep," Alien fired back and they both laughed.

"Shut your eyes on the count of three and don't open them again," Hangman told him.

"Okay," Alien agreed.

"One......two......three."

Both cousins closed their eyes and laughed. Hangman waited for a second before he opened his eyes to make sure Alien wasn't cheating.

Alien opened his eyes at the same time and both men laughed before they both shut their eyes again.

Hangman didn't open his eyes again, not even when he heard Alien laughing. Hangman didn't rise to the bait of checking if Alien was checking on him.

Hangman fell asleep pretty soon. He woke up when he heard someone cough near his head. He pried his head off the ground and saw Viking sitting up.

"You should rest, brother," Hangman rasped.

"You need it more than I do," Viking croaked. "I'm okay."

"Drink some more Gooji juice. You need it."

"I already did. I just sat up to change my position. I'll lie down again soon."

Hangman sat up and examined all of Viking's wounds. The gash on his face had swollen up.

"How bad is it?" Viking growled. "Tell the truth."

"It's no worse than your other scar. Don't worry. Your wife will still love you."

Viking looked away. "I wasn't worried about that."

Their conversation woke up Alien. He sat up and scowled at Viking. "Shouldn't you be resting?"

Viking only grunted at him. "It looks like you and Hangman need more rest than I do."

The others woke up around then. The wounded sat or propped themselves up. Some drank some more Gooji juice before they lay back down. Then Viking lay down, so that settled that.

Kalo and the boys returned a few hours later. They had been out all night.

They delivered a massive load of freshly cooked Stalkion meat to Hangman and the men on the ground. Then Hitro and Ethio climbed up into the canopy to give the women and children an equally large portion of freshly cooked meat for them to share.

The boys departed immediately without explaining themselves to anyone. They must have been curing the rest of the meat at a distance from the band to protect everyone from discovery.

Their behavior gave Hangman too many ideas. He left his men lounging on the ground, climbed up into the canopy, and went back out to the hills flanking the taller eastern mountains. Mora called them the Gorlock's Spine. It was as good a name as any.

He stayed in the branches and observed more and more Renegades all traveling north along the same line. His band made it past them. He and the other men killed all the Renegades who saw the Godless crossing that line of hills.

None of these remaining Renegades diverted or came after Hangman's band. None of the Renegades knew Hangman's band was here.

He watched them for a long time, but watching them didn't put his mind at rest. Where were they going in such numbers? Wherever it was must be somewhere pretty important.

All the territory Hangman and his companions worked so hard to cover—it all lay to the north. Renegade country lay to the north.

Hundreds of fighting men must have passed that way before and after the Godless fought their way through. All those Renegades traveled in the same direction.

They must have all been traveling to the same place for the same purpose. The Renegade force might number in the thousands once they all got there. No other Clan gathered in such numbers. One territory couldn't support so many people.

A population that size would attract too many creature attacks. The other Clans lived in small bands to stay hidden and mobile to avoid training the creatures to hunt from that one location.

All the Clans did it that way. This was the reason all the Clans developed the gatherings—so the small family bands could marry their young people to each other without anyone encroaching on anyone else's territory.

That many Renegades assembled in one place might offer advantages when it came to attacking and invading another Clan's territory.

That many Renegades assembled in one place also might offer significant disadvantages—disadvantages strong enough to make a force that size an absolutely terrible idea.

Hangman could think of a few terrible outcomes that would eventuate from the assembly of such a force.

For a start, a force that size couldn't travel through any stretch of jungle without attracting attention. Krakelows would attack a force that size.

The men wouldn't be able to escape from the Krakelow. Too many other men would block anyone from escaping in any direction.

The sound of Krakelows attacking would attract more Krakelows, Abnormits, ants, Coffincreep, Demonex, and a whole lot of other creatures.

A smaller band could escape or evade a Krakelow. A smaller band could run far enough away into the jungle to avoid getting caught by the same Krakelow or others drawn to the same spot by the noise.

The human race didn't develop these practices over thousands of years for no reason. No territory on the planet was worth assembling a force that size—not unless the people in charge actually wanted to sacrifice hundreds of men along the way.

Maybe the Renegade leaders didn't care how many men they sacrificed. Maybe the Renegade leaders thought the cost of attrition would make it worth the benefit of taking that many armed men into a neighboring Clan's territory.

The nearest neighboring territory belonged to the Godless, but the Renegades invaded and conquered territory with forces much smaller than this. Did the Renegades plan to attack someone else this time? Who would it be?

Hangman couldn't think of anyone else nearby—except the Followers. They didn't pose a threat to the Renegades. The Followers never fought anyone. The Renegades could have just moved into Follower country and taken over without ever drawing a weapon.

The Followers would either leave or they would become captive slaves like these women. The Renegades didn't need such a large force for that.

Maybe another Clan Hangman didn't know about lived on the other side of Renegade country to the west. Maybe that Clan did pose a threat to the Renegades—or maybe the other Clan could defend itself well enough that the Renegades needed this force to take the country.

So why did the Renegades assemble the force on the eastern side of their territory—as far away as possible from this hypothetical Clan?

None of this made any sense—unless the Renegades planned to carry out a mass invasion of Godless country, wipe out all Godless, and start living in that country themselves.

That explanation made more sense than any other that Hangman could think of. He thought it over on his way back to the band.

He really needed to get his people moving, but that didn't look very likely to happen with so many of his men still injured.

Alien was right. Traveling with pregnant women and children slowed the whole band down. The long camp did offer some advantages.

The women and children stayed there, far behind the Clan's territorial boundary, while the men went out in fast-moving hunting, scouting, and war parties.

He didn't have that option. He would just have to come up with a different strategy—at least until he got these people back behind Godless lines and established somewhere safe—wherever that was.

Chapter 43

M ora shifted her position on the hilltop. Lying on her stomach made her uncomfortable. She had to roll sideways onto her hip to take the pressure off her stomach.

Hangman lay next to her. The rest of their band spread out down the hilltop on either side of her. The Godless looked down the hill toward the valley that separated these lower hills from the steep Gorlock's Spine on the other side.

Dozens of Renegade villages dotted the valley. The Renegades all lived close to each other with smoke coming from the rooves of their tents and houses.

Men, women, and children walked between all those houses. The people worked, talked, butchered hunted animals, and conducted every other kind of business.

Villages covered the valley floor as far north and as far south as the Godless could see. The Renegades created an impassable barrier between Hangman's band and the Gorlock's Spine.

"What are we going to do?" Cheina asked from down the row.

"We can't go out there," Kalo added. "We would never get through."

Mora turned to Hangman. "I have an idea."

"What is it?" he asked.

"We should go back to the gulley and follow it either north or south. I don't suppose it matters much which direction we go, but following the gulley will keep us hidden until we can travel away from and around all these Renegades."

"Traveling north will take us straight back into Renegade country," Alien pointed out.

"We're already in Renegade country," Hangman corrected. "Traveling south will take us into Renegade country, too."

"All those Renegades are in the north," Alien went on. "We would be traveling straight into them. We could wind up somewhere we wouldn't be able to get out of at all."

"Our country is in the north," Red interjected. "We could continue north and rendezvous with our home band. They would be happy to take us in."

Hangman cocked his head. "Interesting."

"We can't go out there and we can't go back," Mora told him. "North and south are our only options and the gulley is the only way we can travel without the Renegades seeing us."

He nodded. "You're right. We'll go north. We can climb these hills on occasion until we see that we're clear of all the Renegades. Then we can either cross to the Jagged Points or keep going to Red's territory."

The party retreated down the rear side of the hill. No one stood up until they got all the way to the flat ground at the bottom of the hill. Then everyone re-entered the gulley and started walking.

Mora stayed behind Hangman. All the men stayed near their wives in case anything threatened them. Mora still carried her blades, but she hadn't used them in weeks.

The injured men traveled as slowly as the pregnant women. The gulley offered enough protection from the Renegades so everyone could stop and rest as often as they needed to.

The gulley didn't offer enough protection from the creatures. The gulley's isolated position seemed to bring out the creatures like nothing else. The band traveled all day, but constant creature attacks slowed the party down more than injury or pregnancy.

The men kept having to break away to go fight some attacking creature or deflect a creature that might have been thinking of attacking. The men had to leave the women and children unprotected when this happened.

The party kept hiking for hours. Mora dragged her feet. She could barely keep this up for a single day, much less weeks or maybe even months.

She barely noticed when the men broke away to go deal with a Gorlock that prowled too close to the band. The women kept stumbling forward in a numb trance.

Mora wound up in the lead. The other women followed her because she was Hangman's wife. She only stayed on her feet to set the other women an example and keep them going.

If she stopped, they would stop. If she took it easy on herself or complained, they would think they could do the same thing.

The Gorlock's roar echoed through the treetops. She glanced behind her, but she couldn't see the creature's head above the canopy anymore. Did the men bring it down?

A yowl startled her into facing front. She skidded to a halt when she realized she was turning a corner in the gulley. A pack of Demonex stood right in front of her—two large males and seven good-sized females.

They saw her before she saw them. They were already glaring at her in murderous fury by the time she dragged herself out of her stupor enough to realize the danger she was in.

The other women and children crowded in behind her. None of them could see around the corner, either—not until it was too late.

Those in the front stifled screams when they saw the party facing these massive creatures. Mora's hands flew to her blades, but she couldn't fight these things. She couldn't fight even one of them.

She thrust her hands through the loops and drew her blades from their sheaths. Every woman and child behind her carried weapons, too, but she didn't put much faith in them, either.

The Demonex glared at her and the other women. Then the creatures' eyes dipped to the children. Children offered an irresistible temptation to every jungle predator.

Children were too small, too weak, and too slow to defend themselves—even smaller, weaker, and slower than adult humans. Every creature hunted children. Every creature favored children as prey.

The sound of weapons scraping free of sheaths drifted to Mora's ears from behind her. How long could she and the other women and children hold their ground before the men came back?

The men didn't even know the women and children were in danger. Mora didn't once consider running away. A full-grown Demonex could run her down even before she got pregnant. Forget about now.

The two males pivoted in her direction. Then all the females did the same thing.

The bigger of the two males took a few loping strides forward and then broke into a run. The other Demonex copied him and leapt across the ground in big bounds to attack the party.

Mora braced herself for the worst. The women behind her yelled to their children to get ready. The Demonex picked up speed and the biggest male launched off the ground soaring straight for Mora.

She followed all the instructions Hangman taught her, ducked at the last minute, and raised her blade to gut the Demonex down his belly.

She missed her timing and he fell right on top of her. His weight flattened her underneath him. She only cut him enough to enrage him and he turned on her in snarling fury.

She caught one glimpse of his fangs lunging toward her face. She ducked under her arms and raised her blades between herself and the creature. She couldn't think of any other way to protect herself.

She buried her head under her arms and his jaws closed on her blade, but that only made him madder.

She thought fast and stabbed her other blade into his upper abdomen from under her arms. The blade sank into the hollow space beneath his sternum, but that didn't slow him down one bit.

The creature roared in feral rage, sprang sideways just enough to bowl her onto her back, and attacked her.

She stared up at the creature's hideous, snarling face coming straight at her. She raised her blades again, but he avoided them, dove past them, and turned his head sideways to go for her throat.

Her mind shut down when she saw her efforts come to nothing. She lacked the strength to use her blades effectively. His size, strength, and weight completely overpowered her no matter what she tried to do.

At that moment, Hangman dropped out of the sky from directly above her. He must have been in the trees overhead.

She didn't see him until he landed right on top of the Demonex from behind. Hangman used the momentum of his drop to drive his kukri into the back of the creature's skull, twisted it, and cracked the Demonex's head open.

The Demonex's body thumped on the ground next to Mora. Hangman bared his teeth in a brutal snarl when he ripped the kukri out of the creature's skull. Then he sprang away to go deal with all the other creatures attacking the party.

The men fought all over the gulley. Hangman helped Alien defend Viking against the other largest male. Viking stood alone in front of four women and three children until Hangman and Alien got there to end the creature.

Viking's axe fell to the ground the minute his cousins dispatched the creature. Viking didn't have his old strength, either.

Mora sat up on the ground, but she couldn't get to her feet. She fought to breathe. Her limbs turned to water and her head swam. She could only sit there and watch the men finish off two more Demonex females before the rest ran off into the jungle.

Hangman went from one person to another making sure no one got injured in this latest battle. He and the other men herded all the women and children down the gulley to continue on their journey.

Mora stayed where she was until the very last minute. She kept telling herself to stand up and keep going. Her resolve and her strength failed her even then. She was still sitting there when all the other men, women, and children passed her.

She fought down despair watching them walk away. She was weaker now than she had been the first night she came to join the Godless.

Katha and the other women would come up with all kinds of terrible insults if they saw Mora now. She couldn't even raise a weapon to defend herself anymore.

She didn't look up when Hangman came over to her and squatted down in front of her. She fought down tears and choked out, "I'm sorry! I tried, but I can't fight the way I used to."

"You don't have to," he murmured. "You won't fight again. I don't want you to strain yourself anymore. You can't be the leader of these women anymore. Let someone else take the lead and put themselves in danger."

She tried to shake her head. "I'm sorry I can't be what you need me to be!"

"You are what I need you to be. You're much more than I need you to be. Do you think I value you less because you're carrying my child? Come on. You can't stay here. The men will camp soon and you can rest before we leave tomorrow. You're no weaker than any of the other women, but you'll need to fight again if the Renegades find us."

He took her hands, but she still found it almost impossible to stand up. He wound up putting his arm around her from behind and physically lifting her off the ground.

She limped over to pick up her blades. Why did she even carry them anymore if she couldn't use them?

She hobbled along the gulley floor. He didn't let go of her.

They overtook the rest of the band only a few hundred yards farther up the gulley. The band camped on the ground. The pregnant women couldn't climb.

Mora collapsed with the others. The men built a fire even though they didn't need one. The gulley walls would block the Renegades from seeing the light.

Mora curled up on the ground right away. Cheina handed Mora some of the dried Stalkion meat Kalo and the boys gave the band. Mora chewed the food lying down.

Hangman squatted next to her, but he didn't disturb her. She wasn't the only woman who collapsed right away.

The women curled up one by one. The men and children stayed up later.

The last thing Mora saw before she passed out for the night was the men and boys casting worried glances at the women. All this strain and exhaustion couldn't be good for anyone.

Chapter 44

H angman stopped at the top of a high mountain peak and observed the country in front of him. Jagged mountains lined the horizon to the north. He didn't recognize these mountains.

He thought he recognized the mountains to the south. They looked a little bit like the Jagged Points, but he couldn't be certain.

It didn't matter now because they were too far south. His band had been traveling for months—always following the gulley toward the north.

He and his men ventured into the eastern hills every couple of days to check the Renegades' valley. The men always saw too many Renegade villages there. The band had to stay in the gulley and continue traveling north. The band never found a single opening to travel east to Godless country.

Hangman didn't have a clue how far south he would have to travel to make it back to Shadow's territory—if Shadow's band even still lived in that area. Shadow should have taken the band farther east long before now.

Red kept insisting that Hangman's band should rejoin Red's original family band. Hangman couldn't see any better option than that.

Red climbed the hill behind Hangman and joined him at the top. Red confirmed Hangman's suspicions when Red saw the mountains and burst into a huge grin. "Home!"

"Do you know those mountains?" Hangman asked, but he could already see that Red did know them.

Red got tears in his eyes and had to clamp his lips shut. He barely spoke above a whisper. "I never thought I would see them again. I never thought I would live long enough to make it home."

The other men climbed up to join them. Red's men all burst out laughing and some wiped away tears and hugged each other when they saw the mountains.

Hangman, Viking, Alien, Cross, Kalo, and the boys stood off watching them celebrate. Hangman struggled against all the emotions warring in his middle.

He would have liked to see his family and his home territory again. Maybe he never would. Maybe he and his people would just have to integrate into someone else's band.

Hangman would fall under another Kral. He would become another man's subordinate, but at least Hangman's people would be safe.

Traveling like this exhausted him, but he never let himself show it. He would give just about anything to get Mora to safety before she gave birth.

Hangman grew up in the jungle. He grew up understanding at his core how much danger young children faced just by waking up in the morning.

He faced all of that as a child, but he never saw it as an adult—not like this—not until all these children became his responsibility.

He agreed with Alien now, but Hangman never said so out loud. The long camp was the only place women and children could stay. The jungle was just too dangerous for them.

Hangman counted down the days before he met up with Red's family band. Hangman would gladly become subordinate to another Kral for the chance to get all these women and children to safety. Nothing else mattered to him, not even his own pride.

Shuffling sounds made him glance down the hill behind him. Mora and the other women struggled to climb the hill. Her big swollen belly made traveling a thousand times harder than it should have been.

The other pregnant women all stumbled, panted, and stopped to rest as often as she did, but she was the biggest and most advanced of them all.

The women slowed the party down to a snail's pace. The men just had to accept it. Nothing would make the women travel any faster.

The men had to accept the danger, too. They compensated by becoming extra watchful and protective. They couldn't deal with the situation any other way.

The only good thing about it was that traveling through the gulley completely hid the travelers from the Renegades. No Renegades ever went down into that gulley.

The men had to fight creatures all the time, but that didn't bother anyone. Hangman would much rather fight creatures than people.

Mora stopped seven times on her way up the hill. She didn't let herself sit down. She leaned her arms against the hillside or propped them on her knees while she gasped and rasped for breath. Then she pushed on.

The gulley made traveling easier, but only for the first month or so. Then the gulley started climbing into the mountains.

Hangman's one consolation was that the gulley did climb into the mountains—the mountains of the Gorlock's Spine that he and his comrades had been trying to climb all this time.

The gulley offered the perfect cover for the Godless to continue their journey undetected. No one saw any Renegades except when the men went to check the valley.

The valley dwindled as the band continued north. Sheer mountain cliffs took the valley's place. The Godless couldn't get through that way, either. They just had to keep going.

The gulley ended just a few miles behind where Hangman stood right now. The mountains in front of him looked higher, steeper, and more treacherous than anything he'd faced yet.

Alien broke the silence by saying what everyone else was thinking. "The women won't be able to climb that."

"We can find pathways through the mountains," Red insisted. "The pathways aren't as steep as the gulley has been these last few weeks."

"Where is your Kral's territory?" Hangman asked. "Is it behind those mountains?"

"Not behind them. It's in them—there." Red pointed at one of the highest, steepest, most imposing mountains.

"Where?" Alien demanded. "There is no territory there. It's just stone."

"No!" Red exclaimed. "Not at all! It's lush and abundant! You'll see."

"I don't know about this," Viking murmured.

"You'll see!" Red repeated. "Where else would we go if not there?"

Hangman looked behind him again. The rest of the women floundered on the hill trying to make it to the top.

The country between here and the distant mountains looked vast. It might take the band another six months to travel all that way—or maybe even longer.

Red read Hangman's mind. "You don't have to come. You can go back south to your own country." Red swiveled in front of Hangman, blocked his view of the mountain, and squared his shoulders. "We'll just take our wives with us."

"No," Hangman replied. "We'll all go."

He didn't even have to look south to make up his mind. The country to the south between here and Shadow's territory—it was all so much bigger and even more impassable.

Hangman never once considered breaking up the band. Facing this terrain with only himself, Alien, Viking, Cross, and Kalo's boys—it wasn't an option anymore.

The men waited on the hilltop for the women and children to finally drag themselves up there. Then the women rested for a while before they worked up the energy to go on.

The journey had been like this all this time. The band stopped often, rested a lot, and only traveled short distances before they stopped again.

The sun was already slopping toward the west by the time the party set off down the hillside toward the steep, rugged valleys below. Dense jungle blockaded them.

Hangman already knew what he would find down there.

Red and his men got progressively bouncier and more excited the farther they went. They kept turning around to grin at everyone. The men kept picking up speed to get there faster. Then they had to slow down to fall back and rejoin the band.

The downward slope made walking easier. The party made it to the bottom of the hill in a few hours and entered the jungle.

The men fell into their old habit of surrounding the women, keeping a close watch on all the terrain, and holding their weapons ready just in case.

The valleys between the hills and the mountains dropped downward into steep ravines. The bottoms plunged away into narrow canyons full of waterfalls tumbling over cliffs.

Hangman didn't look forward to going down there and climbing all the way up the other side, but Red and his men found a tiny footpath winding through the jungle before the band got down that far.

The path meandered around and around the valley walls. It climbed, sloped downward, and turned a million corners before it came out onto another, higher stretch of the river.

The water ran over the cliff in a smooth, flat sheet. Red and his men directed everyone to cross only a dozen yards away from the waterfall, but it turned out to be the safest place to cross.

The water shimmered across the rocks only a few inches deep. Everyone could see exactly where to step. The water never got so deep that it put even the smallest child in danger.

The water was also never deep enough for Dushags to swim in—or any other kind of water creature. The band crossed easily and picked up the trail on the other side.

The trail climbed after that, and within a few hours of sunset, the path entered the steep rocks in countless tight, short switchbacks. The going slowed to a crawl again and the sun slipped behind the mountains just a few hours later.

"Where do we camp?" Hangman asked Red.

"We can camp anywhere in the rocks, but we can find an overhang somewhere. It will give us more shelter from the Shrikers."

"The what?" Alien demanded.

"Shrikers," Red repeated. "You don't have them in your country. They live in these mountains."

"What else lives in these mountains?" Viking asked.

"All kinds of creatures you don't have in your country." Red turned away. "Follow me. I know an overhang where we can spend the night."

Chapter 45

Mora let her legs give out and crumpled on the smooth stone under the overhang that Red found for the party to spend the night. She actually loved this cave instantly. It reminded her of her family band's home cave back in Follower country.

The other women sprawled around her. Everyone collapsed—except for the men, of course. Red and his men kept bouncing off the walls, pacing everywhere, and looking out at the surrounding mountains.

She had to admit this was a beautiful country even if it was steep, rocky, and extremely rugged.

The sunset cast the mountains in glowing colors unlike anything she had ever seen. Red and his men kept grabbing each other, shaking each other, and getting emotional over every new sight and change of scenery.

Aliva, Hicia, and Cheina crawled over to Mora, sat down near her, and the women started to pass around their food to each other and the children.

Hangman paced the interior of the overhang and inspected all the walls where they met up with the ceiling. Mora certainly hoped he didn't find any flaws in this place. She didn't want to go anywhere else—not tonight.

The mountains outside certainly looked daunting. She didn't look forward to climbing them in her condition, but she wouldn't have a choice.

The promise of meeting up with another Godless band somewhere in these mountains—that was the only thing keeping her going. It was the only thing keeping all of these women going.

The children sat down near their mothers or in their laps. The mothers stroked their children the way the mothers always did when the band settled down for the night. No one had to move again until morning.

"Hey!" Carnage yelled from the edge of the cliff. "We got a problem!"

The men hustled over there to look over the side. Mora couldn't look. The party didn't need a problem right now—not another one.

All the other women cowered on the floor trying to make themselves invisible. Their worst nightmare came true when Hangman spun around and swiped his forefinger at all of them.

"Everybody get up and get out there!" he barked. "The Renegades are coming up the mountain behind us! Everybody move! Get out there and get up the mountain! Hurry!"

He hustled everyone out. He had to go through the party and pull the women to their feet starting with Mora. He barely got her upright before he shoved her away and moved on to the next woman.

Red and his men left the cave first, stationed themselves across the path, and faced down the mountain with their weapons drawn.

Hangman, Viking, Alien, Cross, Kalo, and the other boys herded the women up the mountain. Some of them burst into tears when they started walking again. Others cried out every time they took a step.

The children became progressively more hysterical the more agitated and insistent the women got. Mora didn't dare to look behind her—at anyone or anything. She fought the urge to fall apart, too.

She barely held it together until the men pushed and prodded the women and children up another hundred feet of rocky, treacherous mountain slope.

The path cut around sharp corners, dropped down into hollows, and climbed again. It was the worst possible terrain for these people to get caught.

Shouts and enraged bellows echoed off the cliffs behind the party. The women made it to another rise. The path plunged into a steep valley on the other side with more mountains towering overhead.

Hangman gave Mora one last push. "Keep going! Don't stop! Follow the path!"

He broke away and his brother and cousins disappeared behind the corner. Kalo and the boys went with them.

The noise of clashing weapons rang louder back there and a man screamed somewhere. The women all stopped and turned around, but they couldn't see anything—not without going back themselves.

Mora couldn't wait. She elbowed her way through the crowd to the front. "Come on!" she called. "We have to keep moving! Follow me!"

She started down the rocky path. It twisted and turned as much as ever. Walking downhill like this turned out to be even harder and more dangerous than climbing up.

Someone lost their footing every few feet. The impact of stepping down again and again made Mora's knees ache.

The noise of battle kept her going no matter what. It sounded like it was getting louder and closer.

The other women heard it, too. They all crowded forward, but going faster only slowed them down in the end when someone skidded in the loose gravel or missed their step.

Mora stayed in the front and used her own pace to slow the others down. They couldn't get past her through the steep defiles.

The path wound to the valley bottom. A thin stream wound through some scrubby trees there before it disappeared into the rocks heading down the mountains on the northern side.

The ground leveled off before the path started climbing into the high cliffs beyond. Mora expected the women and children to race ahead once they got to flat ground.

She came to the last switchback and jumped out of her skin when the noise of men fighting spiked to an ear-splitting din.

All the women and children turned around to stare as the Renegades drove the Godless men around the corner and onto this side of the hill.

The Renegades completely blockaded the path on the southern side. Hangman, Viking, and Alien stood alone to stop the Renegades from going any further.

The steep cliffs on either side prevented the Renegades from attacking with more than two men at a time. The three Godless defended the pass easily, but the Renegades must have brought a lot more men than the women could see from the valley bottom.

Red and his men leapt into the rocks on either side of the path and attacked the Renegades from either side. The Renegades had to turn and fight almost straight upward to defend themselves against Red's party.

Cross, Kalo, and the boys followed Red's example, swarmed the rocks, and dropped down on the Renegades from behind. The screams came from deeper inside the Renegade ranks as the boys plunged in, killed, and sprang out to safety before the Renegades could retaliate.

The Renegades must have brought a lot of men. The efforts of Red's party on one side and Kalo and the boys on the other didn't diminish the Renegade force that Mora could see.

The Renegades pushed Hangman and his cousins around the corner and started working their way down the slope toward the women and children. The Renegades kept advancing and forcing Hangman and his cousins to withdraw a little more.

The women broke and ran for it exactly the way Mora expected them to. She charged out onto the flat ground to cross the valley bottom before the Renegades made it that far.

She ran twenty feet before a catastrophic explosion detonated right next to her. The impact hurled her away and sent her sprawling on the sand and gravel a few yards away.

She barely dragged herself up into a sitting position before another boom went off fifty feet across the valley bottom. She stared in blank confusion as some kind of rocket released from the high cliffs on the other side of the valley.

The vapor trail corkscrewed through the air, arced as high as the mountain peaks, and then plummeted to explode on the gravel beds between the trees on the riverbank.

The sight surprised her so much that she didn't think to react right away. She'd only ever read about this in books.

She half-expected to find artillery at the military installation near the Jeweled River ammunition store, but she and the Godless never got close enough to the installation to find out.

She stared in stunned amazement as more rockets unleashed from the mountainside. They all seemed to come from the same height and the same strata of rocks. Someone up there must be shooting this artillery.

High-pitched shrieks and the yells of women brought her back to her senses. The women grabbed their children and scattered to the four directions.

They took refuge behind other outcroppings and some of the women retreated as far as the cliff base at the edge of the valley.

Chapter 46

Mora tried again and again to pinpoint where the artillery fire was coming from, but she couldn't see well enough from here.

The noise of battle distracted her. The Renegades obviously didn't understand the artillery bombardment. No one did. Mora was the only person here who knew what was going on.

Hangman and his cousins cast hasty glances behind them when they heard the explosions, but the men had to keep fighting to defend themselves.

Cross saw the situation before anyone else and called the boys to a halt up there in the rocks. The boys were all safe up there where the Renegades couldn't get to them.

Red and his men did the same thing on their side. They stood up straight and stared down at the concussions rupturing the valley floor.

Mora saw at a glance that Red and his men didn't recognize this bombardment. They'd never seen anything like this before. They stared at the explosions with their mouths open. None of the men even remembered to raise their weapons.

That left Hangman, Viking, and Alien to face the Renegades alone. Mora couldn't tell what reaction the Renegades had to the bombardment. They didn't seem to react to it at all or even to be aware that anything out of the ordinary was happening.

They pushed the Godless men all the way down to the valley bottom and onto the flat ground. Hangman and his cousins emerged from the rocks. The three men couldn't defend themselves out here.

The Renegades rushed forward to surround the men and cut them down. Hangman and his cousins broke and ran, but the Renegades ran after them.

They all ran straight into the bombardment. Mora lunged out of position, grabbed Hangman with one hand, and seized Viking by the wrist with the other. "Get behind the rocks!" she bellowed. "Get under cover—NOW!"

They heard her and ran behind the outcropping where she had just been hiding. She yanked Alien away just a few seconds before another artillery shell smashed down on the spot where he had just been standing.

She hustled him under cover with the others. The Renegades didn't understand. The artillery hit some of them and knocked others over.

Their confusion proved their undoing. They looked all around them for their enemies and another barrage from the cliffs took out ten Renegades.

The others ran in all directions. Red's party and Kalo's boys saw the Renegades trying to take cover in the same spots where the women and children were hiding.

That moment of confusion turned the tables. The Godless attacked without mercy and cut down the rest of the Renegades, but everyone had to duck for cover when more rockets whistled through the air and smashed into the ground.

"What's happening?!" Hangman bellowed to Mora over the noise.

"Someone is firing artillery at us—from up there!" She pointed to the ledge. "Someone must be up there! They have weapons from the ancients—like giant firearms with massive projectiles!"

She made a circle with both thumbs and fingers to show the diameter of the shells.

"How do we get out of here?!" Viking yelled.

"Stay close to the cliff face!" she told him. "Skirt around there to the path! The bombardment won't be able to hit us there!"

"What about the other women?" Alien roared. "We can't leave them!"

The bombardment cut out as soon as he said it. Dead silence fell over the valley. Everyone froze to listen. Not a sound disturbed the dangerous silence.

Mora lowered her voice to a husky murmur. "Get around to the other side of the path. Stay close to the cliffs and hide in the rocks. Take any women you can find. I'll go get the others. Wait for us there." She pushed Hangman away. "Go on. The bombardment won't restart if we stay out of sight."

He hesitated, but he left after a few minutes.

She didn't stick around to make sure he did it. She turned away, weaseled her way through the rocks, and eventually climbed the path back up to where Cross, Kalo, the boys, and Red's party stood there staring in stunned silence.

"Follow me," she told them all. "We'll be all right as long as we stay in the rocks and close to the cliff faces. Circle the valley on that side. You'll find all your women and children hiding there."

She steered them where she wanted them to go. They took way too long to advance into the valley. All the boys and men kept stopping every few seconds to stare into the valley. The bombardment didn't restart.

The party picked up all the women and children one after the other. They cowered whimpering in their hiding places. It took ages to get them all to come out.

Mora had to explain again and again for everyone to stay hidden and to keep to the sheltered places near the cliff faces.

The gathering darkness made the task even more difficult. Mora had to follow the sounds of crying to find the last few clusters of hidden children. The party didn't rejoin until late into the night. No one bothered to build a fire or look for an overhang.

The party sat down right there at the base of the path. It climbed in an even steeper zigzag course up perilous cliffs and rock ledges. No one could face that—not right now.

No one said a word for hours. No one asked Mora to explain the bombardment to them. Hangman sat up brooding. Mora's body ached, but her mind kept spinning through all the possibilities.

"You have no way of knowing who's up there, do you?" he finally asked after almost everyone else went to sleep.

She shook her head. "The ancients must have stashed those weapons in the cliffs. No one could have gotten them up there without sophisticated machinery."

"So whoever is up there must belong to one of the Clans," Hangman reasoned.

"I don't see how they could be anyone else. I don't know who's up there, but they must have found the weapons and learned how to use them to defend this territory."

"How do you think they learned how to use them?"

Mora shrugged. Viking, Alien, Cross, and some of his men sat up listening to their conversation.

"Maybe the ancients left instructions on how to use the weapons," Mora suggested. "Or maybe the people up there are former Followers—or maybe they belong to a different Clan that studies the ancients and understands how to use the weapons. I don't know."

Hangman turned to Red. "Do your people know anything about this? Have any of your people ever seen this before?"

"No, never," Red murmured. "We pass through this valley all the time. This has never happened before. Whoever it is must have brought the weapons after we left to go after the ammunition."

"That isn't possible," Mora interrupted. "The machines the ancients used to put those weapons up there would have been huge flying machines. The weapons have been there since ancient times. I'm certain of it. Whoever is shooting them now must have just found them recently. That's the only explanation."

Red shrugged. "I don't know anything about this—and neither does anyone in my band."

"Your Follower friend may have known about it," Viking suggested.

"He would have told us," Red replied. "He would have told us how to use the weapons to drive the Renegades out. They never would have invaded these mountains."

"Okay," Viking conceded. "Good point."

"The question is how we get past the artillery to get deeper into the mountains," Mora went on.

"How do you think we should do that?" Hangman asked.

"I don't know. As far as I can tell, the artillery can't hit us as long as we stay on the path. We'll be too close to the cliffs." She pointed up at the high ledge. "The guns have to shoot their projectiles outward from the cliff face. The rocket launches out there and lands down here. The guns can't shoot backward into the cliff."

"It would be better if we could neutralize these guns," Hangman replied. "Do you have any idea how we could do that?"

"No," she replied. "The ancients must have stashed plenty of ammunition when they installed the guns up there. The ancients had a way of leaving food and other supplies all in one place. Whoever is shooting is likely to have all kinds of supplies up there. It would be a lot harder to neutralize them than it was to destroy that ammunition store."

"We should at least find out who they are and *where* they are," Cross chimed in for the first time. "Then we'll at least be able to avoid them and get behind them if we need to."

"I think we should keep following this path," Mora suggested. "Either it will lead us to that ledge or it will bypass it into the mountains beyond. We'll get where we want to go either way."

"What will we do once we find the ledge?" Red asked. "Those people could shoot us in the face and we would all be dead."

"I don't think so. You don't understand how these guns work. They're huge machines. They can only shoot outward from the cliff. They wouldn't get you if you snuck through the rocks and peeked in from above or the sides. The gunners might not even see you. Then you could decide if you want to go in or just slip away unseen and disappear into the mountains."

No one broke the silence after that and Mora didn't continue the conversation. She heard more in that silence than she let on.

None of these men knew enough about any of this to decide what to do about the gunners. Hangman could only take her recommendation.

Climbing this path was the only option left for the party anyway.

Chapter 47

Hangman sent Red and his men ahead of the rest of the band. Then Hangman ordered the women and children to follow Red's party. Hangman positioned Cross, Kalo, and the boys in the rear to follow everyone else.

Hangman held Viking and Alien back. "What do you want to do about this?" Viking asked.

"Those artillery could be the weapons we've been looking for," Alien remarked. "These aren't the right mountains, but they seem to match Mora's description."

"If she's right, then there's no way we would ever be able to move them or take them with us," Hangman pointed out. "The weapons are no good to us except in this valley. They don't help Shadow's band at all."

"If that's true, then the same would be true even if we found the weapons in Butcher's pictures," Viking added. "They would be too big and heavy for us to take back to Godless country. Even the ammunition would be too big and heavy for us to take back with us."

"Then all our searching has been for nothing," Alien finished. "We've been searching for years and never even found the mountains near the plane of flat stone."

"We aren't here for the weapons," Hangman interrupted. "We're here to get these women and children to a safe camp with other Godless. In the best scenario, I would like to get them there before any of them gives birth."

"Of course," Alien agreed. "We all want that."

"Then these weapons are really just another distraction. We should put them out of our minds. They're no good to us. All we care about is getting past them and meeting up with Red's band."

Viking shook his head and puffed out his cheeks. "It sure seems like a waste to leave them behind."

"We don't have any flying machines to lift them out of place or fly them back to Godless territory," Hangman replied. "We don't even know if these ledges have enough ammunition to make the guns run for very long."

"Then we better get going." Alien turned away. "I don't care as long as they don't shoot at me again."

Hangman and Viking went with him. They caught up with the band pretty soon. The women and children traveled as slowly as ever—if not slower. The cliffsides on this flank of the valley posed an even more difficult challenge.

Hangman and his cousins had to stop every few minutes to wait for the women to advance. Cross and the boys did the same thing. They even sat down a few times. There was nothing else to do.

Hangman didn't correct them. Red's men kept clambering into the high rocks, squatting on ledges and overhangs, and observing the country to the south and on all sides for any sign of Renegades. Hangman would have heard if the men spotted any enemies.

Hangman took advantage of these breaks to turn backward and scan the countryside. He saw plenty of creatures here that didn't exist in the jungles at lower elevation.

One of the creatures up here resembled a large Dushag that lived on the dry rocks instead of riverbeds. He also saw a few of what looked like large Gurlgs, but these creatures had brightly colored scales instead of feathers.

These mountains also gave rise to different species of insects. He didn't see any Bliztwords, but he saw plenty of other fist-sized biting and stinging insects—some even bigger than that.

Red's men swatted these things away and killed as many as possible whenever the insects landed on the nearby rocks.

The rest of the band started to copy the men in everything they did. The children got especially enthusiastic about squashing these insects and any other smallish creatures the children happened to lay their eyes on.

Hangman didn't get a chance to consult with Mora again all day. She toiled away in the middle of the pack of pregnant women.

Hangman would have liked to pick her up and carry her over the mountains to make it easier, but he didn't.

If he did it, the other men would think they could do it for their wives, too. Then the band wouldn't have enough fighting men standing ready to defend the band.

He had to admire her fortitude—and all the women's fortitude. This journey turned out to be so much harder for them than for the men. The men got off easy. They mostly just had to stand around and wait for the women to do the hard work.

Cross and the boys got Hangman's attention when they stood up to follow the women up the slope. The women had put some distance between themselves and the boys, but the boys caught up in just a few seconds. This was hardly fair.

Hangman turned around to follow them, but he had to stop again as soon as he and the others caught up with the women. They had been traveling like this for weeks.

He didn't turn his back to the party this time. He stayed where he was and squinted up the hill to where Burn, Butch, and Wildling had climbed up into the rocks to stand guard again.

The men stayed standing, turned one way and then the other, and looked down over the other side of the mountain. The band must be getting to crest a pass where they would descend into another valley system.

Hangman really hoped the band didn't come across another battery of guns installed in these mountains. He didn't know how he would handle it if he did come across one.

That was the moment when he spotted movement far to his right. He thought it might be another mountain creature climbing through the rocks. It was, but it wasn't a creature.

He stared at three people clambering over the rocks. They came from a spot somewhere in the middle of the cliff face—and then Hangman realized with a wild thrill that these three people were coming from a rock ledge in the middle of the cliff.

He hardly believed his good luck when he spotted a long, thin, narrow opening running the length of the cave. The round ends of five enormous guns stuck through the opening and aimed out over the valley.

He couldn't see any other part of the guns. He could just imagine their size based on those cylindrical tubes. They were massive compared to the handheld guns the Renegades used against the Godless.

The people puzzled him. They were all men and they had painted their bodies totally white with some kind of dye. They had shaved their heads and every other trace of their body hair.

They wore no clothes at all. He had no idea which Clan they belonged to or even if they belonged to any Clan.

One of them crouched against the cliff and turned around to face his comrades. The three men stopped there to consult each other. Hangman saw their faces.

They had outlined their eyes, mouths, and nostrils with some kind of black pigment. The combination of the black against their white skin made their faces look like skulls.

Butch and Wildling turned around on their rock overhang. They faced the party and Hangman caught their eye from behind. He pointed sideways toward the three men coming from the artillery ledge.

Wildling had to hold onto the rock and then scale around the overhang before he saw what Hangman was pointing at. Viking, Alien, and Cross saw the gunners leaving, too.

Hangman flagged Burn and circled his hand above his head to tell the men to cut the strangers off. Hangman waved to his cousins and his brother. The men slipped away from the band while the women kept toiling up the hill at a glacial pace.

Hangman and his cousins darted back down the path until Hangman found another side path he didn't notice before. It was really just a series of ledges leading from the main path to the artillery cave.

He glanced into the cave. Mora had been right again—as if he ever doubted her. The artillery would never be able to target someone standing this close to the cliff.

The guns occupied one massive chamber that looked out through that narrow slit. The guns could target the valley below—nothing else. They were far too big even to maneuver into any other position.

A long cable ran the length of the cave's ceiling. A giant metal cage hung from the cable. Hangman couldn't tell what the cage would be good for or why the gunners might need it.

The gunners left the chamber by another path leading from the opposite side of their battery into the cliffs beyond. That's how the gunners made it that far out onto the mountainside.

Chapter 48

Hangman swung himself down into the battery cave. Each gun stood taller than his head. They even stood taller than Viking.

The cousins didn't have time to appreciate the huge weapons. Hangman and his comrades crossed the chamber and came out on the path the gunners took to climb the cliff face.

Hangman hustled up there to catch up with them. He, Cross, and the cousins met up with Burn, Butch, and Wildling at the crest of the cliff.

The path curved over the mountain's shoulder and descended the other side to another stretch of river winding through the scrubby trees. The three gunners capered down the mountain to meet up with two other men also painted white.

"Who are they?" Wildling asked. "I don't recognize their Clan."

"None of us does," Viking replied. "Their Clan is unknown."

"Let's catch them and question them," Hangman ordered. "You three come after them from the north. We'll tackle them from the south. Capture as many of them as you can, but keep them alive. We'll find out who they are and which Clan they belong to."

The friends split up. Both parties broke into a run heading down the mountain. The rocks offered clear stretches of smooth terrain perfect for running. Hangman pushed himself to run faster. It felt good to run after standing around and waiting for the women all this time.

His brother and his cousins kept up with him. They dropped down to the riverbank and turned up it to intercept the strangers. Hangman's group lost sight of Wildling and the others long before they got there.

The five strangers stood together discussing something under the trees by the river. Hangman couldn't tell what the men were doing down here.

Their behavior didn't look normal. They cavorted around each other, waved their arms in wild movements, made exaggerated faces at each other, and even stuck out their tongues in between snatches of jumbled words.

Hangman couldn't pick up any of their conversation. He didn't try.

He, Cross, Viking, and Alien spread out and picked up speed as they came around the rocks and into the strangers' view. The strangers saw the four men coming, wheeled, and bolted in the opposite direction.

The five strangers ran straight into Burn, Butch, and Wildling coming from the other direction. The strangers shrieked in terrified fury, whirled back the other way, and got trapped in a ring of Godless.

Hangman moved in for the kill and tackled one of them, but Hangman didn't pull his weapons. He wanted to capture the guy alive. The stranger burst into a flurry of hysterical struggling. He screeched in one spine-chilling yowl after another. He didn't sound human.

Hangman punched the guy across the jaw—and again in the other direction. The guy relaxed for a moment when the blows stunned him.

Hangman backed off and grabbed a length of vine from a nearby tree to tie the guy up. Hangman reared off his captive to turn him over, but the guy reacted too fast, seized one of Hangman's kukris, and yanked it free.

Hangman braced himself for a battle to the death, but the guy never even tried to get off the ground. He raised the kukri and slashed it across his own throat.

Hangman realized a second too late what the guy was about to do, dove for the stranger's wrist, and pulled the weapon away, but it was too late.

The man spasmed and dropped the weapon as blood boiled from his neck. Hangman sprang clear to get away as blood spurted in a fountain and formed a puddle around the man's naked body.

Hangman could only stand there and stare in horror as the man's eyes glazed over. His body twitched all over until his limbs curled up in a tight spasm. Then he collapsed, went limp, and his eyes floated shut.

Hangman gulped down the sting of bile in his throat. That did not just happen. He had never heard of anyone taking his own life before. That was just not done in this world. Staying alive was hard enough.

Thousands of creatures and enemies lurked in these jungles waiting to kill a person the minute they popped out of their mother's body. No one killed themselves. Human life was too important.

He almost didn't dare to turn around, but he already knew what he would see. Four of the strangers lay dead in their own blood while the men gaped down at the victims in sinking horror.

Only one of the strangers survived. Butch had knocked the guy out before he could do anything to himself.

"What in the name of God is this?" Cross husked. "How could they do this?"

Hangman couldn't even bring himself to answer. The sight shook him in ways he never thought possible. He never dared to imagine anyone could just throw away his own life like this.

He shuddered, but it didn't help. His agitation drove him forward. He needed answers. He grabbed the unconscious man, bound him hand and foot, and dragged him to a nearby tree where Hangman propped the guy up in a sitting position.

Hangman made sure to put his captive where the guy would be sure to see his dead comrades when he woke up. Hangman squatted down to wait. His cousins, brother, and friends remained standing. None of them said a word.

Hangman found himself studying his captive's blackened features. This black pigment and the white body paint meant something. It meant something important.

This man would have killed himself, too, if Butch gave him a chance. Hangman never doubted that for a second. What in the wide world could be going on in these people's minds?

Hangman waited half an hour before he made up his mind. "Run back up there and tell the women to stay where they are," he told Cross. "Tell them not to go any further."

"Do you want me to bring Mora down here?" Cross asked. "She probably knows something about these people."

"No!" Hangman snapped. "Don't bring her down here. Leave her where she is."

Cross only nodded and took off running up the mountain. Hangman envied his brother. At least someone got away from these bloody corpses.

He would rather have watched someone getting devoured by ants than watch a man take his own life. Anything would be better than that.

Hangman couldn't count the number of times he'd come close to dying. He had even come close to wishing he was dead. He never came close to thinking about ending himself. That was just never going to happen.

He was still trying to figure it out when the prisoner roused. He squirmed and then screeched again when he felt himself bound. He struggled to free himself and then opened his eyes to look around.

He didn't look at the Godless—not directly. He looked everywhere else but at them. He never made eye contact even once. The guy grimaced in misery when he saw all his comrades lying around in pools of their own blood.

"Your friends are all dead," Hangman murmured. "You would kill yourself, too, if I let you go free. Wouldn't you? You would throw your life away. Why? Who are you? Which Clan do you belong to?"

The guy didn't answer. He kept his head turned while he fought to control his trembling lips.

Cross came back just then. He ran down the mountain, slowed to a walk when he rejoined the others, and remained standing with Viking and Alien behind Hangman's back.

"The women are where we left them—or a few dozen paces higher than that," Cross reported. "They haven't crossed the brow of the hill to the other side."

Hangman nodded, but he didn't turn around. "What's your name?" he asked.

The captive still didn't answer. He didn't turn his head or look at anyone other than his comrades' bodies.

Hangman waited, but he already saw where this was going. He got to his feet, but he still found it difficult to leave. He really wanted to beat the ever-loving shit out of this guy to make him talk.

Hangman couldn't do that. Whatever this black pigment and white body paint meant—whatever might be that important to these people—that must be the thing that made them kill themselves.

He didn't understand it. That was the one thing that stopped him from treating this man as an ordinary prisoner or enemy. Hangman was missing some crucial piece of the puzzle here. He really needed to talk to Mora about this.

The guy kept his head turned no matter what. He never even came close to looking at or making eye contact with any of Hangman's men.

Hangman finally turned away. "Pick him up and carry him, Viking. We're taking him with us. Cross, run up there and show the women how to get into that battery. Tell them we'll camp there tonight."

Cross took off again. Viking approached the bound captive. The guy screeched again in high, wordless protest, but Viking ignored him, slung the guy over his shoulder, and the men set off back up the mountain.

That hike was the longest, slowest, and most agonized of Hangman's life. Those four deaths weighed on him more heavily than Butcher's death, Vulture's death, and Magnet's death.

Boxer caused Vulture's and Magnet's deaths. Boxer betrayed his Clan and his own blood kin. Hangman could at least understand that. He couldn't understand this. It made no sense. It violated every law that governed this world.

His every instinct told him to go back down to the valley and reverse what those men did. It would have been better if Hangman and his men killed those strangers in open battle. Anything would be better than this.

He had to pay attention when the men made it back up to the small path leading to the battery. He turned to Viking. "Stay here and keep an eye on him until I come and get you. I don't want the women to see him like this. You can put him on the ground if you want to. Just don't let him out of your sight."

Viking nodded and lowered the prisoner to the ground. The guy kept yowling in wounded rage, but he still kept his head craned in the other direction so he wouldn't see anyone.

Viking, Alien, Butch, Burn, and Wildling stood around staring at the guy in confused turmoil. Hangman saw the same unanswerable questions warring in each man's mind. None of them could understand what they just saw down in that valley.

Hangman tore himself away. The others stayed longer before they finally followed him toward the battery.

Chapter 49

M ora had to be careful when she sat down in the battery cave. She almost fell off. She would have fallen down the mountain to her death, but Jolt caught her and steadied her. He helped to lower her down to the floor.

The other women collapsed all over the floor. They were all too exhausted to care about the enormous guns.

A giant metal cage hung from a cable directly over the battery—right at the edge of the cave opening. She couldn't figure out what the cage might be for, but the big guns fascinated her too much.

She struggled to her feet, went over to them, touched them, and examined every part of them. These were incredible. She always knew artillery pieces were big. She never imagined they would be this big.

Another lower ledge ran the length of the battery against the front wall. She stood up on it to peer as far over the side as she could.

The cliff plummeted hundreds of feet to the valley below. She tried to see the gun's muzzle, but it stuck out too far from the opening.

Not a speck of dust marred the battery chamber, the floor, the walls, or any part of the big guns. Everything here looked immaculately clean and maintained.

She found it impossible to believe that people just came to live here for the first time so recently. People must have been living here long before that.

They might have been living here since ancient times. They might have stayed in hiding from the local Clans so no one found out anyone was here at all.

Whoever they were, they didn't waste their ammunition bombarding anyone who happened to set foot in that valley. Red made it sound like that just started in the last few months—since he and his men traveled south to the ammunition store.

Something might have happened to those ancient people. Maybe they all died out and these new residents just moved in. She couldn't explain it.

She straightened up to look out over the terrain to the south. She inhaled a deep breath of the fresh mountain air.

The temperatures up here got as high as they did in the jungles, but the air smelled dry and crisp and clean. It didn't throb with damp heat and all the pungent smells of the jungle.

She liked it up here. She especially liked this cave. It reminded her of home, too—except for the guns, of course. They interested her, though. She looked forward to studying them, but she had to help take care of the other women right now.

She turned around to step off the ledge when Jolt yelled, "Mora—look out!"

She glanced over her shoulder just in time to see a giant winged creature swoop out of the mountain peaks.

The creature was even bigger than a Ridgebeak, but this one didn't have features. The long, webbed talons at the ends of its wings came to wide, razor points. They looked like some kind of armor fashioned into massive feather-blades.

The creature had a long, narrow, bony body like a combination between a Gorlock and a Boultar, but this was neither.

It rushed the ledge open, swung forward two giant feet with huge, curved claws, and plunged straight through the opening.

She jumped down to get away from the thing, but not fast enough. Its claws slammed into her back. It tried to grab her, but its own momentum sent her somersaulting deeper into the cave.

The narrow opening stopped the creature from coming any deeper inside. The creature couldn't catch anyone else inside. The blow knocked Mora away across the floor. She half-skidded, half-rolled all the way to the back wall, but she didn't stop there.

She didn't realize until she got there that the rear wall wasn't as solid as it appeared. Part of it opened into a narrow compartment behind the wall. The wall had been constructed in a way to hide the compartment.

The floor dropped away and Mora fell down a set of stairs arranged in four different landings. She bumped, crashed, tumbled, and eventually slammed down on another floor below the battery itself.

She landed on her stomach and winced, but at least the fall didn't hurt her—not badly. It didn't hurt her baby.

Jolt, Cheina, Aliva, and Ethio rushed down the stairs and surrounded her. "Mora!" Jolt gasped. "Are you okay? Oh, my God! Hangman is going to kill me!"

"No, he won't," Mora mumbled. "It wasn't your fault."

She tried to get up and failed. Jolt and Cheina grabbed her hands and pulled her to her feet. Then everyone looked around.

"What is this place?" Ethio asked.

"This must be the gunners' secret supply room." Mora paced down a long room. It ran the length of the battery. Crates, boxes, and a bunch of metal cartons stood in high stacks against the back wall.

She recognized some of them as ammunition boxes. These boxes resembled the cartons, cases, and containers from the Renegades' ammunition store.

She popped one of the lids and stared down at huge shells bigger than her head. She probably wouldn't have been able to lift one of them.

She went down the line and read out the labels on the cartons. "That one contains food. That one has medical supplies. That one is extra clothes for the people living here."

"How can you tell?" Ethio asked.

"Those markings on the side tell me what's inside each one." Mora stopped next to a crate. The label on the outside read, *Logistics.*

She flipped the lid up and looked out at stacks of maps, diagrams of the guns, and even instruction manuals on how to load and operate them.

"This explains how the gunners figured it out," she remarked.

Cheina came over to her. "How can you understand this?"

"These symbols tell me." Mora pointed to the printed words under each diagram. "This booklet teaches a person how to use the guns. These are maps of the area. Oh, look. This looks like a map of the battery itself."

"What's a battery?" Ethio asked.

"This is the battery. It's a place where the artillery weapons stay mounted and ready to fire. See? This shows the storeroom where we are now. The battery is much bigger than we thought. These lines show different tunnels and passageways leading to different parts of the mountains. There are four other entrances and exits. We wouldn't have to risk our necks climbing up and down over that ledge."

"Thank goodness for that," Cheina exclaimed.

At that moment, the friends heard a steady hum coming from upstairs. Cross came down the stairs just then. "It's raining," he announced. "Hangman says we'll stay here until it stops."

Hangman followed his brother down the stairs and looked around. "Aliva said you got hurt."

"A creature attacked and I fell down here." Mora waved at the supplies. "This the storeroom I told you about. This place has everything."

"Does it have blankets?"

Her head shot up. "What do you want that for?"

"Just give me one if you have one. A piece of clothing or any kind of hide will do."

She hunted around until she found a crate full of thick blankets. She handed one to him and he left without a word.

"What was that about?" she asked Cross.

He looked away. "I'm sure he'll tell you soon. Come upstairs. The other women are worried you're dead down here."

She couldn't even take that as a joke. She and the others returned to the battery.

All the Godless reclined on the floor. A steady pounding drumroll of rain beat on the cliffs outside. The sound came through the ceiling from the smooth mountaintop behind the battery.

Mora and Cheina settled down with the other women. They passed around what they had left from their last kills down in the gulley.

"What will we hunt up here?" Ethio asked. "We don't know any of the creatures here."

"I'm sure Red and the others can tell you all about it," Mora replied.

Jolt heard them. "We used to hunt the Shrikers. We could capture that one. He seems to understand that people live in this place."

Ethio stared at him. "You would hunt....*that?*"

"It's easy," Wildling chimed in from the other side of the room. "All you have to do is find some brave man to use himself as bait. He stands out on an exposed ledge while his friends...."

"His more cowardly friends," Butch added and made his comrades laugh.

"The Shriker swoops in to snatch the brave man....." Wildling went on.

"The much braver man," Butch corrected and everyone laughed.

Wildling blushed and struggled to control his lips while he went on with the story. "The Shriker comes in and the friends....."

"The cowards not as brave as the man," Butch added.

"The cowardly friends throw a noose around the Shriker's feet when he tries to grab the brave man," Wildling finished. "The friends drag the Shriker to the ground and kill it. End of story."

"That sounds terrifying," Ethio breathed.

"That's how Wildling got his name," Butch announced. "He faced one by himself with no cowardly friends to back him up. He lured the Shriker to attack, roped its feet, dragged it down, and killed it by himself. That's how he became an initiated Godless man."

Wildling looked away. "It was a little more difficult than you make it sound."

"He's always the brave man who stands out there to lure the Shriker," Butch explained. "He's the only one with the balls to do it."

"And he always takes a rope with him," Legend chimed in.

"Why does he take a rope if his cowardly friends are there to noose the Shriker for him?" Ethio asked.

"He takes a rope just in case the cowardly friends lose heart and he has to rope the Shriker and kill it himself," Legend replied.

"It has happened before, hasn't it?" Wildling fired back. "You can't blame me for taking precautions."

Ethio gazed at Wildling in awe. "That sounds incredible."

"Don't try this on your own, kid," Wildling told him. "Wait until you're old enough to initiate."

All talk died just then when Hangman returned. He walked in dripping with ran. Viking followed him carrying a large, wrapped bundle over his shoulder. Viking dripped with ran, too.

Hangman crossed the battery and led the way down the stairs leading to the storeroom. Viking followed him.

Hangman waved at Mora to go with them as he passed. She gulped—and then saw the back side of the package Viking was carrying.

A man's head stuck out of the package wrapped in the blanket she had given Hangman. White paint covered the man's shaved head. Some kind of soot surrounded his eyes, mouth, and nostrils to make them black.

She stood stock still and watched Viking carry the man past all the shocked women and children. Alien, Cross, Wildling, Butch, and Burn followed Hangman and Viking as they carried the stranger downstairs.

Mora went last. She hobbled down the stairs much more slowly. The men pulled back and made room for her to get through. She drew up next to Hangman just as Viking laid the stranger on the floor.

Hangman grabbed the guy and tore the blanket away to reveal the rest of the stranger's naked, shaved body. White body paint covered him from head to foot except for the black around his eyes.

Hangman and Viking had tied him hand and foot. The man couldn't get away. He squirmed onto his side and turned his face toward the floor so he wouldn't have to look at anyone.

Hangman stood back and tossed the blanket aside. "Do you know what this is?" he asked in Mora's ear. "Do they come from another Clan?"

She nodded, but she couldn't tear her eyes away from the man. "They're Hungry Ghosts."

"What?" Burn asked. "I never heard of them."

"The Hungry Ghost Clan. They're a death cult." Mora shivered and tried to look around at the men near her. "They're nihilists."

"What does that mean?" Alien asked.

"It means they don't care about life. They don't reproduce. They don't care if they live or die. They don't care about anything. They shun the gatherings and all other practices of family, community—everything. They look down on other Clans for trying to survive and keep the next generation going." She pointed down at the prisoner. "They call themselves 'Maggots'."

"What's that?" Cross asked.

"It's the grub of an insect from the ancient world." She held her thumb and forefinger close together. "They're like an Abnormit larvae, but only about this big. It's an insult—kind of like your people calling me a rabbit—except that the Hungry Ghosts call each other that."

"He won't talk to us," Hangman told her. "He won't even look at us. He won't tell us his name or anything."

She nodded. "I'm not surprised. They don't interact with other Clans. The Hungry Ghosts think other Clans are like creatures because they reproduce and try to keep their family bands going."

Hangman's features twisted. "There.....there were four others...... They.....they killed themselves.....to stop us from capturing them."

"I've heard that. The Hungry Ghosts will take any excuse to kill themselves. They don't believe life is worth living."

"Then why live at all?" Viking asked. "They fought us. Why not just lie down and give up?"

Mora shrugged. "I'm just telling you what I know. They'll kill their own for the slightest reason. They don't value life, especially not their own."

"So what are we supposed to do with him?" Wildling asked. "What are we supposed to call him? Maggot?"

She found herself smiling at him. "He might respond to that. He would be more likely to respond to that than anything else."

Hangman picked up the blanket and tucked it around the guy. "I don't want any of the women and children coming down here—not even you, Mora. Stay upstairs."

"All right," she murmured.

"The men and I will take turns guarding him. We'll keep him tied up. Maybe he'll come around and maybe he won't."

"And if he doesn't?" Viking asked.

"I don't know what we'll do with him then. If we let him go, he'll probably kill himself. I don't know if I can live with that. Can you?"

No one answered him. They all turned away except for Viking. "I'll stay the first watch. I don't know why, but I feel sorry for him."

Hangman turned away, too. "So do I. I just wish we could get through to him somehow."

Chapter 50

H angman dragged himself upstairs to the battery. He planned to squat down near one wall, but he wound up sitting all the way down and then stretching out on his back.

He threw his arm over his eyes and did his best not to think about those men killing themselves. Why? Why would anyone do that? He would never understand it.

He needed to put it out of his mind, especially now that he finally got the answers he needed about who the stranger was. Hangman didn't actually get any answers. He found out what Clan the guy belonged to and even why the other Hungry Ghosts killed themselves.

None of that explained why they did it—not really. It didn't explain how an entire Clan came up with the lunatic notion that their own lives didn't matter.

How could anyone go that far out of their minds? How could an entire population go that far out of their minds? He wouldn't understand it if he dwelt on it for the next hundred years. He wouldn't understand it because it made no logical sense at all.

Someone touched his shoulder. He knew who it was without taking his arm down.

"Eat something," Mora murmured low. "You must be hungry and thirsty. Then you can sleep."

He couldn't ignore how sensible she was. He never felt so grateful to her for knowing as much as she did about so many things he knew nothing about.

He dragged himself off the floor, sat up, and mumbled, "Thank you," when she put some dried Stalkion meat in his hands, but he couldn't look at her.

He stared down at the stick of dried meat balanced between his fingers. He found it impossible to put it in his mouth. The memory of those men killing themselves—it made him sick. It almost robbed him of the will to live.

"Eat it," she murmured. "Don't be like them. Some of us still need you."

He put the meat in his mouth, bit off a piece, and chewed it. He would never be like them. He was Kral of his band and he was about to become a father. Everyone needed him alive. He would never, ever take his own life. God, no!

He risked his life a thousand times, but he always did it to protect and help his band and his relatives. His relatives—mostly his mother—accused him countless times of trying to get himself killed, but he never did. He never actually wanted to die.

He always fought to stay alive even when he thought it was impossible. He always found a way. He would never throw his life away, especially not now. All the hardship of his early life was finally paying off.

Sure, this makeshift band of his faced some rough times. They would face more rough times in the future, but they would keep going no matter what.

Mora pushed a water gourd into his hands. He tipped it up and swallowed most of the water. He had to keep himself alive for her, for their child, for his brother and cousins, for all his men, and for their whole band.

She rested her hand on his shoulder while he ate. He accepted her care and attention, but he couldn't return it. Today brought him to his lowest point.

He would wake up tomorrow and keep going. He would keep making decisions for these people to the best of his ability. He might fail now and then. He might fail a lot, but at least he would keep trying.

He finished the meat she gave him. She handed him another piece and he curled up on his side to eat it lying down. She stroked his hair in silence. He didn't have to explain anything to her.

He could take one night to feel this deep, gnawing despair. What was life really worth? He didn't have to ask because he already knew the answer.

This feeling would pass in the night. He would wake up tomorrow knowing the answer. Then he would act on it and keep going. It was the only thing left to do.

He was still lying there when he heard people talking across the room. Kalo and his boys had joined their mothers and younger siblings in a mixed group.

Kalo and the boys usually kept themselves apart. They weren't initiated men yet, but they stayed separate from the women and children as a mark of their status that they weren't children anymore, either.

Hangman could remember only a handful of times on the journey when the boys mingled with their families. Tonight was one of the exceptions.

"Why do we have to join the Godless anyway," Alvea asked. "Why can't we stay our own band?"

"Because pregnant women and children can't travel through open country," Hitro replied. "Not without getting eaten by something."

"We've come this far," Hicia pointed out.

"At great cost, I might add," Choma corrected. "We could have made it back to Godless territory in a few days if we didn't slow the band down. We put our own children in danger by traveling over open country."

"Then why can't we establish a long camp of our own?" Alvea asked.

"Where would we do that?" Kalo asked. "We're inside the territory of another Godless band right now. We would either have to go under their Kral or leave the area. Every territory is controlled by someone. We can't just camp wherever we want."

"It isn't safe for us to camp anywhere we want anyway," Ethio added.

Red spoke up from the other side of the room. "We'll return to our family band either way—and we'll take our wives with us. The rest of you wouldn't survive without us."

"You won't be able to take your wives with you if we all decide to stay in our own band," Alvea told him. "You would have to go back to your own Kral by yourselves."

"You would all come with us if Hangman decides to come under our Kral," Red countered. "Then you would all wind up in the same place. None of you women can go alone. We'll be the ones to decide what happens to you."

A few people glanced in Hangman's direction. He wasn't ready to make that decision or even listen to the discussion.

Every eye followed him when he got to his feet and crossed the battery floor. He stopped at the opening and looked out.

A solid sheet of rain drenched the landscape. It covered the whole valley in front of him and extended all the way beyond the mountains to the country the party spent so many painstaking weeks crossing.

"The rain doesn't look like it's going to let up anytime soon," Cross remarked.

"It will rain for a long time," Wildling replied. "The wet season is starting. It will rain like this for days if not weeks."

"Then we'll stay here," Hangman decided. "We're safe here. We can rest for a while before we press on. We can't travel in this."

That decided it, but making the decision didn't solve the underlying issue. These women didn't come from the Godless. They didn't know Godless ways.

They probably didn't think when they paired off with these men that the women would ever have to integrate into a true Godless band and follow true Godless customs.

Everyone got used to doing it their own way according to this band's ways. Joining up with a real Godless band would be as hard for them as it had been for Mora at the beginning.

Hangman didn't envy them the process, but they signed up for that when they married Godless men. Red was absolutely right about that. None of the women could back out on that now. They were stuck with it no matter what the men decided.

He stood there with his back to the room. Mora didn't come over to him a second time. She knew when to leave him alone with his thoughts.

Did he stay in this cave because he didn't want to become a subordinate to another Kral? Was his decision entirely selfish? Did he really just want to stay in charge for the rest of forever?

He didn't think so. He wanted more than anything to get Mora and their unborn child to the safety of a real band and a real camp with enough men living in it to protect these women from all danger.

The Renegade Clan was encroaching on this territory, too. Nowhere would be safe. Hangman needed more fighting men than just this handful. Traveling over all these miles had been treacherous enough.

None of them would have survived if they left that gulley. The gulley alone made it possible for the party to travel undetected through country infested with Renegades.

The men of Hangman's band never would have been able to defend themselves if the Renegades ever found out the Godless were there.

The rain didn't let up. It kept pounding the rocky hillsides. The rain flooded the river down there and soaked the banks and pathways. The rain kept up for hours without a single sign of easing off.

The rain helped him think. He was still standing there when Viking and Alien came over to stand next to him. Legend went downstairs to relieve Viking in watching over their prisoner.

"What's on your mind, little brother?" Viking asked.

"Mora says the supply of ammunition downstairs is limited," Alien added. "She says it wouldn't be possible to defend this place long-term."

"Whoever stayed here might not have to defend it long-term if no one ever found out about it," Hangman replied. "People could stay here undetected—maybe forever. They would have to leave to hunt, but they could do that on the sly so the local Godless never found out anyone was staying here."

Viking cocked his head. "You aren't thinking of doing that, are you?"

Hangman turned back on the opening. Looking at the valley didn't tell him anything.

"No, of course not," he replied. "This is another band's territory—another Godless band's territory. We have no choice but to at least tell the Kral we're here. If he doesn't take us, we have to move on. It's the only decent thing to do."

"You know Red is right, don't you?" Alien asked. "Red and his men will stay behind with their wives. If the Kral doesn't take us, then you, me, Viking, Cross, and Mora will be alone again. What will we do then?"

Hangman shrugged. "Then we'll go back to Shadow's territory. I don't see that we'll have much choice."

"We would never make it with Mora in this condition."

"Then we would make camp somewhere and wait for her to give birth. She'll be better able to travel then. The child will pose an irresistible temptation to all the creatures, but at least we won't have to worry about the Renegades so much, now that we're in Godless country."

"The Renegades are here, too," Alien pointed out.

"What do you make of these big guns?" Viking asked. "They're the same kind as we saw in Butcher's pictures."

"We're nowhere near the mountains in the pictures, so these aren't the same guns," Hangman replied. "They might be deeper inside Renegade country and these might be the same kind of guns, but even if they are, that only goes to prove that we can't move them. We should give up on looking for them. They're useless to us."

Now Viking was the one to turn and look out at the rain. "I suppose you're right. I just hate to give up after all the trouble we went to."

"We have bigger problems, brother," Hangman told him. "Besides, we're on this side of the guns now. We have nothing to worry about."

"Mora says that cage is attached to a release lever that sends it swinging out into the air over the valley," Alien went on. "She found some papers downstairs..."

"I told you not to let the women go down there," Hangman snapped.

"She went down there before you came," Viking murmured. "Before you brought the Maggot in here and told her not to go down. She would never violate one of your orders. Please. She obeys you to the letter—always."

Hangman clamped his mouth shut. He really needed to stop being so testy right now. Those men killing themselves slipped farther and farther away into the past. Their deaths lost the sting and became increasingly insignificant. So why did he keep letting it affect him?

"Make sure you don't tell any of the women about the pictures," he told his cousins. "Keep the secret even here."

"Do you mean to tell me you never told Mora about the guns?" Alien asked. "You never asked her if she saw them in the south?"

"Of course not!" Hangman fired back. "Don't you remember what happened with Zyria? I would never tell her or any woman—and you better not tell anyone, either. Keep it to yourselves no matter what. It can't help us right now anyway."

His cousins closed their mouths, too. All three stood there watching the rain until Cross joined them. Hangman gave him the same command to keep Butcher's pictures a secret along with the Godless' mission to find the weapons.

Cross agreed easily. He always went along with Hangman's orders, too. Cross followed Hangman more closely than any of the other men.

The four men fell silent while they watched the rain. The Hungry Ghosts' suicide weighed heavily on them all. It cast the world in a different light, but it didn't really change anything.

Chapter 51

Hangman looked out over the ledge at the valley below. The rain had stopped overnight after a week of straight pounding all over the landscape.

It left the mountains delightfully cool, fresh, and smelling clean and hopeful. The sun evaporated the water off rocks, hillsides, and the valley floor below.

Mist drifted past the cave opening. The sun shone through the mist and created hundreds of shimmering rainbows.

The women and children exclaimed over the view. "Will we leave this cave now?" Aster asked. "Will we go back to traveling?"

"Red made it sound like the rain would start up again soon," Hangman replied. "We'll see what it does before we decide."

That satisfied the girl. She ran off to play with the other children.

Hangman turned around to watch them. The women and children certainly took to this cave. They appreciated a safe, defended place where they didn't have to trek across country in mortal danger all the time.

Half of him wanted to stay here until they all gave birth. He was coming around to the idea of sending Red and his men to rendezvous with their Kral's band and explain the situation while Hangman and the others stayed here to defend the women and children.

He didn't see any reason to take the women and children with him just to receive the Kral's decision about letting the band stay.

Cross sat downstairs guarding the prisoner. Red, his men, Kalo, and the boys weren't here. They all went out hunting this morning and left Hangman, Viking, and Alien to guard the cave.

The cave didn't need that many men guarding it. The band didn't eat the food supplies in the storeroom. The men didn't have any problem hunting plenty of food from the surrounding country.

Viking and Alien lounged on opposite sides of the cave. Alien sat with Cheina and watched Aster and Lonion play around in the middle of the floor. The four of them had become a real family.

Even Kalo spent more time with his mother and younger siblings, now that Alien was with them. Kalo began to worship Alien even more than Kalo worshiped Hangman. Kalo returned to his family in ways he never did before Alien came.

The arrangement definitely agreed with Alien. He smiled more, relaxed more, and showed a lot more affection to all three children, especially Kalo. Fatherhood came naturally to Alien and he showed it.

Hangman took that opportunity to go downstairs to the storeroom. Cross sat on one of the ammunition crates sharpening his blades.

The prisoner lay curled over on his side staring at a spot on the floor. A bowl of untouched food sat in front of him. He didn't look at it or try to get to it.

"Any change?" Hangman asked.

Cross barely looked up. "None. I tried feeding it to him earlier. He only turned his head farther away."

Hangman studied the prisoner more closely. The guy absolutely refused to eat. The men had to hold him by force and pry his jaws apart to dump water down his throat. He wouldn't drink otherwise. He really was determined to kill himself. He would find a way.

The Godless couldn't keep taking care of him—not like this. Every instinct in Hangman's being revolted against keeping another human being tied up underground like this.

The men couldn't keep him alive by pouring water down his throat. He usually spat it out if they let him go too soon.

He always wound up swallowing some of it, but it wasn't enough to keep him alive. He would starve to death eventually—which was what he really wanted.

Cross kept casting momentary glances at Hangman and then at the prisoner. Then Cross went back to what he was doing.

All the men took their turns guarding this man. Hangman took his share of the turns, too. It gave him time to study the guy.

Nothing about this man made sense to Hangman—except the guy's iron determination to accomplish his aim. Nothing could stop him.

The men didn't discuss the prisoner among themselves. His existence disturbed them too much, but Hangman detected all of his men thinking the same thing about the guy. They admired him.

Hangman couldn't help but respect someone who worked this hard to stick to his principles. Whatever made him want to destroy himself—it must have been something really important to him.

He never wavered. He never weakened. He never gave in. He never once looked at any Godless—ever. He blocked everything out of his mind but his one object. He never took his attention off of it for an instant.

Hangman made up his mind, pulled his hunting knife, bent over, and cut the vines that bound the man's ankles together. Hangman had to loosen the blanket so the guy could move well enough for Hangman to pull him to his feet.

Cross scrambled to get off the crate and stand up. He sheathed his weapon so he would be ready to help Hangman if he needed it.

Hangman straightened the guy up, arranged the blanket around him to cover his nakedness, took hold of the guy's elbow, and marched him up the stairs. Cross followed.

Viking and Alien both jumped up when they saw the prisoner walking around. Hangman gave them a pointed look and they followed him and the prisoner outside.

They used the back pathway—the one leading from the cave's southern side—the pathway Hangman and his men used to overtake the Hungry Ghosts in the first place.

The path led all the way down to the valley floor. The prisoner stumbled a lot and nearly fell over a few times. He could barely stand and his head kept lolling.

Hangman led the prisoner back to the same spot on the riverbank where the other Hungry Ghosts killed themselves. Creatures had carried off the bodies and left bloodstained patches of sand in their places.

Hangman stopped the prisoner there in sight of their former battleground. Cross, Viking, and Alien halted at a respectable distance and watched.

Hangman straightened up in front of the prisoner, took off the blanket, and tossed it to Cross. Cross caught it and draped it over his arm.

Hangman inspected the prisoner again. He was as naked now as the first time Hangman saw him.

The guy still wouldn't look at him. The prisoner kept his head turned and compressed his lips when he looked down at the spot where his friends died.

Hangman grabbed the prisoner by the chin, wrenched the guy's head around, and forced the man to look him in the eye. "Listen to me, brother. I'm going to cut you loose now. If you want to kill yourself, I'll give you my blade. You can do it right now. I'm not going to keep you alive any longer."

The man didn't look away this time. He didn't even look away when Hangman let go of his chin.

Hangman walked behind the guy, cut the vine wrapped around the man's wrists, and returned to the same spot in front of his former prisoner.

"You're free now," Hangman told him. "Here. Take this. You can kill yourself now if you want to. Otherwise, you can go home to your Clan. No one will stop you."

Hangman held out his knife, but the guy didn't take it. He glanced down at the knife and then frowned at Hangman. This was the first time the prisoner ever looked any of them in the eye.

He wavered on unsteady legs for a second and then opened his mouth. "Why?" he asked in a scratchy voice.

"You won't tell me what I want to know whether you're dead or just gone. I have no reason to keep you tied up anymore—and I don't want to. You can go. I hope you decide to live, but that's up to you." Hangman held out the knife again. "Take it. That's what you want. I won't stop you."

The guy only frowned at him. "Why?"

Hangman had to study the guy and think about it before he decided how to answer. "No one in my Clan would ever kill themselves. I don't want you to die. I didn't want any of your men to die. I only wanted to question you. You're the last one. I would save you if I could. I've been trying for a week. We all have, but you want to die too badly. You won't stay alive for us and we won't keep you alive for us. Die if you want to die."

The guy just stood there scowling, first at Hangman, then at the knife, and at the bloodstains. Hangman kept holding out the knife waiting for the guy to take it. He didn't.

Hangman lowered his hands and then sheathed the knife in the back of his waistband. The guy didn't even notice.

"What's your name, brother?" Hangman finally asked.

The guy opened his mouth and stopped himself. He went through another five minutes of turmoil. He didn't speak.

Hangman dug in for the long haul. He made up his mind not to leave until the guy either walked away or killed himself.

Hangman had to see this to the end. He didn't know why anymore, but this man meant something. His very existence meant too much for Hangman to just walk away and leave the guy alone.

The man looked down at the bloodstains again. He didn't look up this time. He kept staring at them for several minutes. Then he squatted down near them where he could stare at them at close range.

Hangman could see the wheels turning in the guy's head. Maybe now he was starting to ask himself all the questions Hangman and his men had been asking themselves ever since they found this man.

Chapter 52

Hangman squatted down next to the stranger, pulled some dried meat out of his shoulder bag, and held it out. "Eat something, brother. You haven't eaten in a week. You can't stand. Eat it and live. You don't have to die."

The man didn't move for a second, but he eventually took the meat, bit off a piece, and chewed it. "Thank you," he mumbled.

Hangman had to think for a long time again before he decided what to do next. He waved to his cousins. Alien brought him a water gourd and then retreated to rejoin the other two.

Hangman held out the gourd to the stranger. He took it, tipped it up, and gulped it down until he drained all of it.

"Where do you come from, brother?" Hangman finally asked. "I've never heard of the Hungry Ghost Clan. Where is your home country?"

"I'm not a Hungry Ghost," the man mumbled.

Hangman's head shot up. "You aren't? But....." Hangman went through a series of rapid mental gymnastics trying to figure this out.

Did Mora make a mistake? She sounded awfully sure about the prisoner belonging to the Hungry Ghosts. She even knew about their habit of killing themselves.

"I belong to the Sacrament Clan," the guy mumbled. "My people live in the east—far to the east."

Hangman frowned. "But....you're with the Hungry Ghosts now .....aren't you?"

The guy nodded down at the ground and stuffed the last of the food into his mouth. Hangman pulled out every last scrap of food he still had in his bag and handed it over.

The guy took it. He picked up speed the more he ate. He must be hungry. He ended up stuffing big pieces into his mouth and swallowing them way too fast.

"Be careful, brother," Hangman told him. "You'll make yourself sick."

"My name is Kuvik," the guy blurted out.

Hangman's eyes fell out of their sockets. "Uh...okay. I'm Hangman. That over there is my brother Cross and my cousins, Viking and Alien. We all want you to live."

"I never wanted to die," Kuvik mumbled. "I never wanted to join the Hungry Ghosts at all."

Hangman's throat went dry. "Why did you?"

Kuvik kept mumbling under his breath and staring at the ground in front of him. He hunched his shoulders in wretched misery. "They captured me. They use torture to change your thinking and make you believe as they believe. They convert anyone who happens to fall into their hands. I went along with it to survive. I was just a boy then—only twelve years old. They captured my whole family band, split us up, and I never saw them again."

Hangman gulped. He didn't want to listen to this, but he had to.

This was somehow so much worse than those men killing themselves. Hangman knew of plenty of Clans that marauded the countryside, raided other Clans, killed all the men and boys, and carried off the women and girls for their own use.

This was so much worse than that. These freaks carried people off and infected them with this poisonous mentality that they had to die for no reason.

Hangman struggled to get his voice working, but he couldn't stop it from shaking. "You don't have to return to the Hungry Ghosts. You could return to your own Clan. You might find some of your relatives there."

"I wouldn't even know where to look for them," Kuvik murmured. "I was too young. All my family is somewhere in the Hungry Ghost s....."

"Some of them may have escaped and returned to your original Clan." Hangman's voice broke. "Don't give up. Your life still means something."

Kuvik lowered his voice to a barely audible whisper. "I remember my original Clan. They weren't nice to children. I saw my cousins die. I don't want to go back there." He looked up and his eyes locked on Hangman with unimaginable power. "Could I stay with you?"

Hangman's jaw hit the ground all over again. "You want to stay—with us?"

"I've seen the way you act toward your people. You care for your women and children..."

"Of course we do. We take care of all our people."

"Let me stay with you. I have nowhere else to go."

"Um.....okay, brother. You can stay. I don't know what to say. You're very welcome. We would love to have you. Just....just don't hurt yourself. Please. We can't stand that. Life is hard enough as it is."

Kuvik looked away. "You're the only one who says so."

"We all say so. Ask any of my people."

"I want to stay with you."

Hangman's mind turned another somersault. He told Kuvik, "Stay here a second, brother," got to his feet, and walked over to his men.

"Go up to the storeroom and bring down a set of the clothes from the storeroom," he told Cross. "A pair of pants at least."

Cross nodded and took off running up the hill back to the cave. Hangman turned to his cousins next. "I want you both to go up to the cave and inform the women and children that this man will be staying with us. Tell them his name is Kuvik and I want everyone to welcome him as a member of our band. Tell them he's under my protection the same as everyone else."

Alien clapped Hangman on the shoulder and the two cousins set off climbing up the mountain at a much more leisurely pace.

Hangman watched them go and then went back to squat down next to Kuvik. "My cousins will go up to the cave and tell the rest of our people that you're staying as one of us. They'll welcome you."

"Thank you," Kuvik mumbled. "You have shown me more mercy than I deserve."

"Not at all."

"What is it you wanted to know about the weapons?" Kuvik asked. "I'll tell you anything you want to know."

"I only wanted to know who you are, which Clan you belong to, and what you were doing in the cave shooting at people who cross the valley. You just told me that."

"We only found those weapons a few months ago," Kuvik replied. "We were crossing this country on our way south and we found the cave. It felt comfortable, so we stayed there. We followed the pictures to learn how to use the weapons. I don't know where they came from or how they got there."

"Don't worry about it, brother. My wife used to belong to the Followers. She was the one who told us about you. She can read the writing next to the pictures. Not even she knows how the weapons got there."

Cross came back just then. Hangman retreated and Cross handed him a pair of dark blue pants.

Hangman used his hunting knife to cut them off above the knees. This would have to be good enough.

He returned to Kuvik and held out the pants. "I'm sorry, brother, but I can't let you walk around naked in front of our women and children. You have to put these on before you go up there."

Kuvik frowned at the pants, but when he put out his hand to take them, he stopped himself with his hand poised in midair. He turned his hand over and scowled at the back of it.

Hangman didn't understand why until Kuvik stood up, walked away, and went down to the riverbed. It tumbled and raged with all the rainwater churning through the channel.

Kuvik squatted there, scooped up a double handful of water, splashed it on his face, and rubbed hard. He washed off all the black markings and white body paint.

Viking and Alien came back while he was at it. They stood off to one side with Cross and watched Kuvik splashing and rolling around in the swollen river.

Kuvik didn't stop until he worked his way down his arms, over his shoulders, and finally waded into the flood to wash his legs and back. He cleaned himself all over and removed every speck of paint.

He still looked bizarre with no hair, but he couldn't regrow it overnight. He actually didn't look that much different from Alien. Kuvik would have looked just like Alien if Kuvik had knobs of twisted hair all over his head instead of a bare scalp.

He stepped out onto the bank and examined himself all over. He turned his arms over and over in the sunshine and studied his own skin in minute detail.

He had a soft, boyish, gentle face with deep, haunted black eyes. He looked like the kind of person who has been hurt a lot and survived the worst.

He looked much more like a muscular young man without all that paint all over him. He didn't look like a skeleton. The paint made him look gaunt.

A week without food turned him thin and wiry, but that would change once he started eating regular meals.

He stood a few inches taller than Hangman, but not as tall as Viking.

Kuvik actually smiled a little bit when he returned to Hangman, took the pants, and stepped into them. He pulled them up and buttoned them at his waist. They fit him a little loosely, so he folded over the waistband to make them tight enough.

They came up higher on his legs than Hangman intended, but they still worked to cover Kuvik up. He looked so much more human like this.

Hangman didn't have to ask if Kuvik felt better. He looked better. He stood more easily and his features softened even if he didn't outright smile.

Hangman inclined his head toward the path. Viking, Alien, and Cross joined them and the five men started the climb back up the mountain.

Chapter 53

M ora stood up when Hangman returned with Cross, Viking, and Alien. She opened her mouth to ask him what he did with the Hungry Ghost prisoner.

Her jaw dropped when she saw the tall young man standing in the middle of the group. He didn't look like the same person.

He had washed all the paint and black markings off his face. His skin shone with a golden hue of vibrant health.

His dark eyes darted around the cave taking in all the women and children staring at him. They all fell silent when he walked in.

Red and the others had returned with haunches of the Gorlock they killed in their hunting trip. They stopped cooking it to stand up straight and stare at Kuvik, too.

He wore a pair of torn pants taken from the downstairs storeroom. He wasn't naked anymore.

Hicia broke the awkward silence. "What is he doing here?" she demanded.

"This is Kuvik," Hangman announced. "He's going to be joining our band—as Viking and Alien already told you."

"What if he turns out to be dangerous?" Alvea asked.

"That's my decision," Hangman replied. "I decide who stays and who goes."

"What can he possibly do for us?" Choma demanded. "Can he give us information about the Renegades' plans—or information about anything?"

"What information did you give us about the Renegades' plans?" Hangman asked. "What can you possibly do for us besides slow us down and put us in danger? I'm your Kral by your own decision. No one is making you stay with him." He waved to Kuvik. "Come over here and sit down with me."

He crossed the floor to where Mora stood there trying to pick her jaw up off the floor. She shut her mouth with difficulty and tried to smile at Kuvik, but it didn't work out very well.

Hangman squatted on the floor where he and Mora usually spent their nights in this cave. "Sit down here, brother. Don't worry about them. They'll get used to you. Mora, will you please give us something to eat?"

Mora hustled over to the nearest fire. Wildling saw her coming, carved off a hunk of the cooked meat, and handed it over without a word.

She raced back, sat down on Hangman's other side, put the meat in a bowl, and started cutting it up to serve to both men.

The rest of the men, women, and children eventually got tired of staring and went back to their own business. The men recovered first, especially Cross, Viking, and Alien.

Viking and Alien returned to their own places. Alien exchanged a few words with Cheina and then snapped at Aster and Lonion to stop staring and go do something else.

Kalo and the boys copied the men and pretended that Kuvik had been a member of their band all along.

Some of the other children stayed longer to study Kuvik, but he looked so normal now that the children eventually got tired of waiting for him to do something extraordinary.

Only his bald head set him apart from the others. Other than that, he looked like any normal young man—except for his eyes. His eyes told a different story.

They told of hardship, pain, loss, and years of confusion and misery. They told the tale of a man who has never known kindness—until now.

Mora handed Hangman a bowl full of meat. He immediately passed it to Kuvik. "Eat up," Hangman told him. "You need to make up for the last week."

Kuvik mumbled, "Thank you," and started eating.

His eyes kept darting around the cave to make sure his behavior matched what everyone else was doing. He slowed himself down so he ate at a normal pace, but he ate a lot—much more than men twice his size.

Mora served Hangman next. Hangman ate while he talked to Kuvik about everything the band had been doing since they left Shadow's territory—and even most of what the party had been doing before they left Shadow's territory.

Hangman even told Kuvik about their attempts to domesticate the Ashtaws. Kuvik's head shot up and his eyes widened. "You really did that? You fed them and got them to follow you?"

"Mora was the one who did it. The Followers use Fogpo leaves to lure the Ashtaws into snares. The Godless didn't know about it before she told us."

Hangman launched into an even more detailed description of the Renegades' endless march north. Hangman speculated on why the Renegades would amass so many men in one place.

Kuvik finished eating while Hangman talked. Hangman handed over his own bowl containing what was left of his food. Hangman pushed it into Kuvik's hands and told him to keep going.

Then Hangman handed Kuvik's empty bowl to Mora for her to refill it. Hangman kept supplying Kuvik with more and more food while Hangman talked endlessly—about everything.

He talked about their adventure blowing up the ammunition store. He talked about his ordeal rescuing Mora and the circumstances that led the women to join his band.

Hangman told Kuvik a lot more in that one sitting than Hangman ever told Mora about what happened after she got captured.

Hangman also told the story of meeting up with Red's band outside the ammunition store and how the men joined the band under Hangman as their Kral.

"I don't know the Godless," Kuvik murmured. "I don't know your ways."

"You'll learn," Hangman assured him. "None of these women were Godless before, either. I told you Mora was a Follower. She had a terrible time when she joined our Clan." He turned to look down at her. "Didn't you?"

She nodded. "It was awful. I didn't think I would survive it. I'm sure it will be easier for you if you already know how to fight and hunt."

Kuvik nodded. "I know how to fight and hunt."

"That was the hard part—learning all those skills that the Godless already learned just from growing up in the Clan. I'm sure you'll be fine."

Kuvik gazed at her. "Thank you," he murmured. "You're very kind."

Mora's heart twisted. Poor guy. He must have gone through hell to get this far.

She had never seen Hangman act this kindly toward anyone. A lot of water passed under the bridge before he started acting that kindly toward her.

He took to this man instantly—in a matter of minutes. Mora didn't have to look too hard to see why.

"You could join the Godless," Hangman suggested. "You could initiate as one of our men. You could be one of us."

Kuvik looked down into his bowl and stirred the meat pieces with his finger. "Maybe someday I will be worthy of that."

Hangman clapped him on the shoulder. "When you're ready."

Hangman went on to tell Kuvik about Godless initiation rites. Hangman related his own initiation. Then he described his brother Cross's initiation and repeated the story of Wildling fighting the Shriker.

"That sounds incredible," Kuvik murmured.

"Think about it," Hangman replied. "You'll tell me when you're ready. Kalo and the boys haven't initiated, either, but they will soon."

Kuvik put another piece of meat in his mouth and laid his bowl aside without finishing it. "I think I need to sleep now. Thank you again for all your kindness."

"Of course, brother. Lie down here and sleep near us."

Kuvik lowered himself onto his side, folded his arm under his head, and curled up on the floor. Hangman stood up, walked over to Cross, and came back carrying the blanket Kuvik used to wear around his body.

Hangman lowered the blanket over Kuvik, covered him up, and left him there to sleep. Kuvik shut his eyes and didn't move again. He was the only person in the whole cave who slept with a blanket over him.

Hangman sat down in the same place next to Mora, picked up his food, and started eating. His behavior toward Kuvik was so sweet and attentive that she kissed him on the neck for it.

He caught her eye and went back to eating. She didn't say what was really on her mind. Kuvik needed kindness more than anyone she'd ever met. He found it when he met Hangman.

Kuvik's presence brought out a side of Hangman that Mora never knew existed. He treated all his men as equals.

He even treated Kalo and the boys as equals. He never showed them affection or tenderness. He never expressed affection or tenderness toward anyone but Mora.

It all came out, now that he found someone who actually needed it. Kuvik needed it more than Mora did.

The hum of activity in the cave returned to normal. The men kept processing their Gorlock meat, cooking it up to serve to everyone in the cave, and drying the rest for storage.

All those melded voices created a steady musical blur of contentment. Families sat, lounged, and held each other all over the floor. No one paid any attention to lovers getting closer, children fussing, and mothers nursing their little ones.

Hangman kept casting glances over at Kuvik's sleeping face. Kuvik didn't stir. All that meat must have knocked him out. He must have been exhausted after a week without food.

Mora hoped he woke up feeling a little more human. Everyone in the band would get used to him pretty soon.

Then he would become just another man of their band like all the others. They would accept him and no one would question his presence anymore.

Chapter 54

H angman peeked over the top of the hill and ducked back out of sight. "The Crammers are in position. We should split up and flank them from three sides. Kuvik, you and Legend come with me."

Kuvik sat crosslegged on the gravel at the base of the channel where the Godless men crouched unseen. He didn't look over the hill at their prey in the distance.

Kuvik spent the time scraping his hunting knife over his scalp from his forehead backward. He used short, quick little movements to shave the hair off his scalp as it regrew.

"Why do you keep shaving your head?" Jolt asked. "Why don't you let it grow back? You wouldn't have to look so much like a corpse if you had hair."

"I'm not Godless yet," Kuvik didn't stop what he was doing nor did he look at anyone. He had a habit of avoiding eye contact even when someone engaged him in conversation. "I'll grow my hair back after I initiate into the Godless Clan."

"You could initiate anytime you want to," Baron pointed out. "Hangman already told you that. You could have initiated weeks ago if you really wanted to."

"I'm not ready," Kuvik replied.

Hangman had heard it all before. He had spent the first several weeks of Kuvik's stay trying to convince him that he could initiate and become Godless whenever he chose.

Kuvik had been a fully accepted member of this band for almost four months and he always said he wasn't ready. He never gave any other explanation.

He never repeated to anyone else that he didn't feel worthy of the honor of becoming Godless. He only said it once in that private conversation with Hangman and Mora. Kuvik never shared this with anyone else.

Hangman gave up trying to convince Kuvik to initiate. The rest of the men did not give it up. They kept encouraging him.

They considered it a travesty of justice that he couldn't call himself a fully initiated man of their Clan. They hated to think of him in the same category as Kalo and the boys.

Kuvik was definitely not in the same category as Kalo and the boys. Kuvik proved himself countless times. He proved himself to be one of the greatest badasses the band had ever known. He even frightened Hangman sometimes with unbelievable feats of daring and selfless courage.

Hangman sensed his men winding up to make another assault on Kuvik's resolve, so Hangman headed them off at the pass.

"Viking, you take Red and Butch to the west side. Alien, you take Carnage and Rapid from the east."

"What about us?" Kalo asked. "Don't think you're going to leave us out of this."

"I'm not leaving you out, little brother," Hangman told him. "I want you and the boys to assault the Crammers head on. Stay out in the open so they see you coming. Attack from this direction. Don't show any sign that there are any other hunters out here besides yourselves. Understand?"

Kalo and the boys nodded. Some said, "We understand." Cross didn't answer at all. He always fought and hunted with the boys for some reason—probably because he was their age even though he had already initiated.

No one questioned this. No one treated Cross as a boy, but then again, no one treated Kalo's band as boys, either, even though they hadn't already initiated.

Initiation didn't seem to be an issue for the boys. Hangman didn't see how initiation would make any difference to how much everyone respected them—just like initiation wouldn't make any difference to how much everyone respected Kuvik.

Hangman turned to the rest of Red's men. "You men wait until the boys engage with the Crammers. Wait until the battle starts and our three groups come in from the sides. The Crammers will start fighting harder. Then you come in and we'll overpower them."

Burn nodded. "You got it."

Hangman said, "Let's go," and the men split up.

Kuvik stopped shaving his head. He had developed an obsessive habit of shaving his head whenever he had a spare moment. He never let his hair grow even slightly. He considered the smallest shade of hair on his head an honor reserved for the Godless—an honor he hadn't yet earned.

He put his knife away, stood up, and followed Hangman and Legend down the channel away from the party's hiding place.

Hangman stayed low and followed the channel to the east. Alien, Carnage, and Rapid came with them for a little way until the channel passed a dense patch of jungle between the party and the Crammers in the distance.

Red and his men taught the band a lot about the creatures living in these mountains. Hangman had never seen them anywhere else.

The Crammers were big—the size of Stalkions, but with a completely different build. The Crammers had thin legs that came to sharp, pointed hooves at the end.

Thick, shaggy fur covered the Crammers' bodies all over. Two enormous horns curved backward from their bony skull.

The Crammers scrambled and climbed up steep, rocky hillsides all over the mountains. They could climb almost sheer cliffs, perch on ledges, and eat shrubs growing there that no other animal could get to.

Some of the Crammers had even climbed the vertical cliff face leading to the Godless band's cave. The creatures almost entered it until they saw people living there and ran for it.

The Crammers got their name by fighting each other in pitched battles. Two Crammers would run at each other and smash their skulls together in a clap of thunder.

The noise echoed through the mountains. The sound echoed across the valleys and reflected off the rocky cliffs. The hunters only had to follow the noise to track the creatures down.

The noise covered up any f sound the hunters might have accidentally made while sneaking up on the creatures.

Hangman peeked out of the channel. The trees hid him from the Crammer herd. He waved Alien and the others ahead, climbed out, and Hangman, Kuvik, and Legend ducked into the trees to hide.

The men tiptoed through the undergrowth to the opposite tree line closer to the herd. The Crammers didn't notice a thing. They were too busy charging each other and pulverizing each other's skulls with brutal power.

Kuvik and Legend crouched on either side of Hangman. They watched and waited. Hangman spotted Viking's group getting into position behind some rocks on the other side of the field. The Crammers didn't see them, either.

Alien, Carnage, and Rapid snuck in from behind and hunkered down in another channel far off to the right. That left the field clear for Kalo and the boys to do their thing.

All of them seemed to grow up a lot these last few months—not only in maturity but also in size. Hangman couldn't be sure if he was tricking himself, but all the boys put on inches and plenty of bulk.

The battery cave had been very good to the party since they moved in. Coming home to a safe, secure, sheltered place every night did wonders for everyone.

Hangman became more and more entrenched in the idea of staying here at least until the women gave birth. They all kept getting bigger, too, but in a completely different way.

They became even less mobile, more easily exhausted, and less inclined to do much of anything. Forget about asking them to travel anywhere. Most of them couldn't even make it down to the river to fetch water. They had to send their children to do it for them.

Mora had trouble walking from one side of the cave to the other, but she insisted on continuing her work as much as she possibly could. Hangman didn't dare even suggest that she leave the cave.

He had resigned himself that the band would just stay here until everyone could travel safely. Then he resolved to send Red and the others to go find their people and get their Kral's permission to join him.

Hangman couldn't spare the men now. He needed them for hunting and defense. They came in especially handy at times like this when the band needed as many men as possible to hunt large creatures in the mountains.

Hangman had to pay attention when Kalo and the boys stood up in their channel. They climbed out, drew their weapons, and set off walking straight for the Crammers.

The Crammers noticed the boys right away. The Crammers stopped their battles and turned to face the hunters.

The Crammers' fights always made them irritable. They never took kindly to anyone interrupting their battles for dominance.

The Crammers pawed the ground, lowered their heads, snorted, and tossed their horns at the boys. Kalo and the others raised their weapons and braced themselves as they got closer.

Kalo and the boys wouldn't be able to take on this many Crammers by themselves. The Crammers escalated their aggression when they saw that they outnumbered and towered over these puny humans.

Kalo made a few side remarks to his boys to give them instructions on which Crammers to attack and how to do it.

The boys nodded, broke ranks, raised their weapons, and rushed the Crammers. The Crammers charged, too, but Kalo must have foreseen this.

The boys ran straight into the herd and then dodged at the last minute to strike at the creatures from the side. Kalo passed his blade along one giant male's throat.

The creature plowed face first into the rock before Kalo spun away to attack another Crammer rushing him from behind.

A bloodthirsty battle broke out right there. The boys dropped three Crammers right off the bat, but the others overpowered the boys exactly the way the Crammers predicted. The boys had to back away and tighten into a cluster to protect themselves.

Hangman tightened his grip on his kukris, and at that moment, Viking sprang out of hiding on the other side of the field. Alien broke cover at the same time.

"Let's go!" Hangman called to his friends and plunged out of the bushes.

He, Kuvik, and Legend took off running for the herd from this side. The three flanks converged and distracted the Crammers from the boys.

The three parties dove in to attack. The boys recovered instantly and re-engaged. All the men succeeded in killing Crammers, but the battle wasn't over yet.

Burn, Baron, Prodigy, Jolt, and the others leapt out of the channel and took off running to join the fight. The Crammers got confused by so many men fighting on all sides.

The Crammers couldn't fight as well now. More of them went down. The survivors tried to break out of the circle and four of them trampled the men in their haste to escape in time.

The creatures bolted for the mountains and left eight of their original herd lying there on the ground. The band wouldn't need to hunt again for at least a week.

Hangman and the others closed around the last five Crammers. They went into a frenzy trying to dive here and there and gouge the men with their horns.

The Crammers' own frantic efforts brought about their downfall—or it would have. One of them wheeled to take a swipe at Kuvik. He danced out of the way and drilled his blade into the creature's neck from the side.

Then he brought down a second blade behind the creature's skull from behind. He cleaved the spine in half and dropped the creature right there at his feet.

Kuvik fought with two stolen Renegade blades. He had to wrench and pry them from the creature's body so he could defend himself from the other Crammers still thrashing and plunging in all directions.

Hangman sprang forward to help his friend, but at that moment, a crack echoed across the field. Hangman's hair stood on end when he heard that sound. He knew that sound only too well.

One of the Crammers crumpled on the spot. That shot would have hit one of the Godless men, but the Crammer's giant body saved them.

Hangman spun around. All the rest of his men did the same thing. They came face to face with a squad of Renegades racing across the field.

The remaining Crammers bolted away into the rocks and disappeared, but Hangman never gave them a second thought. All the dead Crammers at his feet disappeared as though they never existed.

All the Godless men leapt into line to face the incoming enemy. The Renegades fired a few more firearms, but not many. The Renegades got too close too fast. They lost their advantage.

Hangman raised his kukris and the two sides closed in a clash of blades against blades. A different battle broke out with all the men fighting tooth and nail just to stay alive.

Hangman found himself fighting next to Hitro and Ethio. "Run back to the cave!" Hangman yelled over the noise.

"No way!" Ethio countered. "We aren't leaving!"

"Tell the women to arm the weapons! We'll draw the Renegades behind the artillery line! The women can open fire! Go now! We'll fall back and lead them to you! Go now, Ethio!!"

The twins finally got the message. They worked their way to the rear of the pack. Hangman and the others moved together to protect them and the boys sprinted their fastest for one of the secret pathways leading back to the cave.

"Fall back!" Hangman yelled to his men. "Fall back to the valley!"

The others heard and took a few steps backward, but the men couldn't go very far at a time before they had to stop and defend themselves.

The Renegades saw themselves pushing the Godless back. The Renegades doubled down their efforts and attacked hard enough to force the Godless to retreat again.

At that moment, Kuvik sprang out of line and jumped over to the side of the Renegade formation. He attacked from that side and killed two of them before the others realized enough to attack him back.

He eventually had to retreat into position with the other Godless, but he executed this move a dozen times and always landed critical hits on his enemies.

His daring checked the Renegades advance again and again. He came perilously close to getting himself injured or killed for the chance to slow them down and draw their weaponry away from the rest of the band.

Hangman glanced over his shoulder. Just a little further and the men would enter the steep defiles leading back to the artillery fiend. Then the men would swivel into the valley at the base of the cliffs. The Godless would lead the Renegades within artillery range.

Then the men would have to dive under cover so the women could pound the Renegades into the ground.

Chapter 55

M ora stopped in the middle of the cave floor, straightened up, stretched her aching back, and puffed out her cheeks to catch her breath. The slightest effort winded her these days.

She couldn't move very well when she was this close to giving birth. She really wished it would hurry up and happen. She hated being this big and cumbersome.

She hobbled forward to return to the side of the cave where she stayed with Hangman. Kuvik stayed over there with Hangman and Mora, too. Kuvik always ate with them and slept near them.

He had become even more obsessively attached to Hangman than Kalo had been at first. Alien had become the object of Kalo's worship since Alien married Cheina. Now Kuvik moved into that place as Hangman's constant shadow.

Mora didn't resent the connection between them. She secretly thanked the stars that Kuvik was always there to keep an eye on Hangman and pull him out of danger if he needed it.

They never talked about this in front of her or the other women, but the bond between the two men kept growing every day. Hangman even encouraged it. He didn't with Kalo.

Hangman always waited for Kuvik to join him before they left the cave. Hangman never ate unless Kuvik was there to share the meal with him. Hangman seemed to be as attached to Kuvik as Kuvik was to Hangman.

Mora had to pause and plan her moves before she squatted down to pick up the bowls the men used to eat. She needed to clean them, but bending that far over didn't usually work out too well for her.

She leaned over, rested her hands on the floor, and then lowered herself onto her knees. She stayed there while she took the water gourd off her arm.

She should have taken the bowls to the river and cleaned them there, but she couldn't make it that far. The children were all too busy helping their mothers, most of whom were also heavily pregnant.

She dumped water into one of the bowls and started to swirl it around when Hitro and Ethio charged into the cave. They came from downstairs, so they must have come from one of the hidden entrances.

They glanced around, saw Mora, and raced over to her all sweaty and breathless. "You have to.....arm the.....arm the weapons.....Mora .....” Ethio blurted out. "Hangman says.....arm the weapons.....”

She gaped at the boys in horror and then struggled to get to her feet without collapsing. "What?! What's wrong?! What's going on? What's happening?! Why do we need to arm the weapons?!"

Both boys grabbed her and pulled her to her feet, but that hardly helped her. "Renegades......” they panted. "The men.....leading them into the....into the valley.....Hangman says.....bombard the valley.....”

She didn't need to hear anything else. She spun around and yelled out for all the women to hear. "The Renegades are attacking! We have to man the weapons! Some of you get downstairs and bring those shells up here! You children form a fire line!"

The women and children stared at her in confusion. None of them had a clue what she was talking about.

She saw right away that she would have to do this herself. "Some of you get downstairs. I'll show you what to do! You children get on the stairs! Cheina—where's Cheina?!"

Mora looked all around her. Cheina, Alvea, and Hicia were three of the very few women who weren't pregnant yet—or at least Cheina wasn't as heavily pregnant as the others. Hicia was too old.

They weren't here right now to help Mora anyway. She gave up putting those three to work, but they walked in through the side entrance right at that moment.

Each of them carried a large haunch of some animal they had killed together. The three women formed their own hunting party, now that the other women couldn't leave the cave.

Mora pointed at all three of them. "The Renegades are attacking! I need all three of you to mount those guns and prepare to fire as soon as we load the ammunition!"

Aliva's eyes popped and she actually took a step away. "We don't know how to shoot those guns."

"I'll show you! Come on! The men are already fighting the Renegades! We have to help them and be ready to shoot when the men lead the Renegades within range. Get up there—NOW!!"

Mora felt herself about to lose her composure completely, but she didn't have time to be nice about this.

Ethio and Hitro stayed by her side and supported both her arms as she limped toward the stairs. They had to cram themselves between the narrow walls to stay on either of her.

Aster, Lonion, and four other children crowded into the downstairs supply room along with three women. All of them looked too petrified even to go near the supply crates.

Mora couldn't waste time reassuring them. She really hoped Hangman and the men weren't anywhere close to entering the valley anytime soon.

She flung open three different crates. They all contained different sizes of shells. She had spent enough time studying the information sheets on the weapons. She swiped her forefinger at the women.

"Pina—stand here and hand these shells out to the children. You children, spread yourselves out in a line up the stairs. Hand up the shells from one person to another." She raised her voice and yelled up the stairs. "We need some more children down here!"

A bunch of them came thundering down the stairs. She arranged them in three different fire lines running from the three different crates.

She stationed one mother at each crate to hand out the shells to the children. Hitro and Ethio helped her climb back up the stairs. She got the children arranged in their lines.

"Aliva—get up on that gun—NOW!!" Mora ordered. Then she bellowed down the stairs. "Start sending up the shells!"

The fire line started. She positioned some of the older girls nearest to the weapons to stack the weapons there. Then she got the oldest boys who didn't go out with Kalo and the others.

She ran through the fastest, simplest explanation for how they should load the giant guns. The boys were just going through their first test when Cheina stood up from her seat.

"They're coming into the valley!" she called. "The men are coming in!!"

Everyone burst into a frenzy. Hitro and Ethio mounted two more guns the three women couldn't man. The girls and boys raced to load the weapons in time.

Mora rushed from one weapon to another—or she tried to rush. She couldn't move as fast as she wanted to and had to stop often. She panted out instructions and corrected the children's technique for loading the weapons.

"The men aren't coming around the corner!" Cheina called. "They keep showing themselves and ducking out of sight."

Mora leaned on the ledge to catch her breath while she assessed the situation. "They're trying to get to one of the hidden entrances."

"They can't go to the hidden entrance—not with the Renegades right there," Ethio remarked. "That would lead them straight to us."

"That's why the men don't go there!" Mora spun away and pointed up at the women. "You're all locked and loaded! Prepare to fire as soon as the Renegades enter the valley!"

"What about the men?" Choma asked.

"Just open fire! The men know what to do! The Renegades don't!"

The children in the fire line passed up more and more shells. The gunners hadn't started shooting yet, so the girls stacked the shells next to each gun.

The fire lines would probably have to ship all these shells back downstairs when this was over, but it would be better to have too many than not enough.

Mora didn't have anything better to do, so she returned to the ledge and looked out. The men tried again and again to divert the Renegades away from the secret entrance. The battle shifted a dozen times before anyone rounded that corner.

She held her breath counting down the seconds before it happened. Was Hangman even still alive down there?

She spotted Wildling, Kuvik, and Alien in the mix, but she couldn't see beyond the rocks. Then the whole party backed up and she saw Kalo and the boys.

"Oh, no!" Cheina whimpered. "Please be all right! Please be all right!"

"Here they come!" Mora yelled. "Get ready!"

The women tensed in their seats. None of them had ever fired one of these weapons before. Mora herself had never fired one or even come close to one while it was firing.

She knew from her readings that they were loud. Nothing she read prepared her for the first gunshot.

The men retreated the rest of the way around the corner and Hangman backed into view. He glanced up toward the ledge. She waved to him, but she couldn't tell from here if he saw her.

The men responded immediately. They must have been deliberately holding the Renegades back to slow them down and stop them from entering the valley until the women got ready.

The men backed all the way down the path in a hurry. They didn't wait around. The Renegades had to run to keep up and continue to hound the men all the way to the level ground.

The men retreated onto the valley floor, stopped there, and the Renegades charged in to engage with the men. The two sides collided in a hail of blows from their weapons.

Cheina fired. Her weapon boomed through the cave with a deafening report. A bunch of the children screamed, clapped their hands over their ears, and fell down to flatten themselves to the floor.

Some of them dropped their shells to the ground, but none of the shells detonated.

Cheina's weapon hurled itself backward from the ledge. The weapon sat mounted on an automatic base that cushioned the recoil and slid the weapon forward again so it would be ready to fire the next time.

The recoiling weapon collided with one of the young boys who happened to be loading that weapon. The recoil knocked him down. He hit his head on the floor and didn't get up again.

Mora hustled over there to take his place. She checked him once to make sure he was still breathing, but she had to work fast.

All the other gunners opened fire. Mora couldn't look at the battle anymore. She just had to trust that Hangman and the others knew what to do.

They would run into the rocks or near the cliffs. The men would abandon the Renegades in the middle of the valley floor to suffer the bombardment—or the men would drive the Renegades out into the middle of the valley where they wouldn't be able to take shelter.

Mora got too preoccupied with loading Cheina's weapon. The women and the two boys fired again and again. The noise from the guns thumped back and forth across the cave in a steady pounding rhythm.

The children recovered from their surprise, restarted their fire line, and started passing shells up the stairs again.

Mora didn't give herself the option to look outside to see what the Godless men or the Renegades were doing. She just had to keep going no matter what.

She huffed and puffed for air to keep loading the weapon. The shells weighed a ton. Her back and legs ached and she started to feel dizzy, but she didn't dare to stop.

She picked up a shell and almost lost her grip on it. She had to stop there to wipe her slippery hands. That slowed down Cheina. Cheina couldn't fire again until Mora loaded the shell.

A scream echoed through the battery behind Mora's back. She glanced over her shoulder in time to see one of the young girls who had been stacking the extra shells the children handed up.

The girl missed her footing and stumbled on the floor. She fell onto one knee and accidentally moved too close inside the range of the big gun's recoil.

It slammed back the next time Aliva fired. The gun collided with the girl and sent her flying across the floor.

Mora barely put her shell down to rush over to help the girl, but her efforts to help the assault weakened her too much. She tripped, too, and landed hard on the floor.

She roared in pain, twisted over on her back, and felt a crushing grip seize her midsection. She had never felt that sensation before in her life, but she recognized it instantly. The sack of muscle around her baby contracted all the way down her stomach.

It didn't hurt, but the intensity overpowered her in a wave of brutal pressure. She winced and tried to sit up, but she couldn't move.

Cheina scrambled down from the weapon and rushed over to her. "Are you okay? Are you....?"

Cheina took one look at Mora's face and the two women's eyes met. Cheina stopped midsentence with her mouth open. She understood. It was happening. This baby was coming.

"Get back up there, Cheina," Mora husked. "Get one of the women from downstairs to load for you. Keep up the bombardment. Don't stop for anything. Protect the men. Go now."

Chapter 56

Hangman raced through the narrow rock channels in the hillsides beyond the valley. He had gotten separated from his men. They all fought different groups of Renegades in these mountains since the Renegades ran into the artillery bombardment.

Some Renegades must have been fighting Godless in the valley. The battery kept hammering the flat ground with dozens of shells.

He kept trying to get to the secret tunnels that led up to the cave. He swerved around a different corner and almost ran straight into a team of fifteen Renegade fighters.

They weren't coming in his direction. He realized in that moment that they were trying to get to the secret entrance. They must have already known where it was. They were trying to ambush the Godless in their own shelter.

Hangman made a snap decision, raised his weapons, and rushed the Renegades. He roared at them to get their attention. They all turned away from the tunnel and came after him instead.

He checked his speed like he suddenly realized the danger he was in. His actions lured the Renegades a little farther away from the entrance.

He couldn't fight this many, so he backed off a little more. They couldn't surround him as long as he stayed in these narrow channels.

They pressed him harder. He had to fight with all he had just to stop them from killing him, but they got the jump on him.

These men got the idea to swarm up the rocks and attack him from behind. Five of them jumped down into the channel behind him. He thrust his kukris in both directions to hold the Renegades at bay, but he couldn't face both sides at the same time.

One of the Renegades on his left raised a blade to hack him down. He blocked with his kukri just in time, which left him exposed on his right side.

He held his adversary's blade above his head. He couldn't defend himself against another two blades hacking him from the other side.

The battle turned against him. He would go down and then nothing would stop the Renegades from going up the tunnel to the undefended cave. The children and pregnant women wouldn't stand a chance.

At that moment, Kuvik dropped off some high ledge somewhere. He landed on top of the Renegades behind Hangman, cut down two of them in the same instant, and landed there with his back turned toward Hangman.

Kuvik started fighting the last three Renegades on that side. He left Hangman free to fight the Renegades in front of him.

The men backed up another step—another step closer to the bombardment. Hangman and Kuvik wouldn't be able to lure the Renegades into the bombardment. The Renegades already understood the danger.

Kuvik finished off the Renegades on his side, scrambled up the rocks to engage with more Renegades trying to surround Hangman, and then dropped into the channel on the tunnel side.

Some of the Renegades had to turn back to defend themselves against Kuvik. The men remained locked in battle until Alien, Red, Kalo, and three of his boys showed up.

They all piled in, jumped down into the channel, and attacked the Renegades from above. The Godless men cut the Renegades down to the last man.

Hangman pulled his kukri out of one of their fractured skulls—and heard the yawning silence in the distance. "The bombardment—it's stopped," Alien breathed.

"Something must be wrong." Hangman sprang over his dead enemies. "Get to the tunnel! We have to get up there now!"

The men followed him. They raced for the tunnel entrance just as the rest of Red's men showed up. Hangman couldn't wait around for the others.

The men charged up the tunnel and came out in the downstairs storeroom. All the ammunition crates lay open, empty, and tossed aside. The rest of the supplies sat untouched in their usual places. No one was down here anymore.

A scream echoed against the walls upstairs. Hangman bolted up there fearing the worst.

The men charged into the battery to find all the women and children standing around in a crowd. "What's going on?" he demanded. "Why aren't you firing on the Renegades?"

The women turned around to look at him. He couldn't read their expressions—until they pulled back to let him through.

He stared down at Mora on her knees on the ground. Aliva and Hicia knelt on either side of her holding onto her arms while she gasped and grimaced in agony.

The bottom dropped out from under his world when he realized what was happening. It couldn't happen now—not now—not at the worst possible time.

She looked up at him through glazed eyes. Her expression twisted with what he really hoped wasn't some kind of apology. She better not start feeling bad about this.

He tore himself away and faced the other women. "What's happening out there? Why did you stop the bombardment?"

Ethio and Hitro came over to him. Hangman had been so preoccupied with protecting the women that he didn't see the two boys standing at the ledge.

"The Renegades are taking shelter against the cliffs," Hitro replied. "We can't shoot at them from here. We would just waste our shells."

"This is all we have left." Ethio waved at the stacks of shells piled up near the big guns. "We didn't want to waste them."

Hangman paced over to the ledge and looked out. The boys were right. Most of the Renegades who survived the bombardment sheltered right against the cliff directly below the battery. The guns couldn't shoot straight down like that.

Hangman forced himself to turn around. He made another snap decision. "Take Mora downstairs away from everyone. I don't want her distracted by this—or the rest of you distracted by her. Can you go downstairs, Mora? You'll be able to concentrate down there."

"Hangman....." she choked and wound up screaming as another wave of brutal agony hit her.

He went over to her, squatted in front of her, and allowed himself just a few precious seconds to rake her hair out of her face. He kissed her on the forehead and looked deep into her eyes.

"I know you'll be brave for me," he murmured. "I'm trusting you with everything I am. Go downstairs. You shouldn't be up here."

"Hangman...." she stammered. "The cage.....use the cage....." She broke off and roared again as her eyes rolled back in her head.

He frowned at her....and then looked up. "What about it?"

"The cage......" She tore her hand out of Hicia's grip and pointed to the ceiling. "That.....that chain......" She had to keep stopping and bellowing with all the intensity rushing through her.

"How does that help us?" he asked.

"Load....the shells......into the cage......"

Hicia took hold of her arm again. "Come on. Let's get you down stairs......"

"Listen to me!!" Mora thundered and had to draw a few steadying breaths. Her eyes bleared open. She barely focused on Hangman. "Listen to me, Hangman...." she husked.

"I'm listening. What about the cage?"

"Load the shells.....into the cage.....pull that chain down......it will release the cage......leave the door open. It will drop the shells......down the cliff...."

Her head lolled just long enough for her to scream again.

Hangman scowled up at the cage. He didn't know how it worked, but he trusted her. She knew a lot more about it than he did. He assumed she must have read about it in those pages downstairs.

She battled through her turmoil to tell him about this. She must be right. He could only try it. He had nothing to lose.

Hicia and Aliva pulled her to her feet. She kept trying to talk to him and getting caught in more waves of intensity wiping out her mind.

She finally nodded to him and let them lead her away, but she had to stop every few feet, roar out in pain, and double over before she could go on.

The women and children all watched her go. The cloud of dread and doom hung heavy over all of them. Hangman had to break out of that.

"Let's get to work!" he ordered. "Viking, you're the tallest. You women bring him the shells to load. We'll load three shells per swing. Let's go!"

Everyone got to work. Hangman ran downstairs and had to dodge Mora to grab one of the empty crates.

He didn't let himself look to see how she was doing. Whatever happened to their baby was all up to her now.

He had one job—to keep the Renegades away long enough for her to give birth and then to get her somewhere safe after that.

He charged back upstairs, put the crate underneath the cage, and jumped up to pull down the chain.

Viking wasn't tall enough to load the shells into the cage from the floor. He had to climb onto the crate, too. The women handed him three shells and he pushed them inside.

Hangman handed Viking a piece of string to tie the cage door open. No one knew if this would work, but they would only lose three shells by trying.

Hangman waited for Viking to step down from the crate. Then Hangman yanked the chain with all his might.

The cage released from the ceiling, swung out, and its own momentum made it tilt forward. The back edge pointed down toward the floor and all three shells rolled to the very back of the cage.

The cage dropped on the cable and the whole cage swung down and outward. An iron bar released at the same time, levered out through the slit opening, and supported the cage in space hundreds of feet above the valley floor.

The cage slid to the end of the bar, slammed, locked in place, and its own momentum made it swing outward to the limit of its cable.

That swing sent the shells wheeling and tumbling back toward the cage door—and they plummeted out of it to drop right there at the base of the cliff.

All the Godless rushed the ledge to watch. The shells smashed into the ground and detonated right on top of the Renegades.

"Do it again!" Hangman ordered. "Load the cage!"

He pulled the chain. It retracted the cable and the cage slid down the bar back inside the battery. The action of pulling the cage inside made the bar fold up. It raised the cage back into the same place as before.

It locked there, all ready for him to pull the chain a second time. The band burst into fresh activity. Everyone sprang into position when they saw their strategy working.

Viking threw the crate into place and climbed onto it. The women and children scrambled to hand him three more shells. He pushed them toward the back, but he didn't need to.

The cage swung inward the instant Hangman pulled the chain. All the shells rolled to the back. The bar levered off the ceiling and out into the open air above the valley floor. The cage slammed to the end of the bar, pivoted forward, and all the shells rolled out.

The band didn't stop working to watch what was happening. Hangman threw all his weight against the chain to pull it back even before the shells hit their target. The band worked themselves into a sweat dropping one shell after another.

"It's working!" Ethio called over from the ledge. "The Renegades are running for it!"

Hangman stopped what he was doing and looked out. Ten Renegades were just disappearing over the distant hills and vanishing toward the south.

He spun away from the ledge. "All of you pack your belongings!" he ordered. "We're moving out!"

"What?!" Choma gasped. "Now?!"

"Yes, now!" Hangman fired back. "We don't have enough shells to defend this place and these weapons won't help us anyway. The Renegades know about the secret tunnels. They can sneak in here while we're all asleep and kill us all. Pack your stuff. We have to get out of here now!"

He pointed at Viking, Alien, and the other men who came up the tunnel with him.

"Make sure everyone gets ready to move. I'll give you a few minutes." He turned to Kuvik. "Go back outside and round up the other men. Tell them we're evacuating and why. Tell them to meet us up here on the double."

Kuvik nodded and charged away at a run down the mountain path to the valley floor. The guy could move when he really wanted to cover the miles.

Hangman took those moments to go downstairs. He almost dreaded what he would find.

His throat constricted when he saw Mora lying propped against the crates. Sweat drenched her face and hair, but she was smiling down at a crumpled, discolored, shriveled little face wrapped in a length of Stalkion hide.

The thing in her arms didn't look human at all. It looked like an Abnormit grub with eyes, a squashed nose, a pursed mouth, and a dusting of black hair across its head.

"It's a boy," Hicia murmured.

Hangman barely noticed when Hicia and Aliva left to go back upstairs. They left him alone with Mora.

He almost broke down with emotion when she looked up at him all shining with relief and pride. "Isn't he beautiful, Hangman?" She looked down at the baby in her arms. "He's perfect—a perfect little Godless warrior."

Hangman couldn't see her or his son. His eyes stung with tears.

He squatted down next to her, blinked his tears away, and kissed her on the side of the head. He could barely whisper loud enough to make himself heard. "Thank you."

She leaned her head against his. She wouldn't even look at him. She only had eyes for her child. "I heard you bombing the Renegades. I'm proud of you."

He couldn't even speak to tell her how proud he was of her. He didn't want to evacuate the battery—not now. He just wanted to stay here with these two—his most favorite people in the world.

Kuvik came downstairs just then. "All the men are back, Hangman. Everyone is ready to go."

Hangman leaned back. He hated even to look at Mora. How could he tell her she had to stand up and hike across countless miles of trackless wilderness after she just gave birth? He could never tell her that.

She read his mind and met his eye dead on. "I know. I heard you."

He gulped down all the emotion pouring out of his heart right now. She already knew why they had to go. She was so much stronger than he was.

He got to his feet and wrapped his arms around her to help her stand up. She did it much more easily than he expected. She wobbled a little, but she could move much better than he dared to hope.

He looked up and nodded at Kuvik. "Tell everyone to move out. Send Red's men in front and get everyone else to guard the women. Get everyone moving."

Kuvik sprang up the stairs. Hangman didn't have to worry anymore. The other men would take care of the band.

He stayed behind to support Mora. He kept his arms around her just in case she fell or lost her balance.

She had to keep stopping, but she climbed the stairs. She paused there, cast one last look around the empty battery, and then she walked out onto the mountainside to catch up with the others.

End of Book 2.

Keep Reading

R ise of the Giants Series: Book 3: The Fate of All Traitors

Hangman's band of Godless Clan has overcome insurmountable obstacles to find safety in a remote territory where their enemies will never find them—or have they? The band's peaceful existence comes crashing down around their ears when the men discover a traitor in their midst. The catastrophic consequences will uproot everything they've ever known and send them on a new quest in search of safety and a connection to the last people left alive in the world.

The traitor leading the band's enemies to their doorstep is only the beginning, though. Internal rivalries, political conflicts, and family dynamics threaten the band's cohesion from the inside as much or more than all the dangerous creatures and enemies circling on the outside. Everything the band has worked so hard to achieve could fall apart before their eyes just when they think they've found what they most desire. Then everyone will have to rebuild from the ground up so a new generation can rise and prosper in a world of chaos and uncertainty.

You can find it at your favorite book retailer.

Sign Up Once--Get all Theo Mann's free books including brand new releases

S ign Up Once--Get all Theo Mann's free books including brand new releases

In a world where everything is out to kill you, humans must fight for survival every day against huge dangerous creatures and enemy Clans. The Godless Clan has enough to worry about already. They don't need to fight their own.

Sixteen-year-old Shadow knows exactly what to do when he discovers a girl from an enemy band hiding in the jungle. He takes her captive as a prisoner of war, but the Godless have a strict code of honor when dealing with women—even enemy women.

He and Katha will have to fight for their very survival and overcome generations of mistrust before they make it back to their people—who just might be the most dangerous enemies either of them has ever faced.

Sign up at www.theomann.com to read it for free

About Theo Mann

I write 70 books per year—and yes, before you ask, all these books are my original creative work. Nothing written under my name is AI-generated or ghostwritten because I write better than AI and any ghostwriter out there.

People don't read fiction for entertainment or to escape from reality. People read fiction to see their humanity reflected in another person's character and story.

This is my promise to you. When you read my books, you'll see your own humanity reflected in the characters and stories. I take this commitment to my readers very seriously. My books are an intimate form of communication between us. I would never disrespect my readers by turning that over to a machine or another writer. This is my bond between me and you as my reader.

I write 20,000 words per day as my daily work output. If anyone with a public platform would like to challenge me to prove this in a controlled environment, feel free to contact me on this website's contact page.

I worked as a professional ghostwriter for fifteen years. Now I'm on a mission to set a Guinness World Record by writing 700 books over the next ten years and 1400 books over the next twenty years, all originally written by me. See my website for the full book list.

I'm also the author of *Proof for the Existence of God* and the *Crimes Against Fiction* blog. You can find all my nonfiction work at www.crimes-against-fiction.com.

If you have a story idea, or if you would like me to explore a series in more depth, or if you'd like me to explore a character by writing a spinoff series about that character or world, leave me a message on my website's contact page. I answer all reader emails, so ask me anything, tell me what you liked and didn't like, and let me know where you'd like your favorite series to go. I would love to hear your ideas and find out what you'd like to read next.

Find out more at www.theomann.com.

Also by Theo Mann (so far)